THE FORCE OF DESTINY

STARSIDE SAGA BOOK FIVE

ERIC KENT EDSTROM

UNDERMOUNTAIN**BOOKS**

To J

1
———

THE GIRL

The chamber walls flash white and green with the light of mercusine powers. The demayne stands amid the Crown of stones, laughing and stroking the cream-colored cat in his arms. Another cat, small and gray, crouches at the edge of the summoning stones, mewling at the girl.

The girl.

Blond hair whipping around her, she stands like a goddess surrounded by an aura of power. Such light! Such fierce light!

Her friends look on, jaws slack. The hideous boy lies bleeding on the floor. The lovely raven-haired woman circles an eyeless old man who hunches in on himself, arms wrapped protectively around his body. A splotch of blood seeps and spreads over the breast of his robe. A knife has gouged a deep wound into the muscle there.

His heart still beats, but his power is diminished. *Oh, Tenn, you foolish old man. Do you seek nothing but power? What of love? What of honor? You claim the title "Hargothe," but what a shadow you are!*

The girl is demanding the demayne return her cat to her. There is a backpack on the floor, thousands of dragon scales spilling out, their swirling surfaces shining like polished jewels cut from a midnight sky.

The girl. Kila Sigh. Her name resounds in realms unknown to man.

But known to woman.

The mercus flows through her blood, her muscle, her bones. She's alight, like a torch in the darkness. Or a star. So many eyes watch her now, for she has become visible in realms beyond the one in which she stands. All denizens of demaynic worlds turn their heads to look—up, or down, or through, or in—to watch her in the particular way they see. And there she is! See how she shines!

In the chamber she turns on the demayne, the fury upon her. "HER NAME IS NAX!"

Sound becomes light upon her voice. The golden power of godspeak flows across all planes at once. It engulfs the lowly animal, the True Name settling upon it the same way the first gods—who were but one god—named the universes.

Tenn, the old man, the seer known by mortal men as the Hargothe, reels as his force-bond with the small creature is rent from his mind, his very soul.

The girl.

She reels and falls to a knee. The bond returns to her, settles into all the cracks and chasms the theft of the bond had torn into her mind.

KILL HIM! the animal orders.

The girl turns, she is charged to bursting with power. She

seethes. She flames. Her blade, the secretive knife of eldenyore, blurs in mercus violet toward the Hargothe.

But he has pulled from the demayne a promised knowledge, and with his last measure of mercusine power, dymenses.

His vision remains seared with one image: the mercus-flaming figure of Kila Sigh. Demaynic weavings of mercusine illuminate her, so intense they blind his already eyeless vision.

He vanishes in mercus green, a dead chill flashing across his skin as he moves a thousand leagues north in an instant. This retreat he has long planned, though this is not the time he had meant to go. He isn't ready for it, for his force-bond on Kila Sigh has failed.

And yet he vanishes. His mind burns with the silhouette of the fiery girl, like looking at the sun and seeing the black imprint behind one's eyelids.

The girl.

That infernal girl.

NO THINKING INVOLVED

The ragged tail of the storm drifted to the west, dividing the sky between dark and light. Perfect blue over two thirds of its endless dome, black fury over the remainder.

The sea. Dark as bitter beer, it still foamed with the echoing chaos of the storm. The sailors aboard *Sea-Hound* called these unsettled stirrings "Kil's Brew." And in typical fashion for such superstitious men, they made wards against evil with their hands whenever they spoke those words.

Despite the unpredictable rolls and pitches of the ship, they scrambled over the deck, climbed the tattered rigging, and worked bilge pumps deep in its ratty bowels.

Kila Sigh stood at the prow, face to the oncoming wind, arms spread wide. She had thought she would never see the sun again.

The storm had caught *Sea-Hound's* Captain Rin by surprise, coming hard out of a blue horizon. Eight days of being tossed about the Ansin Ocean like a cork in a rolling water barrel had exhausted the crew and the two passengers, leaving them pasty from sleepless fear.

Quinn lay on the sun-washed deck behind Kila, head propped on her hands, black hair splayed on the planking like a dark halo. The sun had only a few hours to live for the day, and both young women intended to absorb every second of its remaining warmth. It glinted from the woman's necklace, an emerald pendant that Kila believed she wore to encourage sailors to attempt to steal it.

"Captain Rin says we've lost another two ten-days," Quinn said. "This two-month voyage will take three. At least."

The first delay had happened early in the voyage, just past the Archipelago of Scin, when Captain Rin had come alongside a spicer to trade news and supplies. The spicer's warning of pirates had sent *Sea-Hound* due north, hugging the coast and beating against stiff headwinds for a ten-day. Once well clear of the purported danger, Captain Rin shot east, far to sea before turning again south for the final destination: Garden Island.

And then, the storm.

While Kila was eager to get off the ship, she was in no hurry to get to Garden Island. All that awaited her there was Ori's Home, the school of the Gentle Goddess. Also at the Garden were the schools of Til and Pol.

Attending school in any religious sect did not appeal to Kila, who did not believe in the gods. Not as they were presented, anyway. Her reason for accompanying Quinn on this voyage was to get as far from Starside as she could. Away from the Hargothe—wherever he was—away from the swirl of danger that seemed to confront her at every turn. Away from the loss of her father and her brother, Wen.

If she were honest, there was one thing she did look forward to at the Garden. She wanted to master her mercusine powers. But the voyage itself had taken her a long way down that path already.

Day after day of nothing to do had lulled Kila into an exploration of the mercusine. It had started much like this, her eyes closed, the sun on her face, arms spread wide. She'd been at the top of the foremast, thirty spans up, the ship below looking small as a rowboat.

Captain Rin had given up yelling at her for climbing in the rigging after the first ten times he'd discovered her there. And when she'd demonstrated skill and balance equal to his most experienced able seamen, he had shown a grudging respect for her.

She had even helped reef a sail now and then, just for the physical exertion. The sailors had taken a liking to her . . . for a while. But then the incident with Barton and Whiln had forced the captain to order the rest of the men to stay away from the young women.

Pity. Two men who couldn't keep their hands to themselves had cornered Kila and Quinn in their cabin. Drunkards. Barton was less one finger now, and Whiln—who had come after Kila—well, he wouldn't be fathering any children in this lifetime.

The following morning, Kila had gone to the top of the foremast and braced her legs in the stays so that she needn't concern herself with balancing. The aftermath of the sailors' assault had left her shaken, despite the ease with which she had pulled Cayne from its sheath and sent it into the Whiln's groin.

Quinn had been wheedling and grooming Kila into some

semblance of a "proper young woman" for weeks prior. The tangles in her hair had been straightened, the filth on her skin wiped clean (daily, at Quinn's insistence), and even her clothes stolen and thrown overboard. That had infuriated Kila, but Quinn merely nodded and waited with a flat look until Kila ran out of curses and blasphemies.

As a Radiant's daughter, Quinn was accomplished in all manner of domestic arts, which included a fine bit of sewing skill. She had altered several of her own garments—of which she had three huge chests stuffed full—to fit Kila's slimmer, flatter figure.

So Kila had perched atop the mast, clean, untangled, wearing a somewhat feminine blouse with a hint of ruffle along the laces that cinched up the throat.

She even wore a waistcoat she'd won off the ship's first-master in a game of dice. A little mercus manipulation may have been involved in that piece of "luck." But the man was tiny, small-boned, and the vest fit Kila as if made for her. Deep blue, and solidly made, she thought it set off her blond locks which were now long enough to brush her shoulders.

Fortunately, Quinn favored trousers these days, so Kila wore fine woolen pants, cuffed to the shin and belted around her waist to keep them on. The surprising outcome of all these grooming indignities was that Kila found she rather liked being clean and wearing clothes that wouldn't stand up on their own when she took them off.

Atop the mast, the wind had whipped across her face, making her collar flutter and her hair fly back. From that bird's-eye vantage, the horizon carved a perfect circle around her. Far off, a whale surfaced to blow plumes into the air.

And it was that morning, in the wake of being attacked by

drunkards, that Kila suddenly relaxed and dropped her mercusine mask.

The mercus heightened her senses, made the salt air richer, the creak and thrum of the ship's rigging more nuanced with harmonies and dissonances, a droning song that never ceased.

The wind was too strong to caress her. No, it swiped across her cheeks and brow like a mother dog licking a newborn pup.

Kila sank deeper in the mercusine, feeling more than the tingle of it. She felt . . . or heard . . . it speaking to her in the language of the senses. A world without names.

And so had begun her practice. She created light, heat, cold, sounds, smells, fire, silence. Every day since—except during the horrendous storm—Kila had climbed to the top of the mast and practiced. Anything she could think of that involved the senses, Kila dabbled with it. Every mercusine feat required combining "bolts" of the senses, just as masking her power required her to create combinations that negated each of the mercusine senses.

Setting the fore-topgallant sail on fire had been a mistake, no doubt, but she'd quickly doused the fire by removing all of its heat. Try as she might, she could do nothing to mend the crisp hole she'd burned into the cloth.

Standing here now at the prow of the ship, the fellstorm carrying its rage to other peoples in other lands behind her, Kila sank into the subtle realm once again. It was automatic now.

She had spent so much of her time in Starside wearing the Voluptuary's queller ring, or using the masking technique to conceal her power, she had never come to appreciate the beauty of it.

The power wasn't merely for ashing people or healing

people. It was, she thought, mostly to be bathed in. She always came out cleaner, calmer.

She was impatient to have the sea voyage done with. Not from eagerness to reach the Garden, but to get away from the ship and the sailors. Her nose had now been spoiled by Quinn's constant grooming, and she could taste the sweat and musk of the men working to restore the ship to order.

Now came Quinn's news that their voyage would last another twenty days, or more.

The idea to attempt dymensing—to move instantly from one place to another—had come to her during the storm, when the ship had climbed near vertical waves only to plummet down the other side, then jerk to a sudden slowdown at the bottom and wallow and pitch in sickening and unpredictable tilts.

But the mercus bolts required to dymense eluded her. She could not conceive of what combination of senses would allow one to travel in such a manner. Marlow had told her there were more than the five senses. She hadn't understood what he meant, but obviously, these other senses were involved in the higher feats. And that meant she had already used those senses without knowing it.

Even if that insight helped her get started toward dymensing, how would she direct herself to the desired destination? Dunne Marlow had once told her that dymensing was incredibly dangerous. One could successfully reach a destination, but a thousand paces above the ground. Or perhaps worse, with only one's head protruding above the cobblestone street, body enmeshed in the pavement.

Kila had performed some powerful feats with her mercusine abilities. Her first had been ashing hundreds of thinnies by heating the iron in their blood. At least she knew how that trick worked. Healing the Hargothe and making Cayne fly? She didn't know how she had done those things. Those feats had happened during moments of desperation and fear. No thinking involved; she had merely done them.

At this very moment, she doubted she could get Cayne to pull from the sheath buckled around her thigh without using her hands. Even so, the question of dymensing nagged at her mind like a child tugging her mother's skirts. It constantly drew her attention, even when she didn't want to think about it.

The reason was obvious. If she could dymense, then she could go anywhere, anytime she wanted. She'd dymense to the Garden now and be done with these smelly men and their terrible food.

She again put the question aside, sinking deeper into the mercusine. It came to her as a web of power, luminous lines stretching away from her in all directions.

A strange pulsing came from the south. She turned her attention to it. She had felt it throughout the voyage, always growing more pronounced. It had to come from the Garden. Why wouldn't it? That was the center of mercusine power and training in the world, home to the most powerful merculyns alive.

But how could it spark so brightly from so far away? She had no idea.

"Your hair is ready," Quinn said. Her lazy voice matched the evening, fading and full weariness.

"Ready for what?" Kila said without turning.

"For me to trim it. It was all different lengths after I cut out those tangles. I can even it up now. You'll look tidier and be more presentable to Voluptuary Kalsi when we arrive at Ori's Home."

Kila didn't care about being presentable. Not too much, anyway. But she did like it when Quinn fiddled with her hair. It was soothing. Her brother Wen had seen to her hair cutting in the past, and his technique was to grab a handful and hack it off with Cayne. There hadn't been much tenderness in it. Poor Wen. If he could have lived to see her now . . .

The two young women didn't say another word as the sun slowly dipped to the horizon and disappeared with the flash of green the sailors called Til's Tear. A pious able seaman sang the Prayer for the Dying Day in a lovely, high tenor.

Kila and Quinn descended to their cabin. But Quinn did not trim Kila's hair that night. Both of them were asleep within a minute of flopping into their bunks.

3

FROM SEED TO BLADE

Highest of Til, Mancin Fley, was not satisfied. Not at all.

He allowed some of his agitation to show by sucking in the skin beneath his lower lip. This formed his mouth into a pursed frown he had practiced in the looking glass. The effect, when matched by the heaviness of his brow and his hard blue eyes, was a perfect expression of displeasure.

Anyone who saw that face knew not to bother him with trifling affairs. And so Dunne Hiln did not speak. The man stood in the sun, face streaming with sweat. His robes were thick wool, inappropriate for this climate. He had certainly climbed from the depths of the arena to bring bad news. That was the only sort of news a man like him would deliver in person.

Seeker Yan also stood by, hawkish face and eyes intense with righteous fervor. He did not sweat, but merely stood erect, waiting to be addressed.

Both men would have to wait until Highest Fley brought

his own mind to heel. Sometimes it took a while. His temper renewed itself each morning, and like a hunting hound, it needed daily exercise to tire it out.

Letting his anger run had become part of Highest Fley's morning ritual. He did so by coming to the Garden Tower roof. He did not enjoy the sea breezes on his face, and he certainly did not enjoy the view.

He flicked a glance at one of his personal Favored, who stood near to him holding a shade pole so that his fair skin would not burn. The woman's robes were sheer, sleeveless, and hugged her figure. It was a great honor for her to serve him, and her appreciation made her pliant to his will . . . and his other needs.

She paced with him as he moved along the parapet, keeping him well shaded with the span of sailcloth stretched on a hooped frame atop the pole she carried. It was a hundred pace walk to the wall that barred Fley from continuing around the roof to make a complete circuit.

On the other side of that wall lay Pol's Fifth of the Tower. Sneering, he turned and went the other direction until he was once again stopped by a wall, this one demarcating the beginning of Ori's Fifth of Tower.

Highest Fley paced back and forth between these two walls, like one of those caged and restless wolves the acrobat shows had brought with them when he was a boy in Flyssn. He wanted the *whole* circle.

He stopped at the midpoint of his arc and looked over the landscape. He had been born far to the north in a land of mountains, goats, and snow. By contrast, Garden Island was a paradise of blue water, fruit, and balmy air.

But the vista was spoiled by the two diverging walls,

continuations of the ones hemming him in. At ground level, they shot away from the Tower, climbing hills and descending into vales as they made their way to the sea. They defined the lands of Til's Tower on the island.

He occupied a slice of cake.

The idea made him want to spit. Til was the Father, the patriarch, the One God. Ori and Pol should not have dedicated Ways, they should not have a portion of the Garden Tower, they should not have devotees and novitiates, they should not have separate rituals and doctrines. They were distortions of the faces of the One God, and they would be crushed out of memory.

Soon he would remove these walls. And the Sensuals of Ori and the Spinsters of Pol would be brought to heel. Not only here on Garden Island, but in all realms.

Dunne Hiln staggered, overcome by the heat. Seeker Yan moved aside so that the Donse Master could fall unobstructed. Hiln slumped onto the rooftop. Yan scowled at the weakness of the sweating man.

"Oh, help him up," Highest Fley said. He approached the men, stopping just before the shade pole would block the sun from the fallen Donse Master.

Seeker Yan obeyed, of course, roughly jerking Dunne Hiln's arm. The man's face was wan, droopy. His lips had gone white.

"Forgive me, Highest," Hiln said. He had a high, quavering voice even when in good health. Now it was a raspy creaking sound. "It is the Champion. He is especially violent with the madness this morning."

"How could you possibly tell?" Fley asked. The Champion

was violent with madness at all times. Without sleep or sustenance of any kind, he raged in his arena prison. Only an uninterrupted watch of merculyns kept the madman from destroying the Tower and everyone on Garden Island.

"He spoke," Dunne Yiln said. He wavered and would have collapsed again, but for Seeker Yan's support.

Fley stepped forward, his Favored followed. Now the shade pole did block the sun from Dunne Yiln. "What did he say?"

Yiln's eyes rolled up. Seeker Yan slapped his cheek and his eyes came down. He blinked stupidly. "Dem-Kisk."

"See to him," Highest Fley said to the Seeker. "Keep shade over Dunne Hiln, Favored."

THE AIR WAS cold in the depths beneath Til's Tower. Like the roof, it occupied one fifth of the sub-levels of the tower. The old tombs and sarcophagi had long ago been dug out and disposed of. The space was too valuable to waste on the dead. A single great room occupied the bottom three levels of the crypts, an arena of sorts. Fley had built it for acolytes and Donse Masters to practice mercusine bolts of fire and lightning in preparation for the war to come.

But with the arrival of the Champion it had been given over to one use: as a prison cell.

The man lay on a thick wooden table in the center of the huge room, wrists and ankles and neck clamped in shackles, chains stretched tight to huge rings embedded in the walls. Accommodation for his bodily wastes lay below the table. They were no longer needed because in an effort to weaken the man, Fley had forbidden him food and drink for a fortnight. It was a testament to the man's insanity—and divine blessing—that he still lived.

Four simple chairs sat around the table, each occupied by a merculyn. They sat still as rocks, eyes closed in concentration. They worked in two hour shifts, focusing their power to maintain control over the madman. The Champion.

Highest Fley's footsteps resounded from the stone block walls as he crossed the space. Dunne Portshalan, an elderly Donse Master who oversaw the quelling teams, accompanied him. The old man shuffled as quickly as he could, but did not manage to keep up.

"He started mumbling last night," Portshalan called from behind Fley. "Unusual, but not unprecedented. This morning he began to froth and strain with more urgency than usual. And his grunts and growls formed into words. Very clear words. 'Dem-Kisk.'"

"Have you asked him about it?" Highest Fley said. He stopped well short of the table. The Champion's body strained against his shackles, every muscle bulging, veins protruding. The corded muscle and tendons at his neck jutted out with such force that his face had gone purple. Cracked lips pulled back in a snarl, and wide eyes flickered all about, wild with insanity. The man was not young, but he looked like a thickly muscled warrior.

"Did I *ask* him, Highest?" Dunne Portshalan said. "The Champion is beyond conversation. You may as well ask a wildcat its name."

Men always thought they knew things they did not. They believed that a lunatic who had never had a moment's lucidity must always be a lunatic. But that was not Fley's experience. There were few certainties in this world, clouded as it was by the war against the One God. Man was beset by lies. He could not trust even his own senses, and so everything must be questioned.

He approached the Champion, stopping at a chalked ring roughly sketched on the floor surrounding the straining man. This was the farthest known distance the man could spit. That alone told Fley the man was aware of his captors.

"Stop your straining, Champion," Fley said in tones of absolute command. "I would speak to you, man to man."

Hard to believe this creature had once been a respectable Donse Master. Harder still to believe he had come to Garden Island by coincidence. No, the One God's hand was in it. Brought by those boys, sent by the Voluptuary of Starside to be a prisoner at Ori's Home.

Fley's words had no effect. The Champion didn't cease his struggle to break free. The effort was remarkable. And depriving him of food and water had not weakened him at all. He had shed all of his doughy flab. His body was like a sculptor's depiction of Til himself: gray headed and bearded, physique carved and full of wrath. The scars of his early whippings had healed and were now mere red lines across his abdomen and chest.

"Dunne Yples, why did you say 'Dem-Kisk?'"

Dunne Portshalan hissed behind Fley. Apparently he didn't want anyone using the Champion's old name. Fley now saw why.

The man doubled his efforts, the shackles tearing into his flesh, blood oozing out. The wooden table creaked, and the chains thrummed with tension. Fley doubted a team of horses could pull harder than this man did with each of his limbs. He was truly possessed of the One God's power, and if loosed would rampage until none lived.

"We will have to add another merculyn to each watch," Dunne Portshalan said. "His mercusine grows by the day."

"Good," Highest Fley said.

It was not good, but showing concern would merely undermine Dunne Portshalan's confidence. "Dunne Yples, listen to me. You are the Champion of Til. I am the Highest. You must listen and obey. Those we despise grow weak. We can destroy them, but I cannot release you to fulfill your destiny until you show control. Do you understand?"

In answer, the man shrieked and strained. A great tearing noise—like a tree trunk being twisted apart—filled the chamber. With a ringing metallic sound, the chain holding his right arm came free of the wall. It chimed as it blurred through the air.

It struck one of the sitting merculyns, making a wet slicing noise as it sent him from his chair.

"By Til!" Dunne Portshalan cried. He raced to take a seat in the vacant chair, then bowed his head to lend his power to the quelling. Highest Fley felt the man's considerable mercusine power joining the three remaining sitters as they steadied their control over the madman.

The injured merculyn was dead, neck cut nearly all the way through by the force of the chain.

Four Donse Masters ran in, shouting and pointing. One held a flask. The others were urging him toward the flailing madman, who now swung his loose chain around like a flail.

Highest Fley was urged backward, out of range. It was all

very disturbing. Had this fit truly been brought on by using the man's name?

This was most troubling, indeed. The Champion had to be brought under control if he was to face his destiny, if he was to finally face the agents of Ori and Pol so that Fley could demolish the evil of the Triumvirate.

After assuring the Donse Masters he was quite uninjured, highest Fley ascended the tower to a different sort of prison. Here, his other prized captive lay on her bed, not chained, not struggling. In fact, she had never once moved so much as a finger. She had come to him paralyzed by some unknowable malady, probably brought on by her extraordinary oracular gifts.

He had stolen Roya Reth from the Way of Ori the day she'd arrived at Docktown. Rather, the Seeker had stolen her. And what a prize she was. She didn't often prophesy, but when she did, her words could be counted on. Assuming one could interpret them.

She had foretold the arrival of the Champion, saying he would be chained at the neck.

The boys who had disembarked from that ship had gone to Ori's Home, the Champion dragged along as some sort of hopeless invalid to be placed under the Voluptuary's power. The man had been as docile as a well fed cow then.

Highest Fley had decided to finally act upon thirty years of plans and schemes: to depose the sitting Voluptuary and put Ori's Tower under his sway. It had required finding just the right woman to become just the right Voluptuary, one who would allow the Sensuals and novitiates he had planted among them to finally exert control over the Home.

And now he possessed both the Champion and the young merculyn who had come with him. Henley Mast.

"Roya Reth, I would speak to you," he said to the immobile, slack-slipped oracle. Her head was kept shorn, her body kept clean and free of bedsores by Favored assigned to her care. The room was freshly aired, blossoms adding a pleasant smell. A window let in ocean breezes and the call of birds.

"Speak." Her voice was soft. A child's voice.

"Roya Reth, you spoke of the Champion. He is here. He said 'Dem-Kisk' this morning and his rage increases. Why? Is Dem-Kisk coming?"

She didn't open her eyes. "Have you read the words of the Theb?"

"Of course I have." He was the Highest of Highests.

"Then you know of Dem-Kisk all that has been said."

He snorted. "No one who has read those passages knows what Dem-Kisk means."

The woman was child-like, which meant she was often petulant. He'd tried to punish the tone out of her, but she was immune to pain. Only bribes of comfort and treats produced cooperation. There was a bowl of dates next to her bed for just this purpose.

He pitted one and fed it to her. She moaned with pleasure, taking her time with it.

"Is Dem-Kisk upon us?" he asked. Scholars assumed it referred to a man, born to hold the fate of mankind in his hands. But to anyone intelligent the passage was no more than the ravings of a madman. The Way of Til taught the common people that Dem-Kisk was a man because people liked to be frightened. The interpretation also fit the Way's view that the

Triumvirate was an untenable construct, a false notion of equality among separate gods. The Way of Til had no choice but to accept it during the Synod of the New Pantheon. They had been weakened by ages of war. But the schemes to undermine the Triumvirate had begun before the wax seals on the Synod Treaty had cooled. Ever since, the Ways had connived and manipulated to take greater control over the hearts and minds of men.

The Way of Til had risen to primacy, and now it was time for the lie of the Triumvirate to be dispelled forever. Roya Reth had prophesied the coming of a Champion. What other purpose could such a man serve but to finally put an end to the Triumvirate?

But the man's mention of Dem-Kisk caused Fley to rethink all of his assumptions. Could it be, perhaps, that the Champion had a greater cause? Could *he* be Dem-Kisk? Or was the Champion's purpose to fight Dem-Kisk?

"Answer me, oracle. Is Dem-Kisk upon us?" Highest Fley urged.

Roya Reth recited: "You will know Dem-Kisk by the flames, by the charred bone, by the ash. You will know Dem-Kisk by the black feather, the red scale, the parting mist. You will know Dem-Kisk by the fallen tower, the creaking gate, the bone chill." She licked her dry lips and added a phrase not found in the prophecy: "Soon it will tread upon fields of red."

Highest Fley knew the ancient tongue of Cigil-Tine, knew the literal translation of "dem-kisk" was "red grass." But who would make the grass red with blood? A man. And the Champion would defeat him, *must* defeat him, and bend him to Til's will. Unless . . .

Frustrated, he leaned over the immobile woman. "Is the Champion Dem-Kisk?"

"No."

A small relief washed through him. And yet his gut churned. He couldn't keep the desperation from his voice. "Has Dem-Kisk been born? Where is he?"

"Dem-Kisk has always been born, from seed to blade to seed again. Red are the blades of the dying age. I see them waving beneath the sun. This is prophecy *to* the gods, not from them: Words cannot contain nor the mind apprehend the unconscious will of time. The force of destiny has meter, but, alas, no rhyme."

She was taunting him. One of her favorite pastimes. Realizing she would not give him a straight answer about Dem-Kisk, he decided to pursue other questions.

He plucked another date from a bowl next to her bed. With a twist, he tore it open and pulled out the pit. Pressing the sweet fruit to her lips, he said, "Why does the Champion strain? He is too strong already. He may destroy us before he has a chance to serve us."

"Every child knows what makes one grow. If you want him to wither, why feed you him so?" She accepted the date, chewed it slowly, swallowed slowly.

Highest Fley demanded more of her. They hadn't fed Yples so much as a crumb of bread. But Roya Reth was gone, faded into the somnolent by-world she spent most of her hours wandering. He knew that no bucket of ice water, no lash of the whip, no glowing brand on her skin would rouse her or compel her to speak again.

But she had confirmed one thing. *Soon it will tread upon*

fields of red. Dem-Kisk was coming. Surely that meant the day he had long sought, the fall of the other Ways, was near.

Surely.

But as he ascended the tower to his apartments, he was troubled by something else she'd said.

Why feed you him so? She would not have said that if his orders were being followed in that regard. Someone was slipping the man sustenance.

Upon entering his rooms, he sent for Seeker Yan. The man was a zealot and often over-eager to deliver Til's punishments on lambs he deemed had strayed too far from the fold. But that made him keenly observant. Fley would instruct Seeker Yan to begin an inquisition into the merculyns charged with keeping the Champion restrained. He would discover who was feeding the Champion, and then he would make an example of him.

But the Seeker did not come. Instead, one of the man's pupils, an acolyte of some mercus sensitivity, arrived. He bowed deeply. "My apologies, Highest. Seeker Yan went to the dock to greet a ship. He said he has sensed a merculyn approaching over the past few weeks. A powerful one."

"And why did he not tell me of this?"

The acolyte had no answer and so did not offer one. He merely kept his head down and waited for instructions.

"Send the Seeker to me the moment he returns."

"Yes, Highest." The acolyte departed, swiftly, leaving behind the stink of relief.

Highest Fley went to one of his broad windows and looked again at his slice of the island. His Favored padded in on quiet slippers, bearing a pitcher of wine. It was too early for it, but he drank down a cup.

The warmth washed into his belly, but it did little to soothe him. His conversation with Roya Reth had left him disquieted. For it had rekindled a worry in him.

The Theb did not mention the Champion of Til. That had been new prophecy from Roya Reth herself. Did that mean there were Champions for Pol and Ori, too? Reth had never answered that question.

4

OBEDIENCE AND PIETY

The harbor at the Garden was hot. Only the faintest lick of wind crossed the half-moon of the bay, and the air merely swirled in hot currents.

Captain Rin had his men push *Sea-Hound* away from the dock the second Kila's foot touched the thick wooden planks. She didn't glance back. She had made no friends on the voyage.

Quinn's chests and a pile of strapped-together pieces of her bed from home lay on the dock where the sailors and a few slowpoke dockworkers had dumped it all.

A trio of Til's-boys were working their way down the dock to meet them. Not unexpected, as the three schools surely would want to guide new arrivals to their schools.

"Remember," Quinn said to Kila. "You're my cousin from the country. Where's Nax?"

"In my backpack." Nax hadn't been keen on getting into the leather satchel, but Kila had warned her that the people of Docktown might not welcome a cat.

Quinn gave a gold skillet to a stevedore and instructed him to arrange to have her things delivered to Ori's Home.

"That won't be necessary," the lead Til's-boy said. He was a Donse Master. His robes were thinner than those worn in Starside, but appropriate for this climate. They were the same drab brown though, cinched by belt of golden cord with tassels that dangled to the knees. The man was tall, of salt-and-pepper hair and deeply tanned face. His aquiline nose and bright blue eyes gave him a hawkish look. Kila felt like prey beneath his gaze.

He was flanked by two acolytes, both gowned in white. Sweat gleamed on their brows. Both were in their twenties and had hair bleached a filthy blond by long exposure to the sun.

"I am Seeker Yan, a Donse Master of Til's Tower. You must accompany me to Til's Tower, young ladies. Ori's Home is no place for respectable daughters of good houses."

Kila couldn't keep her nostrils from flaring, but she managed a smile. "Why would ya think we're of good houses?"

She always fell into the Cheaps-speak when irritated. Three months aboard *Sea-Hound* and Quinn hadn't been able to completely break her of that habit.

"Surely not by your manner of dress nor your tone. But who comes to Garden Island but doesn't seek to enter the schools?"

"And since when do Til's-boys take in young women?" Kila said.

"We do not take acolytes of your sex. But since neither of you are clothed as novitiates, I assume you come under the Rules of Princes, under which the great houses send their young to prepare for their future stations of power."

"We are not *princes*," Quinn said. Her tone was so low and

threatening that Kila turned to see if Quinn had recognized the man. But no. This was just how Quinn was these days. Quick to anger, hand on the hilt of her Shadline blade, Black.

At least she hadn't drawn it. On board *Sea-Hound* she had taken to carrying it openly when on the main deck and giving sailors narrow-eyed glances while she worked the weapon through her growing repertoire of flourishes and tosses.

The Seeker studied Quinn, eyes drifting from her face to the emerald pendant at her throat. Finally he said, "'Rules of Princes' is a phrase from a time long past, a better time, when women were not expected to read and dabble in politics." He continued to move closer as he spoke. His shoulders were hunched forward because he kept his hands clasped before him, hidden in the sleeves of his robes. The acolytes moved out from him, blocking the way should Kila and Quinn attempt to slip past.

The man's eyes were aimed at Quinn, flitting from her weapon to her bosom to her face. His lips parted slightly and his eyes abruptly rolled up into his skull. "Hmmm. There is no spark in you. Nor your companion." His eyes rolled down and he lifted the corner of his mouth. "Please, come with me. My acolytes will see that your things get to the Tower."

Kila was grateful she'd resumed her mercus mask that morning. Had he felt her during their approach? The thought made her queasy.

"We aren't goin' anywhere with ya," Kila said. "We're here fer Ori's Home and that's where we're a-goin'."

The Donse Master unclasped his hands to stay his acolytes, who were on the verge of leaping at the young women. "For a generation, not one family sent a son or daughter to Ori's Home under the Rules of Princes. And now arrive four within three months? That's curious. In the past three years a *hundred* have sent their sons to Til's Tower. You see, don't you, that it is only proper that you come to the school most prepared to guide you? You need not be concerned about being girls. You ladies will have fine, secluded accommodations, and will be trained in the virtues of obedience and piety as becomes your station and duty. At Ori's Home you will surely be corrupted. That is, if they accept you at all. There are strange things happening there. Strange and concerning."

Kila desperately wanted to drop her mercus mask and see what this man was up to. She just knew he was probing at them with his own power, perhaps using scent and sound to charm them. But she and Quinn were much too strong-willed to succumb to such tricks easily.

"Acolytes, please assist these ladies."

The young men stepped forward. Both were strong and tall. But unarmed.

Quinn slipped her blade free and crouched. In doing so, she went utterly silent, thanks to Black's powers.

Kila did not draw her blade, but her mind balanced on the edge of dropping her mask.

"There's no need for violence," the Seeker said, waving his boys back. "I see you will not be persuaded by reason. Typical of your sex. Proceed to Ori's Home. I will return to Til's Tower and speak with the Highest. He will issue a demand to the Voluptuary to turn you over to us. You will see. It will be for your own good."

He withdrew, taking his acolytes with him. Quinn watched until they disappeared into the small crowd waiting at the end of the dock. She returned Black to its sheath. "Idiots."

"Our ship was in view of the docks for long enough for

those morons to get here," Kila said. "Why aren't any Sensuals or Spinsters here to greet us?"

Quinn had no answer. She whistled for the dock men to get her things loaded onto a wagon. A tired mare in harness munched on a handful of grain held in the cartman's hand. He was a lump of a man in a broad-brimmed hat. Quinn glared at him. "Another gold when it all arrives safely. And I'll know if a chest has been opened. Mercusine wards." She flashed dangerous eyebrows. The man nodded and knuckled his brow.

The young women strode down the dock, shoes clunking hollowly on the planks. Kila was still getting used to hers. Hard-soled things, slender, with a silver buckle on the top. Not proper lady's shoes, but sturdy. Quinn had brought some clothes from her younger years for Kila. She claimed she'd worn Kila's shoes when she was fourteen.

Like the sailors, Kila had spent most of her time aboard *Sea-Hound* barefoot. But Quinn had insisted she put on the torture devices to make herself "minimally presentable" to the Voluptuary of Ori's Home.

Docktown stretched along the shore of the small harbor, a lovely and sunny collection of small homes. The shops and warehouses near the docks were all pasted over with a textured coating and painted a light yellow. The roofs, white tile.

The town had been built amidst a great, rambling garden. Every terrace and front stoop was host to potted greenery. Hedges of great red and pink blossoms lined the road from the dock. Towering trees, bearded with green moss, shaded the small front yards of the greater houses.

Sleepy-eyed men sat in the doorways of their shops, in the shade of canopies or arched galleries that fronted the buildings. They came alert as the women passed, then hastily looked away from them.

There were few people about, likely due to the overwhelming power of the midday sun. Those who Kila saw were dusky, plump, and aloof.

"A different sort of life here, huh?" Kila said. She was eyeing a man sleeping in a chair in front of his fruit cart. The strange orbs inside were yellow and lined with faint stripes, and each was double the size of his head. "In Starside he'd be robbed to the last seed before he woke up."

"Not many people live here," Quinn said, "and there's no winter to speak of. Just a rainy season. They only have to contend with fellstorms. Those fruits grow everywhere, I suppose. If food isn't scarce, no need to steal it."

There were lemons and oranges on trees along the streets. Anyone could pick one. Kila was tempted to do so, for in Starside such fruit arrived well past best ripeness.

Some folk were not asleep, and they watched the women pass with open suspicion. Mothers called their children inside when Kila and Quinn came near. Worried faces peered from doorways.

"They don't trust us," Quinn said. "You'd think they'd be trying to sell us their wares or ask us news from abroad."

Skin prickling, Kila looked back. Trailing them by a hundred paces was one of the acolytes. "I suspect he's the problem. I have no doubt Til's Tower frightens these folk. It would me."

I'm too hot. I need to get out, Nax sent. Along with the words came a skin prickling sensation and the feeling of not being able to breathe.

Kila took Quinn's wrist and led her down a narrow alley. "Nax needs out for few minutes."

"Here? That's not a good idea."

"How 'bout you dress all in fur and ride inside an airless leather bag for an hour?"

Quinn relented. They wound through a few alleys, until they found a shady park behind a stand of apartment houses. No one was around, so Kila let Nax out.

The cat stretched and tested the air. *It's full of wet.* Nax's drowsiness came to her as a strong suggestion that they all lie down and nap.

There was no time for that. The acolyte would be upon them soon. "This place feels like Cheapsgate," Kila said.

"It's nothing like Cheapsgate," Quinn said. She breathed in through her nose. "It smells nice, and everyone is well-fed."

"That's not what I meant. It's the mood. I was a thief, so I understood why the Watch was after me. But *everyone* in Cheapsgate feared going into the city. The Watch could arrest somebody just because they didn't like the looks of them. This whole town feels like they're trying to avoid drawing the wrong sort of attention."

"The Watch cannot arrest someone without good cause," Quinn said. "Your view is tainted because of your own fear of being caught stealing."

"Weren't you nearly killed by a man of the Watch for keeping Henley from being dragged off?"

"That was different. That Donse Master was ordering the Watch men to bring him in for the Hargothe . . ." She trailed off, realizing she had just proved Kila's point. "Is it truly that frightening for Cheapsgaters?"

"Not for me, but it is for most. A man of the Watch can

take someone to the Westbunk for going barefoot in Gristen-side, or for talking to a merchant in the wrong tone. They might be released in a day or ten, but they always returned to Cheapsgate quiet and looking like they'd seen a Screamclown."

As Kila spoke, Quinn's face brewed up a storm, eyebrows scrunching, lips compressing. She had her blade in her hand. Her lips moved, spitting out a long string of words that Kila could not hear for the silencing power of the blade.

Nax eyed the angry woman with disinterest. Kila was somewhat amused by Quinn's rage at Starside injustice, as outsized for the moment as her display was. The black-haired woman was extraordinarily quick to temper these days.

A flash of white caught Kila's attention. The acolyte had appeared.

Nax, in the sack. She sent enough urgency with the command that the cat was moving before she realized what she was doing. The backpack lay open on the ground, and it soon bulged and wobbled as Nax hid inside.

"I can't hear a word you're saying," Kila said as she gripped Quinn's wrist. She shoved the woman's hand up so that Quinn could see she held the blade.

Quinn's tirade faltered then she sheepishly returned the blade to her sheath. Kila nodded behind Quinn. "Our Til's-boy is here."

Quinn reached for her hilt. Kila stayed her hand. "Calm yourself. He can't do anything to us but look."

The acolyte stopped at the edge of the park, positioning himself in the shade of a moss-bearded tree. He watched them openly, face passive.

Oly is here, Nax sent.

Kila turned to look at the backpack. *What? How?*

The last time Kila had seen Wen's ornery cat had been in the arms of the demayne, Flaumishtak. And happily so, having volunteered to go with the beast.

He's too far away to talk to. But he's here. Huff, too. Huff is worried.

Kila had known that Henley and Ragin were coming to the Garden. So Huff's presence was no surprise. She looked forward to seeing all of them. But if Oly was there, Flaumishtak might be, too.

What is he worried about?

But it was pointless to ask. If Nax couldn't speak with the other cats she wouldn't be able to find the answer.

Kila hefted the backpack onto her shoulders. It didn't contain much aside from the small hand mirror Her Enlightened Majesty had given her, a bank note from same, and her father's lock-picking kit.

And a cat.

She told Quinn about Oly and Huff.

"This place is strange," Quinn said. "You're right. Something *is* off."

"Ya think? Let's get to Ori's Home and see what's going on."

They went past the acolyte without looking at him. He didn't block their way, but simply followed. They asked directions of the first man they passed. He was short, rotund, and nervous. He didn't stop, but quietly said there were novitiates of Ori just up by Governor's House. Before they could ask anything else, he had picked up speed to put as much distance between himself and them as he could.

They found Governor's House easily enough. It was the grandest building in Docktown, at the top of a hill surrounded by fruit trees and a prickly grass lawn. The novitiates were resting in the shade, eating oranges. They had bushels around them, full of foodstuffs apparently bought in town.

Of the five novitiates, one stood out to Kila. He was the only boy, and his hair was nearly white.

"Ragin!" Kila called.

He turned to look, then slowly stood, mouth silently forming the syllables of her name. He didn't look happy to see her. His first words to her were: "What are you doing here?"

"Happy to see you, too. Quinn's mother finally let her to come to Ori's Home. Aren't I lucky to have come with her?" Not one word true. Quinn would never have come if the Shadline Cloak hadn't ordered her to, but other ears were listening and Kila was not about to go telling everyone Quinn was a Shadline.

Ragin lowered his head, eyes downcast. He sighed as if resigned to some great and unwelcome task ahead. He raised his voice. "Let's all return to the Home. These young women are coming there under the Rules of Princes. We should guide them."

The other novitiates rose, groaning. Not one of them looked eager to return. Kila noted that Ragin had surrounded himself with young women his and Quinn's age. Seventeen or eighteen, slim, mildly pretty. Except one, who was tall and beautiful.

A tinge of jealousy rose in her mind. She squashed it. She had no claim on Ragin, nor any interest in establishing one. Yes, they had endured many trials together in Starside, but Ragin had always been a bit too puppyish, following her about and giving her melancholy eyes. It made her uncomfortable.

"And who are *these* people?" the tall girl said. The sneer on her face was matched by the one in her voice. She eyed Quinn and Kila as if they were bit of atlen dung she'd found on her shoe. There was an oddness in her accent, especially her T's, which she pronounced as D's. "Surely you don'd know them, Raginald."

"I do, Hannah. This is Lady Quinn Peline of Starside. Her mother is a Radiant there. And this is—"

"Kiki," Quinn said before Ragin could spill Kila's name. "My cousin from the country."

Ragin's mouth hung open a few moments too long, but Hannah didn't seem to notice. Or care.

"Such didles as Radiand mean nothing do me," Hannah announced to the other novitiate girls. Though their same age, she seemed to have appointed herself their queen. "Nodice the unseemly manner of dress. Nodice how this one carries a draveler's pack upon her shoulders. Poor qualidy folk, both of them."

Ragin's pale cheeks flushed and his faint brows came down, but he didn't say anything in Kila's or Quinn's defense. Instead, he changed the subject. "Come along. This way."

He led the troupe downslope to a perfectly straight road leading inland. In the distance a green hill—or more accurately—a dome-topped mountain rose to the highest point on the island. Atop it, a circular tower.

Gauging by the distance, it had to be a very large structure. The Garden Tower. The center of learning and religion in the world.

Kila had heard about it, but seeing it gave her pause. She mistrusted those who lived in buildings that rose to great heights. The Citadel in Starside, the spires of the Cathedral of Til—even the greathouses of Gristenside—they all spoke of power. And where power rose high over the land, thousands toiled and suffered in its shadow.

The road was of crushed stone maintained with severe precision. The trees and underbrush of a dense jungle hugged it on both sides making the road a thin line of order carved into a realm of chaos.

As the novitiate girls ranged ahead, led by the imperious Hannah, Ragin held back with Kila and Quinn. He kept casting looks at his fellow novitiates. Mistrustful looks.

"You two should leave the island," he said. "It's not safe here."

Quinn scoffed. "Do you think I haven't dealt with worse bullies than Hannah? Highborn or no, we Radiants breed some nasty adders of our own, believe me. That girl's contempt was all for show. Mark me, she's jealous of us. Besides, we have letters of introduction from the Voluptuary of Starside."

"Hannah is merely the gauntlet at the end of a long arm, Quinn. Go back to your ship and sail wherever it takes you."

Kila grabbed his elbow and stopped him. "What're you so afraid of?"

Ragin sucked air through is teeth, frustrated. Hannah was marching back toward them, hands balled in fists. "How well do you know these liddle girls, Raginald? I think you are doo close do them."

Kila whispered to Ragin, "I thought you'd be glad to see us."

"It's not that. It isn't safe for you here. Put that away, Quinn!"

She had drawn her blade again.

"Blades are nod allowed in Ori's Home!" Hannah said, holding out her hand. "You will relinquish them do me imme-diadely."

Quinn moved so quickly that Kila had no chance to stop her. Quinn knocked Hannah's hand away, spun close, wrapped her arms around the girl's neck, and pulled her face down until Black's tip stopped a hairsbreadth from the girl's left eye.

Hannah growled. Quinn's blade hand began to move back, and her knuckles went white.

Kila recognized the effects of willshift instantly. She'd seen the Hargothe freeze Quinn to immobility with it. Hannah was not as powerful as the old seer. Her nostrils flared and her lips clenched as she strained to force Quinn to drop the blade. Beads of sweat pearled on her forehead and her dark eyes squinted in concentration.

"Hannah!" Ragin said. "You are not a Sensual. You do not have permission to use the mercus outside the Home."

The girl ignored him.

Quinn cried out and thrust the blade back toward the novitiate. She was winning, and Hannah's power was fading. Kila knew Quinn would not stop.

She stepped in, took hold of Quinn's wrist, and pushed up. Quinn's arm thrummed with tension. "Stop willshifting her while you have the chance," Kila said to Hannah. "Or are ya stupid?"

Quinn and Kila stumbled as Hannah released her efforts. Kila got between the girls. They were mirrors of each other, both black-haired, lovely, and full of rage.

"The Voluptuary will hear about this," Kila said. "Quinn, put that away."

Ragin went to Hannah and spoke in low, pleading tones. Kila didn't hear what convinced the tall girl to go, but she finally did. Though not without many muttered complaints about both her and Quinn.

Hannah stalked down the road, and none too steadily. The effort to willshift Quinn had taken much of her strength. The other novitiates had stopped farther along. Hannah shouted at them to keep moving.

Kila knew her type. Being bested in front of her own would fester in Hannah like a sickness.

Quinn had regained her composure. She even looked a bit

chagrinned as she sheathed her blade. Instantly her heavy breathing became audible. "What a pleasant girl you've found, eh Ragin?" Quinn said.

Ragin ignored her. "Where is Nax? Tell me you left her in Starside."

"She's in my backpack," Kila said. "What is wrong with you?"

Ragin looked feverish, and he continued to dart glances at the back of Hannah's head. She kept looking back, and she stayed within earshot.

"Are you and that girl . . . ?" Kila asked, waggling her eyebrows, trying to break the weird mood.

"Shush. You need to ditch that blade, Quinn. And Kila—"

"Kiki!" Quinn hissed.

"Kiki. Don't let anyone see Cayne. Both of you, get rid of them."

"We're not just going to throw our weapons into the shrubbery," Kila said. "How about I put them in my backpack. Nax can make room."

"I'm not parting with mine," Quinn said, hand again on Black's hilt.

"They'll search your backpack," Ragin said. "They don't trust anyone, especially folk coming under the Rules of Princes. You'll have to let me carry your weapons in."

"Your sweetheart will tell everyone about mine anyway," Quinn said sourly. "Let them try to take Black."

The chances either would relinquish their blade to Ragin were the same as them tossing them into the Ansin Ocean. And Ragin's demeanor wasn't inspiring much confidence in him anyway.

"Your beloved up there doesn't like me," Kila said.

"Stop saying that. Hannah doesn't like *anyone* but Sensual Thine. You must not get caught possessing blades or she'll—"

Now Ragin was looking behind them. His manner was so taut, Kila couldn't help but look, too. But there was nothing there except a gravel road fringed by dense foliage.

The blade thing didn't make sense. "The Voluptuary in Starside never forbade my weapon," Kila said. The woman had confiscated it once, but she'd returned it. And on subsequent visits, not even the Iopsis sourpuss Sens Taht had done more than frown at the weapon.

"This isn't Starside," Ragin said. "Did the Seeker stop you at the docks?"

"How did you know about him?"

"He stops everyone bound for any of the schools. He takes them all to the Til's Tower, novitiate, devotee, or acolyte it makes no difference. Henley and I were almost dragged there as soon as we got off *Flyer*. But the Voluptuary—the previous one, that is—had sent a contingent of Sensuals to the docks, too. Sens Gopsil was . . ."

Hannah turned and frowned at Ragin.

Ragin amended his statement. "Though a traitor, Sens Gopsil was a powerful merculyn. I thought it was going to be open warfare for a few moments. But the Seeker and his men were outnumbered."

The tall novitiate slowed until they caught up to her. Ragin went stone-faced. The change was as quick as if he'd been will-shifted into it. Kila doubted he had. There was something about the girl that made Ragin very nervous indeed. And it was more than just her imperious nature or her facility with the mercus.

Quinn sensed this, too, and her face went dark again. Kila

placed a light touch on Quinn's arm. The young woman snatched it away, caught herself in the act, and forced her shoulders to relax. Her hand still rested on Black's hilt.

Kila wanted to ask Ragin more questions, but it was clear he wouldn't be able to answer honestly with Hannah listening.

The group caught up to the overloaded horse cart stacked high with all of Quinn's chests and bits of disassembled furniture. The driver walked alongside his swayback mare, lightly tapping her flank with a crop. The beast moved slowly, head swinging side to side in a dirge's cadence. Poor thing, Kila thought.

The driver took hold of the bridle and guided the horse to the verge so that the novitiates could pass. He was not the man Quinn had given the gold coin on the dock. This man's face wasn't familiar, but he had rather tidy hands for a laborer, and he didn't have the features of a native Garden Islander.

He was likely an acolyte, or short of that, a man hired by Til's Tower to riffle through their things.

Instinct prickled the back of Kila's neck. She said, loudly, to Quinn: "Cousin, I don't feel it right to present myself to the Voluptuary dressed in this rough manner. Perhaps we ought to change into our gowns before arriving at Ori's Home."

Ragin's head swung around so fast she was surprised it stayed connected to his neck. He mastered his own surprise. And well that he did, for she'd been addressing him, partially. He had to remember the lie about her being Quinn's cousin.

Kila had practiced Quinn's snob-tongue Gristensider manner of speech, though Quinn insisted she never truly shed her Cheapsgate habit of clipping off entire pieces of words.

"Oh, yes, cousin Kiki," Quinn said. She was a bit hesitant.

Under Black's influence, she had come to hate skirts as much as Kila did, but she was no fool.

"You wand do change clothes now?" Hannah said. Her lips completely disappeared as she clamped her mouth with impatience. "Here in the middle of the road, you are going do sdrip do your skin and pud on dresses?"

"Driver!" Kila called to the cartman. "Halt a moment. We need something out of one of those chests." Kila shrugged off her backpack and gently set it in the shade.

"Your Gristensider accent is *ridiculous*," Quinn whispered. "You weren't even talking like that in front of *her* earlier." She surreptitiously jerked a thumb at Hannah.

Maybe so, but Hannah couldn't tell. Kila and Quinn fetched dresses from one of the great leather chests on the cart. Kila couldn't see any evidence that it had been opened, but that didn't mean much.

Hannah was still looking at her. "Yes," Kila said. "We're going to change right here. Would you like to watch, Sensual?"

"I'm not a Sensual. Yet."

"Oh, I see," Kila said, putting as much disdain in her voice as she could muster. "Then run along, *novitiate*." She'd heard Quinn's mother, Radiant Junison Peline, speak that way to Quinn. Much to Kila's irritation, it didn't quite have the same effect on the novitiate as it had on her friend, but Hannah cursed and showed Kila her pinky before spinning and marched away, fists clenched.

By rights, Ragin should have laughed. But he merely leaned close. "Be careful with Hannah. She's a tale-teller. If she learns a secret, be assured the whole of Ori's Home will hear about it within the hour. Get rid of your knives!"

"Please give us some privacy," Quinn said. "You may proceed, cartman." He clicked his tongue and the horse strained to get the cart underway.

Ragin went with him, herding the other novitiates along.

The young women hurriedly changed into the gowns Quinn had thought most suitable for meeting someone as grand as Voluptuary of Ori's Home. Kila only had three choices of altered dresses. She chose the pale yellow with white lace. It was a straight-skirted garment that cinched just below her rather unimpressive bosom. She felt ridiculous in it, but as she had realized, the skirts would conceal her blade.

Quinn saw the advantage of this instantly. She grinned as she buckled Black to her bare thigh under her lavender frock. Kila noted with a tinge of wry dissatisfaction that Quinn's bodice was much more amply stuffed than her own.

"If they dare search my person," Quinn said, "I will search their guts."

Kila blew out a long breath. "Yer gonna get yerself in deep if ya don't master yer temper. I've seen better-mannered trezz-fiends than you."

That shut Quinn up. But her grin didn't completely disappear. "I think I liked you better before I tamed you."

"Tamed me!"

"Hush. Let's get on with it."

Nax complained when Kila refused to let her out. *It's too hot! Oly and Huff run free in the wild. Why can't I?*

Have you talked to them?

No. They're too far away.

Then how do you know they're running free?

I just do. Let me out.

Kila shrugged and set Nax free. *Quickly now, into the weeds. Don't trust anyone but me or Quinn.*

The cat sent a mixture of relief and irritation through the bond. Kila hefted her backpack, now a bit lighter without the animal in it.

"That's a most becoming bag," Quinn said wryly. "I hear it's all the rage in Charton."

Charton was a coal picker's town on the coast south of Starside. Not exactly where fashion trends were born.

But Kila wasn't about to put the battered sack on the cart. She wouldn't trust the driver with a moldy heel of bread, much less her mirror, lockpicking kit, and bank draft.

She hadn't given much thought to the bank draft recently. Her Enlightened Majesty had bought Kila's excess dragon scales for a total of 3,415 gold Ravens. An enormous fortune, but only available for withdrawal at a bank somewhere in Docktown.

"How I would enjoy taking you to a Gristenside ball," Quinn said eyeing Kila's transformation. "You'd make for a delightful scandal. They would eat you up. Then they'd spit you out." This was said with affection, oddly enough. But Quinn was like that now. Squalls and sunshine.

They continued up the road as the sweltering, unstirring air baked them like pies. Kila had kept her sturdy shoes on rather than don the slippers that matched the dress. The contrast made Quinn giggle. "You look like Pigalia the Urchin newly made into a lady."

"You look like a Radiant's daughter laughing at a girl who doesn't have the same experience."

Quinn bumped shoulders with Kila. "I'm sorry. I don't

mean to tease. If only you could see yourself and notice the differences from when we first met."

Kila conceded there were many changes, not only the riddance of tangles from her hair and the scrubbing away of layers of grime from her skin. But she didn't like the fact that she liked the changes. The old Kila hadn't been bad. She had been happy as a thief. And she'd been free.

Ragin's reaction to her new clothes made Kila very uncomfortable. "Kil—er—Kiki, you look striking."

"You'd better push those eyes back in their sockets, laddie," Quinn said.

Hannah's jaw throbbed and Kila thought she would soon start spitting out bits of tooth.

Recovering, Ragin shook his head and motioned behind him. "Let's continue."

A LONG INCLINE led up the central hill of Garden Island. Two stone walls converged from the left and right to meet a stone arch marking the entrance to the Garden Tower grounds.

Ragin had explained the division of the island into Fifths, the one containing the road to Docktown being the secular Fifth, to which the islanders and their government were confined. "Each Way has a Fifth of the Tower as well. Ori's Home is down by the shore. A long walk yet."

They passed through the gate and into a narrow courtyard. An arched tunnel led inside where the air was cool and the narrowing forced the breeze into a stiff wind. It was refreshing after the long walk and climb.

A smaller courtyard was host to four more gates. "That one leads to Til's Tower," Ragin said. "That one to Pol's Vale, and this one to Ori's Home."

"And the other?" Quinn asked, eying the closed gate.

Ragin shrugged. "The empty Fifth. The ash-barrens."

They passed through the gate to Ori's Fifth and entered a section of the tower filled with placid-faced Sensuals and harried-looking novitiates. They spared cool glances for Kila and Quinn but didn't speak to them.

Then they exited the Tower and were heading downhill toward the seashore. Walls diverged, spreading away to define the domain of Ori's Fifth.

The landscape was similar to what they'd traversed getting to the Tower, but the road was not paved, just a dirt cart track, rutted and pocked with holes.

Kila stopped. If the only way into Ori's Home was through the Tower, she didn't know how Nax would get there. She looked over her shoulder.

Ragin said, "Yes. Reconsider. Go back."

"No. But the walls look so thick and tall. I wonder how the animals on the island get from one side to the other."

He got her meaning right away. "Oh, there are holes here and there, mostly for water drainage so the foundations don't get undercut. And the trees are not pruned. If someone wanted to climb over or through, there's a spot to be found."

Nax, don't come through the tower. Ragin says there are ways through or over the walls.

The cat was distant, somewhere behind her. *I will find a way.*

Kila's skin tingled as she passed through the arch. Not

from any mercusine ward, but merely from the realization that she had arrived. The long voyage was nearly over.

But given Ragin's odd manner, and his urging them not to continue on, she couldn't help but wonder if she would have been better off staying in Starside.

6

TYING ON STRINGS

"Two more, you say?" Highest Fley said, his back to Seeker Yan. They stood in his office, a plate of fruit and cheese on the side table. A flagon of wine, chilled, but untouched on a tray. He had left the furnishings unchanged since being raised to Highest of Highests. Red velvet cushions, thick rugs of intricate patterns, rich gold leaf on filigreed moldings covering the walls. It was fit for an emperor. Fley did not much care for such things. But Yan did. Despite his fervor, he had a weakness for luxury. Well, who but the One God was not flawed in some manner?

"Yes. Two *girls!* The Rules of Princes were never intended for girls," Seeker Yan said. He hadn't eaten a bite. The man was as taut as a drawn bowstring and his hawkish face and bright blue eyes were aimed boldly at Fley.

"I felt a strong merculyn approaching the island," the man explained. "I thought it a Donse Master returning from one of the far-flung realms. But I did not recognize his . . . flavor."

Seeker Yan was a connoisseur of the mercus and claimed he could distinguish one merculyn from another merely by feeling their power.

"And yet you return alone."

"Only those two girls came off the ship. Neither revealed the spark, though they were strong-willed enough to resist a bit of mercus allure. One pulled a blade."

Highest Fley turned away from his window and took up a plate. He stacked a few berries and cubes of cheese on it and sat at his table, a huge, round piece of polshel trunk, polished to a glorious shine so that the striations of its growth-rings created a rich and lovely texture. It had been the Highests' dining table for over 700 years. Legend had it that the tree from which it was cut had once grown where the Tower now stood, the ungoverned monolith of nature rightly giving over its place to Order and man. He flapped open a napkin and tucked it into the collar of his robe. "Sit, Seeker."

Fley poured two goblets of wine and began to eat. He wasn't hungry, but he had to show that he was unperturbed by events. The fervent Seeker wanted everyone to be as continuously outraged as he was. But Highest Fley was in command here, and he would not succumb to the infectiousness of the man's high-strung state. Yan could not refuse a direct order, so he sat, maintaining an upright posture. He took a sip of his wine, probably doing nothing but wetting his lips.

"The ship that bore them departed immediately, you say?" Fley said after a moment's consideration. "Surely the merculyn you felt continued on. Perhaps going to Ansso Island."

"No. There was no merculyn remaining on the ship. It must be one of those girls. One wore a necklace, likely a queller. A pendant of fine emerald worth more coin than the other girl had ever seen, judging by her uncouth demeanor." Yan had a tendency to spit when he spoke, for nothing would be uttered that did not have the force of absolute conviction in it. A fleck of his rage arced over the table to land in Fley's goblet. "Both belong in Til's Tower," Yan continued. "But now they are at the Harlot's Home."

Seeker Yan did not know that Ori's Home was already under Fley's sway. The man would have them scour Ori's Fifth off the island, turn all the Sensuals of mercusine power into source-taps and make charwomen of the rest. The males would be conscripted as novitiates, put on a ten-year track to correct their thinking, and perhaps rise to Donse Master one day.

Highest Fley sought the same ends, but he possessed two qualities that Yan did not. First was patience. Second was a strategic mind. Destroying the Way of Ori was a great objective, no doubt. But why do so now, when a puppet regime could operate there, luring more merculyns to the Garden? Already his pet Voluptuary was making much-needed changes to the training of the novitiates and Sensuals under her control. No more mercusine feats were being taught to the novitiates and only readings from the Theb allowed into their minds.

Patience and strategy were the exertions of true power. Highest Fley was happy to use a sword when a sword was needed. But the greatest power came from tying on strings and pulling them. It was time to pull one of Yan's strings and redirect his focus. "While you were gone, the Champion killed a novitiate. His power grows. Someone is feeding him."

Seeker Yan shot upright. "Impossible!" More spittle flew

from his rage-purpled lips. The right emotion, the wrong intensity.

"One would *think* it impossible," Fley said, popping a cube of cheese into his mouth. He stared at the Seeker while he chewed. He knew Yan despised his calmness. He swallowed and sipped his wine. "And yet his body strengthens and Dunne Portshalan will now require five men to quell his power. I need you to discover who is feeding him."

"But what of the merculyn girl? Her power was appreciable even a day's sail from the island."

Had that been a note of worry in Seeker Yan's voice? A quiver of nervousness passed through Highest Fley's throat. The Seeker knew mercusine power when he felt it. If one of these girls did have such an ability . . . perhaps Ori's Champion *had* arrived.

"I will look into it," Highest Fley said.

"But how? She's already—"

"I said I will look into it. Concern yourself with discovering how our Champion continues to grow in strength. Find out who feeds him."

Seeker Yan's eyes flamed with combatting outrages. The presence of this supposedly powerful merculyn girl on the island warred with the news of this defiance of the Highest's orders not to feed the Champion.

"I will discover the culprit at once." Yan departed, his robes fluttering in his haste to deliver Til's wrath.

Fley's thoughts went back to Roya Reth's words about Dem-Kisk. *Soon it will tread on fields of red.*

The idea of some new merculyn girl hiding in Ori's Home distracted him. If she wore a queller when she got off the ship, why had she continued to wear it now? More frustrating was the clear violation of the rules of the Synod it represented. All mercusine relics were to be turned over to the Way of Til. Neither the followers of Pol nor Ori had complied, else there would be no quellers remaining in the world. It had been the practice of Highests throughout the long history since the Synod to destroy such things to prevent anyone awakened to the mercus from escaping notice.

Yan had never been wrong about such things before, but the man had grown more rigid in his fanaticism of late. It could have clouded his judgment. And it posed to Fley a bit of a quandary. Should he demand the girl now or wait until Ori's Home was even riper with young merculyn talent?

It was one thing to demand Dunne Yples and Henley Mast be turned over. Quite another to demand a merculyn girl. There remained some powerful Sensuals at Ori's Home who could cause trouble for him. Still, if the girl truly existed, she must be brought to the tower soon.

He leaned back, tapping his fingers together. The notion of making this mysterious girl a source-tap revived a vague idea he'd had about the Champion.

Perhaps the Champion could be made a source-tap. He never need leave his prison if someone could draw upon his power. Someone like Fley.

Dangerous. Very dangerous. Highest Fley wasn't sure he could handle such furious mercusine flows.

Still . . . the idea appealed to him.

Caution and patience. He'd never regretted exercising either virtue. If the girl was truly powerful, she would flare upon the mercusine soon enough. When she did, he trusted the One God would provide him the wisdom to know what to do.

For the moment, all his focus would remain on the Champion. Yan would discover who was feeding him, put an end to the practice, and within a day or two the man would be trembling at Fley's feet and a begging for water.

7

GIVE THEM ME

When Kila crossed the arched stone bridge and saw the gentle creek gurgling away to either side, bordered by soft, mossy banks, she knew she was entering a new world.

Huge trees, trunks as thick as houses thrust from up the sparse grass and spread an immense canopy of yellow and green. Some limbs sprouted thick boles that returned to earth, forming new trunks. In this way a forest grew and thrived, mothered by one original, ancient tree.

There were several of these younger trees, which Ragin called polshels, and only in some places were the limbs pruned to allow splashes of sunlight to reach the ground. The effect was to shade the parklike expanse of the Home while leaving pools of sun to bathe gardens of flowers and vegetables.

The slopes descended gently to the seashore, and the vegetation in that direction was left wild as it tumbled in a green and brownish scrub to the sea.

Ancient buildings stood among the greenery, low and

open, of gray stone caked with gray lichen and festooned with vines. They looked a thousand years old.

At the center of all stood the Dome of the Gentle Goddess, open on all sides. Columns held up a great green dome, each carved in a likeness of Ori, each a subtly different aspect of her character. From Love, to Grief, to Rage. One made Kila rather uncomfortable, for it depicted a naked Ori, face to the sky in a moment of blatant ecstasy.

Beneath the dome, the three pools: Birth, Life, Death.

"The Voluptuary's office and residence is in there," Ragin said to them as they passed the largest building. In a quieter voice he said, "It's also the library and Rose Hall."

It was the only structure completely enclosed, though it did have a large circular stained-glass window at the top of the westward wall. Kila knew there would be another on the opposite side. They were the Sunrise and Sunset Rose windows, where the Sensuals would go to observe the opening and closing moments of Ori's day.

"We should go in," Quinn said. "I have letters of introduction for the Voluptuary."

"She is doo busy," Hannah said. "You will come with me do the novitiades ward, where you can dispense with those ridiculous dresses and pud on proper gowns. Sensual Thine will confiscade your weapons."

Ragin coughed into his hand. "They are here under the Rules of Princes. They must go the Princes Ward."

Hannah arched an eyebrow and looked at Ragin as if he were the stupidest person she'd ever met. "You condradigd me? You, Raginald? You fool."

In pleading tones he said, "Quinn Peline is as close to a

princess as one gets in Starside. Her cousin is of the same family. They are not suited for novitiates' gowns."

"Then I shall require do see their ledders of indrodugdzion. No one is admidded under the Rules of Princes withoud a referral from a Volupduary."

"I'll introduce you to the point of my—" Quinn's outrage ended in a yelp as Kila pinched her.

"We will show you nothing, novitiate," Kila said, voice cold. How odd that she was the one maintaining aristocratic deportment, while Quinn was acting the like a Cheapsgate tough. "And should you speak to us with such disrespect again, I'm certain there is a Sensual would be interested to know."

Ragin was waving his hands to get her to stop, but Kila had learned by Quinn's example. If you were of high station, you behaved as if those beneath you to must act accordingly. They usually did. Sometimes.

It didn't have quite the desired effect. Two of the other novitiates giggled into their palms, likely delighted to see Hannah put in her place. They received a hateful glare from Hannah, but the tall girl relented. "Pennie, you show them do the Princes Ward. I don'd have dime for such nonsense. You others, grab your baskeds and dake them do the kidgens. I will see Sensual Thine and inform her aboud our new"—She threw a sour look at Kila and Quinn—"princes."

She stalked off with a bouncing stride, black hair swishing like the tail of an agitated cat.

"I told you to watch it with that one," Ragin said. But before Kila could ask why, he was following after the retreating novitiate.

"He loves her, doesn't he?" Quinn said to the young novitiate assigned as their guide. Pennie could not have been older than ten. Short, curly headed and chubby cheeked, she nevertheless had the hard expression of a middle-aged woman resigned to a long day of chores.

"No one loves her. Raginalt least of all. Come with me."

PENNIE TOOK them to the outskirts of the compound, passing by long, low buildings that she said held the novitiates wards.

Gardens of flowers and mossy boulders lined the paths, while hedges of lovely and fragrant blossoms grew everywhere else. The air was filled with the call of songbirds and the distant surf.

The Princes Ward was backed by a viny and verdant jungle. Like the novitiate wards, there was a central living area open to the outside, and covered walkways leading to each apartment.

"There is one other here under the Rules of Princes," Pennie said. "There were two, but the other one is gone."

"Henley, yes we know him," Kila said.

Pennie squinted at her, but said nothing else. "You may choose whichever room suits you. I doubt there will be more entering the Home under the Rules of Princes, so you each may take a room for yourself."

With that, the girl turn and walked off.

The first room they opened was obviously in use. A man's jacket hung over the post of the bed. Other garments were strewn over chairs, wadded in the corner, and flung over a standing mirror in the corner. The desk had a few notes and books on it, as well as an empty wine bottle. The bed was unmade. A stack of dirty dishes stood on the floor near the door, leaning precariously.

"Boys," Quinn said. "They're all slobs."

Kila hadn't lived with Henley long, but she'd never known him to be more or less messy than she was. She didn't know why, but she didn't think this was Henley's room.

The next two rooms were empty, the air inside stuffy. Kila claimed one, Quinn the other. A door at the rear of Kila's room opened to a small patio. It offered a spectacular view of the descending slopes and the curling sea.

Quinn came out onto her own patio. "I'm starving. Did that girl mention where the dining hall was?"

She hadn't, but Kila was hungry, too. The last meal on board *Sea-Hound* had been two-day-old bread, a gruel the ship's cook called "glift", and a half-cup of watered down ale.

Nax slunk by, having worked her way through the jungle and somehow coming over or through the wall. She sat in a patch of sun and squinted at the view. A feeling of warm contentment and a full belly came through the bond.

What did you eat? Kila sent.

A leg-snake. A mental image came to Kila.

That's called a lizard.

I ate a lizard.

"Maybe we should go find the Voluptuary ourselves," Quinn said. She was holding the letters of introduction, each scroll sealed with the blue wax and the imprint of the Voluptuary of Starside. "Then we can eat."

Kila didn't get a chance to debate the wisdom of barging into the library and demanding an audience, because a Sensual appeared in Kila's room. "I see you girls have decided to use two rooms."

The woman was tall, thin, with dull brown hair bundled atop her head in the shape of a great mushroom cap. She stood erect, hands clasped beneath her breasts. Her gowns were the usual layers of sheer fabric, each a slightly different color, but they swept to the floor, concealing her feet.

Her face was pinched, cheeks and jaw hard. Her lips did not exist, for she scrunched them together in the tightest circle of disapproval that Kila had ever seen. And in her years as a thief, she'd seen hundreds of housemothers give her that look. This woman differed from them only in that her scrunched mouth had taken a permanent set. When she spoke, her lips were white with their tightness, and when she stopped they immediately snapped back into their inward pucker.

Contrasting with her constricted mouth were her eyes, which bulged, blue and fierce. "I am Sensual Thine." She announced it as if she was announcing the arrival of a queen.

Quinn had come round to see who Kila was talking to. The woman didn't acknowledge Quinn's existence except to hold out a hand. "Your letters. Give them me." She snapped her fingers. "I said give them me."

When Quinn hesitated, Thine snapped her fingers again. The sound was so loud, Kila winced. "Do not make me say it again, child. Give them me."

Kila anticipated Quinn's next move and already had her hand on the girl's wrist to keep her from digging under her skirts to draw her blade.

"We are pleased to meet you, Sens Thine," Kila said, "but the letters are addressed to the Voluptuary from the Voluptuary in Starside. We cannot give you their private . . ." she searched for the word Father had used " . . . correspondence."

"You will address me as Sensual Thine. We do not go in for Starsidian informality here—no we do not. Defy me again and your bottom will learn the meaning of the paddle."

Kila couldn't help but laugh. The woman had just threatened to paddle her. Quinn's body was shedding waves of rage, and she was trying to pull her wrist free of Kila's grasp.

"Get your paddle," Kila said. "I'll wait."

Thine's eyes bulged more, and she seemed to grow three inches. Nostrils flaring, she looked down her narrow nose. "I see you two will be a challenge. Very well. I shall take you to the Voluptuary, who I'm sure will be very interested to hear of your blatant disrespect for a Sensual of Ori."

She turned and strode out. "Come!"

They followed.

8

SPOILED APPLES

There was no conversation on the walk to the library. The woman kept up a fast pace, her head never once turning even a fraction of an inch.

The library was silent. The Sensual must have worn slippers, for her feet made no sound upon the tiles. Kila's heavy shoes clomped with every step, sending short-lived echoes through the high-ceilinged main hall.

She'd never been in a library this size before. The one in the Starside novitiates ward held perhaps a thousand volumes. This one had ten times that many. The tomes rested on shelves all around, most secured by drooping brass chains.

A few novitiates and Sensuals were bent over books at tables under the light coming through a dome of clear glass in the ceiling.

On the third level up, behind a set of carved mahogany doors, was the Voluptuary's residence. Thine motioned them in but did not follow.

They found a luxuriously appointed apartment. Thick rugs

on the tile floor, a spread of windows, all open to admit the sea breezes, white filmy curtains fluttering like ghostly dancers.

An enormous bed occupied one side the chamber, canopied and laden with fringed pillows. A desk and sitting area congregated on the opposite side. But in the middle stood an enormous copper tub supported upon a brass platform, the feet wrought into the shape of dragon claws. Kila had once seen a dragon, so she recognized those claws right off.

A woman reclined in the water, eyes closed, while two novitiates dipped cups in the water and gently poured streams over the woman's head.

The woman in the tub was saggy and pale. Her faced drooped at the sides like a bull-hound's cheeks, lower lip protruding and sagging as she took deep breaths through her mouth.

"Voluptuary," Quinn said. "We arrived in Docktown today. We have letters of introduction . . ."

The woman's eyelids lifted a fraction, showing watery, pale gray orbs, rimmed with red. Kila well knew the signs of too much trezz. The woman was a drunken sot.

"Girls!" the Voluptuary said. "Desist with the water."

The novitiates desisted, backing away a pace and tilting their heads forward to stare at their feet. They froze like that, living statues.

"Gimme your letters," she said, holding up a dripping hand.

Quinn handed them over. The woman put one in her mouth while she broke the seal on the other. She scanned the writing, then dropped the parchment into the water. The first one came out of her mouth and got the same treatment.

"Starside. Voluptuary Marnie Sinlop. Did you know I was

a novitiate with her? She was partnered with that moron, Goolsboy."

"Goolsoy," Kila said.

"What'd I say? Never mind. Rules of Princes!" She fished the now waterlogged letters from her bath and balled them in her hands. "All these years, not a greathouse in the world has sent a boy or girl to study here. Years of my life meeting and cajoling them to do so. Nothing! And now, four in the span of a few months. And not a one of them expected. Or wanted."

She threw the wad on the floor. It landed with a wet splat at Kila's feet. "The Way of Til has a hundred under the Rules. The Highest himself told me. A hundred! Is it any surprise the Way of Til holds such so much sway in the world? Girl, bring my cup."

A novitiate went to a side table and poured something into a goblet. The Voluptuary took it and drank it all down. "Excellent. The Voluptuary gets the finest. I always knew that. My foolish predecessor didn't drink trezz. She was too good for it. All those years she could have done, but she didn't. The greater insult? She sent me away, year after year, to recruit novitiates. 'Bring back the orphans, Gilly,' she'd say to me. 'Bring back the little sparks.' Bah! For what purpose? To bring girls here to worship the goddess and say the prayers and maybe—*maybe*—find *one* who could light a candle with her pathetic mercusine spark. I don't suppose either of you possess the knack? No? I didn't think so. The Seeker would've dragged you to Til's Tower if you had."

Kila was very grateful she'd maintained her mercus mask. And frustrated. She'd agreed to come to the Garden—in part —to increase her skill. But Sensual Thine and the Voluptuary had not engendered much confidence.

The woman handed her cup back to the novitiate. "But now I hold the position I always deserved. Voluptuary! I earned it! Not like you two trollops, born into everything you've got. Bah!"

"We've come a long way," Quinn said through gritted teeth. "We are here to learn. But I was surprised that no Sensual met us at the dock."

"Didn't know you were coming." She pursed her lips and leveled her watery gaze on Quinn's gown. "Probably wouldn't have bothered if I had."

Kila nudged Quinn, who was again reaching for her blade. "The Seeker you mentioned tried to drag us off," Kila said. "He claimed that anyone coming here under the Rules of Princes should be forced to Til's Tower."

"Better the Seeker and his boys had succeeded. Why do I need spoiled apples like you two?"

Kila was going to have to tackle Quinn if this woman kept provoking her like this. "Madam Voluptuary, perhaps you ought to rest. We can return when you are better able to—"

"You will return when I summon you. Not before. Sensual Thine will see to your studies. You will not speak to any novitiate unless she permits it."

Sensual Thine had appeared behind them. "Come, girls." When they didn't respond immediately, she snapped her fingers. "Come!"

Sensual Thine led them back to the Princes Ward. "Confine yourself to your rooms. Food will be brought. I will come daily for your lessons. Now, I will inspect your things."

While they had been with the Voluptuary, the cartman had come and gone. Quinn's furniture and chests were stacked in front of the ward. Quinn chewed her tongue so hard Kila thought she'd start spitting blood. But with Kila's help the Radiant's daughter managed to keep her composure while the Sensual poked through all her clothing.

"I heard you both had blades," Thine said. "I don't find them here, so where are they?"

"Novitiate Hannah told us we could not keep them," Kila said. "So we threw them into the jungle. They were mostly ornamental anyway."

Thine made a lot of disgusted noises as she inspected the fine clothes. Every once in a while she would deliver a judgment. Quinn's small-clothes got a "disgraceful" and her hair brush, pins, and innumerable bits and bobs for decorating her hair were pronounced "frivolous."

Once done, Thine had found nothing worthy of confiscation. She turned to Kila. "And where are your things?"

Lying to authority came as easily to Kila as breathing. "Oh, some of those things you just fondled were mine. That's all we brought." She hoped the woman hadn't remembered her backpack, which she'd tossed onto a corner chair in her room.

Apparently the woman had not spied it, for she gave both girls another once over, sniffed sharply, and marched away. Kila had never felt so openly detested. Even proper Gristensider contempt was no match for this this woman's outright hate.

As soon as the woman left, Nax crawled from under Kila's bed. *She smells strange.*

How so?

Cats didn't seem to have the same sense of sweet, sour, and bitter as people did. But Nax shared the smell so that Kila could experience it. And it was odd. Metallic and bitter.

"We have to leave," Quinn said. She stood at Kila's back door, arms crossed.

"And go where?" Kila didn't disagree with her friend, but she didn't see they had many choices at the moment. "*Sea-Hound* is long gone. Besides, we need to talk to Ragin and Henley and find out what in Kil's name is going on here."

Quinn huffed and hiked up her skirts. She pulled Black from her thigh sheath and started tossing it. She timed her comments with the tosses, for the instant the hilt touched her palm her voice went silent whether or not she was done talking. "There is something very off here." Flip. "I can smell it." Flip. "Can't you?" Flip.

"Nax sure can," Kila said.

Quinn tossed the blade again. "Ragin is scared to talk, and"—flip—"the Voluptuary is a drunk"—flip—"sack of flesh with no sense"—flip—"at all." Flip—"Do you feel safe here?"—flip—"Because I sure don't." Triple flip.

Nax watched with interest as Quinn's bladed flipped into the air and returned to the woman's hand, her head jerking up and down with each toss. She meowed and jumped onto Kila's bed to get a closer view.

"Let's talk to the boys," Kila said. "If they haven't fled the island, it must not be that easy to do."

"There are fishing boats"—flip—"all over." Double flip. "We'll find a captain"—flip—"and pay him to take us over to"—flip—"Ansso Island where we can"—flip—"buy passage." To emphasize her frustration, Quinn made her final catch and hurled the blade to *thunk* into a bedpost.

Nax leapt at Black as it wiggled from the impact. It came free and clattered to the tile. Nax chased after, but Quinn snatched her up by the scruff. "Leave it!"

Nax hung there, looking sullen, fore and hind legs limp, tail curled under, ears flat.

"Quinn," Kila said, voice barely a whisper. "Put Nax down."

Quinn swallowed and gently set Nax on her feet. A war waged on her face, making her brows scrunch in the middle then sag at the sides. She bit her lower lip and offered Kila the most apologetic look she'd ever seen. "I'm sorry, Nax," Quinn said, stroking the animal head to tail. "I'm sorry, Kila. I don't know what came over me."

She stooped and collected Black and returned it to the sheath.

"Yes you do," Kila said.

Quinn paled with shame, but she said nothing as she left Kila's room. The sound of her door quietly shutting stayed with Kila for a long time, like an echo repeating too many times.

9

THE HAZE PARTED

Kila moved a chair to the patio and rested in the sun. She knew Quinn hadn't meant to mistreat Nax, but the girl had to master her blade's influence over her. Already she'd nearly attacked the Seeker, a novitiate, Sensual Thine, and the Voluptuary.

Nax curled on Kila's lap and dozed. The cat wasn't concerned about Quinn's behavior. Maybe because animals understood that survival sometimes required shows of aggression.

Pennie showed up bearing a tray of food. Despite her small stature she easily hefted the platters of smoked pig and bowls heaped with a sticky white grain Kila had never seen before. "I'm not allowed to speak to you," the girl said peremptorily. She put the tray on a table in the common area and left.

Kila ate in silence, occasionally tossing a bit of meat to Nax. She didn't bother searching out Quinn to tell her about the food. She'd heard her friend's door open and shut an hour earlier, and then nothing.

Quinn had still not returned when night fell. Kila assumed she was snooping about, playing at being a thief. That blade of hers was a marvel, and Kila imagined—with a tinge of envy—just how useful absolute silence would have been to her and Wen. Especially in the early days, before Kila had mastered the thieve's-step, a way of sneaking that Father had taught her.

She washed up and set the dishes back on the tray for the novitiate to collect. Sleepiness warred with uneasiness as she sank into her bed. She wore the silly nightgown Quinn had provided for the purpose. It was a flimsy thing, but good for the warm climate. Kila kept Cayne strapped to her leg beneath it. She might be able to ash someone if trouble came, but she much preferred not to unmask herself until she had a better sense of what was going on at Ori's Home.

Nax abruptly sat up, claws digging into Kila's flesh. Her ears were forward, alert. She went to the still-open door facing the sea.

Kila was masked, so her senses were dull. But she heard a thump and a sharp curse outside. Someone was out there. A man, gauging by the voice.

She slipped out of her covers, drawing Cayne. She was grateful that she'd shaded the mercus lamp. Only a silvery haze of moonlight cut through the windows.

She opened the door and peered into the gloom.

The Princes Ward was not in the shade of a polshel tree, so the shrubs and flower beds beyond the ward were awash in moonlight.

Another rustle of bushes drew her attention. Someone was approaching from the direction of the novitiates wards, but they were trying to stay hidden by plunging through the thick hedges. If stealth was the goal, they were doing a terrible job of it. Those hedges were thorny.

Another curse sounded. "Kil and his seven sisters!"

That was a good curse in Kila's opinion. Because she'd coined it. In the Theb, Kil only had three sisters.

"Come out, Ragin," she called. "You might as well be traipsing naked through Dunne Medow Plaza."

Ragin fell from a nearby shrub, scuffing his hands and knees. His novitiate's gown flipped high up his milky white legs. Kila would have laughed except the moonlight caught his pale eyes, revealing stark fear.

He rushed forward, hands clenched in fists against the pain of his new abrasions. "Inside," he said.

He cast three nervous glances back before entering her room. He closed the door, drew the curtains to block the windows and pulled her around the opposite side of the bed. It was so dark only his blond hair and pale eyes caught enough of the bleeding light to show where he was. "You have to leave this island. Tonight."

"There are no ships, Ragin. What's got yer socks in knots?"

"It can't be a coincidence. I thought it was just a bit of my terrible standing with Pol. But when you arrived, I *knew*. I just knew!" He was starting to shake. As Kila's eyes adjusted she saw he was hugging himself and rocking. Kila grabbed his shoulders. "Ragin. Have ya been hittin' the trezz?"

When he didn't answer, she shook him. She dropped her Cheaps-speak and said firmly, "You need to explain."

He sucked in a shaky breath. "A month ago everything was wonderful here." He eased himself onto the edge of Kila's bed. "Henley and I arrived on *Flyer* a full ten-day ahead of schedule. It was as if Pol wanted us here, for the winds were constantly with us.

"We had a bit of trouble getting past the Seeker, but there were Sensuals waiting there, else we'd have been dragged to Til's Tower. Henley didn't like seeing the Donse Master, but he calmed down once he got settled here. He was in this very room under the Rules of Princes. Funny you should choose it over all the others available. The force of destiny makes many crossings. But why?" He motioned with his hands and looked to the ceiling, a pleading to Ori.

"Where's Henley?" Kila asked.

"I'm getting to that. When we arrived, the Voluptuary— the previous one—greeted us at the Dome of the Gentle Goddess in a welcoming ritual of cleansing. It was uncomfortable stripping naked before all those people, but I felt truly clean afterward. Henley didn't have to do it because he was here under the Rules. That was the first time I didn't envy him his freedom. I tried to explain how freeing the ritual was, but he just laughed at me."

Nax climbed into Kila's lap. Ragin stared at the animal, but his eyes—which were mere silver embers—looked right through her. "As the days went on, we were both quickly absorbed in our studies. Whatever we were interested in, there were books, and usually a Sensual who had some command of the subject. Henley began a deep study in the mercus, and Sensual Gopsil worked with him for hours every day. He said Henley was the most powerful merculyn he'd ever met. Can you believe that? Our Henley."

Ragin's story was building to something bad. And it had to do with Henley. "What happened to him?" she asked.

"Voluptuary Kalsi died." His pale face was ghostly and

vague. "She was a hale and hardy woman, Kila. Strong as a yearling atlen. She had another fifty years in her, mark me on that. But one morning she was found dead in her bed. No sign of death throes. Nothing. Just didn't wake up. I hadn't known her more than a ten-day, but I had come to love her. And there wasn't a Sensual but didn't feel the same."

He hiccupped and shook his head. His hand fumbled at his side. Kila realized he was seeking her hand. She hooked fingers with him. His flesh was hot, damp. His hand trembled. His voice croaked as he went on. "That's not entirely true. Not everyone loved her. Sensual Thine surely didn't. She often said there was too much freedom of thought and study allowed here. But we dismissed her sourness. Thine is an odd frog. But not a day after Voluptuary Kalsi died, Sensual Sennikt arrived. She had a dozen new novitiates in tow, and five Sensuals come to visit from far off lands. Voluptuary Kalsi had sent her all over the world to collect these strays and bring them into Ori's Home. And so that day she strode into the Home, and there was a very tense moment between her and Sens Gopsil right under the largest polshel tree.

"Nobody heard what was said. A mercus silence had engulfed them. Henley said Sens Gopsil wasn't the one who made it. But we didn't need to hear them to know they were arguing. When the silence lifted, Sensual Sennikt announced that she was the new Voluptuary. Seven Sensuals, including Gopsil, stood to bar her entrance to the Dome of the Gentle Goddess to take the vows. But they were brought to their knees by mercus power.

"Henley didn't see who did it. But gauging by the Sensuals' expressions, it was frightfully painful. The self-proclaimed Voluptuary announced that all seven of them were banished.

They were required to leave the Garden that very day. That moment. They were not allowed to collect their things. They were lead out of the compound by Sensual Thine and the new Sensuals Voluptuary Sennikt had brought. Her passel of new novitiates—including Hannah—looked on with approval and none would talk to any of us. The Voluptuary immediately announced the discontinuation of all the old rites. There are no sunrise or sunset calls anymore. And the only novitiates allowed to train in things mercusine are the ones she brought here."

"Ragin. Where is Henley?"

Ragin leaned away from her, lips going slack. He licked them with a pale tongue and said. "Before Voluptuary Kalsi died, a contingent from Til's Tower had been pestering her about Henley. They came at least once a day. They demanded that the Voluptuary turn Henley over to them. They called out loudly, voices enhanced with mercus power so that all could hear. They said that any Sensual or novitiate who delivered Henley to them would be greatly rewarded. None of us were concerned because Henley was universally admired and the Til's-boys equally despised.

"On the third day of her rule, the new Voluptuary received this same contingent in her private office. Novitiates called to serve food and drink whispered of a night of debauchery and drunkenness to match the Winternight revels in Starside taverns."

"They took Henley," Kila said, knowing it was true. It's why she hadn't seen Huff, who would surely have come to greet Nax. Her cat stirred and let out a mournful meow.

Ragin released a long breath. "The next morning, Henley

was pulled from his bed and thrown into acolyte's robes. His hands were bound and a strange cuff placed on one wrist."

"A queller," Kila said.

"A queller, but not mercusine. It was spiked on the inside. A mere tug on the leash would drive the spikes into his flesh. It must have been enough to discourage him. Henley had developed some facility with his power. Especially with warding his mind. That was all he would say about it." Ragin shivered and mumbled something about it being an appropriate skill for him.

"Where's Huff?" Kila asked.

"I don't know. I haven't seen him for twenty days. Maybe more. I left food out for him for a while, but Sensual Thine caught wind of it and put me in penance for it. Those were a hungry few days for me."

"And Oly?"

Ragin raised an eyebrow and looked at Nax, this time truly seeing her. "I should have realized you'd know he was here. Has either cat spoken to Nax?"

"No. They're too far away. Nax thinks Oly is with Huff. But I saw Oly disappear from this world. Flaumishtak took him. I don't know how he got here."

"Oly . . . Now, *that* was strange. Flaumishtak came to us on *Flyer*. We'd only been at sea for a few hours. He appeared as always, in a swirl of mercus green. He claimed he'd been given Henley's life. But in exchange for not killing Henley he made him promise to take care of Oly. The beast said he couldn't take him where he was going."

Kila disentangled her fingers from Ragin's. She rubbed his sweat from her palm on the bed linens. "Nax says both cats are in that direction." She pointed.

"That's where the Garden Tower is. Remember that Til's Tower occupies a Fifth of it? Huff must be staying close to talk to Henley."

Nax, are Oly and Huff safe?

Nax sent the equivalent of a mental shrug through the bond. She didn't seem worried about her litter-mates and Kila knew from past experience that Nax would be very alarmed if she thought them in immediate danger.

Nax. Answer me.

I don't know. They live.

Kila had never been able to pin down just how far away a cat could be and still communicate with a litter-mate. They always knew what direction their mates were in, but the communication distance seemed variable. Perhaps it depended on the amount of urgency one of them felt.

She realized that Ragin had gone quiet, though his breathing was a bit ragged.

"We obviously have to get Henley out of there," she said.

"You think we can sneak into Til's Tower the way we did at the Abbey?" Ragin said, voice sad and full of skepticism. "You've seen the Tower. The only way in is through the gate."

"Or over the wall, right? That's how Nax got here."

"Nax is a small animal. The Donse Masters' wards would catch a person trying to get into their Fifth of the Tower. No. If you go in, you will never come out. Mask your power, sneak like a shadow, go invisible if you can, but you will get caught. And then they will use you for whatever end they please. Henley is lost unless he can—"

"Listen to yourself, Ragin. We're talking about our friend. Maybe he's being smart and pretending to accept his fate. Maybe he recognizes this is an opportunity to study the mercus with masters of the art. He may be lying in wait for the day he can slip out. The Donse Masters don't know about Huff. They don't know that Henley can talk to us."

"You said they're too far away," Ragin said. "He can't talk to us."

Kila sent, *Nax, do you think you can get close enough to Huff to talk to him and me at the same time? If he's close enough to Henley—*

I understand.

Nax stood and trembled a bit as she stretched her fore-limbs. Then, without so much as a look back, she went to the door.

Kila opened it and Nax faded into the darkness like a ghost.

"Tell her to beware of dangers in the jungle," Ragin said.

"Like what?"

"Snakes, hog-ferrets, hawk-spiders, wolf-lizards, corpse-lice, hundred-legs, stomp-ants . . . the list is endless. Just wait until the night grows deeper. You'll hear the war of nature just beyond your door. Nothing weak or careless lives long out there."

Nor in Cheapsgate. But Kila didn't say it.

Be careful, Naxie, she sent.

This was answered with a particularly human-like feeling of don't-tell-me-what-to-do. Kila sent back a scolding feeling. Nax had no experience in this environment. She might step right into a hawk-spider's web. Just the thought of what such a creature might look like made Kila shiver. She decided she'd rather not know.

"I have to go," Ragin said. "Sensual Thine has her minions

do bed checks every half hour. I can make it back in time if I go now."

Kila wanted him to stay. She had so many questions. But fear sent Ragin out her patio door and into the night.

Nax's presence in her mind faded as the animal worked her way west. Kila found herself alone and feeling a bit helpless. Short of dragging the Voluptuary out of bed and demanding answers about why she had given Henley away, she didn't know what to do.

She decided to tend to her hair, which she had discovered to be a rather soothing ritual. She went to Quinn's room and borrowed the young woman's hairbrush, a silver-backed thing with an ivory handle. Quinn prized it, and said it had belonged to her grandmother.

Kila dug her hand mirror from her backpack and unshielded one of the mercus lights. She began the process of brushing her hair, moving the mirror all about to see herself from different angles. She felt a guilty flush in her belly for indulging in such vanity. How many times had she mocked young women for doing this very thing when she was younger?

But that had been her way of coping with her life then. The idea of owning such a mirror, much less having the luxury time to care about her appearance, would have been laughable during her thieving years.

Her *thieving* years.

They were behind her. She didn't need to rob a drunkard ever again. She had 3,415 gold Ravens just waiting in a bank for her. An unimaginable sum.

She was about to put the mirror down—face down to avoid Pol's wrath as Quinn had taught her—when she saw it casting a white glow on the table. It was the same color as the moonlight shining through the curtains.

She lifted the mirror, wondering how it could reflect so much light. But the light was coming from within the glass.

The mirror had frosted over, like a window on a cold winter night. Kila scraped a fingernail across it, but no strip of frost came up. The glass wasn't even cold. It brightened at her touch.

Her Enlightened Majesty had told Kila the mirror might reveal its secrets to her. She'd assumed that the woman had merely meant the reflection would show Kila that she was not the Cheapsgate waif she had always claimed to be—had taken pride in being.

But now the mirror was truly showing her something. She held it up, amazed by the glow, but also mistrustful of it. Obviously, there was something mercusine afoot. And Kila knew that Her Enlightened would never give away a relic of significant power unless it served her own aims.

The haze parted, just like wispy clouds breaking, to reveal the moon. To Kila's astonishment, she saw stars beyond it. And then the image shifted downward, bringing a distant castle tower into view.

"By Kil's five fingers and his throbbin' handle," she said. The tower continued to drift close. The view through the egg-sized oval of glass was like seeing the world from a bird's perspective. But unlike when Kila perched atop *Sea-Hound's* mast, this perspective was a dozen times higher up.

The image began to draw closer to the ground, showing a blasted land of tree stumps, not sawed cleanly, but jagged as if the trunks had been twisted by great hands and torn free. The few remaining trees were gnarled and leafless, skeletal things bent like crones. Surrounding these dead husks was a landscape of ash. All was tinged silver from the moonlight.

The castle drew closer. A crumbling wall surrounded it, and a long stone-paved roadway lead toward it, guarded by columns now choked with brown, dead vines. Many columns were broken and lay across the road in sections like fallen logs of carved stone.

The image stopped moving, as if the bird had alighted at the entrance to the road. A half-crumbled archway gaped like a mouth, smiling in dire greeting. The decay had shifted some of the stones, so that they protruded like jagged teeth. In all, it gave the impression of a skeletal jaw of a once mighty and enormous beast.

Beyond it, the roadway wound and narrowed as it climbed to the tower. The path pulled at Kila's memory. She wanted nothing more than to walk upon it and go to that strange tower. There was something familiar about it. She was sure she'd never been there. How could she have been? She'd lived her entire life in Starside.

The memory of being there grew until she began to doubt herself. Had she been there? Her head sprouted a pain at the base of her skull and it flashed through her temples, sharp as a calf cramp.

She dropped the mirror on the table and bent to hold her head in her hands. The memory faded and the notion that she'd been to the tower collapsed—like waking from a particularly frightening dream to discover oneself twisted in sweat-drenched blankets. The same sort of relief filled her now. The pain subsided.

It had just been the mirror. Some mercusine spell, forcing falseness into her mind.

Climbing into bed, she pictured the tower the mirror had showed her. What was it? Where was it?

Kila had seen a lot of weird things in her sixteen—or was it seventeen now?—years: demayne, mercus feats, a dragon. This was just another minor miracle in a long stream of them. She resolved to sleep, for she would need her energy to face whatever the next day would bring. Hopefully, Nax would get close enough to talk to Huff and get word to Henley.

10

A DULL THUMP

Life as an acolyte of Til was not nearly as bad as that of the Hargothe's prisoners. This Henley told himself like a mantra. He had food, a bunk to lie in, and he didn't have to worry about hiding from Donse Masters. He was surrounded by them.

That he was still a prisoner was undeniable. But now that he was deep inside Til's Tower, he saw certain advantages to it.

First, he didn't have to conceal his mercus power. In fact, the Donse Masters required he use it. They assumed he was a simpleton, without the first idea of how to perform simple feats with the power. In that, they were in error. But he got to practice aspects of his power freely, and that was nice. He enjoyed the mercus.

The second advantage was that they had grouped him with the novitiates tasked with keeping Dunne Yples from killing everyone. The trick to blocking the insane Donse Master's mercus was quite interesting. If only he'd known it those times the Hargothe had tortured his mind.

Dunne Yples had grown in power since Henley had been neighbors with him in the dungeon cells deep beneath the Cathedral of Til in Starside. Yples had likely been among the more powerful Donse Masters in Starside. Here he would have been an average spark.

But something had happened during the sea voyage to Garden Island. Henley had kept the man sedated using the supply of drugged boluses provided by Finta Sahng. Perhaps the prolonged stupor had allowed the man to find refuge in the mercus and thereby increase his power. Or perhaps he truly was the Champion of Til, as Highest Fley said, and his immense power was a divine gift.

Henley sat in his chair at Dunne Yples's head. Not because he was special outside of this great chamber, but because he was the most powerful merculyn on this shift and that meant he controlled the power the others produced. The others—four of them now, as one had been added since Dunne Yples had decapitated Acolyte Erron with a chain— served as source-taps for him. That, too, was a valuable thing to experience. Their power was considerable, and it all flowed to him.

Those serving as source-taps found their two-hour shifts dull, as they were not allowed to read or talk to each other. But Henley enjoyed his shifts, for the power he received was more than what was required to keep Dunne Yples from getting up to any mischief. This meant he could practice other skills without notice.

Nothing too elaborate. His first experiments were to deaden the stink of Dunne Yples's waste buckets. Removing odors had proved to be rather easy once he understood the principle of it. Blocking the madman was what gave him the idea, since he had to form continuous bolts of negating senses and encircle Yples's mind with them.

Dunne Portshalan, the kindly old Donse Master in charge of the quelling crew, had marveled at how quickly Henley had learned the skill. Henley had not told anyone that he had once performed a time-reign to keep Dunne Yples from killing Kila Sigh.

"In Til's Tower, secrets are power," Novitiate Oppsilin had told him. The dark-skinned boy had been talking about his trade in gossip, but Henley had understood a deeper wisdom in the words.

The other four boys serving as source-taps at the moment were not friends of Henley's, but they showed him grudging respect due to his facility with the mercusine. Uliq and Viniq were brothers. Rean and Tornlin were both twenty and not ever going to be Donse Masters. Both had the fat apathy of men who had given up all ambition and resigned themselves to being bossed around, given tongue-lashings both deserved and undeserved, and whose sole aim was to hoard food and drink for occasional overindulgence during free time.

They fed Henley power. And now he fed a bit of it—just a trickle—to Dunne Yples. Henley thought it a pretty fancy trick. He had some theories about how food provided a body sustenance, some of it learned during his own lean weeks after his father's greathouse had been burned to the ground, leaving him homeless in Cheapsgate.

Even as he barred Yples from accessing the mercusine, he fed some to him. It was not as sustaining as actual food would have been, but so far he'd kept Yples strong—maybe made him stronger in some ways—by trickling a bolt of mercus into him. It was a very general bolt, including the taste of fresh bread, the thirst-quenching feel of cool water on the throat, the soothing sound of a mother's song, the smell of hard black tea, and the vision of a blue sky. Henley had started the bolt seeking to calm the man, to ease his apparent suffering. It hadn't worked, but Henley was patient. Only after a week of doing this during his three daily two-hour shifts did it occur to him that he was sustaining the man.

Without water, the man should have died by now. There had to be more to Henley's mercusine elixir—a term he had coined—than even he understood.

The sound of the huge wooden door being unbolted and creaking open on its great hinges brought Henley's head up. He cut off his rogue mercusine bolt.

The next shift was ready to take over. Henley stood, still maintaining the quell on Yples. He waited until he felt Dunne Dee form his own quelling bolt. At a nod from Dee, Henley dropped his bolt and Dee took over.

The source-taps were stretching and yawning. Henley led them from the chamber. An enormous novitiate called Wad— who had no mercusine spark—served as a door-master and guard. He was at least thirty and would have been better suited to serving in an army or a city watch. But he was devoted to Til, small black eyes full of serious piety. He slid the thick iron bolt into place and returned to his chair.

The novitiates trailed after Henley to a small side room where food was always laid out for queller teams. Fruit, bread, smoked meat. It was good. Henley stuffed his face. No words were exchanged. They were not friends with each other, except the brothers Uliq and Viniq. They were not great conversationalists anyway.

Henley had gotten used to being alone among all these

men. The women were another thing entirely. The Favored of Til were slaves in all but name. As a novitiate, Henley was not permitted to talk to them. But he thought about them, dreamed about a few of them. One in particular.

He didn't know her name. There was no way to find out without asking, and he wasn't supposed to talk about them, much less ask their names. He gave this one a name. Suin, after the heroine of a story he liked as a boy.

She kept this room stocked with food. He usually saw her when he arrived early for his second shift of the day. She was in her mid-twenties, slim, pretty. There was a difference in her eyes from most of the other Favored. She looked unspeakably sad. The others looked placid, resigned.

Not Suin. Her soft brow furrowed when she noticed him noticing her. Not from anger or irritation, but from caution. Sometimes he'd spy her from the hall and just stand there and watch her. He liked how her lips moved as she worked. She was singing, but without sound. If he focused his mercus senses, he could hear her breath forming words. He longed to hear her sing out.

"Novitiate Henley Mast!"

Henley jerked up, startled to hear his name fill the small room. The other novitiates twisted to look at the door, mouths open to expose unchewed bits of food.

"Do not make me repeat myself." It was Seeker Yan. If there was a man Henley hated more in Til's Tower, it would only be Highest Fley himself. The Seeker had tried to abduct Henley and Ragin right at the docks when they'd arrived at the island.

He stood and went to the Seeker, schooling his face into what he hoped look like obedient curiosity.

"Come with me," the Seeker said. He didn't wait for acknowledgement, but turned and strode off. Henley kept pace, but chose to stay behind the man. The Seeker was very sensitive to position, so walking alongside him might be seen as reaching.

The man led Henley up three flights of stairs and into the observation loge, where the highest ranking Donse Masters used to observe the training in the arena below. All that one could see now was Dunne Yples straining against his chains.

"That man should be dead," Seeker Yan said. "He has been without food and water for four weeks. But look how his muscles bulge, how his brow sweats."

"He is possessed of a great madness, Seeker," Henley said.

"No madness can drive a man's body beyond its Til-granted capabilities. Someone is providing him with food and drink."

A slight tremor passed through Henley's mind. Was the man probing him? The Seeker was a babe compared to the Hargothe. Henley knew how to ward his mind from such intrusions now if he chose.

"How is that possible?" Henley asked. "To slip him food would require the cooperation of an entire queller team."

The Seeker wouldn't be taking Henley aside if he didn't suspect Henley of aiding the man. Had he felt Henley's little mercusine reinforcements flowing into the man? If so he was more sensitive to the mercus than Henley had suspected. He had been so careful.

"You . . . suspect me?" Henley said, forcing the soft tone of amazement in his words. He'd never been a natural liar. "I see. You suspect me because the other queller teams are led by full Donse Masters."

The hawk-eyed man stared at Henley without saying another word. "Kneel."

Henley knelt.

The man placed his strong, slender fingers on Henley's head. The mercus was a haze around the man, and Henley felt the bolts forming around him. So slow compared to the Hargothe, who always struck like lightning.

Henley's scalp warmed as a syrupy, silky peace flowed through his head and shoulders. He noted the use of honey flavor and the sound of a mother's humming as distraction bolts as the man plunged into Henley's mind.

Henley could deflect the intrusion. It would be as easy as pushing away a tired old dog seeking a bit of meat from his plate. But Henley knew any such defensive move would be as good as admitting guilt.

The man tightened his grip and his breath whistled in his nose. Henley felt the spine-curling horror of spidery legs probing inside his head. He knew the feeling well.

"I see you are hiding something," the Seeker said. "What is this little thought you wish to conceal?"

Henley scrunched his shoulders, body instinctively seeking to escape the filthy mercusine intrusion into his mind.

What is happening? Huff sent from far away. *The Hargothe?*

No. The Seeker. He knows I'm helping Dunne Yples.

A feeling of exasperation came through the bond. *You help a man who would kill you and Kila?*

Huff's capacity for empathy was reserved for Henley, his litter-mates, and those bonded to his litter-mates: Kila and Fallo. And it wasn't much empathy to begin with.

An abrupt shift in the Seeker's exploration caught Henley by surprise. The man occupied a new place in Henley's consciousness, and he felt his resistance flutter way like a leaf on a strong wind. "You are feeding the Champion."

"Yes," Henley said without qualm, though part of him knew it was stupid to admit it so easily.

"How?"

"I feed him the mercusine."

A pause, the fingers tightened their grip, tilted Henley's face upward. "Open your eyes."

He obeyed. The Seeker's severe blue eyes met his. Nostrils flared, showing dark hairs inside. His lips were flat, beard stubble patchy where his Favored had failed to shave him evenly.

Now that the secret was out, Henley saw no reason to continue to allow the man to stay inside his head. With an easy bolt of negated sound, he tripped his own ward, severing the intrusion.

The Seeker's reaction was entirely out of proportion, for his fingernails clawed into Henley's scalp and his body shuddered. The blue eyes rolled up into his skull and he trembled as if falling into a fit. Henley tore free of the man's grip and crabbed backward.

The Seeker regained control, swaying. Gathering himself he stalked forward. A bolt of mercusine lashed out but struck Henley's mind with as much effect as sunlight on a stone. Henley's defensive wards were all in place now.

Henley returned the favor, casually, not meaning to hurt the man, but merely to put him off. A bolt of light and heat, tossed with the same reflex as a man blocking a blow, struck the Seeker.

But something went wrong. Henley used too much power. The man flew across the room, struck the window, broke it and fell through. A short-lived scream resounded in the arena, ending in a dull thump.

A soft cry came from behind Henley. He spun, expecting a horrified novitiate or Donse Master.

Instead, it was the Favored girl he liked. Suin.

"Quickly!" she said. "With me!"

11

HOT BLOOD OF THE YOUNG

Kila lay awake staring at her thoughts, feeling Nax's presence so far away. Moonlight painted her room in a gray haze. The sounds of the jungle rose, slowly at first, then grew riotous. The chirps of insects battled the croaks of frogs. The low moans of some creature in heat answered the sudden chatter and shriek of a far-away animal Kila couldn't begin to picture. An occasional grunt sounded nearby, followed by a crash of limbs and a squeal. The jungle was a cacophony of struggle and strain.

Remembering Ragin's litany of wilderness dangers, she worried for Nax. Perhaps it had been a mistake to send her out there alone. But Nax had survived the roofs and alleys of Cheapsgate well enough; Kila had to trust the animal to take care of herself here.

But a snake could strike out of darkness. And what about a hawk-spider? Did such build a web? Did it fly?

Kila shivered and drew her blankets to her chin.

A small cry rose just beyond her patio door. It was weak

and high-pitched. It sounded like the meow of cat. It wasn't Nax. Kila knew she was miles away now.

She got out of bed and slipped into the night. The ocean breeze lifted the hem of her nightgown and caressed her bare legs. With the deepening night, the air had cooled. It sent a wave of gooseflesh over her limbs.

She drew Cayne.

The feline cry came from behind the Princes Ward. Kila edged around the structure and peeked into the dimness beyond. The moon was high now, and Kila's eyes quickly adjusted.

Pressed close to the rear of the Ward was a cat. It wasn't Huff or Nax or Oly. This one was larger than any of them, and yet unmistakably a kitten. Its fur was sleek and black, and its paws were twice the size they should be for its body. A kitten, yes, but of a breed that would grow to the size of a bull-hound.

It was hissing now, and out of the foliage crept the reason. Or *reasons*. A pack of strange, low slung, four-legged beasts. They waddled as they walked, long, snake-like tails dragging on the ground behind them. Their protruding lower jaws hung open, and flickery tongues flashed like lightning from between hooked fangs.

The creatures reminded her of the dragon she'd met in the Eerie above Starside. Somewhat. But these creatures had no wings, and the scales were rough and drab. And though much larger than the cat they had cornered, none weighed more than Kila.

They grunted and clicked through their wide nostrils, communicating with each other as they fanned out, approaching the cat from the flanks and front.

Two more held back, patrolling in wide arcs, ready to leap should their quarry get past the first ranks.

The cat hissed and cried. It held up one paw, claws out. Fangs bared, it pressed against the wall.

Kila twirled Cayne. This would never do.

The nearest lizard divided its attention between her and the cat. It kept swinging its ugly face toward her and coughing strange warnings.

She feinted at it. It sidestepped and honked. One of the back-rank sentries dashed at her, body undulating side to side as it ran.

Its speed caught Kila by surprise. She leaped straight up, somersaulting and doing a half-twist as the beast passed beneath her.

She lashed out as she landed, sweeping Cayne in a wide arc. The Shadline edge—keen as death itself—hewed through the tail. The lizard recoiled and flailed. Kila was upon it, stabbing flank, neck, belly. Finally, the blade pierced the eye and the beast went still.

Kila felt the approach of other lizards. Her mercus mask was gone, dropped by instinct. She heard the scuff of claws on the turf, tails dragging, clicks and grunts and high-pitched squawks.

Kila spun, Cayne projecting from her fist like a shard of blackness. The cat was still pinned back, hard pressed by two lizards. The rest of the beasts had turned on her.

She became death.

Teeth gnashed at her, but she was gone. Slash. Stab. Lizards bled. A weird peace came over her as she dealt death, using her mercusine senses to feel the movements of her foes.

Her blade came up to meet a lunging lizard, taking it

through the bottom of the jaw and out through the top of its snout.

Momentum carried the wounded lizard past her, wrenching Cayne from her hand. She became aware of another presence. A figure in a white shirt, slashing at lizards and kicking their heads.

The cat shrieked and attacked, rolling across the ground in a frantic embrace with the final lizard. And then it was loose and disappearing into the jungle, the last lizard giving chase.

The white-shirted man pinned it to the ground with a vicious downward thrust.

Kila retrieved her blade and went about stabbing brains to make sure all were dead. When she was done, she turned to the young man standing amidst the carnage. His white shirt glowed in the moonlight, except where it was torn or splotched with lizard blood. His hair and eyes were dark but nevertheless shone with moonlight and the delighted rush of physical combat. He was breathing hard, hands on hips, his dagger hidden away somewhere.

"Are you hurt?" he asked. His voice was soft, lightly accented.

Kila inspected her limbs. She had no scratches.

He did. She pointed to his thigh where a ragged tear in his trousers exposed his flesh and an ugly gash.

He looked down and gasped. He hadn't known. "It doesn't hurt. But this is not good. I must find a friendly Sensual. Those claws are filthy and give men blood-fevers."

"I can see to it," Kila said. She felt like she was half dreaming. Her mercus senses were alive with the scents and sounds of the night. The jungle had gone quiet during the battle, but now it erupted with chatter as the frogs and bugs gossiped about what they'd just witnessed.

"I thank you," he said. "But this will need a merculyn to—"

She ignored him and knelt to inspect the wound. He flinched and tried to move away when she widened the tear in his pant-leg. She told him to hold still. She cupped the other hand and started a swirling motion, as if rolling dice for a throw.

The combination of mercusine senses she brought into existence were so complex she didn't truly know what she did. But she felt it.

A red glow appeared in her hand, and she continued to swirl and stir it through her motions. "This may not feel good," she said.

"You're a merculyn." He was astonished and somewhat afraid. "But how . . . ?"

"Hush." She gently tilted her cupped hand and poured the mercusine light onto his wound. He hissed and shuddered, but he managed not to pull away.

The wound knit closed. "Do you want a scar or no?" she asked. She sounded distant even to herself.

"A what?"

"A scar. Do you want your flesh to hold a memory of this or do you want it erased?"

"A scar. Yes. Leave a memory."

Kila had watched Wen sew up a wound once. He had such nimble fingers. She remembered how he had clamped his tongue between his teeth as he concentrated on the work.

She did the same, focusing mercusine bolts she did not understand to burn away the wrongness in the wound. She flattened her fingers and traced the wound, knowing she could make the skin perfect. But before it was smoothed away, she stopped, leaving a slender line of white puckered skin. The scar looked like a wound healed over ten years past.

The mercusine light faded and the whirl of sensation that had come with it did, too, leaving only the feeling of her fingers on his skin. He was warm.

The young man sighed as pain and mercus chill drained out of him. And then he grew dizzy and squatted to keep from falling over. Mercus healing pulled much of its power from the subject. Or so the Voluptuary of Starside had once told her.

The young man's face was level with Kila's. Beneath the sweat and grim and splatters, he was . . . pretty. No, that wasn't the right word. Neither was handsome. But she liked his face.

So she knelt there, lizard blood wetting her bare knees, liking his face. He looked at her with amazement. "No one can do what you just did."

Suddenly uncomfortable under his stare, she stood and put up her mercusine mask. He had been shedding too much heat, anyway. Yes, and he'd been looking too deeply into her eyes. She didn't know him.

He straightened and flexed his healed leg, tested his weight on it. "May I ask what you were hoping to accomplish by engaging with these monsters?"

Kila toed one of the dead beasts. "They'd cornered a cat. What are these Kil-kissin' things?"

"Lizard-wolves. They hunt in packs."

Kila grabbed a lizard by the tail and started dragging it toward the trees. "They stink."

"That, they do." He started to help, though he kept throwing glances at her. "Why are we doing this?"

"Because I don't want the Sensuals to find them and start asking questions."

Together they hefted and tossed lizards—and a few severed pieces of tail—into the dense foliage. There was still blood on the grass, but nothing to be done about it. Or the blood on their clothes.

"And why would the Sensuals care that you killed lizard-wolves, aside from it being a foolish thing to attempt?"

She rubbed her hands on her nightgown, only then remembering how scantily she was dressed. She cinched the gaping neckline in a fist and looked at him. "They said I couldn't have my dagger. They wanted to take it. I lied and said I'd thrown it into the jungle on the way here." She shot a suspicious glance at the fine blade on his belt. Apparently the rules were different for men. If there was a universal truth in life, that was it.

He was suddenly very close. Not in a threatening way, but like a friend who wanted to speak to her in private when there were others around. Except there was nobody there but the frogs and insects and dead lizards.

"You have something—just here . . . " His hand rose and approached her face. She leaned away, but he clicked his tongue. "I'm not going to poke you in the eye. Hold still."

He rubbed the flat of his thumb on her cheek. It was a grimy thumb, but big enough to make her feel tiny. He showed it to her. Blood. He moved a lock of her hair from her face and pushed it back.

"You look like a lady, but you swear like a sailor." He sniffed. "And you smell like lizard-wolf guts."

"So do you. I guess you're the slob from the other room in the Princes Ward."

His brows rose. "You sound like my mother." Instantly hearing the mistake in his words, he tried to fix them. "Just that she is always on me about picking things up and not leaving dishes lying about." His voice dropped and he inched closer. "You don't truly sound anything like her. Or look anything like her."

Voices rose beyond the Princes Ward. Kila started away, not wanting to be caught in the night by a Sensual. She sheathed Cayne and tried to mask the bulge it made under her gown with her hands.

She rounded the corner, the young man stupidly following. Sensual Thine came to a stop. Hannah stood behind her, holding up a blazing mercus lantern. Kila squinted against the glare and held up a hand to block the light so she could see.

"I felt the mercus aflame," Thine said. Her constricted mouth was open as she gulped for air. "Who did it? Is there a Sensual back there?"

Kila shrugged. "I didn't see one. But they are all over the place here."

The young man snickered into his hand.

The Sensual paused, her eyes taking in Kila's gown and the young man's torn trousers. "Well, I see how it is," Sensual Thine said. "I warned the Voluptuary of this risk. I warned her of the hot blood of the young."

"Lizard blood is surprisingly cool," Kila said.

"Is thad druly blood all over you?" Hannah said, her lips curled back in disgust.

"I had a tussle with a lizard-wolf on my way back from my hike," the young man said. "This young lady heard the commotion and came out to investigate just as I killed it. There was splatter, unfortunately."

The Sensual's tight circle of a mouth miraculously scrunched in even tighter. Hannah smirked and eyed Kila's bare knees.

"Inside. Both of you." With sharp motions of her hand, Thine waved them ahead of her, and marched them to their rooms. She loudly lamented the lack of exterior locks for the windows and doors. When Kila pointed out that would make the Princes Ward a prison, Sensual Thine said girls should learn to keep their mouths shut. "But a *lady* would know that, wouldn't she?"

Hannah's smirk deepened. Sensual Thine and her lantern-bearer both gave Kila a final sniff of disapproval and stalked off.

Back in her room, Kila found herself trembling. Some of it was due to rage, some of it the left-over energy of killing lizard-wolves. But most of it was provoked by something else entirely.

She picked up her mirror and pressed a hand to her cheek where the young man had touched her. The skin there seemed to burn, not painfully, but with a heat that sank in deep and would not dissipate.

A while later Pennie showed up, bearing a bucket of steaming water. Her eyes were dark, hair plastered to one side of her head from sleep. "Sensual Thine says you are to wash up." The girl had a clean gown over her arm. This one long enough to reach Kila's toes.

"Why does she always send you, Pennie?" Kila asked. "How did you get on the wrong side of her mind?"

"I asked questions."

Kila drew in a long breath and nodded knowingly. In her best snob-tongue she said, "A lady would know better."

Pennie allowed a grin. "What would either of us know about being a lady?" And then she was gone.

Once Kila had turned the water in her basin a muddy red, and her cheeks and limbs a healthy pink, she climbed onto her bed. She stared at the wall opposite her, stared so hard she didn't blink and her eyes went dry.

Behind that wall was a problem. A young man. And she didn't know his name.

12

NECESSARY ENDS

Suin led Henley up a servants' stair, pressing close to the inside curve whenever another Favored or servant passed them going down. A few cast curious looks at Henley, but it wasn't that unusual for am acolyte to take this route.

The thick stone walls muted all sounds except for door slams or the occasional burst of conversation as they passed an opening to one of the many floors of the tower. But Suin kept them climbing, their breath loud in the narrow space.

At any other time he would have enjoyed following her, watching her figure move as she trotted ever upward. He would have memorized the feeling of her hand gripping his. Even now, feeling frantic that Donse Masters would capture him and try him for Seeker Yan's murder, he could not help but notice her scent, the floral incense common to Favored.

"This way," she said, finally taking a passage from the stairs. The corridor was gently curved, following the arc of the Tower. This was a residence floor for the Donse Masters of the

Tower. None were out, but Henley sensed the vague haze of mercus within a few chambers.

And those men would feel him passing by if they were paying any attention at all.

Suin picked up the pace. They were running now.

A door swung open, and white-bearded Dunne Vins tottered out. "By Til, what transpires?"

Henley pointed behind him. "Seeker Yan fell into the Champion's prison. Murder."

"By the Father! I—I—" The man continued to sputter, but Henley and Suin were past him. A corridor turned in, straight for the center of the tower. Suin's feet slid as she cut to take this new path.

The way ahead appeared to dead-end, but she did not slow. At the last moment, a section of the block wall swung in. A Spinster of Pol waved for Suin to run faster. Henley tumbled through and they finally stopped, bent double and gasping for air.

The stone wall ground closed behind them, leaving them in the dim glow of a whale-oil lantern. The Spinster held it up, her face made orange by its light. She was a slight woman of forty, with blond hair going gray. She wore the typical white robes of a Spinster, though her arms were bare. Both upper arms were cuffed in silver, giving her a warrior-like look Henley had never seen in a Spinster.

"Tia, you had better have many answers," she said.

Suin—apparently called Tia—nodded but was too winded to offer explanations.

Henley followed the Spinster through another door and found himself in Pol's Fifth of the Garden Tower. Another Spinster, called Rippa, waited for them there, breathing hard as if she'd been running to meet them. Younger than the first Spinster, this one was also more distraught. Her throat was flushed and she patted her plump face with one hand. With the other, she shoved something small into Henley's hands.

A ring, silver and etched with ruins of a language Henley didn't recognize.

"Put it on!" Spin Rippa said.

It was too small for any finger except his pinky, and even that was a tight fight. But he forced it over the knuckles.

The mercus instantly vanished from his awareness and his senses went dull. The ring was a queller. He was familiar with such relics, since Kila had had one for a while. He'd asked Dunne Portshalan why they hadn't put a queller on Dunne Yples, but the kindly Donse Master had merely shrugged and said they didn't have one.

Relief claimed Henley now, and he leaned against the wall.

"Go tell the Coin he has come. I will take him to a room where he can rest and prepare for his audience with her," the slight Spinster said to the breathless one. With a wordless nod, the plump Spinster ran down the hall and disappeared.

Tia stood next to Henley, face bunched with worry. "I must return, Spin Moirina. The longer I delay the harder it will be to make a reasonable excuse for my absence."

"Were you seen with him?" the Spinster said.

"I was. By servants and one Donse Master, but he is old and not well thought of. His memory is not reliable."

"No. I won't risk sending you back. Your time among them is done."

"But the madman needs me more than ever now," Tia said. "Without Acolyte Henley to sustain him, he will die."

Henley gawped at her. "How did you know about that?"

It was Spin Moirina who answered. "Tia has been watching you since your arrival. We were considering bringing you to the Vale earlier, but the Coin spun ten smiles and ten frowns on the question. She decided to delay until we had a clearer sign." She turned to Tia. "And what was that sign? I only felt a burst of mercus."

Tia clicked her tongue and patted Henley's shoulder. "He killed Seeker Yan."

"I didn't mean to. It just sort of happened."

Spin Moirina frowned. "Things don't just happen, Acolyte Henley. Pol smiles or frowns or turns her back or sits and watches. But the force of destiny guides us all toward necessary ends."

Tia was looking at the door they'd come through, her eyes keen as if she could see through the wood and stone to observe events in Til's Fifth.

"The Coin will want to see you both in the morning," Spinster Moirina said. She handed Henley the lantern.

Tia held back with him as Moirina took the lead, guiding them through hallways that looked just like those of Til's Fifth except that they were painted a bright white. Tia curled her arm through his. "Have you met a Coin before? Perhaps in Starside?"

"No."

"Be polite, not obsequious. Speak only if spoken to. Tell the truth."

"Easy enough. I would behave that way regardless of your warning."

"Good. For the remainder of the night I suggest you pray to Pol. Ask her to smile upon you."

He wasn't about to tell this young woman that he didn't

believe in luck, or Pol, or any of the gods. For one thing, she had saved his life by getting him away from Til's Fifth. For another, he felt an even stronger attraction to her than before. She was too old for him, he knew. She wouldn't have any interest in a boy his age. But he wouldn't say a word that would cause her to release his arm.

"I didn't mean to kill him," he said when they stopped at another door. It led into a sparely appointed room: cot and desk and lantern and nothing else.

"I'll bring food," Tia said. "But first I must change."

Spinster Moirina waited for him to go in. She closed the door and the unmistakable sound of a key working a lock came to his ears.

He was locked in.

Again.

13

CATTLE AND SNAKES

The smell of food roused Kila from her slumber. She rolled herself out of bed and stumbled, bleary-eyed, into the common room. Pennie had set out another tray. This one laden with eggs, bacon, more sticky grains, and a bowl heaped with fresh fruit.

Kila found a pot of tea, still hot, and poured herself a cup. Grabbing a hunk of bread and a few drippy slices of bacon, she went out into the morning sun. There, she sat on the grass and ate her breakfast.

The sea was bright and blue under the happy sun. The day was not yet hot, and Kila savored her delicious food, especially the tea. She didn't get good tea very often in Starside, and *Sea-Hound's* crew survived on a different hot beverage, a dark and bitter brew made by running hot water through ground up beans. Kila had never developed a taste for it, though Quinn had become sorely dependent on it.

Which reminded her of her wayward friend. Kila had gone to sleep before discovering if Quinn had come home. If

Quinn had been holding Black when she'd returned—which Kila thought likely—then she'd never have heard the girl anyway.

"May I join you?"

He stood behind her, teacup and plate in his hands. He was dressed in fresh trousers and a loose tunic meant to lace up the front, but he had neglected to fasten it.

He sat next to her, cross-legged. With his plate balanced on a knee he forked dainty bites of scrambled egg and fruit into his mouth. He swallowed. "You are wise to keep your skills secret from the Sensuals, Miss . . ."

His hair was black as Quinn's, but with a wave to it. Over-long, it drifted into his eyes and he occasionally blew strays away. His skin was tan, like the islanders, but of a different shade. He had very white teeth, which showed when he smiled.

"Miss . . . ?" he prompted again.

"Ki—Kiki," she said.

"Miss KiKiki. It's a pleasure to meet you. May the gods bless your days and nights."

"Not KiKiki," she said. "Just Kiki."

He chewed another mouthful, nodding as he considered this. Pointing his fork at his plate, he said, "The food is good here. The one thing that has stayed true. The rest?" He waved the utensil around, taking in the whole of Ori's Home. "Gone over like a vanan fruit. Beautiful and ripe one day, brown, mushy, and full of nasty little flies the next."

Kila didn't know what a vanan fruit was, but she'd seen other food turn. His comments aligned with Ragin's story from the night before.

But she didn't trust him. Was he trying to lure her into

saying more than she should? Rather than fall into his trap—if it was one—she asked, "What's your name?"

He blinked and stared at her. He swallowed again and wiped his lips on the back of his hands. "The novitiates didn't tell you?"

"No. Should they have?"

This seemed to amuse him no end. He laughed and shook his head. After a long sip of tea, he made a mocking bow. "I am Gian Delp. At your service."

She returned to her own meal and they ate in silence. The breeze picked up, bringing in salt air.

"As I said. It is wise of you to conceal your mercusine. And your Shadline blade."

Kila went still. The way he'd tagged on that bit about her blade made her ears tingle. "Shadline? That's ridiculous."

"A blade that absorbs the blood of its victims? What else could it be? But I won't tell the Voluptuary . . . or anyone else. It's none of their concern. I must say, your fighting style was . . . unconventional. Who is your Cloak?"

Setting her teacup aside she turned to face him. Back erect and chin high, she pretended she was Quinn about to dress down an inferior. "First of all, I had never seen a lizard-wolf before. I fought to kill them, not to score points for a jury of fencing judges. Secondly, if you think your knowledge of my supposed 'secrets' gives you some leverage over me, I encourage you to think twice. I've faced worse than you, and they ran like a frightened rats."

Gian absorbed this with a sideways nod and pursing lips. "You misunderstand, Miss Kiki. I merely encourage you to maintain your secret. Further, I suggest you leave this place— this whole island—at the first opportunity. How you have escaped their notice so far is remarkable, but I doubt you will do so for long. And once they sniff out how powerful you are . . . you will join my friend Henley Mast in Til's Tower."

"You know Henley?"

The first true surprise flashed across his features. "*You* know him?"

Kila felt like clunking her own skull with her fist. She never should have admitted knowing Henley. Well, it was too late now. "He was an acquaintance of mine when we were children. He was from a merchant house, I believe."

"He was. A good lad. He kept to himself when he wasn't training in the mercus. He seemed . . . wounded, but he wouldn't discuss it with me."

Kila pretended not to know what could have caused Henley's wounds. Gian might have been his friend, but that didn't mean he was trustworthy.

"There will be a ship soon," Gian said. "I have paid some Docktowners to come to me when they spy any on approach. I regret I was on a long hike when yours arrived, or I'd be gone now. When the time comes, do come with me."

"And why would she?" Quinn said, walking out to join them. She had dispensed with her dress and wore trousers and blouse. Black was not in view, but Kila knew the young woman had it secreted somewhere on her person.

"Cousin Quinn, this is Gian Delp. He helped me slay some lizard-wolves last night. He claims to have been friends with Hen."

"He hated being called Hen," Gian said, eyes narrowing a bit. "Which you would know if you were friends with him."

"I said we were acquaintances."

In the cool that followed this exchange, Quinn sat next to

Kila and munched on her breakfast. "And where are you from, Gian Delp?"

Again he seemed surprised by the question and laughed softly to himself. "Have you heard of Losstra?"

Quinn made a wry face. "Of course I have. Cattle and snakes and dust, no?"

"No. Music, and wine, and art." He leaned back and straightened his legs. The breeze pushed his hair away from his face. He had a high forehead, dark brows. Kila guessed he was nearly Quinn's age. "And cattle, and snakes, and dust."

"Is it far?" Kila asked.

"Far. South and west."

Kila didn't know much about the lands of the world. She had seen a few maps, but she hadn't committed them to memory. Wen had loved maps. Father had, too.

"Gian says a ship will come," she said to Quinn. "He plans to leave on it, and says we should, too."

"I agree," Quinn said. "About the leaving part. I don't know if we should take him along." Finished with her food, she stood and walked back toward the ward. She stopped abruptly. "Cousin, someone is here."

Sensual Thine stood in the doorway, a huge tome hugged to her bosom. "I have come for your studies. Come. Sit. We begin."

14

A CERTAIN KIND OF SILENCE

The Sensual led them back into the common area. With sharp commands, she bade them arrange the chairs in a half circle centered on her. Hannah was not a pupil, apparently, for she stood near the door, hands clasped, face arranged in a permanent sneer.

Placing her huge tome on a table, Thine said, "Henceforth, your studies will be confined to readings and interpretation of the Theb. I have seen enough to know immorality runs through your veins. Princes or no, you are in need of sharp correction."

She flipped through pages, the paper making a dry crinkling in the silence of the room. Kila and Quinn shared a look. Gian didn't seem slightly surprised, and not at all interested. He had removed his blade and was pruning his fingernails.

"I have a question, Sensual Thine," Kila said. "Why is Gian Delp allowed a blade but we are not?"

The Sensual looked up from her book, brows furrowing.

"Do not interrupt my concentration again. As for your impertinent question, let us make that the subject of today's lecture." With angry swipes, she moved to a different section of the Theb. She read: "And Til spake unto Horice, 'Let man know war and its appurtenances so that fragile woman need not. By their men's valor let woman know their worth. And man know woman's worth by her obedience and piety.'"

The woman looked up and jabbed a finger at Kila. "Think upon those words. From Til himself. Do you know the word *appurtenance*? I didn't think so."

Kila had been about to answer. Her father was always using ten-skillet words. In fact, he had humorously called his lock-picking tools "appurtenances of the thieving trade."

But Sensual Thine rushed on: "I wonder what passes for education in Starside. If you bother to trouble a woman to learn her letters, you might as well teach her to understand a few simple words. 'Appurtenances' refers to the items associated with an activity. Does anyone now understand what the appurtenances of war might be?"

Gian was already holding his weapon, so he waggled it and returned to his grooming.

"That's correct. Weapons. Til commanded that women not know weapons. So you see, the prohibition of weapons from women is prescribed in the Theb. Under Voluptuary Sennikt's guidance we are returning Ori's Home to the example of righteousness and good that it should have been all these years."

"Where in that book does it say Voluptuaries are supposed to lounge drunken in bathtubs?" Kila asked.

Hannah's eyes nearly popped from her face and Sensual Thine slammed her book closed. "You are an impudent little trollop, aren't you? The Voluptuary has led a difficult life. You merely found her in a state of well-deserved relaxation in her private quarters." Calming herself, she went on: "Now I assume you two can also scribble out words on paper. You will write a dissertation on today's reading, citing a minimum of ten more verses in the Theb that explicitly or implicitly forbid weapons to women."

Quinn rose. Kila could see the effort the girl was making to retain her composure. "This is not what I came all this way to study," she said. "I'm a Radiant's daughter, heir to her Radiancy. I came here to study politics, trade, agriculture, forestry, and banking."

Sensual Thine plucked up the Theb. "Those realms of study are available to you. First, enter the Way as a novitiate." She started for the door.

"I should have stayed in Starside. The Sensuals there let me use their library. They did not teach your interpretation of the Theb."

The Sensual stopped but did not turn. Instead she swiveled her head slightly to speak over her shoulder. "Starside is a pit of depravity ruled by a woman unfit to be the madam of a Venral brothel." She departed.

Hannah smirked at Kila and followed the woman out.

"She sounds like a Donse Master," Kila said.

They sat in shocked silence for a while. Gian finished trimming his nails and sheathed his dagger. It was a fine blade, polished, with a gold hilt. "That's the first lesson I've had since the change-over. Interesting. Do you have any doubt that we must all leave?"

"No," Kila said. "But I can't leave Henley trapped in the Tower."

Gain raised an eyebrow. "I thought you were only

acquaintances."

She wanted to slap her own face. A reasonable response did not pop into her mind. Odd, that. She was a facile liar under the most difficult circumstances. But Gian's stupid face made her thoughts all watery.

Quinn was still steaming, hand on Black, she paced the common area. She muttered under her breath about being better off in Starside.

"There are fishing boats," Gian said. "They do not go far out, but a captain might be persuaded to make the passage to Ansso Island."

Quinn stopped. "I had thought the same thing. But it is a long journey for a small vessel."

"We can't leave Henley." Kila looked at Gian for a moment, and a decision settled on her. "Quinn, Nax will be close enough to reach him today, I think. Tomorrow at the latest."

The raven-haired girl darted a glance at Gian, who was looking at Kila with even more interest than usual. "Who is Nax?" Quinn said innocently, covering for Kila's slip.

"Gian was friends with Henley. We have to trust somebody."

"Him? He's a cattleman." The way she said it made it seem like 'cattleman' was on a level with smuggler.

"And I'm a thief. You trust me."

Gian coughed in to his hand. "A thief, did you say?" The dawning of understanding filled his eyes. "You're Kila Sigh." He grinned impishly, proud of himself for having uncovered her secret. "That explains your mercusine power. You were one subject Henley did speak of rather often. Nax is your cat, then? I'm quite fond of Huff. Oly is a little bastard, though."

He shook a hand in the air as if remembering a scratch or bite on one of his fingers. Clearly, he'd met Oly before.

"Kiki, I don't know what this man is talking about," Quinn said. A three-year-old caught in a closet with a stolen pie would have sounded more convincing.

"He helped me kill lizard-wolves last night," Kila said. She added, "There was an odd cat in trouble. We saved it."

The anger bled from Quinn's eyes and face. Finally she gave Gian a once over and shook her head. "I'll leave you two alone. I'll see if I can find a fisherman looking to earn a few extra gold Ravens. But, Kila dear, don't let pretty eyes and strong shoulders make a fool of you." She left.

There's an odd quality to a certain kind of silence, Kila noted as blood rushed to her throat and cheeks. You could wake up to quiet and find it peaceful. You could find a secluded place after hard exertion and rest in a pleasant quietude. She supposed there were some bad silences, too. The one that occupied the common room in the wake of Quinn's last comment was one of them.

Kila decided such a silence couldn't be allowed to linger or it would choke her. Face and chest burning, she said, "Ignore her. She's protective of me, is all." She couldn't bear to look at Gian, who sat in a chair slightly behind her and to her left. If he saw her flaming cheeks, she would die. She felt that she would quite literally burst into flame and that would be it.

"Who wouldn't be protective of you?" he said. "But I don't think you need much protecting, do you Shadline?"

"I'm not a Shadline. I never took the oath."

"Still . . . you can protect yourself just fine."

She didn't nod or say anything. She didn't dare. For reasons she could not fathom, what he'd said about her abilities made her throat burn *worse*. It was like embarrassment combined with fear—fear that this stranger understood her, *knew* her, in a way that nobody should be able to know her without her approval.

"But perhaps you would like to train," he said into the unbearable silence. "I cannot claim to be a blade-master, but I know a trick or two. It will be a good diversion while we wait for your cousin to find us passage off this island."

"I would like that." What? Why had she said that? Quinn was right. Gian was making a fool out of her. "I mean. I would. But it wouldn't be safe. Cayne is . . . dangerous."

"What blade isn't?" He was standing now. "I can fashion wooden ones, good for sparring."

"I need to help Henley, not play at fighting with you."

"Unless you can blow a hole in a wall twenty paces thick, Henley will not leave Til's Tower until they open the gate and let him out."

"Nevertheless, I'm not leaving Garden Island without him. And Ragin."

Gian stretched and twisted, making his ankles and back pop. "I need to move my legs for a while. If we don't speak beforetime, let's meet at moonrise in the south garden. There is a well-lit patch of lawn there, perfect for our needs."

And then he, too, was gone. The silence he left was bearable only because no one was there to see Kila cover her face with her hands.

She allowed her blush to work its course then turned her attention to Nax. The cat was very far to the west. Too far to speak to.

"Hurry up, Naxie," she said to the room. "We've got to get gone."

15

IF IT PLEASES POL

Coin Mos Inlina was tall, lanky, and masculine. She wore her white hair short, cut all one length in the bowl-style of Henley's youth.

She was from Trine, and spoke in a fast, clipped manner, each consonant like the crack of a whip. "The Voluptuary in Starside was a fool to send you here."

Henley said nothing, just as Tia had instructed. But he found himself wanting to defend the Voluptuary, a woman who had no time for fools but who had been kind to him and had given him shelter when he'd needed it most.

The audience chamber was sparse, appointed with sturdy tables and chairs, well used. Nothing was cheap, but neither was it luxurious.

The Coin sat in the largest chair, the only one with armrests. She may have been made out of the same oak, for her back was perfectly straight, her elbows and knees bent at right angles. Her face was pinched, pale, with large black bags under her eyes.

Henley stood before her, looking at her, but not challenging her fierce gray-eyed gaze. He was her guest and he was wearing her queller. He understood the debt he owed.

Spin Moirina and Tia were behind him. Tia lacked the medallion of a full Spinster, though she carried herself like one. Gone was the meek and submissive Favored Henley had known in Til's Tower. Not that he'd known her, really.

The Coin's medallion hung against her flat chest, like a tea saucer on a gold chain. She lifted a long-fingered hand to touch it.

"I haven't slept soundly since that poor devil got here. You say he's mad. No wonder. He's ablaze with the mercus. But there's a constant flow of other merculyns as well. What is Highest Fley doing?"

"Teams of us work together to keep him blocked from the mercus. We have no quellers."

She spurted a humorless laugh. "Idiots. Do you know why they lack quellers? Because they've been destroying them as fast as they can find them. They do not want anyone hiding from their Seekers."

The woman's gaze lifted from Henley and locked onto Tia. "Did they misuse you?"

"There were a few occasions when I had to resort to my protections. Dunne Onnis was particularly free with his hands. Once."

Henley wondered what these protections were, but he guessed it was something mercusine. But if so, it meant Tia had a queller, too. He didn't recall any jewelry on her.

"I was subtle. And quick," Tia said.

"Which is why I chose you. But now you are broken for

that task. Pity. Moirina, do you have another girl to place within the Way of Til?"

"I have two candidates. Neither has Tia's skills."

Henley's queller kept him from hearing as well as he was accustomed to. But the way the Coin's jaw moved, he was surprised he didn't hear her teeth grinding.

"I won't send a girl in unprotected. That's final."

"Yes, Coin."

"So what shall we do with him? I don't suppose he wants to enter into the Way of Pol. We can't send him back to Voluptuary Sennikt, obviously."

Tia shifted.

"You wish to say something, child?"

"Acolyte Henley sustained Dunne Yples by feeding him subtle bolts of mercus, even as he masked him from it. It is a new feat."

Henley twisted to stare at the young woman. For her to have known that, she had to be quite sensitive to the mercus. And for her to have been in their midst without being detected, she had to have a queller.

But she didn't.

Seeing his confusion she offered a smile and raised her eyebrows.

"The Highest believes Dunne Yples is Til's Champion," the Coin said. "Is he, Tia?"

"I cannot say with any certainty. But I overheard two Donse Masters discussing something interesting earlier today. Dunne Yples uttered the words 'Dem-Kisk' recently."

Henley snorted and shook his head. "Did he also say 'thinnies in flames'?"

"What? What?" the Coin barked. "What is this you say?"

Henley wished he hadn't spoken up at all. But he couldn't take the words back. And the Coin looked like she could extract information from him with her eyes alone.

"Did you know that I was the one who brought Dunne Yples to Ori's Home?"

"Yes. Along with Raginalt Keel."

"You had him in chains," Spinster Moirina said. There was a heavy tone of judgment her voice.

"That was for his safety. For everyone's."

"He looked docile enough."

So they had been watching when he and Ragin and arrived. Henley had no idea that the Way of Pol was so sneaky.

"I had a medicine that made him docile, given to me by a wise healer in Starside. The Voluptuary's sister. I wish we had some of it now."

"What is this 'thinnies in flames' nonsense?" the Coin asked.

So now they had come to the heart of Dunne Yples madness and Henley didn't know what to do. He didn't want to draw Kila Sigh into the conversation.

"The thinnies are a reclusive tribe that lives in the Starside sewers. Dunne Yples witnessed hundreds of them burst aflame. A mercusine feat." He looked back at Tia with this last bit. How had she hidden her power without a queller? Was it possible she'd learned Kila's masking trick?

"*You* burned them?" the Coin asked softly. Her hand clenched her medallion, twisted, and removed it from its mounting. She did not blink as she regarded him.

"No. Not me."

"Who?"

The silence stretched. He could claim ignorance. He could lie and say that he'd told her all he knew. But he doubted she would believe him. He'd never been a very good liar.

"A girl," he said. "My friend."

"One of the Peline girls," Tia said. "Kiki and Quinn Peline arrived from Starside yesterday. I heard that Seeker Yan was wroth not to have brought them to the Tower. One must be a merculyn. If Dunne Yples felt her mercusine, he may have recognized it."

A moment of confusion at mention of Quinn Peline resolved in an instant as Henley realized that Kiki was Kila. "They're both here?"

"At Ori's Home, under the Rules of Princes."

Henley swiped a hand down his face. Maybe there was something to all this force of destiny nonsense the Sensuals and Donse Masters talked about. It seemed he would never escape her.

"You're right. But the merculyn's name isn't Kiki," he said. "It's Kila. Dunne Yples tried to kill her. He is convinced she is Dem-Kisk."

The Coin's nostrils flared. "Is she? In your opinion?"

Henley shrugged. "Yes."

"Does Voluptuary Sennikt or Sensual Thine know who she is?"

"I doubt it. I didn't feel her arrival. And trust me, anyone with sensitivity would have felt her. Easily. She can mask as Tia apparently does."

"That powerful?"

"You feel Dunne Yples. In bursts, she outshines him just as mid-day sun blinds the full moon. Although, I'm not certain that's true now. Dunne Portshalan was forced to add a fifth man to each of the queller teams."

The Coin raised her medallion, touched it to her lips. She whispered and closed her eyes. With a slow swing of her arm, she flung the coin high into the air. It arced and flipped, the gold flashing. It made three revolutions before it struck the tile of the floor, sending up a chime-like tone.

The medallion bounced straight up, tumbling and ringing. It landed again, edge on the floor, rebounding to again turn over and over.

Two more strikes, each one on edge, each bounce lower. It finally returned to the floor, on edge. The remaining energy of its momentum turned to a slow wobbling spin, like a top.

The saucer-sized medallion rasped on the floor, the ring fading as the spin slowed. Still it didn't fall.

Henley sucked air through his teeth, hands already raising to form the old, superstitious ward his nanny had used, forefinger and pinky extended, middle fingers tucked.

The medallion stopped, tilting at just the slightest angle. Henley was sure it was going to remain standing, an impossibility.

But then it toppled and clanked flat, showing the image of Pol's smiling face. Henley let out his breath, shoulders sagging with relief.

"Think that is a good result, do you?" the Coin said.

"Isn't it?" he asked.

"What do you think I asked the Goddess?"

"I—I don't know. I supposed you ask if Kila is Dem-Kisk."

"And the smile means . . . what? Yes or no?"

Henley didn't answer. He'd assumed that a smile had to be

good, a frown bad. But a yes to a dire question was as bad as a frown to a happy question. Worse.

"I did not ask if she is Dem-Kisk. It is a meaningless question. A person cannot be an event. I merely asked if her presence brought us closer to Dem-Kisk."

And it came up smiles.

"I've never met anyone who claimed to know that Dem-Kisk is an event," he said. "The way of Til says it is a person. The Voluptuary in Starside thinks it may not mean anything at all, that it is impossible to know regardless."

"She is wise to admit she knows nothing," the Coin said.

From the way she intoned this declaration, Henley realized it was the highest praise this woman could offer to anyone. He shivered to think of being out of her favor.

"If Kila is here, she is in danger," he said. "Voluptuary Sennikt and Sensual Thine will eventually discover her power and turn her over to Highest Fley."

"Don't you find that curious?" the Coin asked. "All these ages, the Ways of Til and Ori have striven against each other to place Donse Masters' and Sensuals' lips close to the ears of power. Ori has done dreadfully in that regard, for their Way is not as easily corruptible as the Way of Til. Yet here we are at the Garden Tower and Ori's Home has been compromised. The idea that a Voluptuary would turn over anyone to Highest Fley is absurd. It is clear to me what has happened. He *placed* her there. Sensual Thine is no devotee to Ori, nor is the Voluptuary. She spent too many bitter years roaming the world in search of novitiates. Someone found her, broke her, then gave her the position she'd always wanted. As long as she obeys Fley, she'll enjoy her station as the Voluptuary of Voluptuaries."

She stood and picked up her medallion. Affixing it to her necklace she approached Henley. She stood a head taller than him. Her boney shoulders were wide. He imagined her holding a sword and found it not too strange of an image.

"Or so she believes," she said. "Highest Fley will not long be content to control a puppet regime in the Home. He wants to possess it. And once he has it, he will turn his attention here."

"How do you know this?" he asked. "Highest Fley surely didn't tell you his plans."

"Tia has the confidence of several Favored in his bevy," the Coin said. "To him they are invisible. He speaks openly of his hatred for Ori and Pol, his contempt for the Triumvirate. The Favored tell Tia these things. Tell him, child. Tell him what Fley said three months ago."

That was before Henley had even left Starside.

"Highest Fley said that he would take the Home after a few dozen more mercusine-skilled novitiates were added to their number. He wants as many source-taps as he can collect."

The Coin lifted her eyes to Spin Moirina. "Can we get Kila Sigh away from Voluptuary Sennikt and Sens Thine?"

"Our girls at the Home are ears only, not prepared to lead an escape. Their coin-code is rudimentary and slow. You should also know that Spin Rippa warns of a coming fell-storm. It will be dangerous for anyone to be out of shelter during the winds."

"We must get word to Kila," the Coin said. "She must leave. Now. If Fley gets hold of her . . . Dem-Kisk may come even sooner, before our own Champion can be readied."

Henley sent to Huff, *Have you spoken to Nax?*

How did you know she was here?

I just found out Kila was on the island. Why didn't you tell me?

We're not ready.

Who's not ready?

Oly and Nax. We are making a . . . line. The image of a chain came with the statement. Henley understood. Ori's Home was too far from the Tower for Nax to communicate with Huff and still be in contact with Kila. So they were putting Oly in the middle to relay the messages.

That would be interesting.

Listen, Huff. Tell Kila to flee as soon as possible. Tell her I said to flee.

Why?

Because there's going to be an attack.

Tia was talking. "It is well that Miss Kila can mask her power. But there was a moment last night when I felt a surge from the Home . . . It was very far away, but it smelled different. It could have been her."

Smelled? Henley thought that an odd way to describe one's spark.

"I felt that, too," the Coin said. "It was fleeting, powerful, but consistent with the types of healing bolts we expect from that Way."

"It must have been her," Tia said. She had walked forward to stand next to Henley. She seemed to have forgotten that she was in the presence of the Coin. Still absorbed in her thoughts, she said, "I need to return to Til's Fifth. We're blind and deaf when we need to hear and see the most."

"They'll know you helped Acolyte Henley escape. You'll be interrogated, broken, turned into a source-tap and worse."

"Not if Henley beat me because I saw him running. First

he tried to kidnap me, then when I fought him, he struck me and knocked me senseless."

The Coin's mouth tightened, the bags beneath her eyes seeming to grow even heavier with the weight of what Tia offered. "You volunteer to do this? Knowing all the risks?"

"I do." Then, shyly, Tia looked up at the Coin. "Would you . . . ?"

"It must be me, my dear child. Are you prepared?"

Tia nodded.

The Coin bent forward, letting her medallion dangle in front of the young woman. Tia kissed the medallion reverently. Straightening, she closed her eyes and murmured, "If it please Pol, I ask the force of destiny to guide me."

"If it please Pol, I ask the force of destiny to guide me," the Coin echoed.

Then she balled her fist and struck Tia across the face. The girl whirled and fell onto her knees. Eyes glistening, the Coin rained four more hard blows to Tia's head and body, until the girl lay curled on the floor, weeping and bleeding.

When the Coin was finished, she nodded to Spin Moirina, who collected Tia and helped her stumble from the audience chamber.

"You are a monster, Henley. How could you do that to her?"

"I did what was necessary," he said, understanding the fiction they had just created. Poor Tia would be found gagged and bound in a storeroom in Til's Tower. She would be questioned, but no suspicion would fall on her or the Way of Pol for Henley's disappearance.

"You may go. I must see to extracting Kila Sigh from the Voluptuary's grasp."

"I have already sent warning to her," he said.

"When?"

"Just a minute ago."

She stared at him, waiting for him to enlighten her.

Taking a deep breath, he began, "Have you heard of Beloved Ones?"

16

OLY IN THE CHAIN

Instead of stewing about how flustered Gian made her, Kila went to the Dome of the Gentle Goddess to find Ragin and tell him they were scheming to leave on a fisherman's boat. She still had no idea how to get Henley free from the Tower.

She didn't expect to find Ragin in the Dome, but she thought somebody there would know where he was. Unlike the Dome in Starside, which held the public baths, there was no Sensual assigned as a door attendant. Maybe because there were no doors, since it was open to the outside all the way around.

The Baths were not for washing in, but for purification and healing rituals. Kila had never seen any of those rites performed. She didn't much want to now that she'd heard Ragin's story of going through it in nothing but his skin.

There were a few Sensuals about, and they studiously ignored Kila or looked at her with outright suspicion. When she approached a novitiate that had been part of the group she'd met in Docktown, the girl fled.

Others watched her and whispered to each other. She approached a young girl with red hair and freckled cheeks. "Do you know where I can find Raginalt?"

"I'm not allowed to speak to you," the girl said, voice squeaking. Her fearful expression reminded Kila of the jungle cat cornered by a lizard-wolf. But it wasn't Kila's fault. The whole mood here had been soured by the new Voluptuary and Sensual Thine.

Lifting her voice, she called, "I'm looking for Novitiate Raginalt Keel. Where can I find him?" Her voice echoed in the dome. All conversation stopped as every eye stared at her. Nobody answered.

"I'm going to keep shouting until someone helps me," Kila said. She cupped her hands around her mouth. "Ragin! Where are you? Ragin!"

Finally an elderly Sensual came toward her, waving a gnarled hand to silence Kila. A sharp snap stung her bottom. The woman had used the mercus to flick her!

Keeping her face calm took a feat of will. But Kila wanted to find Ragin, not get into a mercus battle with this old crone. The woman was boney and hunched, but she moved quickly enough. She took Kila by the elbow. "Come with me, girl."

Kila allowed herself to be led from the dome. Once outside, the Sensual said, "I'm Sens Dooni. I'll not have you disrupting the peace of the Dome. If you need to speak to a novitiate, you must go to Sensual Thine."

Kila started to argue, but the old woman shook her head and interrupted. "I know she'll refuse your request. But that's her prerogative. All novitiates are under her authority. You must accept it." She had not let go of Kila's elbow. She tugged it until Kila bent close. "You would be well to remain in the Princes Ward. Arrange to leave the Garden at the soonest chance."

Frowning, Kila pulled away. The woman's face sagged, and her rheumy eyes would not relinquish their hold on her.

"Mark me," the woman said. "Soonest chance."

"I understand, Sensual," she said. "I do."

She returned to the ward.

THE DAY PASSED IN QUIETUDE. The breeze shushed through the polshel trees and the surf crashed far off. The jungle was alive with bird calls and the cries of unknown animals. But it was a peaceful quiet.

Kila moved from her room to her patio to the common area, bored, worried, searching for Nax and thinking about Henley. And Gian.

When Quinn arrived, Kila jumped up, happy to have someone to divert her mind from its loop of uncomfortable thoughts.

The young woman was grinning. She removed two slim books from under her jacket. "The library wasn't very crowded," she said somewhat mournfully. "I didn't even need Black to sneak in and out. Well, except once."

Kila took one of the books. "*The Annals of the Shadline Cult*," she said. "I don't think the Cloak would like this."

"I want to see if it mentions Black." She held up the other book. "And this one is *A Thief's Notes from the Throne*. It was written by a First Race king who claims to have finagled his way from the alleys of his city to the halls of power. He stole the crown and reigned for fifty years."

"That seems far-fetched."

"Who cares? Better than writing a treatise on how I'm not supposed to carry my own Kil-damned weapon. Can you believe that old pelican? Where did she come from? She'd be better off in Donse Master's robes."

Doing her best imitation of Sensual Thine, Kila said, "You craven harlot! Do you not know that these so-called books have been declared Wrong? I shall report your lurid interests to the Voluptuary. You defile yourself!"

Quinn collapsed in laughter. Soon both of them were on the floor, weak and breathless with giggles. Every once in a while Quinn would say, "Do it again!" and Kila would scrunch her lips into a small circle and say, "Tarts! This is not the deportment one expects of ladies!" She'd put on her snobbiest Gristenside accent so the last word came out "leddehz." Eventually she couldn't get out a single syllable without snorting and collapsing into painful bouts of laughter.

Finally they calmed, and a good silence came over them.

Henley says to flee! Nax's voice came into Kila's mind as softly as the flap of a butterfly's wing. Barely there. Yet it sounded like she shouted it.

Nax! Is Henley well?

No response.

Quinn sat up, faced serious. Kila held up a hand. "It's Nax."

Nax! she shouted in her mind. *Is Huff there? Is Henley alive?* She focused all her attention on the bond, yearning to feel something through it.

Finally, a small voice returned. *Flee!*

Nax. Tell Henley we're going to help him.

There was no way to know if the message got through. Nax's presence was there, far off to the west. Kila had never spoken to her at such a distance.

Henley says attack!

Nax? What does that mean? Flee or attack?

But there was no answer. Quinn started pacing again while Kila lay on the floor of the common room, hands over her eyes to block out all distraction.

"I've lost her. For now."

Quinn offered hand, pulled Kila to her feet. "What is it? You look like you swallowed a bug."

"Henley was talking to Huff who relayed it through Oly to Nax. But Henley said 'flee'. And then he said 'attack'."

"Which is it?"

Kila didn't know. It was the oddest thing. Nax had a peculiar sense of logic, but even she would know those were contradictory instructions.

"We already knew we needed to get off the island," Quinn said. "So I'm going with 'flee.' It was probably Oly throwing in something just to confuse us."

Straightening her skirts and hair, Kila nodded. With Oly in the chain, there was no telling what Henley truly meant.

Quinn said, "I spoke to a fisherman's wife. He was out on his boat. She said for five gold skillets her husband will take us to Ansso Island. I'm going back there tonight to talk to him."

"We're not leaving without Ragin and Henley."

Quinn tilted her head from side to side. Neither refusing nor agreeing.

"Quinn, we can't abandon them."

But Quinn was already gone, leaving Kila alone in silence.

17

AQUAMARINE STARS

Quinn hadn't returned when Pennie arrived with dinner. Kila ate the bread, cheese, and warm salad of a sweet potato-like substance and greens. She tried to reach Nax, but the cat wasn't answering. In fact, she seemed farther away than ever.

Since she wasn't welcome out among the novitiates and was unwilling to write her assignment for Sensual Thine, Kila slept. She awoke to discover night had fallen. The moon was just beginning to haze the trees with silver. The jungle was a riot of noise.

She found dinner in the common room, untouched. Apparently Quinn and Gian had not returned from their adventures.

Gian! She remembered the blade practice he'd mentioned. Stuffing a hunk of bread in her mouth, she changed into her blouse, trousers, and waistcoat.

In minutes, she was out the door and heading south. The paths through the gardens were lit by occasional mercus lights. The night was warm and breezy. The smell of the island was at odds with the tension in the air. Sweet blossoms Kila couldn't identify shed an intoxicating perfume. And the bugs' and frogs' racket was rather nice. The farther she went, the farther she got from the tangle of the jungle. The calls of the wildlife were audible but distant, less threatening.

Gian was waiting for her. She came upon him slowly, her footsteps masked by the wind. The canopy of the polshels was behind her, and she stood in the open beneath a sparkling dome of stars.

He was moving through a series of blade-forms, motions swift, precise, and smooth. She thought the forms more suited to fighting with a sword, but the fact he held a wooden dagger didn't detract from the display.

He danced through the movements, grunting softly when he delivered blows to invisible opponents. His shoes were tumbled at the edge of the patch of light, thrown carelessly aside.

Kila's shoes joined his.

"You're late," he said without looking at her. He leapt and kicked, then landed in a ready-pose, dagger held close to his cheek.

Mercus lamps were posted around the spread of grass that would be their practice area. Moths flitted about them, frenzied by their madness for light. Gian went to the side of the patch of grass and plucked up another dagger. He tossed it to her. She caught it.

The craftsmanship was excellent, hilt smooth but shaped for a secure grip. The single-edged blade was slender and tapered to a point. It was shaped like Cayne.

"It's sharp," she said, thumbing the edge. It could cut paper, a piece of fruit, surely skin.

"It's a dagger."

Compared to Cayne it might as well have been a stick. A sharp stick.

"I hope you didn't spend too much time on this," she said, waving the weapon. "It would be an odd sort of punishment to be cut by a dagger of your own making."

His eyes gleamed, as if made from chips of the moon. His teeth flashed brighter, reflecting the mercus light. "Come. Let's play."

Kila adopted the stance Yiqa had taught her in their single training session atop the Warren. By Kil, that seemed so long ago now. It placed her side-on, dagger forward, knees bent.

Gian circled to her left. Kila happily switched her blade to her left hand to show that he would gain no advantage attacking from that side. His smile strengthened. Was he amused by her defensive move because it was good, or because he knew it was a lie? Kila could no more fight left-handed than she could pick up a boulder with her toes.

Gian lunged. A blur. Kila barely spun in time to avoid a sharp jab in her ribs. Her wooden blade sliced the air in response

"Not so skilled for a Shadline," he said, side-stepping.

Kila put her weapon through some flourishes. They were tricks of the eye once one understood how to perform them, but they had scared off plenty of back-alley street toughs in Starside.

Their sparring ground was much closer to the sea than to the ward, and the low vegetation between them and the water provided no break for the breeze. Gian's black hair pressed to his scalp on one side, his loose shirt doing the same, outlining his lean lines.

Kila's bare feet pressed the grass as she mirrored Gian's steps, keeping him well out of striking range. She had sparred with Wen back when Father had still been alive. Two kids squaring off with wooden rods. That hadn't been anything like this.

Kila had left even those crude sessions a bit bruised, but so had Wen.

Gian wasn't Wen. He didn't look like him; he didn't move like him. There was a silkiness to his steps, a dancer-like balance to his shoulders, so that they stayed level as he moved. He had been trained by masters.

Kila tried her favorite trick. She charged, fell into a roll, bringing the edge of her blade to his shin.

It cut empty air.

She rolled up, already twisting. Gian was gone. She looked around.

Something thumped softly behind her. His arm wrapped around her, pinning both of hers. His body pressed to her back and the edge of his wooden knife came to rest against her throat. "Very slow. I'm disappointed."

Kila stomped his toes.

Gian cried out and his embrace loosened enough that Kila could drive her elbow into his gut. The wooden edge of his knife, dragged across her throat, burned. Had it been steel, she would be dead.

Always press your advantage in a fight, Father had advised. Kila wheeled, hilt of her blade already sweeping up to catch a man bent double from a gut blow.

But Gian had fallen all the way to the ground. Her blow missed.

He swung a leg, catching both of hers and upending her. Her back struck the turf, dislodging a grunt. The shock made her grip release, and the blade fell into the grass.

The noise of Garden Island was distant now, and Kila heard only her own moans and Gian's gulps of breath. Her elbow had hurt him.

Good.

She scrambled for her lost blade.

By the time she had collected it and scrambled to her feet, Gian was ready.

"Get that Kil-bloody smirk off yer face, ya blaggerdy devil!"

"Now, now. There's no call for obscenity." He lunged. A feint. Kila didn't react. She now knew that his back foot twisted slightly when he lunged for a true hit. A tell.

They returned to circling again. The wind stiffened, bringing the smell of the beach with it. Despite the cooling air, Kila was sweating.

"Who taught you to fight?" Gian said. "A tavern brawler?"

Kila threw her blade at him. The point hit his shoulder, but did not sink into his flesh. He charged, swinging his dagger in wide arcs. Kila ducked and rolled, returning to her favorite move.

As soon as she popped to her feet, Gian wrapped her up and pressed his blade to her throat. "Is that all you've got?" His voice was low and hot in her ear. "It's a wonder you've lived to fourteen."

"Fourteen!" Kila cried. She tried to stomp his feet, but he lifted her off the ground. Grunting and cursing, she tried to drive her heels into his shin. He adjusted his hold. "If you let your foes get you like this, you'll die. You need to learn true skills instead of relying on tricks."

The temptation to drop her mercus mask and set his ears on fire nearly defeated her. But years of living with Wen had trained her to respect skill when she saw it. There could be no doubt Gian was a superior blade-fighter than she, as much as it twisted her gizzard to admit it.

That didn't mean she had to tolerate his taunt. "I'll have ya know I am *at least* sixteen," she said archly. She went limp, signaling that she was submitting. This round, anyway.

He released her. Before she could square off again, he lightly took her elbow. "Hold still." His hand slipped up to her wrist, body lightly touching hers. She felt very small, encompassed by him. "Twist your forearm out like this when you jab." He guided her through the motion. "You are small so you must extend your reach by using the whole length of your arm and weapon. Slicing with a dagger is silly."

His bare foot caught the inside of her forward ankle and shoved it forward. "Bend your knee a bit. Yes. When you thrust, the power comes not from your shoulder, but from your hip." His hand touched the outside of her hip. "Rotate, back foot planted. Let the earth give you power."

He released her and came around to inspect her form. She practiced a few thrusts, quickly discovering how much power she got by rooting her toes to the ground and rotating her hip.

His smile faded. "That's how to strike. The difficult part is learning *when* to strike. Against a more powerful, more skilled foe—like me—you should run."

"Are ya tryin' to make me mad? Cause yer damned good at it."

He tilted his head and squinted. "Do you always get angry with those who have invested time and sweat building their craft?"

She struck. Not the way he'd taught, but the way Yiqa had. Lunging low, she brought up her offhand forearm to deflect his parry. Her point drove at his gut.

And then she was off her feet, Gian behind her, and his blade to her throat. He sawed it back and forth, hard enough to burn, but not to cut.

She gritted her teeth and swallowed her curses. She couldn't blame him for being so good.

"Are you sure you're at least sixteen?" he said. "You fight like you're six." But he was laughing. He released her and they faced off again.

For an hour they circled and threw taunts at each other. Kila was wrapped up so many times, she simply started nodding and saying, "Yep." He would release her and they'd try again.

Her blade never once touched his body. She tried throwing it at him again, an end over end blur, aimed at his forehead. He deflected the blade and it flew off into the bushes at the fringe of their sparring ground. Not satisfied with this, he moved through series of mesmerizing lunges and finally ended up wrapping Kila in his arms gain, his blade pressed her throat.

She didn't resist at all. She was too exhausted and bruised. Gian didn't cut her skin with his wooden blade, thought she knew he could have easily gored her a hundred times over. She felt like one of the chicken-bugs Nax liked to toy with it, helpless and weak against an incomprehensible force of nature. Nax eventually killed and ate the chicken-bugs.

She sagged back into Gian, the fight drained out of her. The ocean breeze felt good on her skin. The curl and crash of the surf lulled her. Gian's body was too warm, but she didn't mind. He was solid. Strong. He kept her upright.

"You give up?" he said. At some point he'd lowered the blade from her throat, his arms no longer pinned hers quite so tightly.

He turned her to face him. His smile was still there, no longer amused or taunting. It was then she realized she was trembling, and not from the exertion of the fight.

His face filled her vision. She noticed for the first time a scrape on his cheek, a line of raised red. Not cut enough to bleed. "Did I do this?"

A force beyond her comprehension compelled her to reach for the wound. There was nothing mercusine about it; she may as well have been a string-puppet for her total inability to resist the impulse.

He flinched at her touch. It couldn't have been from pain. The scrape was a nothing. It would fade overnight. His arms looped behind her. And suddenly his hand was in her hair, hers in his. Their lips joined, softly, then urgently. A thrill like the mercus zing crossed Kila's skin, illuminating all her senses. Gian pressed the kiss more firmly. Kila had no counter, no will to attempt one.

Her mercus mask shattered. In rushed all the senses, the sounds of the far off war of the creatures of the jungle, the susurrations of the waves on the shore and the wind through the polshel trees. Bugs and frogs and nightwake birds called in their infinite varieties, all seeking for something, calling into the riot of sound where no individual voice could be heard. And yet, Kila heard them all.

Gian smelled of sweat and earth. His hair was soft in Kila's fingers but thick as a horse's mane. Heat emanated from him, washed over her and mixed with her own. She was enveloped in an inferno yet did not burn. Somehow it chilled her, raising more thrills along her arms. Luxuriating in it, imbibing it, her sense of balance faltered.

The strength of his arms and shoulders, the softness of his mouth, the urgency with which he searched her lips—it was all a marvel, a wonder. His hand stroked the small of her back. She felt fire melting her even as chills stole her breath.

A mercusine wave swirled around her, an incomprehensible blend of senses. The world came alight in blue, even though her eyes were closed.

"Kila!"

The voice drove a blade into the moment. Their lips parted. Gian's eyes went wide, his teeth showing. Not in a smile, but in the softness of unmasked desire. He looked down, toward their feet, then back to Kila's eyes. "Please put us down." His voice was low, but steady.

"Kila!" the rude, interrupting, voice called again. She recognized it, but the name it belonged to couldn't surface in her shattered mind. She realized she'd not taken a breath in a long time.

Blue light reflected in Gian's eyes. Mercusine. All around them swirled a flurry of mercus light, made from sparkling bits of blue. Like a whirlwind of aquamarine stars or illuminated gems, they floated and shed their light upon them.

"Please . . . Kila," Gian said. "The Sensuals will have felt you." He looked down again.

Kila did, too. Their bare feet hung two spans above the

ground, the grass awash in the blue glow of Kila's mercusine swirl.

"Kila!" called the voice again. "You have to get away from here. The Sensuals are coming."

Tiny lanterns were visible in the distance, Sensuals and novitiates coming to find the source of this raging mercus flow. Kila sensed how much power she used to keep them afloat. She would be a beacon to every merculyn on Garden Island.

She didn't know how to stop it gently, so she slammed her mercus mask into place. They fell. Knees unable to absorb the shock, Kila tumbled atop Gian. How she wanted to lie there with him on the grass of their sparring ground. She wanted to kiss him, to let time fall away, to fill up her senses with him again.

Ragin rushed up. "Get up! Go!" He was pulling at Kila's elbow. She yanked free.

"Were you spying on us?" she said, climbing to her feet. "Why can't you leave me alone? I'm not your novitiate partner. I *never* took the oath you did."

"Kila, Raginalt is helping us," Gian said. "And he's right. We must go."

With her mask back in place, the blue swirl had vanished. Ragin's face was illuminated only by the white mercus lights around the sparring ground. His blond hair was white, his face whiter. Lips trembling, he tried to straighten his shoulders. "Get back to the Princes Ward. Stay there. I'll try to get word to you when I've figured out how to get Henley free."

"You? How in Kil's name will you get him free?" Kila cried.

Gian was trying to pull her hand, trying to get her to leave before the Sensuals came. She strained to get close to Ragin.

"What have ya done so far but sulk an' slink around like a kicked dog? You *let* 'em take Henley."

Ragin's face went stony. His eyes flicked to the lanterns of the approaching Sensuals and then to Gian, who stood close behind Kila, still lightly tugging on her hand. "I've seen enough here," he said, voice ice. "I know what I need to do. I'm going to Til's Tower to join as an acolyte. I'll find Henley."

"Ragin, yer bein' a stupid—"

"Don't call me stupid!" he hissed. "One of us has to get inside the Tower. It can't be you, so it has to be me. I'll get word to you through Huff. Now go!"

He turned away from her and jogged toward the approaching Sensuals. Kila allowed herself to be led out of the mercus lights and into the darkness.

18

RIGHTEOUS WRATH

Highest Fley shot up from bed. The mercus hummed with the slowly fading resonances of a far off eruption of power.

No. Not an eruption. More like a great upwelling. But so powerful! It was so full of tones and complexities he couldn't imagine what mercus feat had been accomplished by it.

He nudged the Favored sharing his bed. "Fetch Seeker—" He cut off, remembering Yan was dead, killed by the boy Henley.

The girl rubbed her eyes and gathered her robe. "Who should I fetch?"

"Never mind. Leave me." He dressed and smoothed back his hair. He followed the girl from his quarters. She went one way, he the other.

His steps were quick as he descended level after level. With the mercusine feat to the east being so powerful, he worried that the Champion had escaped and was already wreaking death upon the Sensuals.

Breathless, he broke into the observation loge overlooking Dunne Yples prison. The glass in the window had not yet been replaced. Fley was relieved to find the man still chained to his table, surrounded by five acolytes and one Donse Master.

Dunne Portshalan shuffled into the room, eyes bleary from sleep. "Highest. I feared the same as you."

"Seeker Yan said a strong merculyn had recently come to the island. Quelled, he believed. I think we have just caught a sniff of what she is capable of."

"She? Surely, Highest, no woman alone could command such power. The Sensuals must have joined in a circle. Perhaps all of them together, like these men do." He pointed to the queller team below.

Fley's eyes went to the straining man on the table. His face was purple with effort as he strove to pull his chains from the wall. Protective wrappings had been slipped under the cuffs and shackles to prevent him from rending his flesh to the bone.

"How will we ever control the Champion?" he asked Dunne Portshalan. "We may need him to defeat this girl if we cannot control her."

"Highest? Who is she?"

"I will find out. Have you tracked down Acolyte Henley Mast? I want him questioned. Why was he feeding the Champion against my instructions and how was he doing it unnoticed?"

"He is gone. I have searched deep within the subtle realm for his spark, but it has vanished."

"Dead or quelled? And how did he slip through our gates? I want answers, Portshalan."

The man bowed and shuffled away.

Fley had relied too much on Seeker Yan. He saw that now. The man's fervor and energy had made him a fast and keen-edged tool. But he'd been too zealous, too confident.

Fley was grateful he'd not left his manipulations of Ori's women to the man. Such efforts required a longer view, and an appreciation of nuance and tradeoffs.

Highest Fley came to the only door in Til's Tower he would bother to knock on before opening. He did so now. Three sharp raps of his knuckles on the wood.

"Come in," came an alert voice.

Highest found Dunne Quiv where the man always was: at his small writing desk, lost amidst piles of papers. Stacks of reports and dispatches from around the world leaned against each other on the floor. A small footpath was all that remained visible of the tile floor. It curved from the door to the desk and from there to the small cot affixed high on one wall. Beneath the cot, wooden boxes overflowed with papers. The single window, set two feet into the wall, was obstructed with yet more papers. Even in daytime, the room would lay in shadow. At this hour, the only light came from the mercus lamp on Quiv's desk.

He looked younger than his thirty-five years. Thin, with weak brown hair, he had a noble aspect, broad brow and shapely nose. Though serious, his mouth was shaped into a pleasant smile. "You felt it," he said, a simple declarative sentence without a hint of question in it.

"I did. Seeker Yan claimed a powerful merculyn had recently come to the island."

"Yes. But which girl is it?" He fished one paper from inside a stack and scanned the notes there. "Two young women arrived aboard *Sea-Hound*. Captain Yabor Rin. He's a minor scoundrel. Lady Quinn Peline and her cousin Kiki. They threatened Yan and his acolytes with knives. They proceeded into Docktown where they rested in a backstreet park before joining with a group of novitiates led by our girl, Hannah. They knew Raginalt Keel, the novitiate who arrived before her with Henley Mast."

"Of the Starside Keels?"

Dunne Quiv nodded. "The youngest of five or six boys. There is a daughter, too. Name unknown." He frowned at the uncertainty. With sharp strokes he made marks on the paper. Probably a reminder to find out the Keel girl's name. Quiv had little tolerance for such gaps in his records. "A Mast and a Keel arriving here together . . . An odd pairing. The two families have enjoyed a long spell of animosity. The Mast greathouse was burned to the ground not long ago, according to my sources."

"The Peline girls come from Starside?" Fley asked.

"Yes. Much too much coincidence, don't you think? Young Henley is a powerful merculyn. And now one of these girls is, too? Perhaps the Voluptuary in Starside has sent them as spies."

Fley considered a moment whether Henley had been the source of the mercusine bolt in the east. But no. Not even Henley could have mustered that much power.

"Send word to Voluptuary Sennikt. I want the girls in the morning. If she even considers keeping them, I'll unleash the Champion and sort out the limbs and ashes later."

Dunne Quiv raised an eyebrow. There was much skepticism in the expression, but he kept his mouth shut on that front. "She will likely be unconscious at this hour. Her trezz habit has grown, I understand."

"Then send word to Thine. I will have both girls."

"Within your rights, Highest. But if I may suggest offering Sensual Thine a small reward. She is as zealous as her brother was, and this presents a chance to deepen her loyalty."

"Do as you think best."

"Should I tell her about her brother?" the man asked as Fley opened the door to leave.

"Yes. Tell her that the young man who killed Seeker Yan is well acquainted with the Peline girls. And the reward you mentioned. Tell her that she can assign Henley Mast's penance once he's captured."

Dunne Quiv inhaled sharply, delighted by Fley's creative solution. "And may she come here for Seeker Yan's death services?"

"Of course. We are men of the One God, are we not? He is the god of mercy as well as righteous wrath."

"I will send my messengers immediately. She will deliver the girls to us." He dipped a quill and began to scribble a note. Fley left him there, knowing the work would be carried out with alacrity. Quiv would make a fine Highest one day, but Fley would be sorry to see him go.

Fley needed to find Dunne Portshalan again. They had preparations to make. Once the Peline girls were apprehended and he had learned which was the merculyn, the queller teams would have double duty blocking both her and the Champion from the mercus.

"Question," Quiv said as Fley was turning to leave.

"Yes," he said, pausing in the doorway.

"What *will* you do if Thine refuses?"

"Do you think it likely?"

"I think it improbable. But possible." Quiv's habit of

answering every question by presenting the various slivers of chance irritated Fley. "I like to be prepared."

"She must be strongly encouraged to comply. If she is bold enough to refuse, then I must assume she has planned to betray me from the beginning. A total scouring of the Home will be necessary. But let us hope it does not come to that."

"Let us hope, Highest."

There was a flicker of something in Quiv's eyes that startled Fley. Was it amusement? Contempt? Or was it just the mercus light? Fley departed, shoving his suspicions from his mind.

The possibility of Thine crossing him had never occurred to him. She was Yan's sister, after all. But now that Quiv had planted that seed he wondered if Yan himself had been merely waiting for his chance to drive a blade into his heart.

A decision settled upon him. He began the long descent, in search of Dunne Portshalan. Preparations for the Peline girls could wait. It was time for him to take a turn on a queller team.

19

DETAILS OF WHY

They had slipped behind a hedgerow, and there they huddled close together, silent. A Sensual was reprimanding Ragin for being out of the novitiates ward at this hour. Kila couldn't see the woman, but she could hear the tightness caused by her pinched mouth. Sensual Thine spat her words as if the taste of her own saliva disgusted her.

"I'm going to Til's Tower," Ragin said. "I merely wanted to enjoy the stars one more time."

"Hurry back to your bed. I will send word to the Tower in the morning. Run along now." Her tone was slightly less acid now that she'd heard Ragin's decision.

Kila and Gian kept still, waiting for the Sensuals to return to their rooms. Sensual Thine wandered closer to the hedge, her form vague through the thicket of limbs. A novitiate walked beside her, mercus lantern held high. It had to be Hannah.

Another Sensual followed along. "Sensual Thine, what

makes you so curious about the grass? Shouldn't we be looking for the merculyns who awoke us with . . . whatever that was?"

"And how do you expect to find them? Anyone that powerful has likely dymensed away. But this grass has been disturbed. It looks like a fight. See how these patches are flattened, and these bits have torn free. No hoof marks, though."

The other sensual gasped. "Hoof marks? Are you saying . . . ?" She didn't finished because she didn't want to give voice to the suspicion.

But Kila knew what she meant by "hoof marks." The woman worried a demayne had been the source of the mercusine disruption. Kila knew she was powerful; she'd been told that many times. Unbidden, her chest warmed with a bit of pride.

"Maybe it was Ragin." The second Sensual's voice was not familiar to Kila, but she could tell the woman was reaching for an alternative explanation. There was a note of subservience in it, too. She'd heard that manner in tavern keeps eager to earn men's coin.

"Don't be an idiot," Sensual Thine said. "The absence of demayne hoofmarks means it was certainly our 'princes' cavorting about here. And that mercus was like a lighthouse beacon."

"Was it truly that bright? I'm none too sensitive."

"I feld id," Hannah said. "Id woke me up like someone had lid my hair on fire."

"As it did me, too, child," Sensual Thine said approvingly. "The boy Gian hasn't the spark. But the two girls . . . Hannah, did you note if either of them wore jewelry. A ring? A necklace, perhaps?"

"The black-haired one has a necklace. The blond one has barely the breeding do wear shoes, much less decoradgions."

"Quinn Peline a merculyn? Interesting. In the morning we must take her to the Dome and initiate her. Her queller artifact will be a valuable asset in the days to come."

"She won't go willingly," the second Sensual said. "She brought letters under the Rules of Princes."

"Rules for an age long past. If we do not initiate her, she will be taken or killed with the rest."

"Yes, Sensual Thine. I will speak to the others and prepare the shriving." She ambled away, taking another lantern-bearing novitiate with her. Soon only Sensual Thine and Hannah remained.

Thine was quartering the yard. Kila wished she could see the woman more clearly, but only bits of her nightgown showed through the branches.

Abruptly, Thine gave up. "Come along, Hannah."

Hannah followed. "Do you think Raginald will live?"

"He has a better chance now than before. Leave it to a Keel to sniff out what others cannot. We should pay close attention to him, afterward."

Kila wanted nothing more than to follow the pair and listen to the rest of their conversation, but it was out of the question. She was too bone-weary from sparring and too shaken up by the aftermath of her mercusine feat lifting her and Gian from the ground.

She led the way back to the ward, trusting her sneaking skills over Gian's. He may be a master with the blade, but she doubted anyone except Quinn could out-sneak her. And Quinn cheated.

Quinn was in the common room, still in her trousers and

blouse. She leaned back in a chair, reading one of her stolen books in the half-shielded light of a mercus lamp.

She didn't look up from the page when they came in, holding hands. Kila extracted her fingers from Gian's.

"I spoke to the fisherman and inspected his boat," Quinn said. "A triangular sail. He'll take us to Ansso for ten gold Ravens."

Kila noted the man's price had doubled since Quinn had first spoken to his wife. She closed the front and rear doors. She pulled a chair close to Quinn's. Gian joined them.

Sensing the seriousness in Kila's manner, Quinn closed her book and set it aside. She straightened her legs, crossing them at the ankles. "I see you two have become better acquainted."

Gian coughed into his hand. Kila was amazed to see his cheeks flushing. Amazed and pleased. But there was no time for such frivolity now. "Ragin is going to Til's Tower to join as an acolyte so he can find Henley."

Quinn nodded sagely. "Of course he is. That fool is going to get himself killed. But it turns out that we have time. The fisherman said a fellstorm is coming. He says his wife feels it in her knees. She's never been wrong. He won't leave Garden Island until it has passed."

Kila closed her eyes and cursed. But better to be on land than at sea during a storm. Even better not to be surrounded by scheming Sensuals who acted like Donse Masters.

"We have another problem. Thine thinks this is a queller," Kila said, flicking Quinn's necklace. "She, uh, felt you using the mercus out on the south lawn just a while ago. She and some other Sensuals are coming to force you into novitiate's robes in the morning."

The confusion Kila expected was not what she got. Instead, Quinn tilted her head. "What have you done?"

"I may have let my mask slip."

"And why would you do that?"

Now Kila was flushing. She looked down so Quinn wouldn't see her face turn bright red. "Gian and I were, uh, sparring. He's good with a blade. He could teach you a thing or two. He does this thing with his hands where he—"

"I'm sure he's very skilled with his hands. Why did you let your mask down? And why do the Sensuals think I did it?"

"The details of why aren't important or very interesting," Kila said, looking at her feet.

At her *bare* feet.

A glance showed her Gian's were bare, too.

They had left their shoes on the lawn. Sensual Thine had seen them. She hadn't said anything about them, but she'd seen them.

"Kila?" Gian said. "Are you ill?"

"We left our shoes there."

Gian offered a wry smile. "It matters little. We can claim we left them there during the day. Besides, we aren't staying here, are we? Once the Sensuals take your friend, they'll discover she's no merculyn. Then all attention will turn to you."

"Someone, please explain!" Quinn barked.

Kila shrugged. "I used the mercus a little bit and it attracted Sensual Thine . . . and some others. They didn't see me. And now they've deduced that your necklace must be a queller."

"Let them think it," Quinn said. "Let them take me away,

and you and Dark Eyes can slip out of the Home before they figure out I'm no merculyn."

It was a good plan, except the rest of the conversation Kila had overheard sounded ominous. Something bad was about to happen in the Home, and it hung over Kila's mind like the impending fellstorm itself.

"Let's at least get a night's sleep," Gian said. "We'll all rise before dawn and leave the Ward. No reason to let them find Quinn at all."

Quinn wrinkled her nose. "We'll need shelter from the fellstorm."

"Docktown?" Kila said.

Quinn waved the idea away. "They're all too frightened of Til's Tower to take in guests like us."

"Pol's Fifth, then," Kila said. "They'll take us in, and they have no love for the Til's-boys."

Gian's face was troubled but he nodded. Quinn collected her books and went off to her room. Kila and Gian sat together, not saying anything for a long time.

"Raginalt loves you," Gian said. There was a question in it.

"He does." It was all the answer Kila could offer. An acknowledgment of a troubling truth. She liked Ragin. He had been more loyal than she'd deserved. She felt responsible for him, for reasons she didn't quite understand. But that wasn't true, was it? It had been her robbing him that had started him down this path.

"I would love to stay up with you, Kila Sigh, but we must be alert and rested for whatever comes. Good-night." He kissed her.

She leaned into it, but this time she kept the mercus mask firmly in place. He broke the kiss and went to his room.

Kila wandered to hers, staggering from an odd weakness in her legs not entirely attributable to physical exertion. Gian's eyes floated in her mind, dark, alluring, amused.

She was reminded of the fisherman's wife and her knees which were never wrong. Kila wondered what her knees were telling her.

SO THAT OTHERS MAY THRIVE

"That was certainly Kila Sigh you felt, Coin," Henley said. He bore up under her stare more easily now, though he was as tired as a hundred-mile-atlen. The swell of power the others had felt had not come to him thanks to the queller ring. He'd been so soundly asleep the Devotee sent to rouse him had resorted to slapping his face. And a little more sharply than necessary.

Word had gotten around about what he had supposedly done to Tia. The Coin had been clear on that front. No one but those in the room for Tia's beating could know the truth, for if the Coin put spies in Til's Tower, surely the Highest had eyes and ears in Pol's. Spin Rippa had given him an apologetic look once the Devotee had scurried away. "Spin Moirina and I know you didn't hit that girl," she'd whispered as she guided him to the Coin's hut. "Pol burdens us only with what we must carry."

Henley said nothing, lest too-curious ears overhear it. Fear of spies was one of the reasons they had left the Tower. The

Coin and a number of Spinsters and Devotees had accompanied him to the Vale of Pol near the north shore of Garden Island. Set between two steep hills of green, and backed by a misty waterfall, the vale held a scattering of wooden huts, all perched atop stilts.

The Coin's hut was no different from any of the others. A one-room circular structure of bamboo with a conical thatch roof. They made do with hammocks instead of cots, great nets hanging from the ceiling keeping the multitude of nocturnal insects off their flesh.

Henley now stood in the center of her hut, hands folded in front of him. The jungle outside was a riot of insect chirps and buzzes.

"How do you know it was Kila Sigh if you were quelled?" she asked.

He shot a glance at Spin Rippa, who had fetched him. The Spinster did not know about the cats and the Coin wisely meant to keep them a secret.

Henley had sought Huff's confirmation about Kila as soon as he'd wiped enough sleep from his eyes to discover the Vale in uproar over a distant mercusine disruption.

Huff, Oly, and Nax had followed him here, keeping to the jungle and stopping frequently to hunt, eat, sleep, and groom.

Kila was still too far away from Nax to reach, though the cat was ranging east in hopes of feeling Kila out. The slopes were particularly dangerous in that direction, infested with packs of lizards, snakes that lurked in low branches, and an infinite variety of large insects with poison stingers.

Huff told him of an enormous cat, all black, and the size of a hunting hound. Henley would have been skeptical of this, except Huff had sent him an image of it. Huff seemed nearly as disturbed by this discovery as Henley.

Did you talk to him? Henley had asked.

Her. And no. She was not willing to let me know her mind.

But Huff had learned from Nax that Kila had been very full of feeling when the mercus swell had happened. Nax didn't know if it was good or bad feeling. She thought it might be a bad feeling. But it might be good.

The Coin was staring at him, expecting an answer to how he knew Kila had been the source of the mercus eruption. He again eyed Spinster Rippa and cleared his throat.

"Spin Rippa, please fetch me tea," the Coin said, understanding dawning.

"Yes, Coin." The plump Spinster did not seem at all pleased to be sent away.

When he was certain she was out of earshot, he said: "It was Kila. My Beloved One has confirmed it." He touched his cheek, which was still hot from the Devotee's slap of awakening. "I do hope we can explain the truth about Tia someday. I'm not well thought of, obviously."

"The current attitude suits me fine. I don't need them becoming friends with you, acolyte."

"Please don't call me that. I did not volunteer to wear these robes. I was at Ori's Home under the Rules of Princes. I don't have my letter of introduction anymore, I'm afraid."

"Rules of Princes." The words did not taste good in her mouth apparently. She sneered and waved her large hand, dismissing her own irritation. "That is as good a solution as we'll find, I'm afraid. You are now entered into the Way of Pol under the Rules of Princes."

Henley was surprised by the amount of relief this brought.

Like dropping into a chair after a ten mile hike and kicking off one's boots.

"That means you must be punished under the Rules of Princes."

"Punished! For what?"

She answered with a slight lift of one gray eyebrow.

"Oh." For beating Tia during his escape.

"I will dole out your punishment at the Pol's Slate in the morning. The water there is cold and soothing, you will be glad of it. Now, this Kila Sigh has foolishly lit a bonfire with her mercusine stunt. Not a merculyn on Garden Island will have missed it. Do think it happened because she was heeding your warning to flee?"

"I don't know. Cats are unreliable messengers in the best conditions. But Nax would know if Kila were dead or in much pain."

The Coin nodded and thumbed her medallion. Spin Rippa came in with a tray. She set it on the floor and arranged a cushion for the Coin's comfort. When she was done, the Coin told her to go prepare a Justice Seat to hear Henley's crimes. This made the Spinster frown and she shot Henley a sad look as she departed.

"That one is loyal and good," the Coin said. "And very sensitive to the subtle realm. Kila's power has shaken her badly. That queller you wear is hers."

"I will happily return it," he said. "But there are those in the Tower who will know my spark."

"Keep it. For now. Just know that Spin Rippa suffers, too. But who does not?" She almost managed a smile. "This Kila Sigh person troubles me. The medallion spins contradictions when I ask Pol's guidance. I would have her here, where I can keep an eye on her."

"Let me go to the wall; Huff and Nax and I might be close enough to have a clear conversation with Kila."

"Not likely. Pol's Fifth does not share a wall with Ori's."

"Then what's over there?" He'd never had much time to think about why the island had been divided into Fifths. Fourths would make more sense, a quarter for Docktown, a quarter for each of the three Ways.

The Coin leveled her mind-piercing gaze on him. "You truly do not know? You, an educated merchant boy of Starside? My, how the Way of Til has rubbed out the etchings of history. And it is right here on this island."

When Henley did not figure out the puzzle she motioned south and east. "That Fifth, Prince Henley, was once Kil's Fifth. It is now a barren land of ash and ruin. I'm afraid that here in the Vale you are farther from Kila than before."

"Then why did you have me come?"

"Because I needed you away from Til's Tower. You are too important to risk."

An itch infected Henley's mind, the harbinger of a thought he did not want to think. The way she looked at him—like he was a prized racing atlen—made him remember the way Highest Fley sometimes looked at Dunne Yples. Partly afraid, partly determined.

"Why am I so important to you?"

"The Way of Til has their Champion. The Way of Pol needs one, too."

"Me? I wouldn't last a minute against Dunne Yples. You'd be better off recruiting Kila."

The Coin finished her tea and unfolded herself, standing over him in the dim mercus light of the hut. Her face was shadowed, but pale enough that he could see her expression. Was that sadness or pity in her eyes?

She placed her huge hands on his shoulders. "Becoming a Champion isn't something one asks of another. It's a mantle placed upon one's shoulders by the Goddess. Kila belongs to another. You are the one Pol has chosen, whether you want to be or not. I have spun the medallion twenty times on this question. It came up smiles twenty times."

"I don't believe in Pol," he said. "I don't believe in any of them. I only came here to escape the Hargothe and to get away from Kila."

"A fellstorm comes, Prince Henley. The Vale offers shelter from the wind. But no matter where you go in this world, you will not find refuge from the force of destiny. It whips about you and Kila Sigh and Dunne Yples, gathering power with every passing day. Soon it will break upon the world, a fellstorm of mercusine, and the Way of Pol will depend on you to see that we survive to salvage whatever remains in the aftermath."

"But I'm not even a devotee of Pol. It makes no sense that I carry that burden. And I'm no match for either of them."

"Would you say your luck has been good or bad this past year?"

Henley laughed. "Pol has made a pastime of frowning upon me."

"No. She merely moves you. Every nudge of bad fortune has urged you here, to this place, this moment. I spun twenty smiles upon the question. You *are* her Champion. And that cannot be for else but good. "

"Good. Ill." Henley made a banker's balance of his hands.

"If Pol exists, she surely nudges me to further her own interests, not mankind's."

"Your mistake is that you see only your own life, and—deeming it miserable—decide Pol is capricious and selfish. But look beyond yourself. Consider that you must suffer so that others may thrive. Just as Devotee Tia and Spin Rippa do in different measures."

This woman was almost as good with dramatic pronouncements as the Voluptuary in Starside. But at least back there he'd just been a miserable boy in need of protection. Here he was a miserable boy being charged with the protection of a religious order he cared nothing about.

"What if I refuse?"

"Can your heart refuse to beat?" She removed her medallion from its mounting and pressed it into his hands. "Go on. Ask and throw. It is simple." She stepped back and cleared her cushion and tea tray to make room.

The medallion was heavy. Solid gold. The workings on both sides were masterpieces of coin-work, sharp and clear: the goddess's face raised from the field of gold behind. The surface was warm and smooth.

"Remove your queller first, so that she might see you more clearly. It's safe here."

He obeyed, cupping the ring in one hand as he hefted the medallion in the other. He considered his question carefully. The gods may be a farce, but the force of destiny had already proved to be a noticeable pressure on his choices. He decided to ask a simple and clear question. Unambiguous.

"Am I the Champion of Pol?"

He tossed the medallion just as the Coin had done before. It struck the plank floor and rang out. After one hop it tumbled onto its side and rolled in a slow circle, first passing the Coin's feet, then his.

The circle shrank as it spiraled in and in until it gave one full spin in the center of the floor and flopped onto one side.

Pol smiled.

21

ARCH DISDAIN

The water in Kila's bedroom basin was clean but had long gone cold. Pennie must have changed it while Kila was out with Gian. She washed up anyway, the cold water shocking her from the silly daze Gian's kiss had put her in. She dunked her hair and wrung it out. Icy tendrils traced down her back, making her skin prickle.

When she picked up her hand-mirror to inspect her work, she saw a sodden-headed girl who looked older than she felt. Her cheeks had once been hollow, but plentiful food and three months of laziness aboard *Sea-Hound* had filled them out. She had once looked boyish, but the face looking at her now was feminine. Had her lips held this rosy color all along?

Dunne Marlow had once called her features "elfin" and said she had all the qualities a young man might desire. She had scoffed then, but now . . . ?

She tilted her chin this way and that, trying to see herself the way Gian did. An angry red scrape crossed her throat. She pressed her fingers to it, wincing at the sting. But the memory of Gian's blade pressing there didn't sting. It reminded her of the strength of his arms. And the warmth of his body pressed to hers.

"You're as foolish as a trezz-addled boy," she said to her reflection. She closed her eyes, unable to force him from her mind. It seemed so stupid, really, that her mind would be occupied with thoughts of him, when Ragin was headed for danger and the Sensuals were conspiring to turn Quinn into a novitiate.

And then there was Sensual Thine's cryptic comments about the importance of Quinn being made a novitiate or she'd be killed with the rest. Kila thought she knew who "the rest" were: her and Gian.

Just let them try. Anger made her throat clench and she saw something in her reflection that surprised her. That look in her eyes was exactly as Father's had been in those last moments of his life. He'd tried to save a stranger's life, an old man being beaten by the Watch.

Good. She was skilled at anger. And it had helped her survive worse than this. She shoved away the thought that it had also resulted in the death of hundreds of thinnies—many who hadn't even known why they were dying—and her mistake of healing the Hargothe.

Gian was clouding her judgment. Quinn was right. She was allowing his fine eyes and strong shoulders to make her a fool.

Straightening, she gave herself a shake. Lifting her head, she practiced an expression of arch disdain. She would have to put Gian off. There could be no continuation of their little . . . whatever it was. She hardly knew him at all. If true danger came from Sensual Thine, Kila would meet it with cold calculation, to secure her own safety and that of Quinn and Nax.

Her posture collapsed, shoulders sagging as her mind returned to pathetic yearning. That kiss. That Kil-damned kiss! She was an embarrassment to herself, for her heart ached just to think of this young man she hardly knew.

The mirror hazed.

She brought it close, eager for any distraction. The haze parted and again she saw from the bird's perspective the strange tower.

The vision soared over the tower with one light in a high window, then wheeled to show a moonlit beach. The waves were silver curls along the shore. Farther away, a sparse constellation of lights. A settlement.

The vision sped and the land passed below in a blur. The sparkle of lights grew closer. Kila recognized it. Ori's Home.

Which meant the tower was here, on this island. Just to the north.

"Why are you showing me this?" she asked the mirror. In answer, the vision faded, and Kila was left looking at her own astonished face.

22

THE FIRE THAT WILL CLAIM THE WORLD

Dunne Portshalan sat on the narrow cot, hands folded in his lap. His long, gray beard gave the impression of great wisdom. But Fley saw it for what it was, merely the accumulation of time and a habit of neglecting one's appearance to cultivate a look of piety.

Portshalan was indeed pious. And loyal. But also timid. Had he not possessed a great knowledge of the mercus—though somewhat weak in the power himself—he would have long ago been assigned to some distant countryside abbey on the continent, where he would have lived out a boring life conducting weddings and funerals for unwashed bumpkins.

"Do you understand the question?" Fley asked. He occupied the only chair in the room. Portshalan had fine quarters higher up the Tower, but he spent most nights here, near the Champion, should trouble arise.

"I understand. But Highest, should you—" He hesitated, then said softly— "Should you fail to establish the tap, the Champion will destroy you. I'm not confident a quelling could subsequently be put in place. The Champion would then be free to . . ." The old man shivered and offered a prayer to Til to ward of such an eventuality.

Patience wearing thin, Fley stood, forcing the man to follow suit out of respect for Fley's station. "Do you think me a total lackwit, Dunne Portshalan?" Before the man could do more than splutter a denial, Fley continued: "I would never put myself or this Tower in such danger. Not without precautions in place."

"Precautions . . . I'm afraid this old man doesn't follow your meaning—"

"I mean to use a mercus relic, of course. More specifically, the Sink Gem."

The old man's face reddened with shock. "But such is forbidden by the Theb: 'Let not the godfire be squandered, for once it is spent, the mercusine shall go dark for every age to follow.'"

He was correct about the quote. But that didn't concern Fley. Like most passages in the Theb, it was open to interpretation. And scholars much wiser than kindly Portshalan had theorized that "godfire" didn't mean mercus, but rather the power of the gods, a separate power entirely, as water was separate from light. The godfire could not be squandered through the Sink Gem, in Fley's opinion, because it wasn't godfire that he or the Champion wielded.

"Will you accompany me to the vault or no?" he said.

Obedience was ingrained in Dunne Portshalan. He'd lived a long life following commands regardless of his opinions about them. This was no different, though he became a bit cooler in his manner.

They went to the vault, a small door mounted into the

bedrock of the cellar foundation. Dunne Portshalan opened it through his own mercus efforts. The door swung open on well-greased hinges.

The entirety of the Way's collection of mercusine artifacts resided in the chamber within. Or . . . That was its intent. In truth, many of the hellers and stones and common casters were dispersed among the Donse Masters of the many realms. And an unknown quantity had simply never been turned into the Way of Til following the signing of the Synod Treaty.

Fley stepped inside the chilly chamber, bringing forth a flare of mercus light to see the items arrayed upon the shelves. He had studied them all since rising to his office, spending hours exploring their capabilities and considering how they might be best employed in the service of the One God. The answer had been discouraging. There was a reason these relics had not been put into use. They were too dangerous for the merculyn who dared wield them. And a few had not shown what their function was at all. All of them had been crafted by the First Race, the builders who had come before man, and who—drawing the ire of the One God—were driven from the lands of the world.

But a few items did have obvious purposes. One was a crystal sword. When granted a merculyn's power, it would encompass the wielder in a sphere of power impenetrable by any weapon. Alas, it had burned the mercus spark right out of every Donse Master who had tried it. Every one of them had gone on to die within a ten-day.

A ornate lantern sat on a shelf alone. It was dark. A merculyn who attempted to light it would produce from it a beacon so bright it could sear the sight from any who looked at it. The light illuminated clouds in the sky and if placed on a high hill, it shed daylight upon the surrounding countryside. But once a merculyn began powering the relic, he could never stop. A quelling team was required to sever the connection and thus the lantern's usefulness was low.

A shelf held three wands, each set end-up on special made wooden stands. Wands were relatively common. All but a rare few had a single purpose: to cast light. Any person could use one, spark or no. But the ones here had unknown powers, and no Donse Master in three hundred years had the courage to study them since Dunne Swere was found dead holding two of them. He had been sitting at a desk chair, apparently probing the wands with his mercus powers. He had left one note: "'Nozzle'—brass?"

No one knew what the term "nozzle" meant. The wands had been placed in the vault and not even Fley had touched one since.

And then there was the Sink Gem, a spherical stone of glass. Its yellow depths were full of tiny bubbles. In size and texture it was like a tap gem, a reservoir of mercus power any merculyn could draw from to increase the strength of his feats. Unlike a tap gem, the Sink Gem absorbed power. Not in the aggressive and deadly way the crystal sword did. It had been found and cataloged by relic scholar Hij Mona, who wrote: "A mercus sink, into which an infinity of power might be poured, never to be felt again."

Fley took the Sink Gem from its stand and hefted it. The cold surface would not warm, no matter how long he held it. The weight belied the notion it was made of glass, for a ball of lead this size would weigh as much. But in his coming experiment with Dunne Yples, the gem might be his only protection from complete annihilation.

"How long until the next change of quelling teams?"

"It will happen directly should you command it."

"I do so command it."

Fley went straight to the arena where the Champion lay in chains. He hefted the Sink Gem and studied the man, calming his own mind to better feel the mercusine bolts flowing through the room. The queller captain received the mercus from the taps, who sat dumbly in their chairs, doing nothing else.

To accept and use such power didn't require exceptional reservoirs in oneself. But it did require the ability to use it. A vast lake could only drain through a canal so quickly before over-spilling the banks and destroying the countryside. But provide a deep canyon, and the same lake could drain as quickly as the force of Nature allowed. And so it was with a quelling captain.

Fley's own capacity to channel power was considerable, though his spark was average. But he was not certain what would happen when he attempted to force a tap upon the Champion. Therefore he had the Sink Gem prepared to receive any excess. It would be a tricky feat in itself, but he was confident in his ability.

First, he wanted a fresh quelling team in place, for should things go poorly, he needed them prepared to jump in and stop the Champion's flows. Dunne Portshalan came in at that moment, a weary-faced group trailing in after him looking like they'd just been pulled from their beds.

Upon seeing Highest Fley, their demeanor changed, spines straightening, chins lifting. He extended a hand and each man kneeled to kiss his ring. He offered a vague blessing, pressing a hand to their heads and shunting a charge of mercus into their minds. A little trick he had learned as a novitiate long ago. The effect was a mild but noticeable brightening of mood. It never failed to spark a look of reverence in a man's eyes. What it did to his Favored was a bit more interesting.

"Take your posts," Dunne Portshalan said.

A middle-aged Donse Master called Dunne Dee took the captain chair. He was a smart man, obedient and rather invisible. He would make a good Highest for a holdfast or small city state on the continent one day.

Fley whispered his intentions to the man, who nodded in understanding. He betrayed no alarm at the proposal, but merely signaled that he had taken over the quelling from the previous captain. One by one the fresh source taps took their chairs. Dunne Portshalan shooed the retiring team away, though they lagged, curious to see what their Highest was up to.

The Champion took note of none of this as he strained and groaned against his chains. His head lashed side to side, spittle flying. The chain binding his right hand was shiny and new, freshly replaced following the tantrum that had killed a novitiate.

Fley took a seat in the chair a novitiate brought to him. Bending over the Sink Gem he began to trickle power into it. Easy. This flow had to be established before daring to tap into the Champion's power.

He sat this way for several minutes, allowing his heart to calm, his breathing to steady. Feeling the Champion's mercus spark upon the subtle realm was simple, for he thrummed there so strongly. The source taps of the quelling team were there, too, like the faint stairs outshined by a full moon. Dunne Dee funneled a thin bolt of mercus, composed of several senses, at the Champion. This was the quelling. Had the Champion not been under the thrall of the witch's medicine when he arrived at the Tower, they would certainly all be dead now. Only the man's confusion and lack of wits had protected them long enough to get the quelling in place. Fley was thankful he had heeded Acolyte Henley's warning on that front, for Seeker Yan had dismissed the warning outright.

Yples had not been so powerful then, and the quelling had been easier. It had required only two source-taps and a master to quell him then. Now there were four taps and a captain, and they were beginning to struggle.

Fley reached toward the Champion, threading his bolts around the quelling flow. This wasn't a delicate effort, truly. But caution would never be regretted. The quelling encircled the mind in the same way a force-tap would. Dunne Dee would drop the quelling in the exact moment Fley slammed his tap into place. The effect would be the same. The Champion would be unable to use his power. The difference was that his power would be accessible to Fley, rather than merely blocked.

"Are you prepared, Dee?"

"I am."

"Now!"

Fley slammed the force-tap bolts into place and the mercusine web shuddered. He had only a moment to react, shunting the Champion's excess power to the Sink Gem. Eyes closed, he bent every bit of his senses to the new awareness that sprung up in his mind.

The mercus spark didn't feel like anything at all when one was untrained. And then, in time, it arrived as a buzzing feeling, a slight dizziness, accompanied by the heightened sensitivity to sounds, sight, and smells. All the senses became enlivened to the newly awakened merculyn. A dangerous time in their development, but also an exhilarating one.

Fley had long ago mastered the feeling, and like most Donse Masters, had developed the ability to numb the senses so that everyday life wouldn't be unbearable.

But with the Champion's spark added to his, the inrush of sensation nearly overwhelmed him. No wonder the man appeared so tortured. The stink of the men in the room—and of the Champion himself—made Fley gag. He formed negation bolts, but that had never been a great skill of his.

Getting the balance of mercusine flow just right was difficult while overwhelmed with senses he could not manage to completely deaden. The Champion was so powerful Fley hissed. He felt he had touched a hot cook pan and was unable to remove his hand from it. He increased the flow into the Sink Gem, relieving the overload until he could finally breathe easier. Behind him Dunne Portshalan was praying and pleading for Til to protect him—not all of them, just himself. So, danger revealed the man's true character. Fley took mental note.

The channel to the Sink Gem was not going to work until he could get the Champion to send his excess directly to it. That required some interesting tricks, but since Fley controlled the mercus, he got the bolts established. He was sweating now, the droplets stinging his eyes.

And now he was full to bursting with power, but not so much he couldn't manage it. What should he do to experiment? The answer came to him instantly. He felt for the acolyte who had brought his chair, a young Iopsi man called Nopil. He slammed the boy with a willshift, and to his shock actually felt the boys limbs as his own. Incredible. He walked the lad about, circling the champion, ducking to pass beneath the binding chains when necessary. He turned the boy about, had him dance a jig, and then opened his mouth and spoke. "I control him. I control him."

But the willshift consumed only a tiny fraction of the available power. So he reached for one of the queller team source-taps who was gaping at him. He clamped the man's mouth shut, stood him up, had him climb onto the chair and stand on one leg. One by one, he did the same with the remaining four source-taps. He was tempted to add Dunne Portshalan and Dunne Dee to his little collection of puppets, but such an indignity was uncalled for, especially if he wanted to retain their loyalty.

He still had excess power to play with. He created light, he manifested ringing bells, he cooled the chamber until his breath frosted into the air and the Donse Masters shivered and rubbed their elbows. Only then did he notice that the Champion had quieted. Opening his eyes, Fley studied the man, all the while keeping the acolyte pacing around the room.

The madman still pulled at his chains but his jaw had relaxed and his lips had gone slack. He looked about, confused by his situation, as if a moment of lucidity had slipped over his eyes. He locked his gaze with Fley's. "She is here. She hides herself, but I know she is here."

"Who is here, Champion?"

"The girl who burned them all. The girl who will burn the world. Dem-Kisk." The words were forceful, but not screamed. Just the torn-throated rasp of a man of total conviction. Fley could do nothing to still the gooseflesh that crawled over his skin at these utterances.

"How do you know she is Dem-Kisk?"

"He told me."

"He? Who?"

"Til, the father of all mankind. Til. His face appeared before me, above the lake of the cavern. He said unto me: 'You will know Dem-Kisk by the flames, by the charred bone, by the ash.' And I knew I had witnessed the first spark of the fire that will claim the world. She must die, lest we all perish."

The first line of the prophecy. Had the man truly seen the face of God, or had it been a delusion brought forth by witnessing a horror? "Did Til not finish the prophecy?"

But the man did not answer, his eyes going vague and his breath slowing. His manner reminded Fley of a hound, having run too long suddenly finding itself prone and stupid in the shade. Fley remembered Roya Reth's cryptic remarks. *"Why feed you him so?"*

"Who has been feeding you, Champion? I would know who has kept you so strong."

The man's eyes flickered back to Fley's, but there was no sign of comprehension in them. In fact, his eyelids began to droop. And then they closed and he slept.

His power was still available to Fley, and the temptation to willshift the man or attempt a mental probe was strong. But that was dangerous to do directly on a source-tap; it could subject Fley to a deadly backlash. Reluctantly, he released the power entirely. "Dunne Dee, prepare your team to resume the quelling."

His command was obeyed. Fley noticed the Sink Gem had grown hot. He passed it to Dunne Portshalan and got to his feet. The effort had taxed him more than he'd expected. He found himself wobbly. "I think I shall retire. Come to me after evening bells. We have much to discuss. Provide food and water to this man if you deem it safe to attempt."

"Yes, Highest."

Fley forced himself to walk with long strides and square shoulders. But when he finally got out of the arena and out of view of the acolyte guarding the door, he had to lean on the wall and rest for a full five minutes before proceeding to the long climb to his quarters.

But physical weariness aside, he was elated. He had done it. It had worked. Now he would call in some relics dispersed among the Donse Masters of the Tower. It was clear to him now that he would be the Champion of Til, and the madman . . . Well, the madman would simply be a madman.

23

LIKE LIQUID FIRE

"Wake up, I said. Wake up." A strong hand shook Kila's shoulder.

She pried her eyes open and found Hannah standing over her, black hair curtaining the sides of her face like an oily hood. Sensual Thine stood behind her, hands clasped beneath her bosom. Her circular mouth made her look like she was trying to swallow a slug.

Gray light streamed through the window. The curtain had been pulled back, revealing a slate sky. Rain pelted the ground, raising a constant hissing sound. A harbinger of the fellstorm to come.

"How do you mask your spark?" Sensual Thine demanded.

Kila rubbed her eyes, partly to clear the gunk from them, but also to hide her face. She was too bleary-headed to take control of her features at the moment. She realized Gian's plan, to leave before dawn, had gone wrong.

"I don't know what—" Kila began.

She was not ready for the back of Hannah's hand. It

smacked her cheek, jerking her head to the side. She was so shocked by it she didn't deliver her customary counterblow. She rubbed her face and blinked tears from her eyes. "Kil be a merry maid! That stung, ya little—"

Hannah's next blow was mercusine. An invisible slap across the cheek like the lash of a switch. Kila yelped.

"Perhaps you'll answer without sass this time," Sensual Thine said.

Kila became aware of other people in the ward, just outside her door.

"I don't have any spark to mask."

"Lies. It is no matter. You will reveal all in the shriving."

Kila pushed Hannah off her. The girl's arm drew back, hand clenched in a fist. Her face was dark, but a curl of smile showed just how much she relished this opportunity.

Kila's right hand rose to deflect the blow as her other snaked beneath her blankets to grasp Cayne. A sudden will-shift stalled her movements. The room resounded with the sharp crack of Hannah's strike on Kila's cheek. Her vision shuddered.

They had Quinn. She didn't know how she knew, but she was certain of it. Sensual Thine had come here to provoke Kila, to trick her into dropping her mask.

Stabbing Hannah—as satisfying as it might be— would solve nothing. For the first time in memory, Kila played weak. "Why are you hitting me?" she said, making her voice tremble. Fortunately the sting of the blows had produced tears. Kila had never been able to fake them.

"Get her up," Sensual Thine snapped.

Hannah pulled on Kila's arm. Kila went limp, like an

uncooperative child. "What are you doing?" she whined. "Let me get dressed."

Sensual Thine snapped her fingers. "Novitiate Ebver, Novitiate Virkki, assist Hannah in moving this girl to the Dome."

The men who entered Kila's room were tall, square-jawed identical twins. Hannah delivered a final slap to Kila's face, then backed away so the two men could pull Kila from her blankets.

"Let me go!" She flailed as they easily lifted her. The fellstorm was bringing colder air, and her bare legs felt the chill.

Hannah gasped. "Sensual Thine. She wears a blade!"

The men restrained Kila, each holding an arm and keeping her suspended above the floor. Sensual Thine returned, steps brisk, forehead crinkled in feigned confusion. "But that is impossible. She assured me she had thrown her weapon away. Hold her legs."

One of the twins took hold of her upper body, while the other gripped her ankles. His hands were so strong all her wriggling and cursing had no effect. Her gown was long enough to reach her ankles, but in the struggle it had worked its way to her knees.

Sensual Thine nodded to Hannah, who smirked as she approached. The sour-tempered novitiate hiked Kila's hem up, exposing her thighs and the bottom half of Cayne.

"A fine weapon," one of the men said. His eyes didn't linger on it but instead traced her bare leg.

Hannah's lips were pursed in imitation of Sensual Thine's, but there was a smile in her eyes. She pulled Kila's gown up higher, until the entirety of Cayne and sheath were visible.

Sensual Thine approached. Despite her earlier concern about Kila's character, she apparently saw no problem allowing

Kila to be exposed, held fast, and eyed by the twins. She had no smile in her eyes, but she knew the humiliation—the wrongness—of what she did.

"Hannah, unbuckle that weapon."

The novitiate fiddled with the buckles and straps, making a point to pinch Kila's skin between her fingernails.

Kila endured it with a stifled grunt and a gaze of fury. She could ash these people. She could do it easily. But they had Quinn. Maybe Gian and Ragin, too.

Thine eyed the blade in Hannah's hands. "You have lied to me, broken the rules of Ori's Home. The Rules of Princes do not shield you from punishment. Strip her." She left.

Her gown was off her head before she realized what was happening. Hannah stood at the door, openly grinning now that Sensual Thine was gone.

"This way," Hannah said, motioning Kila out the door. The girl drew Cayne from its sheath, admired the blade. "Don'd worry. I won't cud you. Sensual Thine would see. Bud you must walk. Or do you wand Ebver and Virkki do carry you?"

She did not. Neither man held her now as she huddled in the middle of her room, trying to cover herself with her hands and arms.

They wanted her to drop the mask. Perhaps Quinn had endured this treatment. Perhaps she had spilled Kila's secret. But if she had, why hadn't Sensual Thine said so?

Kila dropped her hands to her side and strode past Hannah, chin high. Only the gooseflesh on her skin betrayed her discomfort.

They marched her along the garden pathways to the Dome. Novitiates and Sensuals lined the paths, some stony-faced, others gawping in horror. Others smirked and whispered foul notions to their neighbors.

The twins followed her.

She arrived at the Dome of the Gentle Goddess to find the Voluptuary and Sensual Thine waiting for her. They stood next to a gilded table holding an ewer. The twins brought Kila to them, then stepped back.

The fellstorm stirred the atmosphere with building fury. The polshels bent under stiff winds out of the east. The rain increased, and the area under the dome didn't remain dry as the wind drove drops sideways. They stung Kila's bare skin. The cold seeped into her bones, making her legs tremble.

She saw now that the Voluptuary and Sensual Thine were shielded from these gusts by a thick column carved in Ori's likeness in the pose of judgment.

"You will receive punishment for violating Ori's Peace with your hateful blade. But that will come later. Now you will be shriven," Sensual Thine said. She snapped her fingers and Hannah handed Cayne to her. "Come here, girl."

The mask was not something Kila paid much attention to. She'd maintained it so easily for so long, it had become like wearing a garment. But now it weighed upon her, like a shirt of lead. She could so easily release it, burn these people to ash, and walk away.

A curse and cry rose behind her. Three men brought Quinn. She wore the gown of a novitiate, and a black bruise darkened one eye. She shot glares of fury at her guards and then at Sensual Thine.

Gian Delp walked beside the guards. He was free. He didn't meet Kila's gaze. Quinn did. And upon seeing Kila naked and shivering, she released a tirade of swearing and blasphemies that would have made a sailor blush. She finished with "Do you know who I am?" But the words cracked from her worn-out voice and their power was stolen by the wind.

Sensual Thine let Quinn swear herself out, then nodded to one of the guards. At Sensual Thine's signal, he casually drove his fist into Quinn's gut. She would have doubled over, but the other two men—both novitiates—held her up.

Quinn retched and coughed, face going red as she fought to regain her breath. Black was no longer on her hip. It was in Gian's hands.

"Bring Kiki Peline here," Sensual Thine said to the twins. They gripped Kila's upper arms and carried her forward. Her knees scraped on the tiles as they thrust her down.

"Hold still," Thine said. "I will have them restrain you if you move." She grabbed a handful of Kila's hair and tugged it up. "Harlot," she muttered. She sliced Cayne through Kila's hair. There was no resistance, for Cayne was a Shadline blade, sharper than a razor. Thine let the clump of hair fall. Damp from rain, it looked like a bit of frayed rope sailors cut away from storm-ravaged rigging.

Kila drew back, lips curling. A hiss escaped her, just like a cat's. And that's how she felt. Like that jungle cat cornered by lizard-wolves. Thine took hold of more hair, sliced it off.

Quinn screamed, then went silent as a novitiate struck her face.

Gian did nothing. Kila twisted, searching him out. All the hate she felt for Sensual Thine was nothing compared to what she felt for him. He had learned her secrets, had lured her to divulge more, to give him more, and he had betrayed her.

He looked through her.

"I said hold still," Thine said, her voice was full of acid. "Hold her, Novitiate Virkki."

The man knelt behind Kila and engulfed her in an iron embrace. It was how Gian had held her, but at the same time *nothing* like it. He pulled her to him and squeezed. She could only move her head. Thine stopped that by taking hold of her ear and pulling. "If you move so much as an eyelid, I will remove this ear. Do you understand?"

Kila could make cinders of this woman. Of all of them. But she wasn't certain she could do them all before the novitiates hurt Quinn. And that's what stopped her from dropping her mask. She would endure this humiliation. And then, when she and Quinn were out of immediate reach, she would deliver retribution.

Sensual Thine continued to shear Kila's hair until all that remained was an uneven patchwork. The rain and wind chilled her stinging scalp. The Sensual set the blade on the gilded table. The Voluptuary stepped forward, put a pale finger under Kila's chin, forced her to look up.

From this vantage the woman looked tall, imperious. But her face was sallow, eyes heavy. She was drunk already. Or still. "A merculyn? This one? I don't feel the faintest spark."

Sensual Thine hefted the ewer from the table. "She masks it. Isn't that correct, Gian?"

Gian didn't answer.

As she always did in times of distress, Kila sought Nax. But the cat's presence was faint. More distant than it had been the last time she'd spoken to the small gray. Was this what Nax had warned Kila about, this violation? But how could it have been? How could Henley have known they'd do this to her?

Thine mumbled some words and then upended the ewer, spilling icy water onto Kila's head.

No. It *wasn't* icy. It was hot. The heat increased, becoming so hot it scalded Kila's scalp, her cheeks. It washed over her shoulders, coursed down her back, blazing her skin like liquid fire.

The novitiate no longer held her. She flung her arms about, trying to shake off the pain, but it stuck to her like honey. She screamed.

Now writhing on the tiles, helpless to escape the flame-like agony engulfing her, she sought the only remaining power left to her. The mercus. Her mask flew apart, the bolts to remove heat from her skin already forming.

"Take her!" Thine shouted.

Something hard and cold clamped around her head, stabbing into her temples and over her ears. Two more spikes drove at the back of her skull. One final stab took her between the eyebrows.

A willshift hit her so hard, so completely, she could not even writhe in the agonies of her burning skin and pierced brain. She could not even open her eyes.

She was frozen, still as stone, and yet her skin felt like it blistered, crackled, and was melting away.

The power she had sought to soothe her pain dissipated, like Quinn's shouts in the wind. Her friend's cries came from a long way away, voice torn with horror and fury.

Kila again reached for bolts of mercusine, to send them at Thine, to blast the woman into pieces so small the fellstorm would carry her away as if she'd never existed.

The force of her effort met a counter-force of equal

strength. The recoil of power shot through Kila's mind, adding a new searing pain, but this one inside her head.

Nax!

And then the pain was gone. All of it.

A muffled voice came to her awareness. "Take her to my quarters. Do not touch the *vaz'on*."

"Yes, Sensual Thine. Shall I dake the blade?" Hannah's voice.

"You may. But do not cut her."

"Thank you, Sensual. I won'd."

Kila was limp now, inert. She knew that hands gripped her and lifted her, but she couldn't feel them. She couldn't feel anything. Her father had once said that numbness could be a blessing. She'd never understood it until now.

Her flesh must have been seared away entirely. She wanted to cry; she *needed* to cry. But she didn't think she had eyes anymore. She couldn't see anything.

The sound of the raging storm muted as a door closed. And then another door closed. She lay in absolute blackness, smelling nothing, seeing nothing, feeling nothing, hearing nothing.

But she tasted one thing.

Blood.

24

A FALL OF HAIL

Henley was bound to a post shoved into a hole atop a great flat rock next to Pol's Falls. The torrent poured in a misty veil from a black cliff in the mountain above. Gusts bent the trees and the sky had dropped low as shreds of black cloud whipped overhead, a vanguard of the coming fellstorm.

The view was magnificent, though he couldn't particularly enjoy it at the moment. An array of stony-faced Spinsters stood on the rocky shore of the mountain lake, waiting for his punishment to be carried out. Their robes whipped about them as they stood waiting to witness his punishment.

The Coin was not in the habit of play-acting at justice. When he pointed out that *he* was play-acting at having committed a crime, she had merely shrugged. "We often bear burdens that we do not deserve. Surely you know others who have endured worse."

It was no consolation that he did, in fact, know others

who had borne more than deserved. Kila was one of them. As was her brother, Wen. Even poor Dunne Yples.

But Henley had also arrived on this island carrying a heavy past. His house burned to the ground by the Keel family, his father murdered. Torture and captivity at the hands of the Hargothe. And now this.

The Coin carried a short whip made of three knotted leather cords attached to a polished wooden handle. Her thin lips and wan face gave her a stone-carved aspect. This was a woman used to making decisions that made others miserable. She did not relish it, but she did not shirk her responsibilities. She would, no doubt, have gotten on well with the Voluptuary in Starside.

She lifted her voice to address the witnesses. "Under the Rules of Princes we have the authority and responsibility to correct wrong behaviors in Princes so that they will not exhibit such when they return to their lofty stations in the world. Henley Mast stands accused of beating Devotee Tia On'Liette. He struck her face and body with such viciousness her nose was broken and her vision impaired in one eye. She will heal, though she will have scars for the rest of her life." She turned to Henley. "Do you admit to these crimes or must the Justice Seat spin their medallions?"

The Justice Seat was composed of three Spinsters, two women and one man, all elderly. They stood off to the side, bent and weary from the ascent to the falls. But their eyes were keen. Just then a peal of thunder tore across the sky as if a god had struck the earth with a great hammer. The Spinsters of the Justice Seat did not flinch.

Henley wondered what they'd spin up if he called for them to do so. What if their tosses showed he was innocent? But he knew his part in this farce. And for reasons he didn't completely understand, he had decided to play it.

As crazy as it was, he trusted the Coin. She was one of the few people he'd met who had earned any trust. It was her brutal honesty. Not exactly an endearing quality, but certainly one he could respect—notwithstanding the nonsense about him being the Champion of Pol.

Huff, I'm going to have a lot of pain soon. I will be fine. It is necessary.

Huff was watching from the trees with Nax and Oly. He hadn't seen them, but he knew they were there, huddled somewhere sheltered from the brunt of the storm. He hoped Huff kept quiet when the lashes fell. The last thing he needed was Spinsters rushing to grab his cat by the scruff. While the Way of Pol was not as set on killing every cat they found, many apparently still held to the superstition that cats were possessed by demayne.

"I admit it," he said to the Coin. "I am ashamed. If Tia were here, I would beg her forgiveness."

The three Spinsters of the Justice Seat looked a bit disappointed that they would not get to toss their medallions. But with his admission, they came forward to stand behind him. They would watch every lash fall, witnessing the parting of his flesh on behalf of the victim and the entire Way of Pol.

Spin Heleen, a portly, pleasant woman with wavy hair hustled forward with a white sheet. She folded it into a wide belt, then wound it around his waist and cinched it tight. "For the blood," she said.

The air was hot despite the wind. Sweat prickled on his naked back, though his heart was cold.

"He has admitted his guilt and his shame," the Coin cried.

"As Pol seals the past into history, let us so seal his crimes. Pol is not vengeful, Pol is not merciful. Such scars that remain, let them remind us that the price of violence is pain."

A whistling in the air was Henley's only warning. The leather strips struck his back, three lances of flame in one blow.

He gasped with the first lash, eyes tearing and body clenching with the shock. They'd bound his hands with leather bands, and the edges dug into his flesh as his body struggled to break free. Already the pain was too much.

"The community punishes you for your crimes," the Coin intoned. She swung again. The lashes landed with a slap and digging agony. Henley gritted his teeth. He could not endure a single more lash, much less three more.

"When you beat Tia, you beat us all."

The next lash landed, scalding him like spray of hot coals. A cry tore from his throat. If not for the queller, he would certainly have sought refuge in the mercusine. He may even have struck back out of pure instinct.

I'm here, Huff sent. The cat's presence was full and near.

As he had done in the past, Henley clung to the bond. The same way a cold and sodden kitten would cling to its mother.

The lashes struck again. Henley didn't know if he screamed or gasped. He sank into the bond, the pain surrounding him like walls of fire. The wind of the fellstorm whipped him, too.

The Coin was speaking. Her words meaningless. The whistle came again. The pain flared anew.

And again.

And again.

It was too much. One lash for every blow Tia had suffered

was fair, but this . . . It was beyond cruel. The fire of pain became a vision before his tightly clenched eyes. Pillars of flame filled his mind. They transformed to the fire that had claimed his house.

Ragin had been there, had ushered Henley to his bedroom window, urged him to climb down. The only way to survive was to flee, to run, to hide.

Henley had done little but run and hide since. The pain and deprivations he'd suffered hadn't been the consequence of any of his actions or choices. It had been the unrelenting world trying to kill him. And for what? Were Pol and the other gods that capricious? Did they sit in their cloud-top palaces and watch him scream and writhe, laughing and growing drunk upon his agony?

"Henley?"

"Henley!"

Cold water splashed on his face. He sputtered and pried open an eye. The world was dark and full of fury. His flesh steamed. The Spin Heleen brushed back his unruly ginger hair.

"It is done," she mouthed, words lost to the strengthening winds.

She laid a cool, damp sheet over his shredded back. The bonds securing him to the whipping post were cut and strong hands kept him upright.

"To the lake waters," the woman said. "They will soothe and clean the wounds."

He couldn't keep his eyes open, so when his feet plunged into cold water he stumbled. His guide gently helped him to sit in the shallow water. "Lie back."

He did. The water lifted him as it probed into the gashes

on his back. A new sort of pain sliced into him, but he lacked the strength to fight it.

He floated on his back. The sky whirled with vortices of gray cloud. The roar of the falls merged with that of the wind, blocking the sounds of the world. Someone was talking nearby, but their words were nonsense.

You let them hurt you, Huff sent.

Yes. It was necessary.

But had it been? He was going along with this fiction because the Coin worried there were Til's spies in their ranks. Shouldn't she be able to flip her medallion for each Spinster and Devotee and ask Pol if they were true followers?

Your kind is strange, Huff sent. *You would do better to not let others hurt you.*

"Come, Henley, we must return to the Vale. The fellstorm grows." The Coin stood on the shore, looking like a colossal statue from his perspective in the water. What little daylight that seeped through the clouds shined so brightly off her white hair Henley couldn't look directly at her.

His wounds still flamed, but it was a tolerable pain. He waded out of the lake. The wavy-haired Spinster wrapped a light robe around his shoulders. He discovered he was shivering.

He looked again to the Coin, seeking some affirmation that he'd done well and that she truly *knew* what she'd made him endure. But she was conferring with a breathless young devotee. The boy was Henley's age, soaked with sweat, his bare chest heaving from having run all the way to the falls.

The Coin bent to hear his answer to her last question. Her head snapped toward Henley. "It's Kila Sigh. She's been unmasked and taken to Sensual Thine's rooms."

The boy said something else, just two words.

The Coin's face clouded and her jaw thrust forward. "They shrove her under the Dome of the Gentle Goddess."

"Fortune strike me!" cried the Spin Heleen. This earned a disapproving frown from the Coin. The chasten woman apologized profusely and set about checking Henley's wounds.

"Shrove? What does that mean?" He winced as the woman wiped a poultice across his ragged flesh.

Once he could stand, the Coin helped steady him as they descended into the Vale. She leaned close to him so that he might hear her narrative about the Ritual of Shriving. With every step his anger grew. As much as he feared what Kila had become, and as much as he resented being constantly pulled into her maelstrom of madness, she was his friend.

"What will happen to her?" he asked as they came to the winding stair leading into the relative shelter of the Vale canyon. His voice was suddenly too loud in the stiller air.

"The coin-talker didn't say. The novitiate wasn't privy to that information."

"Coin-talker?"

She touched her medallion. "A mercusine trick that a few of our number have mastered. We infuse another's medallion with our own power, like a signature. In deep meditation upon the mercusine web, we can feel the orientation of the medallion. This allows the one in possession of it to move their medallion to communicate in code. Smile and Frown in a series of turns form words and phrases. That is the coin-code. In legend, some were powerful enough to turn a coin in someone's hands, allowing for brief conversations."

The potential of such a skill drew Henley's mind away from his pain and his worry about Kila for a moment. "How much distance can stand between the coin and the Spinster who marked it?"

The Coin didn't answer for several steps. Finally she said, "There is no limit to the distance."

That meant Spinsters could communicate news from afar. "You have these coin-talker people—You have them every-where? In Starside, too?"

Again a long silence. But the Coin betrayed her consterna-tion with a deep furrow of her brow. "I would that it were so. But Coins in their towers have drifted from trust. They see coin-talkers from afar as spies. My web of talkers has thinned in the past ten-year. Starside has been silent since our talker there died. Coin Eppol sometimes sends coded letters by packet ship to keep me apprised of events in Starside. When she chooses to."

"Did she tell you of Kila?"

"Only that a powerful merculyn girl had awakened in Star-side. I fear Coin Eppol found the demise of my talker an opportunity to loosen the reins of my authority. She shares as little as she can."

Huff, is Kila hurt?

I don't know. Nax is in dead-sleep. Then came the image of Nax sprawled over the exposed and mossy roots of a great tree. It wasn't the posture of sleep, but of a sudden unconsciousness that had come over the animal mid-stride. This same thing had happened to Huff when Henley had been tortured by the Hargothe.

"Kila is not well," Henley said, swaying as the feeling Huff received from Nax swept into his mind.

"The shriving is pure agony to one with the spark," the Coin said. "It has not been used since the establishment of the

Triumvirate. I did not know that any of the shriving urns survived to this day. Voluptuary Sennikt must have discovered one on her journeys."

"What does it do?"

They had arrived among the huts. They stood at the base of the ladder leading to the Coin's hut. The woman's nostrils flared. "It was supposed to sear away ones crimes, to purify the soul to come into the service of the gods. It flays and burns as its water pours over the flesh, yet it leaves no marks. It is pure agony, and against it no one can remain unawakened to the mercusine if they have the spark. If they do not have it, they feel nothing at all."

Henley was terrified to think that such a relic might get into the hands of the Way of Til. Every Highest in every abbey would seek to awaken merculyns through torture.

"I didn't feel her lash out," he said, grasping for hope. He knew Kila was in a bad way or Nax wouldn't have fallen into the dead-sleep. But if Kila was attacked, why didn't she used her power to answer it?

"Sennikt and Thine would have been prepared for that. Perhaps they circled to prepare a quell on her, just as you did with Dunne Yples." But she didn't sound convinced of this. She looked worried, as if some other possibility had occurred to her. "Can your Beloved One rouse the Sigh girl's animal? We need to know what's happened."

Huff. Wake Nax.

How?

I don't know. Bite her ear or something.

Huff replied with a flush of exhaustion and irritation.

Just do it, Henley sent. *But don't hurt her.*

Her ear is wet now and I've got fuzz in my mouth.

You lick yourself constantly.

That's different. Oly says he can wake Nax.

Tell him to do it.

He says he wants to go back to Flaumishtak.

Henley had hoped never to hear that name again. The demayne, Flaumishtak, had come to him aboard *Flyer* during their sea voyage. He'd claimed to own Henley's life, but had granted it back to him if Henley promised to look after Oly for a while. The demayne had said he couldn't take the cat where he was going.

I don't control Flaumishtak. He'll return for Oly when he chooses. Henley suspected the beast would never return for the ornery cat. It had probably found Oly's attitude too odious to be tolerated.

Oly says he won't wake Nax unless you promise to return him to Flaumishtak immediately.

"Are you speaking with your Beloved One?" the Coin said.

Henley realized he had lost focus of his surroundings. He and Huff didn't usually have conversations this lengthy. Cats rapidly grew bored with talking. A prickly feeling had started to crawl over his scalp, sent from Huff. The cat was about to cut off the conversation and take a nap.

"Do you know how to summon a demayne?" Henley asked.

The Coin simply stared at him.

He sent to Huff, *If Oly can wake Nax, then you can, too.*

Resistance came back. And something else. A new feeling that Henley had never received from Huff before. It felt like secrecy and shame. Huff was keeping something from him.

The Coin urged him to climb. They entered the hut from

the bottom and stepped into the cool shelter. It swayed sickeningly in the wind.

What is it that Oly is willing to do that you aren't?

There was a long silence, during which the Coin pressed something into Henley's hands. A teacup. He sipped at the floral tea, barely tasting it. His mind held fast to Huff's.

We have to help Kila. But to help her we have to talk to her. To talk to her, we have to wake Nax.

You wouldn't like it.

If I was back with the Hargothe and you were like Nax again, would you want Oly or Nax to do this thing? Whatever it was. Henley was picturing someone dumping a bucket of water on the cat, but that wasn't what Huff had in mind.

You will feel this, Huff sent. *I'm sorry.*

Before Henley could ask what Huff meant, he felt it. Huff's presence in his mind vanished. The tea cup shattered on the floor, the splatter of the hot liquid staining Henley's clothes.

He joined the pieces on the floor, his breath squeezed out of him by the sudden vacancy in his heart.

This was what Kila had suffered when she'd lost Nax to the Hargothe. An unbearable feeling of absence, a gaping wound where the glory of living had been.

The Coin stooped to help Henley to his feet. She was talking. Was he ill? Was Kila dead? What was happening? Her words were a fall of hail, hard, loud, and meaningless.

Huff!

No answer came. No answer could come. The bond was severed.

"He's gone. He just vanished."

"Who? Your Beloved One? Why?" The Coin had stopped

trying to lift him to his feet. There was no way he could stand. He didn't want to stand. He wanted to disappear just as Huff had. He wanted to die.

The lashes had hurt his flesh, but this . . . The ache clenched his throat and burned his eyes. The loss of his house and his father had left him dazed, angry, and frightened. The loss of Huff was pure agony of the soul.

"Come back. Come back. Come back!"

Now the Coin's strong arm was around his shoulder. She had stopped trying to pry answers from him. Now she crooned and stroked his hair.

Sobs took him and he collapsed into her arms. And she kissed the top of his head and told him all would be well.

But nothing would be well again.

Not for him.

25

TAKE HOLD YOUR MIND

Knowing that she was going to die did not bring the peace Devotee Tia On'Liette had hoped for. It was nothing like what her grandmother had described. But Grandmother had been very ill and very old when she had declined toward Lumne's wakeless realm. In her last weeks, a sort of transparency had come over the woman, despite her trembles and milky eyes. To be near her was to be at peace. "I feared this for so long, but now that it is upon me, I see nothing to fear at all. I simply see."

For Tia, imminent death revealed nothing to content her. The closer she came to her objective, the more her stomach churned and her hands slicked with sweat. The Coin's orders had been simple—and nearly impossible to fulfill.

Release Dunne Yples.

"You'll catch another fist if you tarry longer," said Plina, another of Til's Favored who served Highest Fley. She was older, desired less for her loveliness than her competence. But she was loyal to Fley, so she was dangerous.

Tia leaned close to the looking glass and smudged on the last of the concealing ointment Plina had given her. It didn't soothe the bruises on her face, but it did mute the deep blue color.

"Tia!" the older woman snapped.

With one last swipe of her trembling finger, she stood and draped a scarf around her neck to hide a few more bruises and filed out of the Favored's Hall. The other women were attending to their duties. Some had not returned from the previous night, having been required to warm a Donse Master's bed.

Nothing unusual about that. Til granted his Donse Masters total dominion over the Favored. It was one of the reasons Tia had volunteered to serve as the Coin's spy. She wanted to get close enough to Fley to return an old favor.

Ideally it would have involved a blade into his eye, but now she'd have to settle for releasing his pet monster. Her sister had been a Favored, stolen off the streets of Trine and made the plaything of then Dunne Fley, who had later taken her with him when he was raised to Highest of Til's Tower.

The stories her sister had told were dry tinder for the fire in Tia's heart. And no abuse would deter her from her aim. She had finagled a position seeing to the queller team's needs. Mostly food and drink for them. They were so tired most of the time that they rarely attempted much else. And those who had? Well, they didn't have the seniority to have their complaints of her sharp-kneed defenses heard.

Most of the boys weren't too bad. Some were even sweet and kind. There were several Donse Masters who meant well. Dunne Portshalan was one. That poor man was likely going to die today, too. But did he not deserve it for remaining silent in his knowledge of the corruption of the Way of Til?

She moved as quickly as her aching legs could take her, circling down a winding stair to the basement level holding Dunne Yples's vast prison cell.

The kitchens sent the platters down with acolyte boys, since they were too heavy for young women like Tia. That's what she'd told them anyway.

All she had to do was arrange things in the small dining chamber to make sure the queller teams had their favorite treats in abundance and tidy up all their dirty dishes when they were done.

It was a task of a few minutes. She swept the floor, emptied a waste bin, rearranged some chairs. It was good, honest work that got her limbs moving.

Fifteen minutes later she was standing before Acolyte Wad, the pious guard who watched the great door to Dunne Yples's chamber. Tia held out a plate of squash cake, his favorite.

"Wad. I have a treat for you."

He lifted his eyes, coming out of a deep prayerful state. His gaze lingered on her bruises. "I will kill him when I see him."

He was talking about Henley Mast. She honored his vow with a curtsy. "I fear he is far from here. Perhaps gone from the island."

"Fellstorm. No one is leaving. I will crush his skull in my fist." He took the platter and ate the cake in one bite. "Why are you feeding me?"

Wad was devoted, but not particularly bright minded. He should have asked the question before swallowing. Now all she had to do was wait. It didn't take long. All of the Coin's spies had stashes of drowse-draughts and kill-quaffs.

Wad blinked furiously as the effect of the drops she'd soaked into the cake drew him to Lumne's permanent embrace.

Tia was struggling to slide back the locking bolt on the door when someone cleared his throat behind her. She spun, hand already going to the fold in her flimsy dress where her small knife was concealed.

A pale-haired lad stood before her, wearing fresh robes of a newly inducted acolyte. The creases from the folds were still sharp. He watched Wad choking on the floor. The huge man was grasping his throat, face purple.

Tia curtsied. "Can you help him, acolyte? I was just going inside for help."

The boy knelt next to the dying man, face soft with concern. His eyes flicked to the shattered platter, crumbs peppering the clean floor between the shards.

Tia didn't want to stab him. He was broad-shouldered and clearly stronger than her. But if he did start calling for help, he might raise enough response to ruin her plan. A plan that must not fail.

She felt the bone handle of her knife. She needed only to step close, pretend to care about Wad. And then, with a simple motion, cut a furrow in the lad's pale throat.

"Do you know an acolyte called Henley?" the boy asked. He lowered Wad's eyelids and straightened.

This made no sense at all. An acolyte should react to the death of another acolyte with great alarm.

"I knew him," she said carefully. "He beat me."

The boy scanned her face. Just like Wad had done, his

attention lingered on the barely-concealed bruises around her cheeks. No. Not like Wad. There was nothing possessive in the look, just skepticism. "He did no such thing. I count him among my closest friends. He would no sooner strike you than he would a child."

Feigning indignation, she looked down her nose at him. "And who are you? If you are so familiar with him, why have I not seen you before?"

He looked behind him, checking for eavesdroppers. "Like him, I came from Ori's Home. He did not come here by choice. I know how they treat Favored here. Help me find him. I'll get him away from here. Maybe you, too."

She pulled her blade, held it up. "Tell Highest Fley he will never have me. Nor any other Favored again. I'm ending this."

The boy raised his hands and stepped back. "I've never met the Highest. I say again, Henley never touched you. I don't know why you lied, but I think it's because you're helping him hide. Dunne Vins says you were with him the last time he was seen. And it looked like you were leading him somewhere. Voluntarily."

The lad had been asking around. He had a haughty face, but not unkindly. She'd seen enough like him to know he'd come from money. But if he was truly a friend of Henley's, then perhaps he could help her.

"Unlock that door," she said, flicking the point of her blade at the iron bar. "I'll tell you where Henley is."

The boy moved slowly, but deliberately to obey. The bar rasped in its holders as he shoved it aside.

"Step away," she ordered.

He obeyed.

"I helped Henley escape to Pol's Fifth of the Tower. I can't help you do the same. But flee this place if you can."

His eyes narrowed. He seemed to take notice of the door and realized where it led. "Is the Champion in there? I knew him, too. Dunne Yples. Henley and I brought him to Ori's Home from Starside. What are they doing to him?"

"They're breaking him. And then they'll forge him into a weapon. I'm going to free him. He'll bring this tower down around their heads."

She pulled on the door and it swung open a foot. Backing in, she said, "Run, lad. I can't save you."

Once inside the prison arena, she pulled on the door. It stopped a fist-width from closing. The boy had shoved his hand in the gap. Hissing with pain, he squirmed his arm through an pried the door open.

"Let me help."

Shrugging, Tia turned to the center of the chamber where the Champion strained atop a table. There were five men seated around him now, the one at the man's head focusing the others' power.

"I'm Ragin," the fair-haired boy said. "Dunne Yples is mad, but he doesn't deserve this torture."

She could see how the lad would think the man tortured. Yples strained against chains shackled to his wrists and feet. His muscles bulged, veins popping to the surface as he continued his endless struggle for freedom.

The acolytes serving as source-taps did not hear them enter. They did not hear Tia and Ragin walk toward their captain.

She whispered, "Once the Champion's mask is down, he will break free. Everyone in this chamber will die." She felt warning him was fair, but his insistence in accompanying her didn't earn him the right to argue with her. So she ignored him when he tried to.

One of the source-taps, a twenty-year-old boy named Tornlin, noticed her. His slow gaze encompassed her, and recognition that she should not be there slowly dawned on his slack face.

She stepped behind the leader, Dunne Dee, and cut his throat. Sputtering and choking, the man fell sideways. Whatever control he'd had over the mercusine bolts blocking Dunne Yples faltered. The source-taps, unexpectedly released, flew back from their seats with the recoil.

"Kil's toes!" Ragin cried. He rushed to Yples, who was now jerking and shaking his chains.

"Dunne Yples, it's me Raginalt. Calm down."

In answer, the man roared, "DEM-KISK!"

The walls trembled. A chunk of block wall fell away and smashed to the floor. With a huge groan, the Champion tore one chain free from the wall. It whipped over Tia's head, singing through the air like a demaynic scream.

The second chain came free, adding to the ringing cacophony of metal links clanking. The air sizzled with the speed of the chain's flight.

Yples sat up, gripped the shackles around his ankles and ripped the metal apart. The stink of mercusine hit Tia's nose.

Ragin lunged at the man, tried to press him bodily to the table. "Calm yourself! Take hold your mind!"

With the slightest shrug, Yples tossed Ragin away. The boy struck ground and did not move again.

Tia dropped her knife. She did not want to kill this man.

She wanted him to become a weapon, just as the Coin had commanded.

"Champion of Til!" she cried. "Kill Highest Fley! He blasphemes Til and claws for mortal power so that he might enrich himself. He lays with women who are not bonded to him under Til's laws. He murders for his own aims in Til's name. Destroy this hive of infidelity and do Til's will!"

Yples leapt to his feet, body still straining as if pulling against invisible chains. Sweat poured from his brow. His lips pulled back and he howled with insensible rage.

"THINNIES IN FLAMES!"

What he did next Tia did not understand. Balls of blue fire formed above his hands. And with an upward thrust, he hurled them toward the ceiling.

The world trembled and shifted under her feet. The ceiling fell, and all was lost in an unending assault of falling rock and the screams of mortal men.

26

TERRIBLE KNOWLEDGE

"The blade, the mirror, the bank node, and this curious canvas roll," Hannah said. "I swear thad is all she possesses aside from her clothes."

"Very little indeed for a girl of her station," Sensual Thine said.

Kila couldn't see the women. She couldn't see anything but a gauzy blanket drawn over her face. It was thin enough that her breath passed through the weave without making her feel like she was suffocating. Light passed through, too, bright and white. Mercus light.

But it was sight and she drank it in, like cool water on thirsty lips. Sounds flooded her awareness. The riotous thunder of the fellstorm registered as vibrations in her bones, but the wind—the unceasing wind—drowned out all else.

"This mirror is fine work," Thine said. "But she has no brush of her own? No mementos of her parents or sisters? Doesn't that seem odd to you? And this bank note, written by

Starside's strange queen. Why would *she* grant this child so much coin? Suspicious. It is all very suspicious."

A knock at a door. A murmured conversation. Kila heard the exchange. A man asking if the girl was ready.

"Come in. Come in. She'll not be a threat to you." The scuff of feet, heavy and booted. "There. Voluptuary Sennikt says you may speak with her here."

"Speak? But we are to take her back to the Tower, no?" The man's voice was young, abrupt.

"No."

Kila thought a whole lot of meaning ran through the silence that followed. She smelled the man now, behind the clean scents of Thine and Hannah came the sour sweat and pipe smoke of a Donse Master.

"Highest Fley's orders were clear," he said. "She is to be taken to the Champion, subdued, and made a source-tap."

"She will go to the Tower when I say she goes. But I have received assurances that Henley Mast will be returned to me. He killed my brother. Where is he? I don't see him in chains at my feet."

"You have my condolences, Sensual Thine. But I'm expected to return with both of the Misses Peline."

"Bring Henley Mast to me and Quinn Peline is yours."

"I was to bring them both."

A far off rumble sounded and the surface under Kila vibrated for a half a heartbeat.

"What was that?" the man asked.

"An earth tremor," Sensual Thine said. "Common when a fellstorm is upon us. Now go."

The door closed and Sensual Thine's quick and stiff footsteps came near to Kila. She could picture the woman staring down at her shrouded form, her lips pinched with that lemon-sucking tightness.

"Sensual Thine, is id wise to andagonize the Highesd's man so?" Hannah asked in a surprisingly small voice. The girl wasn't accustomed to questioning her mentor and it brought out a particularly pathetic childlike quality in her.

"Antagonize? I don't antagonize anyone. I was offered the Mast boy in return for this girl. I would be a fool to relinquish her until I have him. He murdered my brother."

Far off, a flare of mercus power erupted. It came to Kila across the mercusine web, shockingly bright and searing. Again the floor trembled. Kila's skin flashed cold and a wave of nausea made her gag. It passed as the flare subsided.

"Who is thad?" Hannah said.

"Yples. They've released him."

"Bud they cannod condrol him. He will kill them, no?"

Thine had no answer for this. "Clearly they have found a way to do so or they would not have let him spark so brightly upon the mercusine." Her voice trailed off, and then in a tone that betrayed her awe, she mumbled, "Such power." Collecting herself she sniffed. "We must hurry with this girl. I mean to have her secrets."

Kila tried to open her mouth to offer a snide comment about nobody asking for her opinion in the matter, but her lips wouldn't part.

A warm, languid feeling weighed upon her. The thought of moving so much as a finger seemed an enormous undertaking. She attempted it but nothing happened.

She could close her eyes. She could breathe. That was it.

She reached for the mercus, conceiving of tactile bolts needed to push the shroud from her face. But her efforts encountered a glassy obstruction. The mercus was present to her, enlivening her senses and even visible as haze around Thine and Hannah. But her will slipped against an impenetrable mercusine surface.

Alarm forced her breath faster until the fabric of her covering sucked into her nostrils on every inhale. She didn't want the women in the room to know she was awake, so she willed herself to slow her breathing. It made her feel like she was suffocating.

Her body thrummed with panic. She had to get away. The sleepy, heavy feeling vanished. But no matter how she tried to move, her limbs did not respond.

She sought the mercus again and was again denied by a seamless and infinite barrier. This was not like being masked, this was like being caged.

"She stirs," Thine said. The snap of her fingers cracked in the air and Hannah came close to pull the shroud from Kila's face. The sour girl's chin tucked in as she bent to inspect Kila's eyes.

"She's awake. Her irises are flecked with red, as you said they would be."

"I have experience with the *vaz'on*. Clean the penetrations or the flesh will become corrupted. We don't want her to die. Not yet, anyway."

"Would thad be bad?"

"Hannah child, don't be petulant. Jealousy is making you irrational. This girl has a purpose. She came to *us* for a reason." Thine appeared over Hannah's shoulder and watched as the dark-haired girl fiddled with something attached to Kila's head.

"Will you allow me do condrol the *vaz'on*?" Hannah asked slyly.

The woman considered the request but shook her head. "Not until you are a full Sensual. But it may not be up to me if Highest Fley delivers the boy. Oh!"

Again the flare shot across the mercusine. Kila clenched her eyelids shut, a groan rumbling in her throat. The acrid taste of flashtaper smoke came to her mouth, a manifestation of the mercusine power being wielded across the island. If it was Dunne Yples, his power had grown a thousand fold during his time at Til's Tower.

Hannah cried out at the same moment. "Whad is he doing? Highest Fley should pud a *vaz'on* on his Champion."

"Some secrets remain to the Way of Ori. But surely that is not Dunne Yples controlling that power. He would destroy the Tower. Fley must have discovered how to use him as a source-tap."

"Such power would overwhelm him, no?"

Thine remained silent to this question. "Distractions. We must explore this girl. It may be that she must die before Highest Fley claims her."

With the shroud removed Kila felt the coolness of stirring air upon her shorn scalp. And a tightness, too. Seven points pressed hard into her skin, one at each temple, one centered between her eyebrows, one over each ear, and two at the back of her skull.

She shifted her eyes all around, looking for someone else, anyone else. Someone to plead with.

"The *vaz'on* is secure," Hannah said, wiping at Kila's forehead with a damp cloth. It came away bloody.

Bloody.

No matter how Kila strained, she could not see what these horrid women had clamped onto her head.

Hannah moved aside and dipped her rag in a basin and wrung it out. Sensual Thine took her place, bending over Kila. Her tight mouth pursed as she observed Kila's face. "You hid your mercusine power from us. Why?"

Kila blinked rapidly. How could she answer if her lips wouldn't part? But then they did. She licked her lips and drew in a breath.

"Answer," Thine snapped.

"There was a Seeker at the docks." Her voice broke, and a sticky thirst made her tongue slow. "I didn't like my welcome to the island."

"And you also concealed this from me." The woman held up Cayne, the black blade naked and cruel. "A Shadline blade, if I'm not mistaken. That means two Shadline women came to Ori's Home. Why?"

Kila forced herself to look away. She didn't owe this woman any information. She had been stripped, humiliated, and tortured. What she owed Thine was retribution.

"Speak."

Kila said nothing.

Her breath cut off. Her mouth remained open, but her lungs stopped mid-inhale. The suffocating sensation triggered instant panic. She couldn't move so much as a finger, couldn't do anything but widen her eyes and beg Thine to stop doing whatever she was doing.

But the woman looked down her nose and watched Kila's silent suffering.

"I will allow you to breathe. When I do, you will answer

my question. Else I will let you pass out next time. It takes longer than you might expect and is most unpleasant."

Kila's lungs filled with glorious, sweet air. Her chest heaved with relief. "The Voluptuary of Starside sent us. We gave letters to Voluptuary Sennikt. I'm no Shadline. Didn't take oath. What are you doing to me?"

Hannah came over to watch the questioning. She smiled, but her eyes were full of worry. She kept looking over her shoulder as if expecting an unwelcome visitor. "He's coming," she said softly. "Sensual Thine. Why is he coming here?"

"Stand," Thine ordered.

Kila stood, though her will had no involvement in the movement. Her body merely went through the motion of sitting up, swinging her legs from the table, and slipping onto her feet.

The shroud fell to the floor, leaving her naked. The impulse to cover herself with her hands was met with immobility. She stood stiffly, arms at her sides, head down, shoulders slumped.

"Turn toward me," Thine commanded.

Kila refused in her mind, but her body obeyed. It was the strongest willshift she had ever experienced, and she had been subjected to it by both the Hargothe and the demayne, Flaumishtak.

"Look at me."

Kila's eyes lifted. Thine rounded the table, hands clasped before her, shoulders erect and severe.

"Hannah, the mirror."

The novitiate moved a stand mirror from the corner and tilted it so Kila could see herself. The girl's hands trembled and she bit her lip. Another burst of power flashed across the mercusine. Whatever Yples was doing, he was throwing massive bolts around.

Nostrils flaring, Hannah's head snapped up, as if she could see through the roof. "Father's grace!" she whispered.

"Look upon yourself," Thine said to Kila. The woman's face was screwed up like a soldier bracing for an amputation.

Kila gasped at the sight of her reflection. The only part of herself she recognized were her eyes and nose. But her hair . . . It had been hacked and scraped until nothing remained of it but a few patches of uneven fuzz here and there. In most places her scalp was red and bumpy and bare.

But the crown she wore drew all her attention. She wanted to lean forward and inspect it. She wanted to reach for it and pull it off.

Thine positioned herself behind Kila and gently place her hands on Kila's shoulders. "Inspect the *vaz'on*. Go on." The willshift released and Kila found herself free to move.

Stumbling, she approached the mirror, hands raising to touch the slim band of gold on her brow. Not merely on her brow. In it.

Her eyes clamped shut as yet another glare of mercus pierced her mind.

"Sensual Thine! Did you feel thad?" The girl flinched and hugged her elbows. She had no interest in Kila now.

"Yes, child. Hush."

Whatever Yples was doing, Kila didn't care. The crown— the *vaz'on*—was her only concern. Gems at the temples, between her eyebrows, over her ears and at the back of her skull were not merely decorative. They were finger grips for screws that penetrated into her skin. And now that she saw them, she felt them.

The metal bit into the bone of her skull. How deep did they go? Frantically she pulled at the gems at her temples. They did not move. She twisted. They tightened.

"Enough!" Thine snapped. The willshift slapped into Kila with such force she would have fallen to her knees, except she no longer controlled her legs.

She wanted to scream, to beg for Thine to remove the horrid thing. Knowing it was there pulled all of her attention to it, so that screws piercing her head felt like they went all the way through and out the other side.

This horrible headpiece was what blocked her from reaching the mercusine. This put the glass wall there. This gave Thine—whose mercus spark was not half as strong as Hannah's—total control over Kila's body. This was not something a Sensual should use. This was a tool suited to the worst sort of Donse Master, people like the Hargothe himself.

This was evil.

Thine said, "The *vaz'on* was created by the builder race, to subdue merculyns of too much power and assure that they serve the good of all. You, child, are well-suited to wear it. Your power is great, but your character is poor. You are a liar and you are not devoted to any god at all. This will not be tolerated. The Ways of the New Pantheon have been corrupted. The day of renewal is upon us. The Champion has come into the world to cleanse us. The Triumvirate will cease to exist and there will be but one Way. The Way of righteous truth, humility, and order."

Her tirade was too much to follow. The woman spoke with such fervor, spittle flew from her squished mouth.

The floor trembled and a strong gust howled outside.

Limbs cracked under the strain, followed by the rush and hiss of the wind ripping through the polshel leaves.

"Merely the fellstorm," Sensual Thine said to Hannah. The girl had moved to the far corner, where she squatted and covered her head. "Don't be a goose, child."

"So much power!" Hannah moaned.

Yples's exertions upon the mercusine were constant now, like the booms of a great drum.

"We all must become accustomed to such beacons upon the mercusine. The new era will have hundreds of source-taps under the command of righteous merculyns. Our world has not seen such feats for an age of ages, but they will soon be commonplace."

She addressed Kila now. "You are not Lady Quinn Peline's cousin. What is your true name?"

Kila's mouth opened and a low moan came out. Willshift could make her speak, but it could not compel her to speak the truth. But she saw no advantage in suffering more to conceal information that made no difference. Relenting, she said, "Kila Sigh."

"Bring the chair, novitiate," Thine said to Hannah.

The girl emerged from her corner, dragged a straight backed chair behind Kila, and then returned. "Id's doo much. Id's doo close. Can'd you feel him? Id's all hade and fear."

"Sit, Kila Sigh," Thine ordered. Beads of sweat had formed on her brow. Her face had drained of blood and taken on a green cast. Thine was terrified.

Kila sat, Hannah's fear now infecting her. The mercus remained forbidden to her, just on the other side of the glassy barrier in her mind. But she could see the haze of mercus potential around the other women in the room.

Thine cleared her throat and patted her brow with her sleeve. "Now that you are awake, we can proceed with peeling you. The pain you suffer will be your choice. But first, let us finish your grooming."

Thine raised Cayne and tested the edge with her thumb. Her nostrils flared with satisfaction to find it razor sharp along its length. She placed the edge on Kila's scalp and scraped, removing a patch of longer hair she'd missed the first time around.

To Kila's heightened senses the sound was similar to what she'd just heard when Hannah had dragged the chair legs across the tiles. A rash of heat prickled on the newly shaven skin.

As Thine continued her deliberate work of removing Kila's remaining hair, she spoke. Like telling a child a story. "I do not believe in prophecy. The gods do not know what they mean to do from one day to the next. Mostly, they do nothing. That is because those we call Ori and Til and Pol are merely ideas. They do not call themselves by these names, nor do they acknowledge their supposed specialties. Ori is no more a healer goddess than Pol is the goddess of hunting hounds."

She scraped along the edge of the *vaz'on*, slipping the blade between skin and crown to remove a bit of hair hidden under the golden band encircling Kila's head. "The force of destiny is separate from the gods. It is like the metal of this blade, or the blood in your heart. It is like the mysterious power that makes a dropped object fall to the floor. It is thoughtless. It is a principle. In the parlance of the philosophers, the force of destiny lacks agency, because it does not seek any particular end for any particular reason, but merely because its path is headed toward that end, in the way a ball rolling downhill comes to rest where it does. No reason, just a consequence of where it began its journey. That is an apt metaphor. We must not think about ends, but of beginnings. Why we are here is because of how things were started. And who started you? Tell me of your father."

"Wenton Sigh. He died when I was young. He was a locksmith and—"

Pain over her left ear. What a spike driven into her skull would feel like. In the mirror she saw the gem flash a brilliant red, the light painting the walls crimson.

Thine moved Cayne from Kila's scalp and placed the flat of the blade under her chin. The woman's hand trembled. "The *vaz'on* says you are lying."

"He was a thief!" Kila blurted. The light vanished and the pain faded. She still felt the stab of the seven screws in her skull.

"And your mother?"

Searing pain wracked her brain. Thine didn't allow her to bend forward and grip her head, nor did she allow Kila to close her eyes. And so she sat there, immobile and suffering. If her earlier lie had sent a spike into her head, Thine's question drove in ten. Nausea followed immediately after, but Kila's wasn't free to respond to it. Pressure built in her belly, but her throat remained clamped tightly shut.

"Tell me your mother's name."

Kila was given control of her mouth. Her lips were wet from drool. The need to heave up the contents of her stomach was not answered. "Father was a locksmith before he was a thief."

"I did not ask about him. Your mother. Tell me of her."

The red gem did not glow but the pain from inside her

head intensified. Blurs of light covered her vision and the room began to tilt. A rushing sound, like waves upon the seashore, filled her ears. She realized she was hearing her own blood flowing through her veins.

"Who was your mother?"

"I don't know!" A high-pitched cry came from her throat. "I don't know! She died!"

The red gem flashed onto the walls and the lie spike pierced into her head.

"Liar! What is her name?"

"I don't know."

"Where was she from? Starside?"

Kila gagged. The red gem had darkened and remained so after her last answer. Thine set Cayne aside and came to stand in front of Kila. She put her thumbs under Kila's eyes and pulled the skin down. "The vessels in her whites have gone fully red. This fit of hers is not the *vaz'on's* doing."

The woman cupped Kila's cheek and extended her thumb across her eye to touch the gem between her brows.

The world went purple. Kila's mind erupted. Someone screamed.

When her vision cleared. Sensual Thine was being held upright by Hannah. Blood trickled from the woman's nose. "Fetch Voluptuary Sennikt. Quickly now."

"Bud you are nod well."

Thine gathered her strength and straightened. "Go. Now."

Hannah fled. It was then that Kila noticed tiny flecks of blood splatter on the walls and felt the hot trickle of it on her cheeks. It was her blood on the walls.

Nax? I need help.

The cat's presence was very far away, to the north now. There was no response.

Sensual Thine fetched the damp rag Hannah had hung up to dry. Hands shaking, she dipped it into the basin and returned to Kila. With hard strokes she wiped blood away from Kila's face. It burned, but only from the force of the rubbing.

"The *vaz'on* likely saved your life just now," Thine said. "The eruptions on your skin are small and will heal quickly."

The woman moved in a business-like efficiency, mouth set tight as she attended to a task that had to be done and best done quickly. Now she was glancing at the ceiling, and her mouth parted to form a perfect circle.

She fetched a sheer gown from somewhere and willshifted Kila's arms up so that she could pull it over Kila's head. It wasn't long before Voluptuary Sennikt and four Sensuals arrived, Hannah leading. The woman's face had a yellowish cast, and the bags under her eyes had darkened since Kila had seen her last. She was breathing hard, as if she'd run all the way from her library residence.

"What is it, Thine? I do not appreciate being summoned when we face imminent attack."

"Attack? No. Surely Highest Fley merely experiments with the Champion as source-tap."

"There's smoke carrying on the wind from the west. I do not think the Highest controls his Champion at all."

Thine took in a deep breath, mouth nearly disappearing as she clenched it. "We have another problem. The girl's mind has been occluded to keep knowledge of her mother from her. Terrible knowledge."

Something she said made the pain flare in Kila's head. Not

as bad as before, but enough to make tears flow. "Why are you doing this to me?"

"Occluded?" the Voluptuary said, eyes narrowing. "How so?"

Thine gestured at the gem between Kila's brows. "See for yourself."

The woman approached warily. Her finger reached for the gem.

Again, Kila's world exploded in purple.

27

OFFSPRING OF SIN

The girl stands on the shore of a mountain lake, her bare toes just touching the icy water. A high and narrow waterfall sheets from the cliffs to her right, plunging into a cloud of mist as it meets the lake.

The vale is all noisy silence. The crush of the falls, the call of waking nightskirls, the wash of trees in the wind. But behind that is the stillness of a held breath, full of an ever-growing need for release.

Across from her, high up on the cliff face is the enormous carving of a man's head. The beard is a hang of pale moss. But the girl wonders if the face was made by man or by the water and wind. The thrusts of striated rock that form the brows are not even, nor is the noble nose so symmetrical as to suggest the intentional craft of trained hands.

The little lake is held in the vale like tea in a cup, the great blank eyes of the strange face peering into the waters as if seeking some dark augury in the depths.

There is no way into this vale save a steep climb down the

cliffs. Had she done that? the girl wonders. Her memory is just as misty as the base of the falls.

She is hungry. Mother has not come, though she has said she would. She has promised to come here and meet her daughter so they can finally be together.

The girl moves away from the shore and finds a dry, flat boulder to perch on. The air is growing colder. It will be another miserable night.

If her flesh must be cold, then perhaps her heart can be warm. She hums a little tune and allows her mind to float. She imagines her thoughts to be like the trout she sometimes pulls from the lake: aimless, unthinking, sometimes moving slow, sometimes darting in quick lunges. In this way she allows time to be, and her longing for her mother fills her without breaking her.

At some point, after the sun goes down and darkness claims the sky, she sleeps. She doesn't see the violet glow appear in the water. She doesn't see it grow brighter until the cliff walls and the trunks of the pines are ablaze with it.

A face emerges from the lake, surrounded by black hair that falls in glistening sheets over pale shoulders. Wide eyes blink away the last streams of water and fix on the sleeping girl.

The water spirit, Semūin, presses a hand to her heart and weeps. She lives outside of time. Her daughter is trapped within it.

The spirit watches until the sky begins to lighten. And just as the girl stirs, Semūin slips below the surface and swims to her grotto behind the falls.

Til has cursed the water spirit for disobeying him and indulging her desires for a mortal man. The offspring of that sin now haunts the vale, unattached and wild, a child that was and is and might yet be.

Semūin weeps in her grotto. And schemes. If the child's father is not good enough for Father Til, then she will replace him with one who is. It is of no matter that the child has already been born, for Semūin can swim through time. Any man can be the father.

But she needs one who is not merely a man, but one whose veins still course with a bit of godfire.

The child rises from where she's been curled. Her muscles are cold and stiff from lying on stone all night.

The falls still roil the water.

She thinks that perhaps today will be different. Perhaps today Mother will come.

28

THE MERCUSINE STORM

Kila Sigh awoke with a great gasp. Her heart slammed in her chest and hard-driven chisels sought to chip through her skull from the inside. The paralysis of the hated crown did not allow her to move. She was on her back again, though the white shroud had not been thrown over her face.

She moved her eyes side to side. Thine stood to her left, Voluptuary Sennikt to her right. Both women looked haggard. And worried.

"Who is your mother, child?" the Voluptuary said softly.

The only thing Kila could do was clamp her eyes shut. Her arms would not raise the way instinct demanded, so that she might grip her skull to keep it from exploding. "I don't know. I don't know. I don't know!"

"Occluded. But *I* saw," the Voluptuary said. She tapped her knuckles together and began to pace. "This is . . . unexpected. Do we dare turn her over to Highest Fley now? I can't imagine that wise."

Another Sensual spoke. Kila couldn't see her, but she thought it was old Sens Dooni, the woman who had told her to leave the Home when she'd gone searching for Ragin in the Dome. "If what you say is true—"

"Touch the Eye Gem if you doubt me," the Voluptuary barked. Her voice trembled, and so did her hands.

Kila's eyes flicked back to Thine. The woman's mouth had parted in a tight circle and she drew shallow breaths through the orifice, betraying her nervousness. "If she is *her* daughter we cannot allow Highest Fley to have her. We must kill her."

"No," the Voluptuary said. It was the first time Kila had seen the woman exert her authority over Thine. "She wears the *vaz'on*." A fingerlike pressure probed inside Kila's skull. She realized the woman was using the crown's power to delve into her mind in the way the Hargothe had done. "The Earth Gems are there for a reason. Perhaps it is time to test Fley. Perhaps our old plan must be thrown out. He was never meant to stay in power anyway. He enjoys his Favored too much to reign in righteousness once the Triumvirate falls."

Kila couldn't track the woman's logic because she couldn't understand half of what she said. But given the Voluptuary's love of trezz, she found the sneer about the Highest's lack of piety ridiculous.

"Safer to be done with her," Thine said. "Why risk making an ash-barrens of the whole island?"

Sens Dooni stepped into view. It was indeed the same one who had warned Kila away. "Perhaps it best to remove the *vaz'on*. Who are we to stand in the way of the force of destiny? If this girl is to contend as a Champion, then so be it. Something dire approaches even now. Though he has the form of man, Dunne Yples is no longer mere man. His mind roils up a fellstorm of greater power than that which now blows across the island."

The thrum of Yples's presence continued to grow in Kila's mind. She could hardly bring herself to care. If he destroyed these hateful women, all the better.

"Surely that is Fley we feel," Thine insisted, a note of desperation in her voice. "He would never release that monster if he could not control him."

The floor shook, making the table Kila lay on shudder and slide a few feet to the left. The surface beneath her thumped against her spine and shoulders, and she could do nothing to soften the blows.

"What in Ori's blessed name was that?" the Voluptuary said. "Hannah, go check to see if the Dome collapsed or—"

BOOM!

"He's here!" the novitiate cried, her eyes rolling up into her skull until only red-streaked whites showed. Foam formed on her lips. "The fire! The rough wind. Searing hade!"

Kila felt it all now. And no wonder the women around her were terrified. She had never felt such power, never conceived that such could exist. As if the sun itself had come to roll over the earth.

The room shook. Something glass fell from a table behind Kila and shattered. The ceiling loosed drifts of dust that fell onto the Voluptuary's head. She grabbed Kila's table to keep herself upright. Thine squawked and stumbled against a wall.

"Let me move!" Kila cried.

"Thine! If she gets crushed by this ceiling . . ."

Kila's limbs released. She curled into herself and rolled from the table. The floor tiles slammed her shoulder. She didn't care. At least this pain had a cause she could understand. She scrambled under her table.

If she hadn't known she was on the floor, she was would have sworn she was lying on the bed of a wagon racing over rutted roads. The floor bounced and swayed. Tiles cracked. The table juddered and slid.

The other women dropped to the floor, hands spread as if they could stop the insane motion through the strength of their arms. Another boom sounded. Kila couldn't tell what direction it had come from.

And then came the scream. A throat-rending call of a man possessed with the fury of the gods.

"DEM-KISK!"

Dunne Yples had come.

Kila! Run! Nax sent.

Where are you?

In ash. Come!

Still in control of her limbs, Kila climbed from under the table and staggered to the door. Thine and the Voluptuary lay on the floor next to Sens Dooni. Hannah stood to bar Kila's way, her hair wild and eyes still rolled up. She held Cayne out, the tip wavering as she shivered with fear. The mercusine storm had obliterated the girl's senses, but her hate for Kila did not require rational thought.

Kila stepped close, gripping the girl's wrist. With a quick jerk, she bent the girl's arm to the side. Cayne came free.

Kila caught the blade before it hit the tile.

She spotted her backpack on a table across the room. Five steps and it was in her hands.

"DEM-KISK!" came the inhuman cry from outside. Closer now.

The floor shook again and Kila barely kept her feet. Something cracked in the ceiling and the far wall simply fell away. A timber collapsed, striking Hannah on the crown of the head and driving her to the floor. Her mercus spark vanished.

Rain and wind pelted through the new opening, stinging Kila's face. The polshels bent and twisted in the fellstorm gale. Kila ran into the madness, leaping over the dead novitiate.

"No!" Thine cried.

Kila didn't care about the wind. Just escape.

"No!"

Willshift clamped Kila's muscles tight and she lunged forward as her legs refused to continue their steps. The soggy ground met her face.

She bounced and rolled until she lay face up.

Thine staggered into the wind, holding her hands up to block the pelting rain. Her robe pressed hard against her body, the loose skirts whipping like a flag atop a mainsail.

"Stand!" Thine commanded.

Kila stood. The finger-probe returned to her mind as Thine laid claim to Kila's mercusine power. The penetrations at her temples grew hot and she saw green light shed onto the ground before her, beaming from the *vaz'on* gems that gave Thine access to her mercus. A glow formed around the Sensual and her arms spread wide in ecstasy as she filled with Kila's power.

A blur appeared behind the Sensual, black and oily.

Sensual Thine's mouth opened to deliver another command, but then it relaxed and her jaw dropped, light lips finally loosening. Her eyes went wide.

She fell to her knees, then onto her face. Her grip on Kila's power and body vanished.

Quinn stood in her place, crouched and holding Black, the blade already absorbing Thine's blood. "Come on!" she mouthed. "We've got to run!"

Released from Thine's willshift, Kila obeyed her friend and together they plunged into the fellstorm.

29

CRACKLED WITH POWER

Henley came awake sucking in a huge gulp of air.

Huff had returned.

The emptiness had crushed him, and his sobbing had grown so bad the Coin had called for a Devotee to bring a special blend of sleep tea and hanose oil. The liquid had gone down hot and thick, but Henley had welcomed the numbness it had brought.

But now that was gone, and the return of the bond shot him to his feet.

Huff was very far away, but he could feel the bond.

Don't ever do that again! he sent with all his might. He wiped sleep and tears from his eyes.

I woke Nax as you commanded. Huff's voice was faint. *Kila is free. The storm grows worse.*

Storm. That's what that raging sound was. He'd thought it an aspect of his own confusion, perhaps the rush of blood in his ears. But no. The trees outside his hut were bent over, and a driving rain pounded the world.

The hatch in the floor of his hut lifted. Spin Heleen peeped in, her wavy hair wildly askew. "Good, you're awake. You must come down. The huts aren't safe during storms this strong."

As if the gods wished to emphasize this, the hut swayed, floor tilting. The Spinster squawked and disappeared. Henley clambered after her.

Outside, gripping the ladder to descend, he was nearly blown free. He had to slide down and hope the Spinster had gotten out of the way.

Water streamed down his face and his body was instantly soaked. The lash wounds on his back rebelled with every motion.

The sky was charcoal-colored and streaked with whirling gray clouds. Flashes of lightning flared among them. The canopy of the surrounding trees waved like hard-blown seas.

The Spinster gripped his hand and pulled. He followed her through the skin-burning wind, leaning forward and shielding his face with one hand. Each rain drop stung like a thrown pebble.

But he didn't care.

Huff had returned.

What did you do? he sent. The Spinster led him toward the path that ascended toward the falls. He saw the wisdom in it, there were many caves along the cliffs that way. Other Spinsters and Devotees were joining them, struggling forward against the blast of the fellstorm.

I joined Nax, Huff sent. It was clear from the feeling of annoyance coming through the bond that Huff didn't have the words to describe what he'd done. But it had worked.

Where is Kila?

Loose. Hunted.

Ahead of him a Spinster moaned. "So much power. How can one person have *so* much?"

The path curved toward the cliffs, to the mouth of a cave. The vertical crack, aglow with warm light, beckoned to him.

Who is hunting Kila? Henley sent.

Who doesn't?

That was a fair point. Henley felt the same way about himself. But he needed more answers.

Is Ragin helping? Is Quinn?

No. Yes.

From far off came a clap of thunder that shook the ground. But it hadn't been thunder from the storm, but a great impact upon the earth.

A Spinster had stopped in the path and was holding her head. "It's too much!" It was Spin Rippa. Heleen collected her and they continued into the dry safety of the cave. The entrance narrowed and wound through several bends. The wind became a constant low howl, as if a god played upon a horn the size of the world.

Dripping and chilled, Henley staggered to a brazier where several Devotees and Spinsters were warming themselves. He tugged off the queller.

Instantly the mercusine crackled with power. To the south a great chorus of it thrummed upon the subtle world. To Henley it was not as difficult to tolerate as it was for the merculyns around him. Perhaps a benefit of the Hargothe's experiments.

He handed the queller to Spin Rippa, who seemed to be suffering the most. "Put it on. You need it more than I do."

The woman shook so badly she dropped it. Henley

stopped it from rolling away by stomping on it. He collected it and placed it on Rippa's finger. With a moan of relief she embraced him, weeping.

"Henley Mast!" the Coin called. She tromped toward him, her fists balled, her stern gaze fixed on him. "What transpires?"

"That storm you feel on the mercus is Dunne Yples."

The woman's mouth moved as she struggled to comprehend that one person could be the source of so much power. A strangled look crossed her face as if she now realized something she should have seen before. "And where is Kila?"

"My Beloved One has returned his bond to me. Kila is free, but she is hunted."

"Where is she? Exactly."

Huff, where is Kila?

And image flashed of Ori's Home.

"Ori's Home."

"She must come north. When she gets to the wall marking the northern extent of Ori's Fifth, she must climb it. Then she must run as fast as she can across the ash-barren to the next wall. Once she climbs it, she'll be in Pol's Fifth and we may be able to shield her." She didn't sound particularly convinced of this last part. And Henley didn't blame her. Dunne Yples power was so vast that his very presence glowed like the sun. Henley wondered if the power he'd fed the man had somehow accumulated, filling him the way the butcher used to inflate pig bladders to entertain children.

Have Nax tell Kila to find the northern wall and go over it, he sent to Huff.

He didn't get an answer. Huff felt tired, beyond tired. Just as Henley did.

A devotee handed him a dry robe. He wiped his face with

it and looked down the passage, toward the entrance and the world beyond where the fellstorm reigned.

"Is there a path to the south wall from here?" he asked the Coin.

The woman shook her head. "Don't be a fool."

Henley laughed through his nose. A feeling of sadness cloaked him now, familiar and comfortable. He had been running from Kila and her whirlwind of danger for months, and look where it had gotten him. Right back into it.

Perhaps he had pushed against the force of destiny too long. Maybe now he would be better off letting it carry him to his fate. If it was a bad fate, better to have it done with.

"If you go, the whipping will have been for nothing," the Coin hissed in his ear. She gripped her medallion. Her eyes were wide and urgent. "I spun on you. Pol has plans for you. I'm sure of it. You spun for yourself. You saw."

"And what if her plan is for me to help Kila Sigh this very night?"

She removed her medallion, whispered to it and flipped it. The goddess's faces flashed in the brazier light and the metal sang out a high-pitched ring as it turned in the air.

It clanked onto the stone floor of the cave, not on edge, but flat one side. It didn't bounce, but stuck to the floor as if the downward face was covered with glue.

Pol's face frowned up at all who bent to look.

The Coin considered this result for a moment, then barked out, "Bring a satchel of food, and an oil-cloak." She turned her heavy stare on Henley. "Our Prince is leaving us this night. I would not send him out unprotected."

30

A FLICK OF INSTINCT

The wind pounded Ori's Home, tearing the upper branches from the polshels, and carrying them away never to be seen again. Some branches skittered and tumbled across the ground. One slapped Kila's bare legs as it passed, sharp and painful as a lash. Three red lines appeared on her calf and wept blood that was instantly washed away by the sideways torrent.

Quinn was shouting something, but her words flew away like scraps of paper. And that's what Kila felt like as she stumbled from tree trunk to tree trunk, following Quinn.

Her dark-haired friend had sheathed her blade so that she could talk to Kila, but her hand kept going to the hilt. Only obvious effort kept her from drawing it.

"Where are we going?" Kila shouted.

Quinn turned, her mouth forming an irritated "What?"

Kila waved her on. This was ridiculous.

Another concussion shook the ground. It was not from the fellstorm, but from the tempest currently raging upon the mercusine. It was as if Yples was leaping into the air and impacting with the weight of a house-sized boulder.

Kila's head throbbed with the power coming from the west. But very close now. She heard his distant scream of "Dem-Kisk" again, enhanced by mercus bolts to carry for miles.

The man had the strength of a god and apparently the Highest of Til had decided to unleash him. She was ablaze with power, too, but she did not know if she could match Dunne Yples even if she could use it. She tried to throw up her mercus mask, but the crown prevented it.

They darted across a garden, keeping low to provide as little exposure to the wind as they could. The gale thrust them with hard shoves toward the Princes Ward. The doors were closed, the windows shuttered.

The door to the common area opened as they approached. Gian stood inside, waving to them.

At the sight of him, Kila drew Cayne and charged. He had betrayed her. He had betrayed Quinn. None of this would have happened if he hadn't told Thine who she was and what she was.

With cat-like grace he sidestepped her awkward attack and wrapped her up, him embracing her from behind, her blade somehow in his hand and poised near her throat.

But not touching. She struggled in his grasp, but he overpowered her. She tried to lash him with mercus fire, but her grasp upon the power slid away against the wall of glass inside her mind.

"Let me go!"

He released her. Quinn leaned against the door and

slammed the bar in place. The roar of the wind lessened, but not by much.

Soaked through, Kila shivered and dripped as her trembling fingers went to the gems on her crown. She twisted, seeking to pull the screws out of her skull, but a turn in one direction did nothing and other only tightened them.

Gian gaped at the relic and mouthed a curse.

"Help me get this off, Quinn," Kila said.

Her friend came to her and fiddled with the gems. She tugged and even probed between the metal band and Kila's naked scalp to see if Black would cut through one of the spikes.

"They do look like screws," Quinn said, "but the gems just turn freely in this direction."

Kila realized that some mercus trick was required to engage them. That way only a merculyn could remove the crown. The *vaz'on*.

"I guess I'm Kil-damned and kissed," she said in frustration.

Climb the north wall, Nax sent, voice very distant, very desperate. *Henley says.*

"North wall?" Kila said aloud. *Why?*

She stepped away from Gian, putting a chair and table between them. He flipped Cayne, caught it by the tip, and presented the weapon to her, hilt first. When she didn't take it, he set it on the table and slid it to her.

She plucked it up and assumed a guard position.

Huff says Pol's Vale is that way. Safety. Help.

"Kila, why are you angry with me?" Gian said. "Do you truly think I betrayed you to the Voluptuary?"

"To Thine, more like. I saw you guarding Quinn when

they brought you to the Dome for my little ceremony." Her throat constricted at the memory of the agony, of the humiliation of being naked and cold and having her hair chopped off. She realized the white gown Thine had put on her was soaked through, making it mostly transparent as it clung to her skin.

She shook out her limbs. She would not allow humiliation to cloud her mind just now. Maybe later, if she lived through the next hour, she would have time to be mortified.

Quinn's lips moved, but no sound came out. With a frustrated jerk, she sheathed her blade. "He didn't betray either of us. They came for me first. I got doused with that urn, too." She shrugged as if trying to loosening a too-tight shirt. "But nothing happened. I didn't feel anything. But they had found Black. Gian got hold of it somehow. He talks smooth."

"I merely suggested that as a skilled bladesman, I would be best suited to guard her."

"When they did what they did to you . . . " Quinn said. Her dark eyes welled up, but she firmed her jaw, forced the emotion back from where it had come. "I'm sorry. I wanted to stop them."

"And what about you?" Kila ask Gian. "Did you want to stop them?"

"I . . . It is not a simple decision to begin killing Sensuals. My family depends on me to maintain good relationships here. My feelings for you had to . . . remain unexpressed. I knew they would not kill you. Well, I hoped they wouldn't."

"So you allowed them to scald my flesh from my bones and scrape my scalp?"

"We could not see the cause of your pain. They poured water over you. It didn't burn or smoke. It was just water."

Kila looked at her arms, her legs. In the moment of the shriving it had felt like molten iron pouring over her body.

"As for the shaving . . ." He shrugged unapologetically. "Do I risk everyone's life to spare you humiliation and put my own family's interests in danger? An easy decision to make. You are strong enough to live through a haircut."

Somehow he had ambled close while he talked. Now he rounded the table. She kept the tip of Cayne pointed right at his heart. He showed no concern, but neither was he threatening.

Cayne trembled, the point carving a wild squiggle in the air. Kila had never felt so cold, not even when she'd climbed to the Eerie above the Citadel in Starside.

"Haircut?" she said, throat constricting around the understatement. "This is a little more than a haircut."

"You have a shapely head." He grasped her wrist, gently moving the blade down and away. Then his hands were on the sides of her face, thumbs stroking her cheekbones. "My feelings for you never altered. But I have my responsibilities. I was going to press them hard to release you, to see if reason and diplomacy could prevail. But then Pennie came." His eyes lifted and he looked over Kila's shoulder.

She turned to find the young novitiate standing in the hallway. She looked small and fragile except for her world-weary expression.

"She said they were torturing you. With this." He tapped a finger on her crown. "That, I could not abide. How can my family trust a Voluptuary who will resort to such things? Especially against one who is here under the Rules of Princes?"

"He came to me," Quinn said. "I was ready to do anything he asked. For you. Anything." Her eyes glimmered again and this time she did not fully master her feelings. Though her face was strong and arrogant, a tear tracked down her cheek. Seeing it, Kila's throat ached and her eyes began to burn.

"Where you go, I go, Kila Sigh," Gian said.

Kila could not draw her eyes away from Gian's. She wanted to believe him, but she didn't understand what he was talking about. Who was this family? Why would a merchant's son need to be so diplomatic with the Way of Ori?

"You're not a merchant's son," she said.

"I never said I was."

A roar blasted from the sky. "DEM-KISK!" The ward shook with the declaration.

Another inhuman roar carried to them on the wind and was followed by a tremor in the earth. Kila could not help but imagine Dunne Yples had become a giant and every step smashed huge footprints into the land.

Gian smiled. "We can discuss my family later. But know this: I swear to help you however I can, but I am no merculyn. Whoever it is that calls so loudly, I cannot fight him." He smiled. Such a soft expression. "But I've always known that you do not need my protection."

Kila wanted to fold into his arms, hide in his warmth. She wanted to say, "Yes I do. I need it. I have always needed it." But she said nothing as her arms wound around him and pulled him close.

"I'll protect you," she said after a long moment. "But I can't do it with this Kil-damned tiara bolted to my skull."

"I can help with that," Pennie said.

The girl came forward, and with the imperious gesture of a teacher motioning for a pupil to approach, she curled her fingers.

Kila noticed the faint haze of mercus around the child and hope sprang to her chest. She disentangled herself from Gian's arms and knelt, head bowed.

The girl came alight with mercus and gently touched the gems at the back of Kila's skull. Then the ones over her ears, then temples, and finished with the one between Kila's brows.

The crown released with seven sharp clicks, a satisfying sound like the shackle of a heavy lock releasing. The pressure on Kila's skull eased.

"This will hurt. The gem-spikes go deeper than you'd think," Pennie said. She set about unscrewing each of the gem-spikes.

"How do you know so much about this thing?" Kila asked.

The girl merely looked at her and blinked, the world-weary expression suddenly explained. She knew about the crown from direct experience.

Kila felt the rasp of metal against the bone of her skull. It made her teeth buzz and ache. Quinn gagged and turned away.

Gian knelt by Kila's side, rubbing her back and making soothing sounds. When the crown came off, Pennie shook it so that droplets of Kila's blood fell from the seven sharp spike points.

Quinn brought a towel and pressed it against Kila's wounds. It came away splotched with stark red stains.

"The holes will have already sealed," Pennie said. "But there will be scars."

Kila probed the area of each spike penetration. The skin was whole, but tender. She shivered, and was overtaken with an immediate need to get out of her soaked robe. Her room was as she had left it. The Sensuals had not bothered to collect her trousers, top, and vest. With a little feat of power, she dried herself.

She had just strapped Cayne to her leg when Yples's voice erupted.

"DEM-KISK! THERE!"

The ceiling shook and rattled. The wind increased, and the sound of a tree being rent in half tore through the air. She realized that Yples hadn't been able to find her while she had worn the *vaz'on*.

"We have to go to the north wall," Kila said, running back into the common area. "Pol's Vale."

"Wouldn't it be better to hide in here?" Pennie asked. "There's a storm."

"DEM-KISK!"

Much louder now. The man was close. Now that Kila was unmasked to the mercusine, she'd be like a lantern in the dark to him.

She slammed her mask into place.

Too late.

The roof tore off the Princes Ward, shrieking and grinding as timbers split and nails pulled free. The fellstorm caught it, and with a great whoosh it shot skyward and disappeared in the gray haze of the cloud-cover. Water sluiced from the sky, drenching Kila and her friends.

Now masked, Kila did not know where Dunne Yples was. "We must run," she said. She sheathed Cayne and hefted her trusty backpack over her shoulders. "Follow me."

She didn't know the way. Not specifically. But all she had to do was follow the pull of her bond with Nax. Not waiting for the others to agree or disagree, she pushed through the door and into the wild wind.

A path to her right led toward the novitiates ward. Straight ahead were gardens and the long downward slope to the seaside. To the left the fringe of the jungle angled away, north and east. In clear weather she could have sprinted straight for the tree-line, but the wind forced her to stay low, and gusts continuously challenged her balance. Gian and Quinn followed, shouting words lost to the storm. Pennie remained in the doorway, shifting from foot to foot, face stricken. The *vaz'on* dangled from one small hand.

"Come on!" Kila mouthed, waving her arm for the girl to follow.

The fear in the girl's eyes vanished, replaced by determination. Head down, Pennie dashed to join Kila. "The wall is very high," Pennie shouted once she'd caught up. "How will we get over?"

Kila hadn't seen too many walls that could keep her out. They'd figure it out when they got to it. Kila had never found much use in planning ahead. Events always seemed to spin toward the unpredictable for her. She took the *vaz'on* from the girl, intending to fling it away. But a moment's hesitation forced her to reconsider. She knew nothing about it, but such a powerful mercusine relic would be valuable. And just throwing it into the wind would not keep it from the Sensuals or Donse Masters. She had Gian stuff it in her backpack.

The four of them pressed toward the jungle where the trees were leaning over so hard it looked like a vast invisible hand was mashing them down.

Behind them, the polshels were swaying, too, but the multitude of secondary and tertiary trunks they sprouted helped keep them rooted. For such trees to be so big, surely they'd survived more than one fellstorm.

The rain fell in wispy sheets now, the drops so close together they struck like water thrown from buckets. Kila had never seen anything like it, even in the rainiest season of Starside.

Thunder rolled from one corner of the sky to the other and flashes of lightning flickered above. Pennie tugged Kila's arm and pointed up. Against the strobing sky the silhouette of a man descended, borne upon plumes of mercusine fire.

His feet impacted the ground, sending up splashes of mud and making the world roll and shake. His bare chest heaved with huge panting breaths and his muscles were corded with fury, each striation standing out with the maximum exertion. The contraction never relaxed. His chest, arms, and thighs were in a state of permanent strain. The effort made him hunch, like a bull-shouldered man-beast.

Kila had seen Dunne Yples only briefly before, long ago in the subterranean cavern city of the thinnies. She had been so focused on saving Nax from drowning, she hadn't spared him more than a glance.

Then, not long ago, this man had tried to kill her in the Hargothe's chambers, while Kila had been in thrall of the ancient seer. She had not seen Dunne Yples then, either.

But here he was, thin hair plastered to his scalp and runnels of rainwater pouring from his sodden beard. He wore ragged breeches, ripped at the thigh by his straining muscles.

His form was monstrous in its pose of constant exertion. His muscles were carved so deeply, he looked like a moving statue of Kil himself. Lips pulled back in a snarl and his jaw thrust forward, he leered with unmasked insanity.

"Kila Sigh!" he growled. "DEM-KISK!" He pointed his

finger and started toward her, hands stretched out as balls of swirling mercusine light formed above his upturned palms.

Kila recognized the mercusine thrum. He'd been using this same feat before he came to find her. She wondered if any at Til's Tower still lived.

Quinn had Black in her fist and she already circled to flank the man. Her hair flew wildly in the gale, and her black cloak flapped behind her like crow's wings. Gian, too, had a weapon out.

Kila pushed Pennie behind her. She would end this now.

She sought the iron in Dunne Yples blood. The man felt her mercus, and with a twitch of his own mind negated the heat she summoned in his veins.

Of course he would be prepared for such an attack. This was what she'd done to all those poor thinnies. It was that display of power that had driven Dunne Yples mad and made him certain that Kila was Dem-Kisk.

He threw his arms forward, hurling the glowing balls of mercusine. They shone blue, and blurred straight toward her, unaffected by the wind.

Kila's mercus senses heard the doom-toll in the bolts and felt the strange tingling power each globe contained. But she didn't understand what she sensed, except for the dire power it contained.

Something darted before her just as both spheres struck her chest and threw her off her feet.

Her limbs twitched as jolts of mercusine coursed through her muscles. If she screamed she didn't hear it. When she struck the muddy turf, all her breath burst from her lungs. Muddy water poured into her mouth, choking her. The scent of burning flesh stung her nose and then was gone in the wind.

Coughing, and convulsing she dug at the earth, straining to raise her head from the mud. She was alive. It was all she could say. Her mind couldn't grasp how she'd even come to be where she lay.

A sharp cry brought Kila's attention to the present moment. It sounded like Pennie.

Kila pushed up, arms feeling as weak as lengths of slack rope. Her will was all that remained to her now. She dug for it, like rooting in the garbage heap behind an inn for a bit of unspoiled food. There was never much sustenance to be found in such places, but Kila knew from long experience that if she just kept digging, a morsel would turn up. And so she groped deep inside herself and found a crumb of will, enough to get her onto her feet and leaning into the wind.

Her body still tingled with the effects of Yples's mercusine attack. That it hadn't burned her to ash or blown her apart was a miracle. She knew how much power the man had put into the attack. And yet she'd lived.

Now she saw why. Gian lay on the ground, arms splayed out. His blade was still clutched in his hand. One foot twitched, up and down. His free hand, too, moved in quick jerks, as if his fingers were manipulated by some unseen puppeteer.

He had come between her and the attack, absorbing into his own body much of the power meant to destroy Kila.

Dropping her mask, she shot her senses out, seeking Dunne Yples. There. She looked up in time to see him plummeting toward her. The same spheres of power already formed over his palms. She saw into the mercus bolts now.

She formed her own, latching onto Cayne with her power and pulling the blade from its sheathe without use of her hands. With a second manifestation of her power, she shot the blade in a blur of violet at the descending madman.

He sent one of his glowing spheres to intercept the blade. Kila was not quick enough to divert Cayne, and the two forces met with a thunderous boom that concussed like the hammer of Til upon the spine of the world.

Though she was not holding the hilt, the repercussion on Cayne shot pain through Kila's forearm and elbow, striking her arm numb. Yet she kept her mercusine grip on the hilt, now two hundred spans away, and pulled with all the strength of her mind to arc it down toward the descending man.

Yples again struck ground, another spout of mud and water shooting up from his feet. He was in mid-stride, already charging Kila, hand back and prepared to hurl his next blow at her.

Sparing a fraction of her effort to control Cayne, she formed bolts of tuber-rose scent and the caress of a spring breeze and the soft whispered songs of a gentle mother crooning to her newborn. These she formed upon a bolt of warm amber light and thrust toward Yples.

The charm caught him. His steps faltered and his lips went slack. His remaining sphere of power dissipated in sparks and crackles. Cayne curved down, its speed making a hissing noise as it cut through the air, leaving a trail of steamed raindrops behind.

Dunne Yples shook his head and stamped like a bull, fighting Kila's charm. Of all the attacks he might have anticipated from her, the hard press of allure was not one.

It bought her time.

She ran for Gian, dove for him as Cayne struck Yples in the temple. She didn't see the blade go in, but she heard a horrific sound like metal sheering through metal, followed by a hard thunk.

Clods of dirt, rocks, and pats of mud splattered all around. She shielded Gian's face with her body until the last of the debris landed.

Turning back, she sought the remains of Dunne Yples. They were not hard to find, for they were intact and standing.

A thin slice of his temple was missing, exposing a glistening portion of brain beneath. Either he had dodged just the fraction needed at the last moment, or he'd used his own power to deflect Cayne's course.

He arched backward and roared at the sky. With this swell of rage arose a new mercusine charge, something Kila had never seen or felt before. Cringing away, she reflexively raised a hand to deflect the waves of emotion flowing from the madman. A useless gesture. Weak.

But the emotion wasn't the attack, merely stray power shed by whatever mercusine feat he brewed within his madness. And now she could see something forming around his feet. Smoke.

She had seen Flaumishtak and the Hargothe dymense, vanish in swirls of mercus green. What Yples was doing now formed a similar swirling cloud at his feet. But this was as black and oily as ink. It reached upward with liquid fingers, clawing from the earth itself. The fellstorm winds did not cause so much as a wisp of the smoke to blow away.

Cold wafted from the cloud, then heat. The smell of flashtaper smoke slid past Kila, made her nose burn. The eerie tentacles elongated, twisting and writhing in an obscene dance as the mercus black continued to thicken and grow around Dunne Yples. Faster it lifted, now spinning as it rose, twisting until it formed a twirling storm unto itself and Dunne Yples was lost inside of it.

Kila plunged her own mercusine awareness into the funneling black, searching for Yples, searching to make sense of the chaos at the center of this twisting column of undulating vulgarity.

Stomach clenching, and throat tightening with suppressed gags, she felt for mercusine bolts formed of the basic five senses. But there were none. It took her five long breaths before the truth struck home. Dunne Marlow had once told her that the higher mercus feats were formed from bolts of senses beyond the five of humankind. He had spoken about senses of the demaynic realms. She hadn't been curious enough to ask what he'd meant, but now that she felt it . . . she knew.

The bolts Dunne Yples was forming were woven *from emotion*. And in seeing it, she understood how her own higher feats had worked. Healing Gian had come from feelings she couldn't even name, as had the ashing of the thinnies. What she felt pouring from the black cloud was a stew of rage, hatred, righteousness, and the vile stirrings of animal hunger.

"Gian. Get up," she called.

His eyes were open, staring blankly at the storm above. His hand still twitched. She shook him, slapped his mud-spattered face. "Get up."

Something small and warm embraced Kila. Pennie. And Quinn joined her, huddling close, face a white oval of fear. Her raven locks were plastered to her head from rain, from mud. She looked so much younger now. She shouted something, but she was silenced by her own blade.

"He's dead," Pennie shouted, pointing at Gian.

No he wasn't. Kila wouldn't allow it.

Forming bolts from pure instinct, she plunged her mercusine senses into him, felt his heart and lungs.

"DEM-KISK! THINNIES IN FLAMES!" Yples' voice shattered the air, yet remained distant to Kila. Her attention was only on Gian.

"Kila!" Quinn's voice was nearly carried away on the wind. She had thrust her blade into the mud, though her hand hovered near the hilt. "Either kill Yples now or get us away from here."

Gian's heart still beat in rare convulsions, like the last weak flaps of a dying moth's wings. Each slow convulsion barely stirred his idle blood. His chest did not rise in breath.

Placing her hands on his head, Kila probed for his thoughts. This was what the Hargothe had done to her so many times. A vile intrusion. She didn't care about the right or wrong of it.

Wake up, she sent into his mind. And with that sending, she wove a knot into his consciousness. Another trick she'd learned from the Hargothe. A force-bond. The mercus connection slipped tight and she felt him.

Wake up, Gian!

"Kila!" Pennie screamed.

A concussion shook the ground, the footstep of a giant. Kila glanced back to see the black whirlwind surrounding Dunne Yples had taken form. Towering over her was a figure as tall as a polshel, each leg as thick as a tree trunk and arms that ended in wisps of black smoke. The head was an incoherent smear of black punctuated with eyes of fire.

GIAN! she sent.

He jerked up, eyes rolling into his skull and limbs trembling. She didn't wait for him to gain control of his body, but grabbed his arm and pulled. Quinn took the other. Together they got him onto his feet.

His convulsions stopped and he sagged, forcing the women to support his lead-solid body. Kila sought Cayne which had buried itself in the earth after slicing through Dunne Yples's head.

With a mercusine pull, it flew toward the black monster Yples had summoned. Or perhaps the hideous creature was entirely Dunne Yples.

Amidst the flows of her own power, she felt the slow build of his next assault, a blend of hate and rage. It filled the air with an icy carrion stink and made the rain turn to pellets of sticky black that scalded her skin.

Pennie huddled behind Kila, crying and screaming, "Stop. Please stop!"

But it would not stop. Not until Kila put an end to it. She didn't know what sort of attack Yples was forming, but she doubted it would be the glowing orbs that had failed to kill her. This was something vaster, deeper—a power pulled from the rancid heart of death. That it was taking these long moments for Yples to collect spoke to the enormous amount of mercusine he was bringing to bear.

Kila's legs were trembling, her body shivering. She hadn't recovered from the abuse of the *vaz'on*, let alone the power of the storm, the blows she'd taken, or the stark fear Yples's madness had driven through her gut.

She didn't know how to kill him. Or stop him. Or even defend against what he was preparing to throw at her. If she were the only one in danger she would stand and fight, end it forever—one way or the other. But her friends would die by Yples's hands merely for being near her when she took the brunt of his assault. She couldn't allow that.

Quinn was right. They needed to leave.

She felt for Nax. North. Past the wall.

"Hold onto me. All of you." She hugged Gian's limp body close.

Raising her fist, Kila let go of thought. Desperation guided her to form bolts she'd seen but had never attempted. A swirl of green fog rose from the ground at her feet. And then, with a flick of instinct alone, she wielded the mercusine bolts and let them go.

The storm muted. The raging black monster of hate blurred behind a shimmering wall of green haze. And then the chill of ice-water flowed down her back and the world vanished.

31

SUPREME AMONG THEM

Til's Fifth of the Garden Tower had fallen. Mostly. Muted cries arose from the rubble spilling downhill from the tower. Highest Mancin Fley stood at the newly formed ledge in his bedchamber and leaned out to peer into the still-smoldering wreckage.

His Favored tugged his sleeve, urging him back. "It is surely not safe to stand there," she said.

He yanked free of her grip. But she was correct. Not only was the floor trembling, but the fellstorm winds were capricious and pulled at him one moment and pushed him the next. Moving backward he went to the broad desk where now were arrayed the mercusine relics he'd demanded. The various Donse Masters who'd possessed them had been vociferous in their objections, but Fley had simply stared them down. They didn't have much choice, unless they wanted to be expelled from the order.

The One God had surely been protecting Fley and this

assemblage of relics. Another sign that Fley—not the madman —was the true Champion.

He winced as a great burst of power coursed over the mercus, another of Yples's outbursts. Somehow the man had gotten free. Til's Tower was destroyed, and hundreds of Donse Masters and acolytes were dead. He did note that the remaining Fifths of the Tower appeared to be unscathed, no doubt the One God's doing.

Fley felt for the mercusine sparks of those trapped in the rubble. There were a dozen or so, many too deep to be helped. Unless he could establish his force-tap once again upon the madman. But to do that would require the man be quelled, and now that he was in the agonies of his full power, that seemed an impossibility at the moment.

He had a more pressing problem. The stairways were gone. He could ascend to the roof, though. And with some effort, he thought he might scale the wall to Ori's Fifth. From there he could descend, assuming the Sensuals in the tower would allow it. If they didn't he would deal with them most severely. He did have some powerful relics in his possession now.

He set about attaching them to his belt or stuffing them into a leather satchel. The jewelry, he donned. A simple wide band of gold slipped over one finger. Known as Roop's Wild, it was a heller of general purpose, doubling the wearer's mercus power. Excellent. Next was a bracelet carved into the likeness of a crane, wings wrapping around his wrist and head and beak protruding over the top of his hand. It granted the wearer the ability to throw a gust of wind more powerful than the fellstorm gales that whipped his open chamber even now. The necklace was of three chains, one gold, one silver, and one copper. The only known power it bestowed was a sort of protection from steel weapons. Fortunately there were few blades of bronze or wooden bludgeons in use on the island. Besides, who would attack him with a blade? No one. But he'd rather have it than not.

A slim wand that appeared to be made of bits of conch shell slipped into his belt. It was a simple light caster, but again, he'd rather have it than not. The wands from the vault remained in the vault. But the lantern would come along. He'd have a strong acolyte carry it. Unfortunately the ideal man, the one who stood guard at the Champion's door, had been crushed in the collapse. He'd find someone else.

The crystal sword was too dangerous. He'd left it in the vault as well.

Instead he had chosen the dagger, a relic he'd kept in his office all these years. A Shadline weapon, and one of the only such known to still be in the Way's possession. When it pierced the flesh it sapped heat from the victim. The effect was quick at first, freezing a victim in place as their limbs turned to ice. But the dying was slow. It was called Bone Chill.

He dumped the remaining few heller rings and cubes into his satchel, along with the light-caster relics. A plan was forming, though it lacked much detail.

What he needed was that strange witch bolus the boy Henley had fed the madman on the sail to Garden Island. But that had all been used up. It gave him an idea, though. The Sensuals must have more bark-burners in their midst. He'd go to the Home and hope anyone survived Yples's rampages there. How, exactly, he would get the man to consume the concoction would be yet another problem to solve. But if enough merculyns were armed with hellers, and if they would submit to being source-taps under his control, perhaps he'd have a chance.

The Sensuals did not interfere with his descent from their Fifth of the Tower. He was not the only man to have thought of it. Dunne Quiv met him as he exited at ground-level, where throngs of acolytes and novitiates milled about, all wondering what had happened.

A wide section of the dividing wall between Til and Ori had fallen during the collapse, allowing him to move back into Til's Fifth and scramble over the rubble. Quiv followed, brow furrowed.

Far off the madman surged upon the mercus while the fell-storm began to throw sheets of rain over the world of flesh. Ragged Donse Masters and acolytes picked through the crumbled block and stone of the tower, calling for survivors. Those strong in the mercus could easily feel if someone with the spark lay buried alive within.

"Assemble all merculyns along the gap in the wall there," Fley ordered Dunne Quiv. "We must go collect our wayward madman."

Quiv raised an eyebrow but didn't argue.

A strong-spined Sensual approached, face full of pity. Fley recognized her as Sensual Harrisan Minn. She was powerful in the mercus, but was not allied with Thine and Voluptuary Sennikt. That made her an enemy, which she surely knew. She had the round, sturdy body of a farmwife, and clear blue eyes. She nodded and said, "If your people need healing, I've got some girls with skill ready in the Tower Gate. Do you want help rescuing those buried?"

He forced a pained smile. "It would be a kindness, Sensual. I must take a party to subdue our—"

"We will join you. Of course you will expect us to submit as source-taps, no?" She was matter-of-fact. He thought she would make an excellent Sister of the Way one day, but doubted she would readily submit to the particular rules he intended to establish once the Ways were united under the One God.

"I will, indeed," he said. "It does you credit that you offer to help us."

"He'll kill us all if I don't."

Fley realized this woman was in command of the Sensuals of the Garden Tower. Voluptuary Sennikt should never have left such an important post occupied by one who had not sworn allegiance to her. But this was no time for such concerns. "Spare all you can, and what hellers and relics may be needful," he said, though bile stained his tongue merely uttering the words.

She turned and began issuing orders in a low, calm voice. Novitiates scurried away, and Sensuals bobbed their heads.

Fley found himself irritated that such a woman had eluded his attention. But now that he was thinking on her, he remembered Dunne Quiv saying she had been the likely successor to the previous Voluptuary.

Dunne Quiv was pulling searchers off the rubble and getting them assembled. Fley noted the faint sparks in the ones remaining to find survivors were placed under the command of Dunne Upps, a freshly raised Donse Master who wore a bloodstained bandage on his head. Three dozen men lay about in the rain, dazed or unconscious. The mangled bodies of the unlucky were being dragged downhill and placed into an orderly row.

Fley turned away from the disaster and toward the ranks of

merculyns assembling for the battle to come. He approached them, already feeling out the relative mercus power among them, preparing to arrange them in squads of four, each with a captain. That captain would receive power from his team. Fley would receive the combined power from the captains.

But none of this would matter if they could not get to the madman, and that would require a downhill trek to Ori's Home while a fellstorm pounded the island.

The men and women stared at him, most dazed, some furious. The men straightened under his gaze, the women's eyes narrowed. There was no trust there. But none disputed his right to wield the power, for he was supreme among them as Highest.

Novitiates streamed from the Tower bearing oil-cloaks to ward off the rain. Most were too small for the men. All such gear possessed by the Way of Til was somewhere buried in the rubble.

Sensual Minn approached, thrusting her arms through one such cloak and pulling the hood over her head. "I shall begin a circle of my own, Highest. If you have any astute merculyns, they should study what I do."

Before he could protest or even inquire what she intended, she began to receive the combined mercus power of a dozen women. She formed bolts of heat and touch that bubbled up from her and soon encompassed all of those in her circle. Rain steamed from an invisible dome of mercusine that now sheltered them, and the power of the wind barely stirred their cloaks. Sens Minn's brow furrowed in concentration as she maintained the protective shield.

Understanding the wisdom in the effort, while simultaneously fuming that such a feat was unknown to the Way of Til, he nodded to Quiv. Soon the man was barking orders and ten such domes were forming to encompass the Til teams. Fley would expend no effort in such a task, for it would fall to him to face the madman.

He took the lead in the march to the Home, sheltering in Quiv's protective dome. He noted that it was not as impermeable those cast by the Sensuals, and spatters of rain occasionally struck his head. No matter. It was just water.

He handed his satchel of relics to his Favored. A Sensual had given her an oil-cloak, he noted. "Keep up," he said.

Fley bent close to Dunne Quiv as they moved east. "Did Thine refuse my command to send us the Peline girls?"

"Not outright. She merely stalled. Our man did not get a good look, but he was told by a novitiate that the entire Home had been assembled to witness a shriving. Thine obviously knew she had a merculyn trying to hide her powers. I did not get word on which girl it was."

"She should have complied instantly!"

Quiv arched an eyebrow. "But perhaps it is well that she did not."

Fley took his meaning. If the merculyn girl Yples hated had come to the Tower, the madman would have directed all his power to destroying her there. And then Fley himself— along with those who had survived his escape—would likely already be dead.

The force of destiny was with them. What was it Roya Reth had prophesied? *Soon it will tread upon fields of red.*

Reth was certainly dead, along with so many others. Fley hoped she rotted in some demaynic hell for eternity for all the good she'd been to him.

"But now that you mention it," Dunne Quiv said softly, as

if continuing a conversation Fley had not been paying attention to, "if the girl is so powerful, perhaps we may have to confront her, too."

Fley scoffed. A single girl would be of no consequence against Yples. Nor would she be so much as a mosquito to him once he'd aggregated the combined powers of this army of merculyns.

Thunder rumbled above, a stern warning of a yet greater storm to come.

32

WORLD AWASH

A raven wings over Garden Island, uncaring of the fellstorm's power.

Why won't you fly? Kila Sigh. Why?

See with my eyes, child. See the wild drift of time!

It squawks and dives, fluttering as it lands atop the ancient tower. The man inside paces, hands clasped behind his back. His fingers are heavy with rings, all but one a heller or wardskeen. The last is special, set with garnet. It flashes in the firelight.

The bird taps on the window. He opens it and holds out his hand. The raven hops onto his wrist, and from there to his shoulder.

"Sweet one, welcome. Dire one, begone."

The bird stays.

THE GROUND WAS STICKY, and the mud smelled of wet ash. A bit of it had squeezed between Kila's lips. She spat it out, choking and fighting for air.

To the south, Dunne Yples's swell of power continued to build.

Quinn helped Kila stand. The ash-muck squished between her bare toes. Gian sat up, supported by Pennie. His head turned this way and that, but he seemed unaware of what was going on around him.

Pennie's face was wan, soaked hair pressed to her skull making her look like a dream-wanderer come to take the soul of the dying.

Quinn was painted gray with ash-mud on one side. She must have fallen when they'd arrived. Kila had struck face down, so her front was clumped with it.

Come! Nax sent. *Quickly!*

Kila knew the direction. She turned and pointed. The rain had thinned and the wind had lowered, though not by much. Gusts buffeted her so hard she would have fallen without Quinn's support. "Nax is that way." Though why the cat had come into this place she had no idea.

She looked to Gian. He was trying to stand. Pennie was too small to help much. He swayed and looked around stupidly. "Where are we?"

There was nothing here but ash-mud and burnt stumps. She remembered seeing such a landscape through her mirror. The tower she'd seen must be nearby.

Nax, have you found shelter?

Yes! Come!

"This way." She started to trudge, slow sucking step by

slow sucking step. Thunder grumbled above, the sky itself discontented with their presence beneath it.

"You dymensed us," Quinn shouted into Kila's ear. "I didn't know you could do that."

"Neither did I."

Again it had come down to desperation. In the last moment before utter obliteration, her mercusine instincts had saved her. If she weren't so tired, she would have wept with relief.

Part of her wished she could tell Dunne Marlow about it. He'd be so jealous.

Her breath caught. Alarmed, she threw up her mask. Dunne Yples had surely felt her presence here. She cursed herself for not masking herself the moment she arrived. She just hoped Yples couldn't dymense, too.

Her muscles rebelled when she tried to increase the pace. Will alone could not produce more strength than her body possessed. She wished she had dymensed them closer to their destination, wherever it was.

"Where are we going?" Quinn shouted.

"There's a tower ahead. Somewhere. Nax is near."

"How do you know about a tower?"

This wasn't the time to explain the mirror visions to Quinn. Fortunately, Gian had caught up. He seemed to have gathered his wits. "There's a ruin north of Ori's Home along the shoreline. You can see it from the beaches below the gardens. We're obviously within the ash-barrens now."

Kila focused on Nax. The cat was very near. The way ahead was shrouded with rain and mist.

Pennie straggled, lips drooping, eyelids sagging, limbs leaden. Kila motioned her forward and put her arm around the child's shoulders. She linked arms with Quinn and pushed ahead. More of Gian's strength returned with every step. Soon he ranged ahead, a gray blur in the gloom.

Kila realized she could feel him up there, a sweet knot in her mind next to Nax. He felt . . . different. The bond wasn't the same; it didn't fit the way Nax's did. But it didn't constrict like the mental noose the Hargothe had once tried to slip over her consciousness.

Can you hear me? she sent to Gian.

What? What's that?

It's me, Gian. Kila.

How—how are you doing that?

You feel me. You know where I am.

A long pause. Gian was lost in the haze ahead. The wind began to increase again and distant thunder warned that another band of the fellstorm approached.

The ground squished under Kila's bare feet, the wet ash sticking in clumps to her soles. The remains of broken-off tree trunks loomed around them, like twisted cemetery stones. All was charred black, even the huge rocks that thrust up from the ash like the knuckles of buried giants.

I feel you, Gian finally answered. A shrugging feeling came through the bond. Not one of carelessness, but of trying to loosen a tight collar. Kila knew it well. She had been bonded to Oly for a short time. That had not been pleasant.

I will release the bond.

Yes. You will.

She had bonded him to save him. Now he lived. There was no reason to maintain it. She had no right to force-bond anyone.

But his response hurt her. She pushed the feeling away,

angry at herself. She should have released the bond the second she remembered it. It seemed there was a lot she should do that she didn't. The pang of guilt warred with her deep desire to keep Gian close. That only made it worse.

Already she mourned losing the sweetness of his presence in her mind. Letting go of the bond was harder than merely dropping the mercusine ties. It was like severing her own hand.

But it *wasn't* her own hand. Frustrated, Kila wiped her eyes, clearing the ridiculous tears that came unbidden.

I can't do it now, she sent to Gian. *I have to lower my mask, and Yples will spot me. I swear I will as soon as I can safely use the mercus.*

The answer was few moments too long in coming. *Very well.*

Neither Quinn nor Pennie noticed the tears that tracked down Kila's cheeks, for her face was already wet from the rain. She sniffed and cleared her throat. "We must be getting close." Nax was so present in her mind, she should be able to see the cat.

A gray form emerged from the gloom. A wall. It was part of a building. The ancient masonry still held together, though the crisped remains of vines thrust from cracks between stones like weird, insectile feelers. The roof was mounded with muddy ash, which overhung the eaves in gloopy festoons.

They rounded the corner and came into the lee of the structure and into the relative protection it provided from the wind. Gian stood there, soaked and shivering, peering through a doorway.

When he turned and nodded, his face was haggard. And

hard. He motioned for Kila and the others to go in. They filed past him and finally found respite from the storm.

Pennie slumped onto the damp stone floor, a waterlogged doll of straw. Though the roof was intact, water had long ago found or formed many cracks and crevices through the walls. The floor was damp, the air redolent of rot. The mouldering remains of barrels and wooden crates were stacked in the back of the space. A storage building.

A ladder climbed to a loft, though only three rungs remained. The loft itself was full of holes, the raw edges worn smooth by ages of decay.

"It smells like chickens," Kila said. A distinct odor that she was well familiar with. But faint. That she detected the smell while masked to the mercus spoke of how thick the stink truly was. There hadn't been a chicken here in a hundred years. Maybe a thousand. Nothing lived in the ash-barrens except the four human interlopers and three cats sheltering in this building.

The cats peered from the loft, six eyes aglow with different shades of welcome, curiosity, and disdain.

Those last belonged to Oly, who meowed and turned to show Kila the underside of his tail. Nax leapt directly to Kila's shoulder and pressed her soft face to Kila's cheek. Huff meowed and stayed put, obviously mistrustful of Gian and Pennie.

Tell Huff that Gian and Pennie are friendly.

Pennie's eyes were locked on Nax. Kila knelt next to the girl. "This is Nax. She is my friend. You can pet her if you want."

Pennie shrank back, shaking her head.

Gian eased down next to the girl and stared at Nax, too. His jaw bulged and his eyes flicked from the cat to Kila and back. It was like a veil had lifted, and he now saw that Kila was not who he thought she was.

"She won't hurt you," Kila said to Pennie. She raised her fingers to Nax. The cat presented her white chin for a scratch.

"The tower ruins must be near," Gian said, changing the subject. His tone was cold, businesslike. He was obviously regretting the whole "where you go I go" nonsense now. Everyone got dragged into her usual whirlwind of trouble without truly understanding how vicious it would be.

She shrugged off her backpack. The *vaz'on* inside clanked dully as it struck the stone floor. "This must've been a storage building for the groundskeepers or . . . something." She had no real idea how such a keep would operate.

"There might be some dry enough wood in this mess to get a fire going," Quinn said, picking through the wet lumps of old crates. She eyed Gian, clearly sensing the tension between him and Kila. As a Radiant's daughter, she'd grown up in a society where the subtlest comment or lift of an eyebrow communicated volumes. Kila was from Cheapsgate, where people tended to blurt out what was on their minds. But she was sensitive enough to other's expressions to know coldness when she saw it in Gian's eyes.

The force-bond had ruined everything. She wanted to tell him that she hadn't looked into his thoughts, that she hadn't toyed with his mind. She had just done what was needed for him to live.

"I said there might be some dry wood here," Quinn said, more loudly this time. She was trying to break through the silence and refocus Kila on survival. Quinn was a good friend.

Kila could make a fire easily if she dropped her mask. But she didn't dare, lest she attract Yples to her. Exhaustion weighed upon her now that she'd stopped moving. She doubted she'd survive another confrontation with the madman. She wondered if he was still gathering his mercusine into some hideous feat at that moment. He had to be or she would have felt its release, if only as a boom or a tremble in the earth.

Pennie was shivering and hunching in on herself, cold, terrified, and obviously fearful of the cats. Kila couldn't blame her. The girl had likely grown up hearing that such animals were possessed by demayne.

Quinn tested the loft ladder. It creaked and the lowest rung cracked under her foot. "I suppose it'll burn," she said. She gave the ladder a hard pull and it came away from its braces on the edge of the loft. With little effort, she broke it into small sections.

"All we need is something to spark a blade on." She resumed her search of the building.

"I didn't get a chance to collect my things before we left," Gian said. "I had a flint. But couldn't Kila just . . ." He made a combustion motion with his hands.

"That madman will feel me the second I drop my mask," Kila said. Seeing Gian's blank look she explained how she kept herself unseen upon the mercusine. "That's the mask I was telling you about. Before."

"Ah." He clearly didn't understand what she was talking about, but he accepted it. "What about you, girl?" he said to Pennie. His voice was so flat it made Kila flinch.

"Me?" Pennie said.

"You can do it," Kila said to her, grasping at the idea. But mostly wanting to agree with Gian. Wanting to be on his side. "I've felt your power. If Yples feels it, he'll just think you're a Spinster in Pol's Fifth."

"I'm not allowed to do anything with the mercus." The child hugged her knees and rested her cheek on them. "I don't have any skill. Not compared to you."

Kila couldn't imagine what it had been like for the girl to see what she and Dunne Yples had done. Terrifying, no doubt. But it was no surprise that Sensual Thine had forbidden Pennie to use the mercus. That was typical for a person jealous of power.

"I can teach you."

"We don't have a ten-year to make a fire," Quinn said. She'd found part of an old brass lantern and was futilely scraping Black on it. She didn't even have any tinder prepared to receive an unlikely spark.

"Pennie doesn't need a ten-year. I can teach her now."

Nax, this girl is afraid of you. Would you please go make sure Oly isn't doing something awful?

He's licking himself.

Go bat his head with your paws. He's done something bad recently, I'm sure.

I will distance myself from the child.

Nax hopped from Kila's shoulder, bounded to a crate, and then slipped into the loft through a hole. A moment later Oly hissed.

You were right. He was doing something awful.

Kila didn't ask. Her attention was on Pennie. "Will you let me teach you? We need you to make fire for us."

With Nax out of view, the girl unfurled. Some of her world-weary resolve returned to her face. "How do I do it?"

"Has anyone taught you how to make a sensation?"

"No."

"Close your eyes. Feel the dampness in your clothes. Feel how they stick to your skin."

"I don't need to close my eyes to feel that."

"Do it!"

The girl's eyes snapped shut. "I'm doing it."

"Notice it. Where is it the most uncomfortable?"

"On my belly."

"Focus on that. Do you feel it? Do you feel how the fabric sticks to your skin, how it chills it?"

"Yes."

"Now instead of that, feel it warm and dry. Do it gradually. At first your belly is cold and damp. But now it is starting to feel warm. Feel that warmth. The cold is going away. It's being filled up with warmth. Do you feel it?"

"Maybe."

"Notice the dampness. It's doesn't cling to your skin as much. You feel the fabric resting on your skin, but it's becoming and dry. When its dry it doesn't stick does it? Make it feel dry."

Kila stopped talking. She wanted to drop her mask and simply take hold of the girl's mercus and do it for her. That would teach her more directly than Sens Goolsoy had once taught Kila. But she couldn't do that. Nor should she. The mercus needed to be explored and discovered on one's own.

"My belly is dry." Pennie's eyes remained closed, but her eyebrows had climbed up her forehead with amazement. She rubbed the patch that had dried.

"Now the wood," Kila said. "Put your hand on it. Feel that it is cold and damp. Then feel it becoming dry. Imagine hot, dry air is pulling the moisture from the grain. Feel the heat and dryness under your fingers. Put more heat and dryness into it. More. And more. Soon it will be too hot to touch. Before it begins to glow with heat, you will see that glow. You will add to the heat and the glow until it fills the wood."

Pennie leaned over the chunks of broken ladder, face fixed, eyes lost in concentration. Quinn watched, absently flipping her dagger. Gian leaned in, urging the girl to succeed. His face was pale, his hands unsteady. Though his strength had returned, he still suffered from the shock of Dunne Yples's mercusine attack. Or maybe it was the after effect of Kila's force-bond.

Kila put her hand next to Pennie's. The wood was cold and damp.

"You can make the wood dry and hot, Pennie. Just as you made that patch of your robe warm and dry. It will be very gradual at first, but then it will go quickly. We need fire to warm us. We need you to do this."

"I'm trying." There was no whining or anger in her voice. Just a statement of fact.

Learning to light a candle with the mercus took Donse Masters years. Not because it truly took that long to build the strength and skill to do it, but because they relied only on the five senses.

Kila did not. Pennie would not.

"Imagine Sensual Thine's face, Pennie. Imagine her squished up lips. What did she say to you when she sent you to bring us food?"

"She said I would never be more than a servant to her. She said when I came of age, she would send me to be a Favored in Til's Tower."

Kila didn't know what a Favored was, but she knew that the Til's-boys didn't take women acolytes. From the tone in Pennie's voice, serving as a Favored wasn't much of a privilege.

"Sensual Thine hurt me. She humiliated me," Kila said.

"She wanted to hurt you. She wanted to humiliate you. Now put heat into this wood, girl!"

The wood remained cold and damp.

Too much. Kila had pushed too hard. She had counted on the girl summoning anger, but she had only provoked tears.

Pennie dropped her head, sniffling. Tears fell from her eyelashes. An upwelling of sympathy overtook Kila. She had been a bit older than Pennie when Father had died. But Wen had been there to look after her. Together they'd been a family. But what family did Pennie have? The Sensuals? Maybe some were compassionate, but Kila understood how people's minds worked. Growing up in Cheapsgate had taught her that even the most generous-minded old crone would steal from an orphan to feed her pet crow. When Voluptuary Sennikt and Sensual Thine had come into power, who had stood up to them?

According to Ragin, those who had were sent away. So who remained to lend a comforting hand or voice to Pennie? No wonder the child had such a worldly look. She had survived the best she could. Through obedience and inconspicuousness.

"I'm sorry," Kila said. She scooted close to the girl, put an arm around her and awkwardly kissed the top of her head. She'd never looked after a child before, but the gesture seemed appropriate. Pennie had saved Kila's life by removing the *vaz'on*, the least Kila could do was offer compassion. "We'll find another way to make fire."

She looked to Gian. His lips were pressed into a thin line. He looked about to fall over. His rally to strength had been short-lived, perhaps driven entirely by will. Quinn started to scrape Black on the brass piece of lantern, but she shook her head. It was going to be a cold night.

A hard band of rain struck and the wind screamed past the doorless entry. Beyond it was a world awash in water. The storage warehouse could have been a league beneath the sea and the view would have been the same.

"Rest, Pennie. Maybe you can practice by drying out our clothes a little once you've slept."

Kila patted the girl's shoulder and got to her feet. She meant to clear a relatively dry spot and lie down. Maybe forever. Sleep would soon claim her one way or another. If Pol smiled, perhaps Dunne Yples would discover her while she slept and end her before she woke.

"I haven't given up," Pennie said softly.

Quinn stopped mid-scrape. Kila turned back to the girl.

A tendril of smoke rose from between the girl's fingers.

Kila didn't dare breathe lest the sound break Pennie's concentration. Quinn, too, held still. Gian wavered, apparently oblivious to what was happening.

Kila wished again to drop her mask, to see and feel how close the girl had come to making fire. But she didn't need to, for Pennie gritted her teeth and cursed hard and low: "Sens Thine is a goat-sucker's sister!"

Flames burst forth and Pennie fell back. The wood crackled and sparked, and coils of thick smoke rolled upward.

"More wood," Quinn said. "Quick."

Kila and Quinn frantically collected wood from pieces of

the mouldering barrels and crates. It was all damp and rotten, but Pennie's flames were fueled by mercus rage and the wood succumbed.

Later, as the heat seeped into Kila's bones, Pennie leaned against her and slept. Nax curled on Kila's lap, grooming her white feet, and occasionally sparing a lick for Pennie's eyebrows.

Gian had passed out, but his breaths came in slow and strong cycles.

Quinn tended the fire, reading one of her stolen books. When Kila told her to sleep, Quinn refused. "I'm a Shadline. I keep watch."

That's all they needed. Quinn reading Shadline lore and putting on the airs of a storybook's code of honor. But the raven-haired woman would not be dissuaded and Kila was too tired to argue.

She eased Pennie to the floor and curled up with the girl. Nax footed across Kila's flank, kneading Kila's ribs until she found just the right spot, then she balled up and went to sleep.

Kila didn't dream.

When she awoke, at Nax's insistence, she knew she'd only slept an hour or two. The fire had died down to embers, and Quinn lay sprawled on her back, blade in one fist, book in the other . . . snoring silently.

What is it, Nax?

Henley comes.

From the loft came Huff's soft meow. It sounded mournful and tiny against the roar of the fellstorm wind.

Nax, why did you three come here?

Oly made us.

Why?

Because he's Oly.

Perfect cat logic. And from the tone of finality in that pronouncement, Nax thought it all that needed to be said.

Kila lay back and slept.

33

SOME FIRE-SCALDED REALM

The voice floated upon the fellstorm winds, faint as a ghost's whisper. Yet it was rage-filled.

"Dem-Kisk."

Henley knew that voice as well as he knew Huff's. He had spent a brief eternity locked in a black cell next to Dunne Yples, listening to the man rave about "thinnies in flames" and "Dem-Kisk" until the man's voice had given out.

The Highest must have released him from his prison. Why he would do so was a mystery.

Henley rested in the calm provided by the south wall of Pol's Fifth. It was an ancient structure, made from porous rock plucked from the island's shoreline and stacked with extraordinary skill. Each stone fit with its neighbors like a puzzle piece. Not one showed sign of having been worked with tools.

The wall was ten-spans high, perhaps thirty feet. He had never been a skilled and fearless climber like Kila. Even Fallo had been better at it. But Huff was on the other side somewhere. And so, too, was Kila. That meant Henley had to go up and over.

He reached out for his cat, sensing exactly where he was. Huff had not said much since the great booms had sounded from far to the south. Only that Kila had fought with Dunne Yples and somehow escaped.

During the battle, the mercusine flows had stunned and enthralled him. The sheer power of those distant feats had brought the mercus into his body such that he trembled to release it with his own bolts of fire and light.

He wanted to blast a hole in this wall so he didn't have to climb it. But even if he knew how, he wasn't about to risk drawing Dunne Yples's attention. Or anyone else's for that matter.

The wall was wet, but the stones were rough and gave good purchase under his fingers and toes. As he ascended, he wondered what the purpose of such a wall was if it was so easy to climb. Maybe it was just a border marker.

As he finally topped the wall, the wind thrust hard against him, threatening to blow him back into Pol's Fifth. He hooked a leg over the other side and flattened himself on the broad surface, quickly sliding to the other side and lowering himself.

Now the wind pressed him against the stone, like a firm hand supporting him. The climb down was easy.

His feet sank into gray mud. Ahead, the world was shrouded in rain and fog, as if the storm clouds had sunk to the ground.

Huff was his marker, like a bright candle in a distant window, and only his heart could see it. He moved toward the cat, bent against the wind and soaked to the bone.

The ash-barrens offered little shelter other than the occasional stump thrusting from the gray mud. He clung to these when he could, resting and catching his breath. The charred wood blackened his hands. Whatever had happened here must have been a horror to behold. If Henley didn't know he was still on Garden Island he would have thought it a demaynic landscape, some fire-scalded realm not meant for man.

He forged ahead and soon a ribcage emerged from the gloom. Like the keel of a wrecked ship, the fossilized bones arced up from the muck to join a great spine that trailed away to be lost beneath the surface. No sign of a head.

Dragon bones.

At any other point of Henley's life the sight of such a skeleton would have been the greatest thing he'd ever seen. He would have walked among the ribs, touching them with reverence, imaging with awe the glory of the creature's flight. Now the sight chilled him more deeply than the rain and wind.

He recalled a peculiar line in an old song his father used to sing: "To the souls in Lumne's womb, our world is but a fearful tomb. What a horror-land we tread, we who dare to not be dead."

The fellstorm landing just as Yples and Kila began their battle was no coincidence. The force of destiny pressed upon this island, the powers of nature, gods, and mercusine converging.

But to what end?

He wove between the upthrusting ribs, hands holding to them for support. And they were warm still, after an epoch of decay.

Henley's foot slipped in the mud as his soles pressed onto something hard and very slick. He fell to a knee, which also impacted something buried in the muck. Like a patch of hidden ice. But such was not possible on this island. He probed into the gray sludge and curled his finger back to expose the strange surface hidden there.

Even in the bleak light, the shine of garnet red, polished and clean as his mother's finest dinnerware, was unabated. Heart hammering, he dug for the edges and found them. With a sucking pull, the round, smooth miracle came free of the ash-mud. He stared at it dumbly, no longer caring about the rain and wind. In his hand he held a dragon scale, red as blood and translucent as glass. A moments exploration revealed the ground all around him strewn with the scales. He collected several more, nesting them together like plates. He slipped them into his satchel.

Head down, he trudged forward. Toward Huff and Kila. Toward destiny. Whatever it was, he wanted it done.

34

STRATEGY AGAINST MADNESS

His army of merculyns—now counted as one hundred and twelve strong—strung out on the path behind Highest Fley. The teams staggered into the Home, haggard and breathless from the swift march. Several had been forced to reassemble their teams with new captains in order to maintain their protective domes.

But not Sensual Minn. The woman had ranged ahead of Fley to announce their arrival to any Sensuals who might take an invading force of Donse Masters the wrong way. But Fley could already see she would find no significant force to contend with. The buildings of the Home were flattened. Not even the Dome of the Gentle Goddess stood. The magnificent polshels that had sheltered the parklike expanse had been burnt to their stumps, ash carried off into the invincible wind.

The gardens and shrubs and grass: all scorched.

Sensual Minn flared slightly in the rain-hidden distance, forming new bolts that Fley did not quite catch. When she returned, she led a pitiable string of novitiates. Heads hanging, they had neither the strength nor the inclination to so much as glance at the assembling merculyns who continued to follow Fley into the Home. Without looking back, the novitiates continued up the path, toward the Garden Tower.

When Sens Minn returned to Fley, her lips were pressed into a hard line. "Those were all who remained alive here. Not a single Sensual among them. Voluptuary Sennikt and Sensual Thine are among the dead, I'm afraid."

She didn't seem too mournful to announce that last bit of news. Fley's head hurt. Not merely from the trials of the day, but due to the impossible forces that the madman had wielded here. But he hadn't been alone. There had been another spark upon the mercusine. As impossible as it was, both Sens Minn and Dunne Quiv had agreed that it was single person: the girl. Kiki Peline. As abruptly as she'd flared, she'd vanished, leaving Yples's torrential flows to wrack their brains as they drew nearer to his unceasing tantrums.

"He has moved north," Dunne Quiv said.

There was no shelter here for his army. No time to rest if there had been. He surveyed his weary merculyns who continued to form ranks in the windswept ruin that had once been Ori's Home. He noted the Sensuals and novitiates were fitter, more alert, than the Donse Masters and acolytes he'd brought. That Ori's Way had a number of strong merculyns had been no secret. Seeker Yan had long complained of it, as sensitive as the man had been. But these women were physically more hale than the pasty-faced men of Til. Souring on the state of his men, he resolved that once the present crisis had been dealt with, he would institute mandatory exercise protocols for the Way of Til.

He noted that the captains of the Ori teams—some mere

novitiates—were maintaining their protective domes with apparent ease, while their counterparts on the Til teams strained. It wasn't absolute power, Fley knew, that made a merculyn dangerous. But this showed it in very stark terms indeed. And he was not the only one who noticed. There would be many shamed men after this day was through, and no doubt, many women who would feel a new contempt for the Way of Til.

But enough chewing on the bitter roots of these revelations. What was he to do? The madman had gone from here. "Quiv, Sensual Minn. A council apart from curious ears, if you please." It burned him to offer such politeness to the woman, but he needed her.

For her part, she seemed unsurprised that he would seek her advice. Bah! This was not good at all. Both were captains of their own dome teams, so each had to hand off the task, releasing source-taps and seeing the domes reformed before turning their attention to Highest Fley. The Ori team had no interruption of their dome, exposing yet another bit of lore they'd mastered that Til's scholars had not.

Sensual Minn took it upon herself to form a dome to contain the three of them, and they walked a hundred yards ahead of the main body to stand where the great library had once stood. All that remained was charred stone and ash. Not a single page of paper flittered in the wind. The sight of the destruction turned Fley's stomach watery. He could not imagine what feat the man had used to wreak such destruction.

As if reading his mind, Quiv offered, "Like dragonfire. Not that I've seen such firsthand. But it matches the many descriptions I've read."

"You will see true dragon scorch soon enough," Sens Minn said. "The battle has moved to the ash-barrens."

"A long walk, I expect," Fley said. "And a wall to climb. Perhaps the main tap-force need not climb over. I can accept their flows across a fair distance."

"It will not be much attenuated," Quiv said, agreeing. "But . . ." His hesitation was not his usual play at deference. The man looked tired, and afraid. He was at home among his books and dispatches, but not here. Not beneath the naked rages of the storm and in closer proximity to the most powerful merculyn of a dozen ages.

"Speak, Dunne Quiv."

"I thought, perhaps, it might be wiser to split the force. Put perhaps ten merculyns forward, each supplied with ten or so source-taps. If armed with hellers and what relics might be of use, such a team might be able to subdue the Champion with greater likelihood of success than one alone."

"Brute power against brute power," Sensual Minn said. "That is a sure strategy for destruction. A battle in which no side wins, but which all who inhabit this island must surely lose no matter the victor. Dunne Quiv is quite astute, Highest Fley. Let us instead apply strategy against madness."

Fley saw the wisdom in it, though he hated the idea. Once arrayed so, he would not be able to command each individual unless they were within earshot. In this storm, that meant they'd have to be close at hand. That would render them useless. They needed to surround the madman, throw attacks and feints and mind probes all at once, giving him no chance to deflect them all. It was how his own seekers sometimes had to subdue and bring in the newly awakened.

But he recalled his objective. To make the madman his

source-tap was the ultimate goal. So be it. And perhaps this merculyn girl and the madman would weaken each other. He lowered his eyes so that they would not reveal so much as a hint of his deeper schemes. Both Quiv and Sensual Minn were keen-eyed and intelligent. Surely they were mulling over what he might do once Yples had been subdued. And of the two of them, Sensual Minn surely saw that she would be in the gravest of danger, no matter how much she had helped him get to that point.

"I will not forget your contribution to this great battle, either of you."

They nodded, but said nothing else. "Arrange your teams as you see fit. Assign captains strong in defensive feats, mind probing, willshift, and immobilizations. I do not want to kill either of the combatants if at all possible." He removed the Sink Gem from the relic satchel and told Quiv to disperse the rest of the items to best advantage. Sensual Minn said her teams had a few small hellers, but nothing else to contribute.

A lie, Fley knew. But he would confiscate whatever they did have in their possession once this was over. For now, he had three priorities. Subdue the madman, defeat the girl, and —since Ori's Home was lost—conquer the rest of Garden Island to finally join the Ways into one.

Fifteen minutes later, he and ten others—including Quiv, Sens Minn, five more Sensuals and novitiates, and three Donse Masters—strode into the jungle and toward the northern wall of Ori's Fifth.

Far off, power flared and raged.

35

GLORIOUS HATE

There had been no sign of Dunne Yples. Kila's ears were alert, but she kept her mercus masked.

Though sheltered from the brunt of the storm, Kila did not feel safe. They needed to move. And she knew where to go.

"The tower looks sort of like a fortress," she said to her friends. She *hoped* Gian was still a friend. "Someone lives there, and I'm sure I'm supposed to go there."

"How do you know that?" Quinn asked. She had braided her hair so that she now looked like depictions of Sephie, the archer of On'lin Keep, the legendary heroine who had driven the nosg from the westlands. The resemblance was no accident. Quinn had just read about her in one of her books. Apparently, Sephie's bow had been a Shadline weapon.

Kila wanted to tell her friends about her mirror-visions. But Her Enlightened Majesty had been clear that the mirror was jealous of its secrets and might refuse to reveal more if Kila divulged its power.

But she'd also learned from the Voluptuary of Starside that twisty words often served where the truth couldn't be stated outright. So now she spoke like the Voluptuary: "The force of destiny has led us here. The tower *is* nearby. I saw a light in a high window once. Someone is there and they may be able to hide us."

Gian leaned back on his hands. The color had returned to his face. His thick black hair was pushed back from his face, a bit tousled, but giving him a regal aspect. His eyes held no warmth. "The tower is visible from the beaches below Ori's Home. I think it a bit too far away to know if a lantern burns in a window. Perhaps you saw the sun reflect from the glass."

"We have fire right here," Quinn said. "The storm has not lessened. That madman hasn't found us. Why move when we have just dried out?"

Quinn was right. If they went out, they would be soaked through and chilled to their spines. Perhaps it best if Kila went on alone. She'd already put them in enough danger.

"We should at least wait until Henley comes," Quinn said. Huff sat next to her, allowing her to stroke his body. Oly was still lurking in the loft and Nax refused to talk to him or about him.

Nax sat a few feet away from Pennie, despite Kila urging her to leave the child alone. But Nax liked Pennie and was determined that the feeling must be returned. The child hugged her knees and looked into the flames of their renewed fire. She occasionally glanced at Nax, each time inching slightly away from the cat. Nax would immediately shorten the distance an equal amount, sit primly, and squint into the flames. If they kept it up, both would make a complete circle around the fire before long.

Nax, give her time to get used to you.

Nax returned a burst of flick-tail irritation through the bond. *I am.*

It would be easier to distract Pennie than to control Nax, Kila decided. "Pennie, can you feel what he's doing?" She didn't have to say who "he" was. If the girl had the power to make a fire, she could surely feel Dunne Yples's immense power.

Pennie's face tightened. "Nothing now. He was just . . . building and building. The power gave me a headache. It made my teeth all buzzy inside. And then?" She snapped her fingers. "It stopped."

"Point to him."

The girl jerked a thumb over her shoulder. "He was that way when it stopped. Where we left him."

South. He hadn't moved. But why not?

"How long ago did he stop?" Kila asked, chills rising.

"Hours ago."

Gian leapt to his feet. "How many hours?"

Pennie's answer was silenced by a great rending as the roof of their shelter began to tear away. Clumps of rotten boards fell around them.

A creamy white blur jumped from the loft, landing on Kila's head and bounding to the floor. Oly hadn't spared her his claws, and pinpricks of pain lanced over her scalp.

She didn't have time to complain. Jumping up, she drew Cayne. Quinn already held Black, and Gian held his blade, a dirk pulled from his boot.

The roof flew upward and the storm blasted in. Pennie screamed and covered her ears. Nax cowered beneath Kila, hissing.

The sky was black, but not from the fellstorm. The huge creature of oily smoke loomed over them. It gripped the remains of the roof in its amorphous hands and ripped it apart as easily as Kila could break a warm biscuit in twain. The creature flung the pieces away and they landed with a crash somewhere in the gloom.

Fiery eyes, pits of molten hate set deep into the smoke creature's cloudy head, gazed down at the people it had uncovered. This thing was Yples, but also more than Yples, for it radiated hate as a fire radiates light and heat. The feeling infected Kila and she felt her lips curl back and a deep snarl rumble within her.

Surely this beast had to be rich with mercusine. She decided she had no choice but to drop her mask.

The sun could not have out-shined such power. But this was a black shine, a soul-gobbling darkflame that emitted nothing but the hot stink of a charnel house.

That second—the moment she'd dropped her mask—those eyes flared even as they narrowed. She felt the gaze fall on her. A furnace-blast of heat flowed from its eyes to singe her.

She pulled the heat from the air, a trick of negation she used all the time. "To the tower!"

"Where is it?" Quinn yelled, her voice ripping away into the chaos of the fellstorm.

"This way!" Gian shouted.

They ran, Kila holding fast to Pennie's hand. The cats sprinted, heads low, tails lower. Oly shot ahead, outpacing even Gian. Nax struggled as the wind scoured the ash-covered ground.

Jump up! Kila sent.

Nax obeyed and Kila tucked the animal into the crook of her elbow.

Out of the corner of her eye she saw that Quinn was carrying Huff in the same way, her Shadline blade clenched in the other fist, for all the good its keen edge or the silence would do her now.

"It's coming! Now!" Pennie shrieked.

Kila felt it. A release of the mercusine like the tumble of rock from a mountainside, unstoppable, unavoidable, and certain in its lethality. She didn't look back.

An arch of stone stood ahead, just as she'd seen in her mirror-vision. It emerged from the fog-shrouded world ahead. Gian was already passing under it. He stumbled and fell, balled up and rolled, then popped to his feet.

An explosion concussed the air and the ground to Kila's left blew apart, sending gouts of ash and earth skyward. Another impact struck behind her, pelting her back with chunks of rock.

Quinn reached the arch and she, too, fell as she passed beneath it. Gian had his hands to his mouth. He was shouting for Kila to move faster.

Pennie's breath was ragged, and her grip on Kila's hand began to loosen. Blood bloomed from the back of the girl's head where a stone had struck.

Kila spun and hefted the girl onto her shoulder. In that moment she saw what she had been feeling. The enormous power Yples had summoned was not formed of any of the base senses, but of hate, disgust, yearning, and a feeling she could only identify through the resonances it evoked in her own body: righteousness. She knew that Yples had pursued her, driven by an absolute conviction that she must die. Not for being Kila Sigh, thief girl. But for being what he imagined she was: the destroyer of the world.

The bolts of emotion surged from the fire-eyed giant of oily smoke as it stomped on mist-shrouded legs toward her. Kila backed away, at once fascinated by the monstrosity and thrilling with terror. Her teeth chattered and again the hatred curled her lip.

She couldn't understand what purpose this show of power served. Wouldn't have Yples been better served to throw a thousand glowing spheres at her than to take on this hell-form?

"Kila, I can't see," Pennie said. "It's all black."

Or had he realized something from their first encounter? Perhaps that she would not be easily defeated by such attacks. Perhaps this new strategy reflected some truth about her that even Kila hadn't understood yet.

"I can't see!" Pennie cried. She wriggled and wiped her eyes with her filthy hands, sobbing with terror.

The little worm had no appreciation for the risks Kila had taken to protect her. All she could do was complain. All she could do was whine and sob like a—

The hell-form shrieked, an ear-shattering call of a million tearing throats. And it released its attack. Black zags of power arced from its nebulous fingers, stabbing toward the earth, toward Kila. She threw the hateful child from her, not to save the girl but to free herself from the burden. Nax shrieked and wriggled free.

The black bolts struck Kila's chest as she released her answering bolts of hate and revulsion. Her vision blanked, and her body flushed with a trillion pinpricks. Arms and legs convulsing, she dance upon the muck in jerks and hops beyond her control. It was no willshift, but the natural freaks of muscle tissue under the overwhelming power of the black bolt attack.

The taste of rotten fish and ash filled her mouth and her stomach rebelled. She doubled over, but could not produce more than gags.

She should be dead. She knew it. No one could withstand such a force as the Yples hell-form had delivered. Yet she stood there, vision slowly returning. The storm had muted to her ears, though the wind whipped harder than ever.

Someone was tugging at her. Pennie. She back-handed the spiteful child. "Yer a stain upon the floor, ya Kil-kissin' little—"

Kila felt her scalp tingling with the momentary thrill of warning as the hell-form prepared another strike. She let her own mercus response fly, not a counter attack but a thrust into the earth beneath her feet. The consequence was to send her skyward, just as Yples had done at Ori's Home. It wasn't flying so much as a mercus-powered leap. But it carried her free of the black bolts arcing toward where she'd stood.

A man had come. He scooped Pennie up and backpedaled just in time for more arcs to fall harmlessly into mud. He threw up a mercus ward, much too weak to defend against another strike. But it didn't seem intended to do so. No. It went opaque, merely shielding him and child from the hell-form's sight. Pitiful!

Kila twisted as she rose, guiding herself by mercusine pulls and thrusts as instinctive to her now as had been her leaps and tumbles over the Starside roofway. She flew ever upward until she hovered before the hell-form. Arms out she gloried in the power coursing through her. She grinned, full of hate. Yes.

This was glorious hate. Hate for the demonic giant before her. Hate for her friends. Hate for all the world.

Why should she feel anything else? They were all ants. They were beneath ants! Specks of dust, of no note, of no worth. How she despised them all.

The hell-form's arms reached for her. No mercus boiled within it now, aside from Yples's inexhaustible spark. But he was forming no bolts. The fiery eyes flared and yet softened with what she felt was a kind of affinity. This was what hate fully manifested could be. She could become such a thing. She could surpass it!

Huff says it's a trick, Nax said into her mind.

The sudden sending annoyed her. *Leave me.*

The black arms encircled her and began to close in. An embrace, a hateful embrace. And there was nothing in the world she desired more.

36

EVER DOWN

Henley backed through the arch, barely able to carry the girl and walk at the same time. Gian and Quinn were there, both pitifully wet and ragged. Gian looked the worse off of the two. Henley had admired the young man, looked up to him during their time together in the Princes Ward. That seemed so long ago. They had a strange reunion, consisting of sharp nods, an even briefer glance, and a return to the awesome display of mercus before them.

Henley shouted to be heard above the gale. "Since when can she fly?"

Quinn took the girl from him. The poor thing was sobbing and bleeding. A novitiate from the looks of her. Henley didn't know her name, but he'd probably seen her any number of times at the Home.

Nobody answered him, and from the stunned looks on their faces he knew this was a new feat for Kila. He opened himself to feel the bolts, but whatever she was doing, it was too complex to follow. Aside from the stench of a charnel house and the vague taste of rotting fish, he couldn't make any sense of what Yples had done either. It was just hate. Constant, pure, hate.

Huff leapt, Henley caught him. He peeled his eyes away from Kila and the enormous smoke giant and nuzzled his cat.

Tell her again, he sent.

Nax is telling her. She's not listening. She's being mean, Nax says.

Henley found himself quite furious all of the sudden. He spun on Gian and Quinn. "How could you let this happen?"

Their faces had darkened, too. Quinn was saying something, but she was holding Black and her words were lost. Gian pulled his blade too and backed into a ready stance, facing off against both of them. Pennie lay on the stone pavements, having been shoved aside.

It's a trick, Huff reminded him.

Henley caught himself and shook his head at the insidiousness of the creature's attack. He backed away from his friends. "Resist!" he shouted. "That feeling you feel is not coming from within you. That hate is from Yples!"

He'd felt the feeling building over the last mile of his trek through the ash-barrens. But he'd recognized it as having a source outside of himself. He realized now that was because the brunt of it was aimed at Kila. Yples was trying to infect her with his hate. To what end, Henley didn't know. But now that he saw her floating before the fiery-eyed head of the smoke giant, he thought it was to lure her into some sort of submission.

He'd seen Kila slap the girl. Surely out of character for Kila, even if the child had been annoying her. No. She'd succumbed to Yples's spell. And Henley knew that was because at the core of her black-witted humor and prickly nature was a deep resentment for all that had happened to her. Henley understood it perfectly, for he felt the same way.

Yples was pulling to the surface what lurked in the depths of every woman and man on earth. Seductive, powerful, hatred.

"Quinn! Gian! The hate you feel is not real. Think! Why would you hate me?"

Gian faltered, stared at the blade in his hand, then lowered it. Quinn followed suit, though the battle to command her heart showed more plainly on her face.

Huff! What's happening to Kila?

She is . . . Huff did not have a word to express it, so he merely passed to Henley the emotion he was getting from Nax: a seething, almost joyful anger. The kind of anger that makes one feel powerful, but also justified for lashing out, and relishing the chance to inflict well-deserved suffering on others.

Kila was no longer visible, for the smoky arms of the hell-spawned giant had engulfed her. But Henley could see her mercusine haze, like a blur of white against the black of the monster.

His companions had shaken off most of their false-hatred, and both looked apologetic and embarrassed. But also determined. "Get to shelter," he called to them. He pointed beyond them to a vague shape in the gray wash of rain. A tower, as ancient and decrepit as any described in children's tales.

Pennie—who had apparently not succumbed to Yples poisonous spell—climbed into Gian's arms and he trudged after Quinn. He kept throwing glances back and up, toward Kila. Henley recognized that look. Another mortal pulled into the maelstrom that was Kila Sigh, and who now resented it. But there was nothing Gian could do to help her. That would fall to Henley. Which made him chuckle with the dark humor of a man tip-toeing through a graveyard.

But what could he do to help her? If Nax had no influence, how would he talk sense into her? Especially since he couldn't talk to her at all at the moment. He hadn't the faintest idea how to fly up to where she hovered. And as committed as he was to meeting his fate, he wasn't eager to get closer to the giant oily beast than he was now.

Time-rein? He'd done it once to save Kila from Dunne Yples. No idea how to do it again. That had been pure desperation. He needed to distract the Yples-beast. He reached for a rock the size of his own head. Not with his hands, but with the mercus. Such feats had been beyond the Sensuals he'd studied with at Ori's Home, but they'd taught him the principle of it.

He felt the contours of the stone. Closing his eyes, he grasped the stone and threw it with all his power toward the hell-spawn's head. He opened his eyes in time to see the stone plunge into the depths and disappear. The beast neither noticed nor cared. It was, he noted, a thing of demaynic properties, unaffected by the wind. Surely, nothing else of the material world would wound it.

At least he'd learned something. And he was relieved, because he doubted he could throw enough rocks to have much effect against such a giant anyway. Next was the mercus touch formed into a thread, the trick he'd learned from the Hargothe.

And so Henley plunged, shoulders hunched, fingers flexed and clawed. He had vowed to himself never to resort to such intrusions. Another promise gone by the board. And probably not the last, in the unlikely event he survived the next few minutes.

Eyes closed, he stood there, ankle-deep in the ash mud, face pelted with sharp snaps of rain. But all bodily sensation faded as he sought the mind of the beast, which was a man's mind. A sane mind was treacherous seas for an inexperienced diver, but a madman's brain roiled like a storm strewn ocean. Henley dove, feeling his way through the disordered and senseless byways, churning currents, and sucking vortexes. Ever deeper he delved, for there is only one direction to go when seeking the heart of something vile. Down. Ever down.

Kila is changing, Huff called into his mind. The cat felt distant, though the animal pressed close to Henley's shins. *Nax is afraid.*

Where is Nax? Henley asked, barely noting his own question.

At the center. In the black.

In the haze beneath Yples and Kila, a mournful mewl arose. Nax could not reach the sky-dancing Kila, so she had slunk as close as she could get.

Call her back!

She will not come.

Get her.

Henley did not hear or feel any response from his bonded cat, for he had finally probed to the black-pulsing core of Dunne Yples's madness. And he cried out in despair, for there was naught he could do. If he touched it, if he dared plunge deeper, he would be consumed by the insanity and there would be no Henley Mast.

He opened his eyes, keeping his mercus tendril in place, at

once seeing both the horrific tableau in the world of man and the sickening pit in the soul of man. And Kila, a mercusine blur lost in black, formed a new feat that pulled power into a swirl around her. A fog of aquamarine began to take giant-form shape to match Yples's hell-form of black.

Henley did not understand it, but he *knew* it.

She *was* Dem-Kisk. She would release that power and not one speck of the Garden Island would remain.

Nax is holding her! Huff sent.

Henley didn't know what that meant. Not exactly. But the implication was clear. Kila was balanced on the brim, and Nax was keeping her from plunging over the edge. Did the fate of mankind rest upon the will of a cat? It seemed so. But it could not long remain so.

A burst of power to the south. It caught Henley unawares, and he jerked his awareness there. An impossibly bright light flared into existence, making the rain glisten like crystals and the clouds reveal their angry black bellies. Spreading from this light east and west, a group of new powers had suddenly awakened. Each was stronger than any single merculyn save Yples and Kila. But who were they? He sniffed the wind, felt it trail through is fingers. He recognized flavors there. Yes. He detected the spark of Dunne Quiv and several novitiates he'd noted when he'd been taken into Til's Tower. The others were strangers to him. And lesser sparks behind them. Far behind.

Source-taps! And ten captains.

And Highest Fley in the lead.

They sent bolts toward the hell-spawn. Fire, ice, and violet plasma flashed inside the dark giant, like lightning within storm clouds. The red eyes erupted with anger and the beast turned. The piercing light caused tendrils of its corporeal fog to wisp away.

With a world-juddering shriek, it flashed black arcs into the distance. And from the mass of Yples's hate-void mind, Henley watched new tendrils burst forth. He pulled back his own probes lest he get caught up in these outward reaching limbs. These were not true limbs, but representations of thought. Of the dividing of Yples's attention to deal with the intruders.

The air filled with mercusine bolts, and Henley's teeth buzzed with their resonances.

Huff. Bring me Nax. If the foolish cat was in the center of that battle, and she was all that held Kila back, then she could not remain where she was.

In my teeth?

If you must.

I—I cannot. I can only . . .

Steeling himself, Henley sent a command to once again rend from himself his most cherished part. *Join her!*

And then Huff's presence was gone.

The gaping maw this absence left nearly swallowed Henley this time. Only the repeated assurance that it was only for a short time and that Huff would soon return kept him upright. But the heart is never fully convinced that any suffering is temporary.

What more did he have to give? He couldn't think of single thing. And he lacked the knowledge to throw the mercusine bolts the attacking teams were hurling.

But he had another trick to try. One he'd learned from old Sens Dooni. Forming the bolts, he swallowed his sobs and called into the wind. "KILA! REMEMBER WEN! REMEMBER NAX! REMEMBER ME!"

His bolts made his words boom above the raging storm that erupted within the hell-spawn giant. His shout shook the ground and even he was shocked to feel his ribs and knees vibrate with his voice. He repeated his call. Again and again. He must get through to her. He must.

And then Nax and Huff ran from the mist and huddled at his feet. They cowered, ears flat, tails flat, fur matted with mud and ash. He scooped up a cat in each hand and backed slowly toward the tower.

Remember Wen. Remember Nax. Remember Me. He urged her to remember Fallo and Dunne Marlow and Critt Sanglo and every other name he recalled that might evoke a recollection of love or friendship or the slightest good feeling at all.

Yples shot forth a flurry of black bolts, but none came toward Henley. He didn't understand why, except that each time a limb emerged from the man's vile black brain that came close to Henley's mercusine probe, Henley darted in and snipped it. Each touch made him shiver and his nose filled with the rot of the grave.

His voice wore out, and now his mercusine bolts powered raspy commands into the fray. Remember, Kila Sigh. Remember!

Huff hadn't returned the bond for some reason. Henley desperately needed to feel that connection. In the worst trials with the Hargothe, he had been able to latch onto that bond. Even when the Coin had lashed him for a crime he hadn't committed, Huff had been there. Not to absorb the suffering, but to strengthen Henley's will.

"Come back, Huff," he said, giving the cat slight shake. But Huff did not return. Both animals hung limp as he clutched the scruffs of their necks. He pulled them into the crooks of his arms. He shouted to Kila. He whispered to Huff.

He staggered up the debris-filled roadway leading to the ancient tower. Dunne Quiv fired strange bolts at Yples from a mile to Henley's left. A novitiate girl named Roon pushed a different sort of bolt two miles beyond. Henley couldn't make sense of either effort. It appeared that five merculyns kept up a barrage of fire, plasma, and a strange sort of liquid ice that flashed in jagged bolts.

Yples responded with black arcs and spheres of blue. Huge gouts of mud went skyward, and two of the merculyns vanished, their sparks extinguished forever. The crystalline light accompanying Fley charged closer, held aloft by a young man charging a hundred paces ahead of the Highest. Henley winced to see how the mercus was ripped from the lad to feed the lantern. But the light continued to press against Yples, tearing away more of the oily fog that comprised his body.

Kila hovered next to the giant, a pinpoint of immense power compressed in her mind, ready to release and end them all. Her giant-form had limbs now, the smear of a head sparking alight with eyes of garnet-fire red.

Remember Wen. Remember Nax. Remember me. Remember your father. Remember Starside. Remember love, Kila. Remember it. Remember it. Please. Please remember!

37

PULLING BACK A VEIL

Like sitting atop the foremast on *Sea-Hound*, hovering twenty spans above the ground while the wind whipped past her filled Kila with a strange euphoria. Arms spread wide she let the wind take her, and she felt as though she was the source of the power.

Yes. She *was* the source of all power.

Yples's hell-form had turned its lava gaze from her. He threw bolts of hatred into the storm, striking at unseen merculyns in the rain-shrouded distance. Each jagged bolt of blackness—like inverse lightning—sent wafts of death-pyre stink to Kila's nose. Revulsion and hatred spun all around her, through her. And it was glorious.

A strange light shone from the intruders, casting stark daylight upon the ash-barrens. A tiny pinpoint, like a star born upon the ground. Yples recoiled from it and threw rays of crimson hate toward it. A furrow opened in the mud, and the light-bearer tottered on the brink.

Kila yearned for him to fall. She longed for him to remain. The light burned, the light soothed.

Yples arced black hate at the light-bearer. But the arcs did not reach him. Another man rushed up to pulled him away from the chasm.

Tearing her attention away from the light, Kila turned inward. She had accumulated a mass of mercusine. Just as Yples had collected and formed his own power into the hell-form, so too had Kila. She had no purpose in mind, other than to concentrate it, tighter and tighter. All of her rage and the malice she'd hidden away in the black corners of her mind came out, like greedy hands, to pull more power in until she thought she would burst. But still she wanted more, yearned for an ultimate release that would be her final judgment upon the world.

Kila! Nax sent.

Hateful animal. Intrusive beast.

"REMEMBER WEN!" came the call, rumbling forth on mercusine waves. "REMEMBER NAX!"

She recognized the voice. She formed the bolts to negate the sound and it fell to silence.

Yples had been right. She was Dem-Kisk. Not because she'd been chosen, but because she chose to be it. In this moment, charged with this superabundance of power, she accepted the mantle of Dem-Kisk. Whatever the forgotten prophet had meant by the warning, it mattered not. For Kila would make the moment mean what *she* wanted it to mean.

More eruptions came from the puny merculyns arrayed around her. Only six remained of the original ten. They threw tiny blows at Yples, who absorbed them or deflected them or simply ignored them. Three wielded more subtle powers, seeking to willshift or paralyze the man who was not a man. They may as well be mosquitos biting a horse for all the damage they did. But the lantern bearer pressed forward, the chasm having filled with flows of ash-mud.

She could lash out at these ants to more effect than Yples did with his black bolts of hate.

Kila. Remember Wen. Remember Me. Remember Henley, and Huff, and Startle, and Lop, and Fallo, and Critt Sanglo, and Marlow, and Her Enlightened, and Finta Sahng, and—

Kila interrupted: *Remember the Hargothe! Remember Parlo Odok and Jocko and Dox Viller and his hounds. Remember the thinnies!*

In answer, Nax sent the stark fear of drowning in the thinnie cavern lake, trapped in a box sinking into lightless depths. The chill crept over Kila's skin. Her rage shifted to the thinnies, the vile people who had sought to sacrifice Nax to appease Kil and cure their town of sickness.

Yples wants to kill you, Nax sent. *He makes you hate what you don't hate. He lures you.*

I'm right here. Why doesn't he attack? Uncertainty broke through Kila's anger, gave her pause. Her heart slammed in her chest and her limbs felt impossibly strong. Without knowing how, she had infused her flesh with mercusine bolts that would magnify all her physical efforts. Meanwhile, she continued to keep herself aloft through buffeting winds she controlled by pure instinct.

Henley says not every attack is a blow. He says you know that as well as he does. You are feeling Yples's feelings. Nax seemed uncomfortable with this notion, as if uncertain what it meant. But she had dutifully passed along Henley's words. Kila noticed that her cat was terrified.

Yples shrieked as his attackers coordinated a strike, not of fire or lightning, but against his mercus control. It was an attempt to sever him from his powers. Kila saw the bolts as whirling tentacles lashing from the darkness toward the hell-form's smoky head. Another such tentacle, hair thin and unnoticed until now was already attached to Yples's mind. That was from Henley, she realized. It was a perfect imitation of the Hargothe's technique. What was that pathetic insect doing?

Remember love! Nax sent, sending with it a wave of emotion. She felt the soft dry brush of Nax's fur against her cheek, the small, firm feet kneading her belly as she tried to sleep, the vibrating purr of content closeness that they'd shared nearly every night since the bond had first formed.

Remember yourself, Nax said.

And Kila did remember. And in remembering she nearly lost control of the enormous power she'd gathered. She needed to shed some of it or she would obliterate herself. Light and heat would drain it most quickly, so she sent forth rays of white-hot light that outshined even the strange lantern.

Her outward burst fluttered the hell-form's body. Yples shrieked and turned back to Kila. "DEM-KISK!"

The oily arms again reached for her, hate flowing down on her like a waterfall.

Remember!

The attackers rushed forward now, each latching onto Yples's mind.

The lantern-bearer rushed into the black fog, light destroying blackness. Kila joined her light to his, tearing away enormous clouds of Yples's body.

Abruptly the lantern went out. The bearer fell into the mud, dead.

But the merculyns had laid claim to Yples's mind, and all at once the hell-form dissipated and finally it did feel the wind, which whipped the smoke westward and into oblivion. All that remained was the man, shirtless and shivering upon the mud of the ash-barrens. He held his hands over his head, cowering.

Kila knew she could smite him with fire and end him. She had the power to leave a crater the size of Starside where he stood. And despite the draining hatred and the rising remembrance of herself, she saw no purpose in letting him live. Mercy had only delayed this battle.

But then people stumbled close to encircle him. Sensuals, novitiates, Donse Masters. One possessed the strongest tie to Yples's mind, a tall, stern Donse Master. He barked commands and several of the merculyns released their holds on Yples, while he pressed his more strongly.

Henley was just a speck in the distance, a luminous figure near the old abandoned tower. Nax and Huff were with him, safe. His slim mercus probe had pulled back from Yples's mind and vanished.

A Sensual wrapped Yples in an oil-cloak and tipped a flask to his lips. The man shivered, lips blue, hair and beard matted with mud.

The lead man called out. "I am Highest Fley, master of this island. Descend and submit yourself into my care. I will see no harm comes to you."

No harm?

She still hung high above the ash field, held aloft by her mercusine flows, and flooded with power. The aura she'd created had barely drained any of it. She let it grow, throwing heat and light in all directions. The tiny merculyns raised their hands to block her glare. She laughed and mimicked Henley's voice-casting trick, making her words carry over the wind. "Yer a Kil-kissin' idiot, ya are."

They all flinched. Several covered their ears.

Fley raised his arms. Something in one hand flashed. Mercus began to coalesce around him. "I see your power, girl. You cannot control it."

He struck. The force of the attack caught Kila off guard. No bolts approached her, but instead went to still the winds keeping her aloft. She fell, legs pumping and arms pinwheeling.

She threw down a bolt of desperation that cushioned her landing. Spouts of mud flew up from her impact. The mercus strength infusing her legs kept her upright. Still shining and shedding heat to dissipate her excess mercus, she stalked toward the man.

As she had done so many times before, she formed bolts by instinct. This time she took inspiration from Dunne Yples, calling forth spheres of power which she hurled at the man.

Dunne Quiv struck them aside and countered with will-shift. She deflected it with annoyance.

Moving with inhuman speed, Fley rushed at her. So, the man knew some tricks, did he? And his power . . .

She saw it then. Fley had not only quelled Yples, he had claimed the man's power. She sensed the flow coursing from madman to Highest. The others had retreated and had begun to circle her. Their mental probes darted in. She blocked them easily.

Fley flung a strange bolt at her, a mixture of gong resonance and pressure that impacted her in the chest. Had she not been so infused with power, it would have flung her onto her back, likely shattering her breastbone and spine into the bargain. As it was, it simply knocked the breath from her lungs.

The Sensual who had taken Yples under her care shone brightly for a moment and Kila felt herself grow calm. A powerful charm of sedation. She smelled the plumeria and incense and tasted the sweet milk. It was harder to resist than the others' attempts.

Fley lunged, not with an attack, but an intrusion. The five other merculyns followed his lead. Kila fell to her knees, gripping her skull. Not again. Not this. Not the slimy finger probes into her mind.

Kila! Henley can help you.

She felt him there, a mercus spark to her left, far off. And she felt that hair-thin bolt of mercus brushing against her mind, even as Fley and the others jabbed hard trying to overcome her will through sheer force.

She hurled spheres of power and jagged green bolts and flame and ice back along the web-strands of her enemies' intrusions. One struck, the others glanced from protective wards. Explosions rumbled in the ground as her blows landed. But the intrusions persisted.

Kila! Nax sent. Let Henley join you.

What?

Surrender to him. He can help you.

Kila didn't know how to surrender. She had been taught to fight, to scrape, claw, crawl. To slog through bone-chilled nights, robbing lordlings and drunkards for enough coin to pay for shelter, for Wen's medicine. When confronted by those set on her destruction, she destroyed them.

To surrender to someone else . . .

He knows the ways of the Hargothe, Nax sent.

Kila knew them, too. She had endured his assaults. What made Henley think he could defend her better than she could?

He knows what Fley is doing.

Kila pulled her hands from her head and got to her feet. Fley had moved closer while he and his force of merculyns had pressed their attack. He was powered by Yples's strength. They were supported with hellers and she saw now streams of mercus flowing from a hundred more merculyns to the south.

Her own power could be measured against that, but like Yples, she could not divide her attention among so many powerful attackers.

Let Henley join you.

She didn't know what that meant. Nax kept putting emphasis on "join" as if it meant something more than simply letting him into her mind.

With a surge of frustration, Nax sent the catsight. Kila's vision blurred and refocused. Fley was not before her now, but Henley was. Viewed from the ground, he appeared to be a giant, with the old tower looming behind him. He squatted and spoke. "Kila, listen to me."

His voice came through Nax's ears and into Kila's awareness as if she were right there. "Huff has taught me something. He used it to wake Nax when you were unconscious. I can help you if you let me."

The catsight vanished. Kila bent forward and threw up a thin stream of bile. A novitiate's probe touched her mind, found purchase. A second later, so too, did Dunne Quiv's. These were followed in quick succession by intrusions from the remaining merculyns. Kila felt her will collapsing, as if each probe were a finger pulling back a veil to expose the vulnerable flesh of her mind.

Kila! Nax shrieked into her mind.

Henley's touch pressed ever-so-lightly, like a gentle hand on her shoulder. He was seeking permission.

Fley stood a pace from her, a blade in his hand, a shining amber orb in the other. His eyes glowed white with the rush of power surging through him. "Sweet child," he said, "you will serve me well."

He lurched forward, blade flashing toward her. She called for Cayne, sending her own blade forth upon mercusine wings to parry.

Fley scraped with claw-like probes into her exposed mind, and her vision doubled. Steel clanged against steel, then a piercing of ice found her flank. She opened her eyes to see Fley's blade sunk into her side.

His face was close now, so close she could see every pore, every whisker where it thrust from his flesh. His teeth were pulled back in a satisfied grin. A blade in her mind sliced through her mercus, and all her power rushed from her to Fley.

It should have seared him, parted him into infinite pieces. But instead the largest portion flowed to the gem in his hand. It flashed brightly orange. His head tilted back and his mouth opened wide. A groan of ecstasy pulled from his throat. He released the hilt of his blade.

Kila fell backward.

And then she surrendered.

38

TO THE TOWER

The combined powers of the madman and the girl thundered through Highest Fley. Had he not established the spillway of mercus to the Sink Gem he would not have survived it for a second.

Force-tapping Dunne Yples would have been impossible without the assistance of his allies. The same was true for this incredible girl. But now he had them both. Could there be any doubt that he was the Champion of the One God?

Now he need only study the girl's stunning repertoire of feats and nothing in the world could stand against him. All would be united in worship of the One God.

He turned away from the limp form of the slight girl who now lay in the mud. He wished he could take on giant form as Yples had done, but hadn't the slightest idea how to do it. No matter. With such an abundance of mercus he could pull the secrets from the girl. Dunne Yples on the other hand . . . The man likely had no idea what he'd done.

He found Dunne Quiv and Sensual Minn's mercus knots

still attached to the girl's mind. He severed them easily. Same with the others.

But what was this? Another thread, so slight and ephemeral, snaking off to the long-abandoned tower of Kil's Keep. There had been another merculyn present during the battle with Yples. Fley sniffed and reached for the source. The spark was familiar.

The boy he'd collected from the Home. The very same who had accompanied Dunne Yples to Garden Island. Acolyte Henley Mast. What subtle trick was he playing? Why bother with such a thin attempt to control the girl?

Fley sliced at the thread, his effort passing through it as though it weren't even there. But the thread did not part. He tried again, forming mercusine bolts of piercing sound to obliterate it. But they had no effect.

Pausing he studied the strand. Like any bolt, it should be composed of the five senses. But this had none of them. It was . . . he didn't know what it was. Recoiling from the strangeness, he barked orders for Quiv to capture the boy.

Dunne Quiv and the other surviving Donse Master set off, staggering in the wind. The Sensual and two surviving novitiates of Ori remained. Sens Minn had moved from Yples to the girl.

The girl's lips were blue and her closed eyelids had a bluish cast as well. The Sensual had covered her with another oil-cloak, though what good that could do was not apparent to Fley.

"They will both die if we do not warm them," she said.

"To the tower, then," he said. The Sensual motioned to her sisters and both Yples and the girl were gathered up. They began the long walk toward the tower. But Fley was not content to follow. He wanted to strike.

He turned northward. Somewhere in that direction, beyond these ash-barrens of Kil's Fifth, lay the Vale of Pol. He could feel them even now, the sour-faced Spinsters.

They would submit.

Well, those he did not make examples of would submit.

39

CARESSING THE EDGE

Are you still with me? Henley said.

I'm here, Kila answered. *What's happening?*

Horror. Jagged teeth of despair. Gaping wound in soul.

Where's Nax? Ah me! Naxie!

Shhhhh. Shhhh. She is here with me. All will be well. I know how it hurts. Believe me. I had to leave Huff to join you. They are safe inside with Quinn and Gian.

Kila wanted to pant and clutch her chest, but she had no form—no body at all.

Where am I?

We have joined minds. In manner of speaking. Don't ask. I don't truly understand it. Huff showed me.

She reached for her mercus, intent on sparking a floating light so that she might see something of where she stood. But the mercus seemed distant, like a waterfall heard from miles away.

She knew of waterfalls. How did she know? She had never been out of Starside. Had she?

Pay attention, thief girl, Henley said. *Highest Fley has force-tapped you, just as he did with Dunne Yples. All your power is his. For now. Sens Minn is bringing your body to the tower. I can see them ascending the tower path. The others bear Dunne Yples. This is good.*

I can't see anything. Why can't I see?

Because your eyes are shut and only one of us can look out through my eyes at a time. And I need them right now.

The panic of the tomb crept up her throat. She was trapped. Sightless, formless. A soul afloat in a void. She wanted to scrabble for escape, to claw for sunlight and air.

She wasn't breathing. She had no mouth. She had no scream.

Calm yourself, Kila. You're giving me heart tremors. I need to concentrate. Quiv and Mackle are coming for me, I think. Fley is heading toward Pol's Fifth. That's good. That will give us time.

Time for what?

Well, for Quinn and Gian and I to get your body away from these people who have allied themselves with Highest Fley. I'm astonished that Sensual Harrisan Minn agreed to do this. I can only suppose she saw the danger in Yples's rampaging around. I swore she was loyal to the old Voluptuary.

I was stabbed, Kila said, remembering now the grievous wound. *Henley, am I dying?*

He didn't answer right away. *Quinn is laying a fire in the hearth. You should see this place. The hall is . . . Not like anything I've ever seen. Can you believe Kil had a Fifth?*

Don't let those Donse Masters get near Nax. Promise me, Henley.

Nax and Huff have gone up—Wait! Do you feel that?

His presence grew distant. Mercus roared. Kila looked all round, searching for something to orient herself to. She felt like she was standing upside down.

Quiv and Mackle tried to subdue me. They are supplied with source-taps. But they are exhausted, despite their hellers. They're regrouping. Ah, Sens Minn is here. She outshines them both. They are standing down.

Kila's existence was without any physical sensation that correlated with human experience. But she was vibrating with fear. This is what panic that has no outlet felt like. It was similar to how she'd felt before Fley had severed her from the mercus, about to explode with power. Except this was pure vulnerability, the exact opposite of what she'd felt.

My eyes turned black for a while, Henley. It felt so right.

Henley chuckled at the reference. An old sailors' poem about Rilan, who ventured to the ferneaters lands and was cursed with unquenchable desire for their queen. He drank from forbidden gourds and ate the flesh of vergant-kin, a spirit race who occupied the liminal spaces of the world. Neither alive nor dead. And no friend of man.

> *Every desire profane arose*
> *As Rilan trekked the vergant track;*
> *His cup of bloodwine dripped with lust*
> *And all did mark his eyes gone black*

Henley said, *There were days when I was first in Cheapsgate when I would have eaten vergant-kin whole.* She felt him send comfort for a moment, a fleeting, gentle touch. It was as ill-defined as a morning haze: there, but untouchable, then gone. She wanted to hold to it and never let go. She wanted Nax.

Ah, me. What a forlorn sight I must be. Fer all my skillets I'd have but one more sight o' the sun.

You do look rather poorly, Henley said. *They've dragged you into the hall. The fire burns well. Gian pulled a table near to it. They have laid you upon it. Dear me, you are blue. Like one frozen on Winternight.*

Blue? How could she be frozen? Garden Island was hot. *The fellstorm. I was exposed to the brunt for too long.*

No. It was Highest Fley's blade. Sensual Minn has set it aside and forbids anyone touch it. A mercusine relic, she says. Surely a Shadline, don't you think?

Mention of Fley's blade reminded her that she had sent Cayne for a desperate parry. For all the good that had done. The weapon must still lay out in the ash somewhere, likely lost beneath the mud. That had been her last bit of Father, the final connection from him to Wen to her. Was life naught but loss?

Nax! Tearless sobs. No gulps of breath or shuddering shoulders. Just the infinite potential to cry and no release. *Kil's eyes! Nax!* she called again, feeling as helpless as a small girl she'd once seen in Dunne Medow plaza. The girl had become separated from her mother, and how she had wept and called. Kila had not stayed to see if they had ever been reunited. She doubted it.

Nax!

She is well, Kila. But she cannot hear you while we are joined. Please be calm if you can. I must attend to something.

Calm. How could she be calm?

I want out, Henley. I want back into my mind.

That you most certainly do not. Trust me. Now hush!

THE DONSE MASTERS huddled in a dim gallery at the side of Kil's Hall, their furtive eyes catching glimmers from Quinn's raging fire. They were outnumbered, and gauging by their mercusine sparks, well overpowered by Sens Minn and her sisters.

Henley observed all of this with cautious calm. He doubted they could feel what he was doing with the mercus. The bolts were mere whispers and the force of that flowed from Yples and Kila, screams. He kept his tendril attached to Kila's mind. Such a dim country was her brain, frozen to near solidity. Only the vaguest force of life pulsed within her. The deep dagger wound in her side had bubbled out a single, gloopy blob of blood, which had frozen in place, like melted garnet.

Dunne Yples showed more signs of life. His chest rose, though in sharp jerks followed by long, heavy pauses. His eyes were closed, his lips slack. A slice of one temple was missing, exposing gray brain. But it did not bleed. Cut off from his mercus, he seemed to also have been cut from his infinite hatred for Kila. It might have been interesting had Henley not had other concerns.

Quinn and Gian stood on either side of Kila's table, blades out. They refused to let anyone approach her. They had even warned Henley away, despite his insistence that he was on her side.

"There are a multitude of sides," Quinn said. "Kila and I are on one, and the rest of the world is on all the others." She spat at Sensual Minn. "Did you know what Thine was doing to her? Did you?"

For her part Sens Minn was maintaining her calm. Obviously unaccustomed to such a tone from anyone short of . . . well, anyone, she mastered her indignation and merely stood at the very edge of Quinn's stabbing range. On the other side, Gian eyed the Donse Masters and seemed ready to disembowel them if they he decided they wore the wrong expressions on their muddy faces. Henley had seen Gian move through his blademaster exercises. Mercus or no, he'd wager every last skillet on Gian if it came to a fight.

But Kila was not going to thaw out merely by lying next to the hearth. She had been struck down by a Shadline blade. Only mercusine interventions could save her now.

He paused only a second to consider whether it might be better for all involved if she were to die. Yples, too. Fley would lose his tap on their power instantly and the whirlwind of Kila's existence could no longer pull him inexorably toward doom.

But she was family. It was simple as that. He imagined what Fallo would have said could he have heard Henley's thoughts. All he came up with was an off-color comment about Kila's rather striking eyes. But even Fallo—selfish Fallo—would have risked all to save Kila. She brought that instinct out in people . . . at least, in those who weren't already trying to kill her.

"It's a Shadline blade," Henley said softly. He spoke to Quinn. She was the key here. If Sensual Minn could have bypassed her, or moved her out of the way through some mercusine effort, she surely would have. No. Something prevented her from acting against Quinn. Or perhaps it was Gian. Interesting. But again, something to mull over when there were less dire catastrophes in the offing.

"Sens Minn, who is your best healer?" he asked

The woman eyed him, lips pursing. "Novitiate Sliy." A sharp-eyed woman of no more than twenty-two stepped forward, head tilted to one side. Her fawn-colored hair was cut short and parted down the middle. Handsome and serious. Her spark was remarkable, but not the brightest among them.

"Kila is dying," he said. A simple truth. "I am keeping her alive the only way I know how. But unless her body is restored . . . I can't maintain this forever."

"Maintain what?" Sens Minn asked.

Henley couldn't explain it any more than he could demonstrate it. "I suffered at the hands of the Hargothe in Starside. I learned some things. You know I have a bonded Beloved One. He, too, has illuminated some mysteries to me. I hold Kila's mind." He cupped a hand. "Like a chick scooped from the nest."

Sens Minn came close to him, placed her rough hands on his cheeks. She pulled down the bottoms of his eyes. "Flaked with silver." Novitiate Sliy peered over her shoulder, mouth slightly parted as she studied Henley's eyes. "Astonishing."

"Quinn," Henley said. "Allow the novitiate to tend to Kila."

The raven-haired woman spoke, though her words were silent. She raised her own Shadline weapon a bit higher and rocked from foot to foot.

"You are not thinking clearly, Lady Peline," he said, arching his vowels a bit higher than his former station as a merchant's son warranted. "By protecting her in this way, you are surely killing her."

She mouthed a curse, one Henley read easily on her lips. A wildness took over her eyes. Her knuckles had gone white as she gripped the hilt of her blade. And Henley saw it at the same time as Gian did.

Quinn was still infected with some of Yples's hate. And his righteous rage. That she hadn't already attacked spoke to a deep battle within her. Henley wished he could give her more time, but Kila didn't have it to spare. "Gian. Take her weapon. Sens Minn, you see what has come over her?"

"I do."

Gian blurred. One moment he was on the opposite side of the table from Quinn, the next he had leaped over Kila, wrapped Quinn in an iron hold, wrenched her wrist until her blade clanked onto the stone tiles of the floor.

Quinn's answering scream erupted as soon as the hilt left her hand. Gian was as gentle as a man could be who was incapacitating a friend. His arm snaked around her throat and he applied a sharp twist. The light in Quinn's eyes went out and she slumped in his arms.

Novitiate Sliy rushed to Kila even as Sensual Minn went to Quinn. Henley joined the novitiate. The young woman had surely never seen the effects of Fley's blade before. He could only hope she had the skills to explore Kila's state and discover how to reverse it.

He had seen healings before. None were of this magnitude. From her posture, Sliy had never attempted anything like it. He felt her sending bolts of mercus into the wound and into Kila's heart. But Sliy instantly recoiled. Not from disgust, but in pain. She shuddered, arms going stiff. Her eyes rolled up into her skull, and she fell backward, stiff as a plank. Henley caught her and set her down. Her lips were blue.

"It won't work. None of it will have any effect." Dunne Quiv had ventured forth, taking the opportunity of Gian's distraction. He held no mercus at the ready. Judging by his pasty face and the dark circles under his eyes, the only battle he was prepared for was with wakefulness.

He pointed at Fley's blade. "That is a Shadline dagger, Bone Chill."

Even as he said, the man seemed to hear a different meaning in his words than he'd intended. Every conscious person in the room inhaled at once, all recalling the last line from the prophecy of Dem-Kisk. *You will know Dem-Kisk by the fallen tower, the creaking gate, the bone chill.*

"Then she is truly lost," Sens Minn said, kneeling now next to her fallen novitiate. Whatever mercusine curse held Kila in its icicle-fingered grip, it now claimed Sliy. Henley closed his eyes.

~

THE VOICE RETURNED to the blackness, centered in Kila's mind. *You were stabbed by a Shadline blade. It seems anyone who attempts to heal the wound gets . . . frozen.*

Is it a willshift? If so you can send bolts of calming scent and soothing sound. Maybe—

It is not a willshift. You are a block of ice right now. I felt your heart. You still live or you'd already be gone from my mind. But I'm not sure what to do. The remaining merculyns are under-standably hesitant to probe further, considering what happened to Novitiate Sliy. And also considering what they saw you preparing before they stopped you. Some are arguing that the force of destiny has brought you to this state to protect the world from your power.

What she had been preparing . . . The concentration of mercus that might have destroyed the island. The world. At minimum it would have killed Nax, and Henley, and Quinn, and Gian. Had she truly intended to do that? The righteous hate she'd felt then seemed distant now, like a dream half-remembered and quickly fading.

Have you studied the blade itself? she asked. *There might be a—*

Excuse me a moment. Gian is trying to talk to me.

Kila was growing weary of these interruptions. Without a body, or even a *place* to retreat to, she was at Henley's mercy. At least she wasn't feeling as panicky now. In fact, her thoughts were a bit vague. She realized she was sleepy. That couldn't be good.

Henley. I'm getting sleepy. Why am I sleepy?

Gian says you healed his leg after fighting . . . lizard-wolves? Were you truly fighting lizard-wolves with a dagger?

They had cornered a cat. But yes. I healed him. It was a small scratch. Nothing like when I healed the old man.

She had used Flaumishtak's healing tricks to save the Hargothe, who had force-bonded Nax at the time. She'd only done it to save Nax, though.

I'd forgotten about that. You know more healing than all these fools.

She wanted to yawn. She wanted to close her eyes. Lacking eyes, mouth, and lungs, she simply let her mind go quiet. A good long sleep was what she needed.

Kila! Stay alert. I have an idea. It is dangerous for us both.

I can't stay awake.

You're dying.

This information was interesting, but not alarming. Dying didn't seem so bad. *If I'm dying, then it's only dangerous for me.*

Henley was quiet a moment. You *are dangerous for me. I see that's never going to change. I'm going to give you command. Don't get me killed.*

What?

Two pinpoints of light appeared before Kila. They rushed toward her, like distant openings in a pitch-black cavern. With an inrushing gulp of breath, she came alive into the world. Chills prickled her skin and she stumbled. Someone caught her elbow. It was Gian.

Kila! Hurry. I'm already drifting. That was Henley's voice. Inside her head.

"Henley?" Gian said. "Are you unwell?"

Her vision refocused beyond Gian to where a slight figure lay upon a rickety old table. Someone had thrown a cloak over her. It was her own body. Stumbling forward, she struggled with Henley's uncoordinated manner of walking. Her limbs felt wrong. Catching herself on the table, she reached a trembling hand toward her frozen face.

Cheeks smudged with ash, bald scalp pocked with red bumps from Sens Thine's rough shaving. Lips blue. She barely recognized herself. Reflexively she reached for the mercus, and found it. Such a shallow well compared to her own infinite reservoir. This was Henley's mercusine. And now she felt, saw, heard the immense flows leaving her frozen body. The mercus streamed away, passing through the stone walls of the tower, to where Fley still drew upon them.

Kila, please hurry, Henley said.

She felt tired, but not sleepy. Henley had taken on her dying, risking that she could save herself. There was no time. She didn't know what to do.

Something bumped her elbow. Nax had jumped onto the

table. The cat meowed and batted at her, urging her to do something. And so she would.

"Does anyone have a heller?" she asked, choking slightly over the low voice that come from her throat. "Please. A heller."

A novitiate with red hair pressed a small oval stone into Kila's hand. She immediately discovered her power had doubled. Good. Remarkable. Henley was strong compared to most, but not compared to her.

Someone behind her mumbled: "The madman fades, too. The exertion was too much for him."

Kila couldn't concern herself with Yples. He had tried to kill her, had filled her with an infectious hatred. If Til had touched him with such in response to her power, then she would do nothing to save him.

She closed her eyes and tuned her mercus senses, smelling the damp stone, the smoke from the fire, the ancient musty air of the tower. Her senses brought to her the brush of Nax's fur, still damp but soft, as the cat pressed under her fingers.

Soon the shapes of the other people in the chamber came into her awareness, revealed by their heat, the subtle currents of air that flowed past them, the sound of their heartbeats. Even more detail came to her. The arches of the gallery where two exhausted Donse Masters huddled. The curving stairwell that went up, and up, to where long-abandoned chambers held mouldering books, and furniture, and bones. Two cats hid half-way up. And still higher to where birds roosted on half-rotten rafters. There was something up there, on the highest floor, too.

But what interested her was the blade. She grasped it with mercusine fingers and brought it to her hand. The gasps of onlookers washed over her like a soft gust through dry leaves. They did not possess such skills, even with all the power of their source-taps.

The blade alighted in her palm. Cold to the touch, masterful craftsmanship. It fit her grip as if made for it. She'd seen the Cloak attempt to divine the name and power of a Shadline blade once. Cayne had refused to reveal any of its secrets to the man.

She looked deeper into the weapon, but not with her eyes. They were tightly shut. The subtle realms revealed finer detail than one's eyes could ever see. The hilt was covered with hide, the texture at once smooth and tactile, giving the wielder an unslipping hold. She probed deeper. The mercus vision had always revealed metal to her. This did blade had none. None at all.

"It's of bone," she said. "No steel. No iron."

"But look at it," someone said. One of the Donse Masters. "It shines like steel."

It did. But it wasn't metal.

Deeper she probed, now caressing the edge with a mercus touch. Listening closely she sought the resonances that would reveal what bolts had infused it with its power. A tinkling of ice came through quite clearly, as did the roar of wind past a window. A cold, dry smell wafted to her nose, the crisp scent of snow. Flavor, too, recalling the crystal clear icicles she used to pull from eaves of the Cherry Bottom Inn in Starside.

Deeper she probed.

Kila. I . . . are you there . . . I can't hold my thoughts. Kila?

The blade was indeed bone, with a narrow hollow channel running through it. Kila had seen sawed-through beef bones outside a butcher shop. She knew how much of the thickness was chambered through with small voids that held the bloody living tissue so desired by hounds.

This was the same, except for the fineness of these voids. Had she cut through—could she have cut through, which she doubted—they would not be visible at all. The bone would appear as solid as steel.

Upon the resonances she thought she heard a word come to her ears. A whispered roar. The name of the Shadline blade. "Tell me again," she whispered back.

Shinane!

She kept herself from gasping at the name, which any child over four years old would recognize. Having given up its name, the blade now revealed to her its mercusine power. A scholar might understand why it had the power it did, but Kila didn't need such understanding.

The bone chill the blade delivered was a heat negation bolt combined with an emotion she tagged as "persistence." Odd. Persistence seemed like it would require an ever-renewing source of energy, the way the characteristic did in humans. Kila had been blessed with an abundance of it. Or perhaps, it had been bludgeoned into her by the necessities of her voca-tion as thief. In any case, it showed again that higher mercu-sine feats required complex emotion.

She dropped the blade, and it clanked from the stones, sending echoes up to the heights of the tower, disturbing the birds who sheltered there from the storm.

Turning to her own frozen body, Kila formed the bolts needed. Simple and complex. Impossibly subtle, but she didn't think about it. Desperation always guided her, as it did now. She knew it was the needed thing.

Kila?

Plunging into her own body with mercusine fingers, she infused her flesh with heat. Immediately the bone chill struck back at her. But she was prepared with a mercusine ward. A rather simple negation of persistence: despair. It was easy to call upon, because Henley's entire presence had turned into gray despair.

She swirled her hand, forming the crimson brew of demaynic healing. It was easier now than ever, though it took longer due to Henley's smaller reservoir of mercus.

It was odd healing herself, for she felt disconnected from the lump of flesh on the table. There was no tenderness in her actions, no sympathy. Pouring the mercusine brew on the wound, she already knew it would succeed.

And so it did, the blue fading instantly from her body's eyelids, lips, and fingertips. With another flush of power, she deepened her breathing. Her heart, which had squeezed in agonizing slow pumps, lurched to a gallop.

It's done, Henley. No answer. *Henley?*

Her body's eyes opened, going wide, pupils so wide the whole of her eyes were black. Just as quickly they constricted into pinpoints. Coughing and spitting, her body twisted and spat muddy saliva onto the floor. Then she locked eyes with herself.

Henley?

I'm here. This is the strangest thing that has ever happened. Do I really look like that?

How do we . . . get back to ourselves?

Surrender.

She did.

THE HATEFUL CROWN

The effect was instant, and it made her vision swim. Quinn caught her head before it struck the table. Gian supported Henley.

The first thing Kila noticed was the cold. She had never been so chilled. The second was Nax's presence. The cat was already in her arms, and now the bond bloomed in her heart. Arms shaking, lips quivering from cold and joy, she held the cat close.

The final thing she noticed was she was still blocked from her own mercusine power. Quinn's arm was wrapped around her shoulder, and a round-faced Sensual was saying something. The word sounded like "sly."

"My name is Sigh," Kila said weakly. "Kila Sigh."

The woman was shaking her head and pointing to the floor. Kila leaned forward and finally understood. There was a young woman there, as blue as Kila had been. The Sensual wanted Kila to save Novitiate Sliy.

"I can't," she said through chattering teeth. "Fley still has my power."

"Can't you two . . ." The Sensual waved a finger back and forth between Kila and Henley. Henley's face was wan and he appeared unable to support himself without Gian's help. Kila hadn't the slightest idea how to accomplish the joining feat, and Henley did not appear to have the strength remaining to do again. But that was irrelevant, for she would not do that again. Not if it meant she must separate from Nax.

"Teach me then," the Sensual said. "The swirling technique." She cupped her hand in imitation of what Kila had done just moments before.

"You don't need to heal any wound. That is not necessary. Can you form a ward?"

Sensual Minn smiled. "That is my speciality. What senses in what proportions?"

"Sensual . . ."

"Harrisan Minn." Had the woman curtsied just now. Odd. No Sensual had ever shown Kila the slightest deference, not that she thought she'd ever deserved it. "Sensual Minn. The Shadline is infused with a perpetual bolt of persistence. The bone chill lies in wait for any intrusion, and so it will lash out to grasp you, too. A ward bolted with despair will negate it."

The woman's face turned gray at Kila's words. She licked her lips and looked at the novitiates and Sensuals around her. The Donse Master, Dunne Quiv, was eyeing Kila and the frozen novitiate with a peculiar cunning.

"Demaynic mercus," the woman breathed. "I—I couldn't."

"Then free me from Fley's mercus noose and I'll do it. But hurry. She won't last long."

The Sensual pressed her palms on her skirts, visibly trying to collect herself for the task ahead. None of the others stepped forward to volunteer. Kila wondered how much of what she'd said made sense to Dunne Quiv. The other Donse Master scowled in utter disapproval. But what could be expected of such men? Their entire world had been built on denying others what they hoarded away for themselves. Kila felt no fear of them now. She felt nothing but contempt.

Sensual Minn beckoned to her sisters and murmured instructions to them. Each was still accepting flows of mercusine from teams far away, though they did not draw upon it. Now they began to, focusing all they received to Sens Minn. It was a stunning display all by itself. Kila was no expert on how such things worked, but the implications were astounding. If mercus could be aggregated in this manner over long distances, then who knew what manner of feats could be accomplished?

Sens Minn bent over Novitiate Sliy. Kila smelled the usual charms forming around the woman. Sweet florals and calming chimes blended with warmth and the sense of having one's hair gently stroked. It was a charm, but it wouldn't be useful for poor Sliy. Kila supposed it was for those watching, especially the Donse Masters, who the woman likely mistrusted. Savvy, Kila acknowledged. Sens Minn would be vulnerable attempting this feat, and if Dunne Quiv decided to attack, she would not be able to defend herself.

Quiv was smiling, and the other Donse Master had lost his sourness. A mighty charm, indeed. Even Kila felt herself relaxing, letting go of the cold and the fear of the trauma she'd endured.

Abruptly, Sens Minn formed the ward. Quite skillfully for one who had not played with the mercusine realm of the emotions. To produce despair, one had to have felt it before.

And then Novitiate Sliy was coughing and sitting up. The bone chill was banished and her life returned. Sens Minn slumped and herself needed the other women to assist her. But she shrugged them off. "Dunne Quiv, will you help us remove Fley's force-tap on this girl?"

His lips quirked and the charm smile faded. He merely blinked at Sens Minn. Catching the breeze of the conversation, Quinn spun on the man, Black flashing. She mouthed a threat.

"That's enough, Quinn Peline!" Sens Minn barked. "Master your blade or begone. Not every disagreement can be resolved with violence."

Quinn muttered something nobody could hear. She caught herself, once again, on the verge of a reckless act. Slowly, as if she weren't in complete control of her limbs, she returned Black to its sheath. And then, to Kila's amazement, she unbuckled it and set it on the table next to Kila. "Take it. Don't give it back until you think it time."

Relieved of this strange burden, Quinn turned again to Dunne Quiv. Her hair had begun to dry, though it was caked with ash-mud. She shook it out and moved close to him, hands clasped. The smile that spread her lips was magnificent, a mimicry of her mother's. It was a courtier's smile, containing promises and falsehoods, intrigue and threat. "Dunne Quiv. Do you believe Fley a man of character?"

"I do not think on such things."

"Do you believe his aims are righteous?"

"My role is to discover things, communicate things, and to advise."

"And you think it would be a betrayal to free Kila from his . . . force-tap?"

"I think it would be precipitous. And in a storm such as this, who knows what doom might fall from the sky and strike me dead."

Kila didn't follow that part. The word "precipitous" sounded like a ten-skillet word that Father would use. She wasn't familiar with it. But she could read faces, and Quiv had just revealed that he didn't believe in anything. There was no loyalty to Fley. He served his own interests.

Kila respected that. But a way to sever Fley's tap without his help occurred to her. So simple. So terrible. "Where is my backpack?"

They found it with Pennie, who huddled forgotten in the shadows. The girl had fallen asleep, arms curled around the backpack. A sorrier sight had never been seen. Like a fabled mudlin, not a single speck of her but wasn't coated with ash-mud. When Gian tugged the backpack from her arms, it seemed green gems appeared amidst the mass of sludge. She had opened her eyes. They did not lock on Gian, or onto anything. She looked past him. "This is Kila's. You can't take it."

"I'm here," Kila called. Pennie released it.

Gian brought it to her. His jaw was tight, eyes cold. He looked like a man bound by promises he no longer believed in. She took the backpack and dug out the *vaz'on*. The hateful crown.

At the sight of it, Sensual Minn's head thrust forward and her eyes bulged with indignation. "How did you come by that? That relic was stored in the library vault. No one but the Voluptuary herself is allowed to touch such things."

Kila turned the crown this way and that, studying the tap

screws and gems. Once she had gotten it aligned, she set it on her head.

"Only a merculyn can affix it," Sens Minn said. "It will not restore your power."

"Ya think I don't know that?"

"I cannot believe you withheld that from the Way of Til," Dunne Quiv said to Minn, marveling at the *vaz'on*. Ignoring Quinn's threatening posture, he moved closer, careful to keep his hands clasped non-threateningly behind his back. Kila had no fear of him.

"Someone, anyone, bolt me in."

When no one moved to help, she pushed from the table and tottered on her bare feet. Kil's-beans was she tired. "I've worn this hat before. After the shriving, that old bird Thine played with me for a while." Just remembering that caused her head to ache.

"Shriving, you say?" Sens Minn said, voice cracking. "They *shrove* you?"

"Yes, yes. The urn with the boiling water. Then they tapped this on m'skull and had a round of fun with it. Are ya gonna help me or not?"

Quiv was studying them both very closely, calculation in his eyes. He didn't move to intercede. But he was the first to understand why Kila was asking to have the *vaz'on* placed on her head.

"A better solution, all things considered," he said. "I'll do it."

And he did.

"Cut him if he claims my mercus," she said to Gian as the stabs of pain thrust into the seven points on her skull. Falling back onto the table, she lost her senses momentarily as the taps pierced into her brain and the mercus power of the *vaz'on* laid claim to her.

The spell passed and she regained her feet. Since nobody was controlling her through the *vaz'on* she wasn't paralyzed. The mercus Fley had been pulling from her abruptly stopped, as his force-tap was destroyed by the relic. His presence was very distant now. But she could feel the mercus fully. It was hers, her own power, just beyond the glass that the *vaz'on* placed between her and touching it.

"Remove it," she commanded.

Dunne Quiv hesitated only a moment. Surely he knew how much power he could draw from her if he merely reached for it. But such a decision would also be "precipitous" and he struck Kila as the type of man who liked to keep many options open for as long as he could.

With an arched brow and slight smile, he touched the gems. Again the pain, and again the final release. She removed it with her own hands and shook blood from the tips of the screws. Quiv eyed the relic with something that wasn't quite hunger, but desire nonetheless.

Kila gave the *vaz'on* to Sens Minn. "Use it on Dunne Yples now. And I think we can all agree it best if we not remove it."

Now Dunne Quiv did object. "It will be too great a temptation to let him remain alive wearing that thing. Any merculyn could tap his power."

"Then the *vaz'on* must be warded . . . somehow." Looking to Sens Minn, she raised an eyebrow. "You are skilled with wards. Surely you can manage something."

"But she will have access to him!" Quiv whined. And it was more of a whine than an objection. The other Donse Master—Dunne Mackle—had moved forward, his mouth opening and closing as he tried to form an argument. Kila glared at them and brought into existence a bright white light that hung above the assembled merculyns.

"I trust Sens Minn more than I do any of you Til's-boys. I suggest you accustom yourselves to that fact." She sounded a little too much like Quinn just there. Ah well. It worked. The men backed into the little gallery.

Sens Minn placed the *vaz'on* on Dunne Yples's head. Kila went to the man. He looked so frail now. She frowned, recalling the malice he'd radiated like light. Hatred. Righteous hatred. The evil of the Donse Masters was no surprise to her. They were corrupt. The Hargothe had been particularly vile, twisted as he was by his insatiable thirst for power. Had he been here, she wondered what he might have done to claim Yples's power for himself.

But Donse Masters were just men. Some, she supposed, even believed in Til. And nowhere in her experience had a Donse Master taught hatred in such a pure form as she'd felt from Yples. Intolerance, yes. The Way of Til had innumerable rules for how men and women were supposed to live and comport themselves. Most of it was designed to deliver coin into each Abbey's coffers. But what Yples had demonstrated did not align with mere corruption or simple greed.

Something else had seeped into the man's heart. All this time she'd believed that she had unlocked his hate. But what if that black hate had already been there?

"I feel sorry for him," Henley said. He stood next to her, swaying. She put an arm around his waist. They were of a height now. When had that happened? She was a year or two older than he, but his face—his eyes—had the hollow look of someone who has endured and seen too many horrors for a single life.

"I don't think he is Yples anymore," she said.

The *vaz'on* taps went in. The man did not waken. His only reaction was to inhale sharply, but soon his breathing returned to its unsteady cadence. The power surging from him to Fley cut off.

Kila smiled, imagining the fool out there in the storm, reveling in his godlike glow, suddenly severed from it. She hoped he'd been trying her hovering trick at the time.

Someone ran into the tower from outside. A young man in Sensuals robes, wearing an oil-cloak. His hair was plastered to his head. Eyes wide, he skittered to a stop, taking in the strange tableau of the great Hall of Kil. "Sens Minn, there were runners from Garden Tower. They've survivors buried deep in the rubble. But no one has the strength to lift the debris. Pol's Fifth is empty, ma'am."

"The Coin moved us to the Vale," Henley said. "They are sheltering from the storm in a cave. Fley is surely going there."

"We're too exhausted to walk, most of us," Sens Minn said. "Even if we could, it would be half a day's trek. Release the source-tap teams from Ori's Home to help dig them out."

"Yes, Sensual, but . . ."

"Go on."

"Most of those merculyns were unconscious when I left. They had just collapsed when the main battle had ended. Some of the hellers they were given seemed unwilling to release."

The woman was exhausted. But she had her responsibilities. And she had a sense of duty. Those were Til's-boys buried in the Tower, yet she felt compelled to help them. To Kila it was as admirable as it was strange.

Dunne Quiv was arguing with Dunne Mackle who was intent on waiting for Highest Fley to return. In the end, Quiv won. Sensual Minn organized her people. Novitiate Sliy had difficulty standing.

"Leave her with us," Kila said. "Henley and Pennie will stay with me, too."

"You mean to stay in this ruin?" Quiv asked. "Surely the Garden Tower would be—"

"You'll be looking for shelter there," Kila said. "No doubt the Sensuals will offer the hospitality you deserve. But I'm not moving an inch until I've slept and eaten and warmed myself to my bones."

He held her gaze for a beat longer, not challenging, just searching. Sensual Minn shook her head and raised her hands in surrender. Smart woman.

"Leave Dunne Yples here," Kila said. "Place a ward if you must."

Sensual Minn spent less than a minute constructing the ward. Kila paid it no attention at all. She had no desire to access Yples's power, and she knew Henley didn't either.

Before they all departed, Sens Minn brought Kila and Quiv together. "We must talk, all of us, soon. The fellstorm is weakening already. Perhaps tomorrow."

"And what shall we discuss?" Dunne Quiv asked.

"Assuming that Highest Fley has survived, we must decide what to do with him."

Dunne Quiv looked to where Bone Chill still lay where Kila had dropped it. Kila knew he wanted it. She shook her head, ever-so-slightly. He shrugged. "Very well. Let's see who we can rescue from the Tower. We can convene there in a day or two."

"You can come here." Kila turned away from them and didn't look back until the great iron-bound entry door boomed shut. The echoes went on and on.

41

I'VE SEEN YOUR DREAMS

The hall was leaky and cold. But the fire was hot, and the orange light inviting. If they could find bedding, Kila knew it would make for a cozy den. Her stomach rumbled. Even the tables looked somewhat appetizing.

"Anyone have any food?"

Henley didn't say anything. He simply held up a satchel and shook it. Quinn collected it and dug through the contents. She brought out bread, some fruit, a wedge of cheese. These delectables vanished within minutes. Kila's share wasn't enough, but it was something.

She had a hunch there was more food to be had here. But climbing those rickety winding stairs would have to wait until morning. Gian had moved Henley close to the fire and sat chatting with him. Novitiate Sliy had propped her back against the thick table legs and was rubbing her calves to warm them. Pennie joined the boys, and was now combing through her curly red locks with her fingers, removing clumps of dried mud. She looked all about, mouth open in an expression of deep listening. Kila didn't have the energy to attempt a healing on the girl. She'd see to it in the morning.

Quinn stood like a statue by the table where Kila had been frozen. She wasn't looking at the fire. In fact, she still held a heel of bread, apparently forgotten, in her hand.

"It pulls at me," she said as Kila joined her. Black lay on the table where Kila had set it aside. She snatched it up now, determined to fulfill Quinn's request. She would not return it until Quinn had shown some mastery of herself. The raven-haired woman swallowed hard, eyes luminous with feeling.

"I am not as strong as I thought I was. It was leading me toward something." Quinn pulled her gaze from the weapon in Kila's hand to Kila's face. "Toward its own desires. It always wants blood."

"Few blades want much else, I expect. It's what they're for." And now she remembered Cayne, lost out in the ash-barrens. With a flick of mercusine, she drew Bone Chill blade to her hand. To call it "dangerous" would be stupid. All blades were. But this one was another of the undiscovered Shadline weapons. Like Cayne. Like Fallo's blade. On the voyage to the island, Quinn had told her about the Cloak's shock when he revealed the name of Fallo's blade: Telt.

Kila had thought it a large story, probably a crock of atlen dung. Until she had heard Bone Chill whisper its true name.

Shinane.

If Fallo's blade was truly Telt, then two of the three Dragon Tooth Blades of legend had been found.

Kila couldn't help but think the appearance of these blades —at this time—portended ill for her.

"What's this?" Gian said. Then a gasp.

He was removing something from Henley's pack. Round, blood red, shining in the fire like an enormous garnet. He inhaled sharply as he turned the object this way and that.

"Dragon scales," Henley said. "I slipped on one as I trekked across the barrens. There's a whole ribcage out there to the north. You've got several there. Nested together."

Kila and Quinn went to inspect the scales. Novitiate Sliy, too, clambered to her feet and came to see. Even as the heat of the flames washed over Kila, a chill crept over her arms and scalp. "The flames, the charred bone, the ash," she said softly, reciting part of the prophecy of Dem-Kisk. "That could've been me in the thinnie cavern."

"It could be the library at the Home," Sliy said. Her voice quavered.

"The black feather, the red scale, the parting mist," Henley continued the passage from the Theb. "Here's a red scale. I suppose."

"The fallen tower, the creaking gate, the bone chill," Quinn said, finishing the prophecy. "Til's Tower has fallen, it sounds like."

"Bone Chill," Sliy said, teeth chattering.

Kila still held the blade. It fit her hand so nicely. "So we're still missing the black feather, the parting mist, and the creaking gate."

"If it means anything at all," Henley said softly. He didn't sound hopeful.

There was a long silence as they watched reflections dance from the dragon scales. Gian slid them apart and handed them around until all of them held one. Kila pressed the scale to her cheek. It was warm.

You know what has black feathers? Nax asked. The cat had

curled up in Pennie's lap. The girl stroked Nax's fur, all past fear forgotten.

Kila didn't want to answer.

Nax decided the obvious wasn't clear enough.

Ravens. Ravens have black feathers.

They do, Kila sent, admitting nothing.

But she didn't need to admit anything for Nax to know her mind. The cat's response came quietly. *I've seen your dreams. I've seen the raven.*

42

MEDALLION DESCENDED

So this was what the One God could do. And this was likely an unnoticeable fraction of what He could do. Such power was impossible to conceive of, even as Fley bathed in it.

How had Yples transformed himself into that ghastly monster? How had the girl flown? These feats eluded Fley, and it frustrated him. For he now possessed both of their wells of power. Granted, the largest portion was pouring into the Sink Gem. The One God be praised that the relic had remained within Til's Tower's grasp or none of this would be possible.

Fley's mercus skills lay in the mundane. He had managed to light lanterns and candles at rather a young age. It took him only five years, when his peers had struggled for a decade or more. He could warm a cup of tea, though it usually wasn't worth the effort of concentration. Charms and willshift had always eluded him. He had never had much of a sense of smell, so it was difficult for him to manifest them in such bolts.

Pushing things around with the mercus was impossible without at least three source-taps. But now . . . Now everything he saw was at his command. This was power! He saw a boulder ahead the size of a cow. With no effort at all, he lifted it and hurled it at the wall separating Kil's Fifth from Pol's.

He was reward with a satisfying crash, and an enormous section of the old wall broke away. The boulder continued to roll and disappeared into the verdant green jungle beyond. He strode through, feeling like a god himself.

The mercus spark of the Spinsters beckoned to him. Surely they felt him approaching, too. They felt their approaching doom. This made him smile.

The protective dome that kept out the rain was holding up well. He'd studied the Sensual's trick the entire walk to Ori's Home earlier in the day. Clever business. But with his abundance of power, he not only kept the rain off him, he'd heated his clothes and dried them.

The fellstorm was flailing at him, offering its final blows. But already the wind had lessened. He could not but feel it was now retreating in defeat. Appropriate. All that remained was the Vale and the Way of Pol.

Three-quarters of an hour later, he found their hidey-hole. A few Spinsters had gathered just outside it, eyes to the sky and assessing whether it was safe for to return to their stilt-huts in the Vale.

It was not safe, for Fley had destroyed the huts as he'd passed them by.

A gray-headed woman stepped forward to greet him. He recognized the Coin. She had met with him once, long ago, when he'd first taken his seat as Highest of Til. She had offered pleasantries salted with vague warnings and hints that Fley would suffer serious repercussions if he meddled in the affairs of Pol. He had been more blunt, and simply told her he did not see the Way of Pol as legitimate and that one day she would come to serve him.

That day had arrived.

Of course, she could see the power flowing through him. To anyone of the slightest mercus spark he would be a luminous god. Spreading his arms wide, he smiled. "My children, I have come."

The Coin smirked and fiddled with the medallion at her throat. Her white hair was close-cropped, a flop of snowy silk that did nothing to soften her masculine features. "Highest Fley, I see that you have tapped into two sources of power. And is that a Sink Gem I see in your hands? Strange, I thought all of those had been destroyed long ago. But you wear hellers, as well. A bit excessive, don't you think?"

Fley wished he had more skill with charms and mental tricks. A strong willshift to bring her to her knees would be delightful. Instead he merely heated her spine, curling his fingers into a fist as the delicious power flowed from him.

A team of linked Spinsters immediately negated the bolt. Two of them were at the mouth of the cavern, and seven more were inside. This was a stalling effort so that the others might hide. Laughable. None with the spark could elude him.

It irritated him that he would have to squander these women's lives. But since he now possessed more power than he could ever use, a little waste could be tolerated. His bolts of flame were full-force, all the mercus his capabilities could handle. It burst from his hands and engulfed the Coin and all the Spinsters around her.

There were screams. He didn't relish them. He'd never

been one to inflict pain for its own sake. That had been Seeker Yan's secret pleasure. Three of the women became ash, their mercus drifting away to nothingness.

Only the Coin remained. He stopped his attack, for he could not read her bolts while blasting her with his own. But there were none. She merely held to her medallion, face hard as granite. Fury enlivened her eyes, but drained blood from her face until she looked carved from ivory.

The medallion must be a ward-skeen of some sort. Somehow it had protected her. No matter.

"You will assemble your devotees and Spinsters and conduct them to the tower. There, you will turn over all your medallions, all your mercusine relics, and don the robes of Sisters of the One God. The name of Pol will never been spoken again. The tossing of coins and sooth-saying will cease. I have come to deliver us into a new age."

"Soon it will tread upon fields of red," the Coin said. "Is that not what Roya Reth said to you? I have not seen the red grass of Dem-Kisk yet, Highest Fley. You presume that your victory today means something it does not."

With a fluid motion, she removed her medallion and flung it into the air. "Will this man survive this day?"

Her words startled him, recalling to his mind Roya Reth's cryptic prophecy. How had she known?

Spies! But how could they have known? Unless Reth had been speaking to others. To the Favored. Perhaps they had some means to pass messages to the Spinsters.

The medallion spun as it climbed. It flew much higher than it should have. And when it reached the top of its arc, the clouds parted and a beam of pure sunlight struck it. Glimmers and glares of golden light shot in all directions. He was forced to cover his eyes.

But the Coin merely watched, blue eyes unblinking. And by following the path of her gaze, he knew the medallion descended.

Enough of this. With his crane bracelet, he summoned a gust of wind that would carry the medallion out to the ocean. The trees fluttered and bent, foliage torn loose by the fellstorm flew all around. The Coin staggered, but was supported by answering forces from her hidden merculyns.

But the medallion fell straight. It landed on the wet stone path between the Coin and Fley. A thunderous gong sounded, and the ground trembled. Doubt surged in him, weakening his knees even as the mercus continued to fill him from toes to scalp.

A flick of his eyes told him the result. Pol frowned.

The Coin laughed, turned, and walked away.

At that instant, Kila Sigh's power vanished from his control. The shock of loss dropped him to one knee, as if a heavy cable he'd been pulling had suddenly been cut loose.

The Coin stepped over the ashes of the dead Spinsters, clicking her tongue and shaking her head. "Spinsters, to me. I require more source-taps."

Fley climbed to his feet. Even with the girl's power gone, he was full of Yples's seemingly infinite reserves. Though it did seem slightly less than before. He adjusted the flow into his Sink Gem and once again formed the bolts that would burn the interior of the cave and all who hid within in.

Yples' power vanished.

His bolts fell apart, the heat billowing from him and blowing away in the fellstorm's trailing wind.

He still had the hellers. But the contrast between the supreme power of a moment ago and this weak, vague spark that remained, left him gasping for breath. A sob caught in his throat.

The Coin emerged from the cavern, now luminous with the power she drew from twenty Spinsters and devotees behind her. The medallion flew from the path and landed in her hand. She affixed it to her necklace.

With a tilt of her head, several vertebrae in her neck popped.

"As Coin my responsibility is to emulate Pol's impartiality in all things. I see only what is. I serve only Pol's will, which is that everything proceeds as it must."

Fley summoned and threw fire, a weak spout of flame that did not reach her. He stepped backward, now looking for escape.

"Pol is not vengeful," she intoned.

He understood. Fley had always been insightful when it came to hearing what a person meant beneath the words they said. Everyone had desires, needs, aims. His in this moment was to survive. He'd tasted true power. He would get it back. Whatever had happened to the girl and Yples, he would regain his control over them.

"Pol is not vengeful," the Coin said again. A hint, surely.

He dropped to his knees, letting the Sink Gem roll away. Submission would gain him time. "I beg for mercy, Coin. The power was too much. That madman had control of me. Your toss of the coin freed me. You see that, don't you? You must."

Her lips quirked. "Pol is not merciful."

Her mercus bolt burned him, and in the waning moments of agony, he called out to the One God.

He received no answer.

43

WRITTEN IN METAL

Kila awoke from a strange dream. A raven had been circling the Citadel in Starside. But *she* had been the raven. And then she'd been inside the Citadel, looking out over the moon-washed city.

Scratching and yawning she picked herself off the floor. The fire had burned low, but orange embers still shed enough heat to warm the others. Quinn and Henley and Gian all slept, though Quinn muttered, childlike, in her dreams. Dunne Yples slept, too. His breath had slowed, and now rose and fell with the first peaceful breaths he'd drawn in . . . she had no idea. Novitiate Sliy had bound his head, concealing the wound. She was still awake, facing away from Kila and bent over something in her hands. She rocked back and forth as she toyed with the object.

Pennie was asleep under the table. Both Nax and Huff were sleeping atop her slight form. Nax claimed the child needed the warmth, and she had apparently bullied Huff into joining her.

And then there was Oly, who had slipped off to who knew where. Kila didn't much care if she ever saw that nasty animal again.

It was midnight, Kila knew. She had always had good sense of the time of the day. Had she still been in Starside, she'd be creeping along the rooftops, spying on passersby below, looking for a mark. A pang rose in her heart.

She pushed through the huge door, negating the squeaks of its great hinges with afterthought bolts of silence. The air outside was crisp, fresh. It smelled of the distant jungle and mud. The ash-barrens had quickly swallowed the excess rain once the storm had abated. She suspected it would be dusty in a fortnight.

Her feet squelched through the damp ash that covered the approaching road. When she finally came to the site of the battle, she was disappointed to see that nothing distinguished it from any other place. The ash must have flowed in and covered all evidence of the mercus impacts that had scarred the land.

On an out-breath, she closed her eyes and listened: to the breeze passing her ears, to the tiny riot of the jungle to the south. And beneath that, she heard the hum. The whisper. Her mercus touch searched in the mire, and with a sharp flick, she pulled Cayne free. The blade flew to her, shedding all filth behind it. Catching it, she sheathed it.

Relief settled over her. One thing complete.

The mercus spark of every merculyn on the island was visible to her now, like tiny stars glommed in tight constellations here and there. The Spinsters were not the smallest. Ori's Home was sparse with sparks. How many had Yples killed there?

But she turned toward the Vale, letting her senses roam. Fley had been there. She'd felt his diminished power continue for a while. And then it had simply vanished beneath a sudden uprising. Henley said it was the Coin. If the woman had killed Fley, Kila wanted to meet her. Thank her.

But . . . she didn't think that was going to happen.

She'd come here to learn. There was nothing more for her to learn here. She turned back toward the tower and gazed to the topmost window. Just as she'd seen in her mirror, there was a light burning there. Now was as good a time as any to investigate, before the others awoke. Something told her that whoever waited in the room waited only for her.

A glimmer to her right caught her eye. Glass. She discovered a lantern in the muck. A withered, leathery hand clutched the top ring. The rest of the lantern-bearer was lost in the mud. A memory of light made a flush of heat pass through her.

The dead man was none too willing to release the lantern. Kila had to pry his fingers from it, one by one. But she recalled how the light had hurt Yples's hell-form. It had stood against hate. That had to be good. Besides, like the *vaz'on*, she didn't want it to fall into anyone else's hands.

She re-entered Kil's Keep, plucked up her backpack, and began the long, winding ascent. Nax joined her. They exchanged no words. None were needed.

The steps were made of some impossibly hard wood. Seemingly impervious to rot. She paused and listened to them. There. A mercusine infusion of a property she could only describe as "stone-ness." The surfaces were smooth and dusty, cold under her bare feet. What made Kila's stomach clench was the fact that each plank thrust from the stone wall, unsupported from below and unconnected with any other tread.

Kila respected heights, but she hadn't ever been afraid of them. Nevertheless, she would have welcomed a handrail to guard the ever-growing plummet to her right.

The steps became harder to see as she ascended, leaving the great hall below in a haze of fire-tinged gloom, ever shrinking. Her mercus senses remained alive, like cat ears perked for the slightest sound.

Nothing yet. As she climbed she discovered she was chewing her tongue, a nervous habit she'd picked up recently. She forced herself to stop.

Occasional landings gave entry to balcony walkways that circled the tower. Doors punctuated the interior walls, letting into forgotten rooms. But no light shone from beneath them, and the dust at each landing spoke of no recent footfalls in an age.

At the top, she came to a plain wooden door. It was locked. She felt the strange familiarity arise, the same as when she'd seen the tower in the mirror, the feeling that she'd been here before.

The person behind that door would have answers. If only she knew what the question was.

More likely, they would seek to capture her and use her. She hadn't met anyone of power who hadn't. Except maybe Her Enlightened Majesty, and Kila was not at all convinced that she was the benevolent friend she seemed to be. Kila vaguely remembered being sick on the rug in Her Enlightened's private audience chamber. She couldn't remember why.

She knocked. No answer.

She knocked again, harder. "Who's in there?"

With her heightened senses she listened. The soft movement of fabric against fabric, the low creak of a footstep on floorboards. A sliver of light oozed from beneath the door.

There was a keyhole. Her mercus vision showed that the mechanism within was missing all its tumblers. No . . . They were there; they just weren't made of metal.

Kil's teeth, this was frustrating.

Unlimbering her backpack, she invoked a soft glow so she could better see. The canvas roll of lockpicking tools was nestled next to the mirror and her bank draft for 3415 gold Ravens. So much coin, so little meaning.

Grunting a humorless laugh she unfurled the canvas roll. Wen had carried it for years, but Kila had learned to use each of the tools. Not to much purpose, since Wen didn't like them breaking into houses. Except that one time . . . She shook away the memory.

Her fingers drifted over the points and hooks and wires inside. Withdrawing a fine steel probe, she rolled the canvas and clamped it between her teeth.

She closed her eyes and slipped the probe into the keyhole. Her mercus senses were alive, and the glow of the steel tool shined with a bluish haze. The brass lockplate hummed and glowed, too. Kila had never known a locking mechanism to employ anything but metal, most commonly iron—especially in Cheapsgate—but also brass, steel, and other alloys.

But that wasn't entirely true. There was one other lock that had tumblers of an unknown material. The lock in the Rose Hall at the Baths of Ori in Starside. It was meant to be a test of her skill. She had failed to open that one.

She shed the thought, as it was not helping. And neither was the probe. There didn't seem to be any tumblers inside the lock at all. She unrolled her canvas and selected a hooked pick. But dig as she might, there was nothing inside to discover.

She sat back on her heels and stared at the lock. Absently, she returned the hooked pick to its pocket. If there wasn't in mechanism in the lock, then what would the purpose of a key be? Why have a hole at all?

Again the feeling of familiarity struck her. Had she been here before? But no. That was impossible.

Her fingers slid across the other tools, as if one of them would inspire an insight to help solve this annoying obstacle. She didn't want to blast the door apart with the mercus. That would be rude, even for her.

Her finger paused on a tiny mirror. A clever tool, the sliver of reflective glass was attached to the end of a probe, its shaft a series of ever-smaller tubes allowing it to be extended.

It wasn't a lock-pick, but a way to look around corners or . . . She had never noticed before, but the glass emitted a soft, yellowish glow. Gold? But mirrors weren't gold-backed. They were silvered.

Frowning, she pulled the mirror tool free of its sleeve and held it close. Astonished, she brought it closer still, until her eye was nearly pressing to it. "There are words written here, Naxie." Written in metal. Behind the glass of the mirror. Behind the silvering, in fact. The letters would never be visible without the mercus vision.

"By Kil and his axe-edged teeth!"

Fallo's words fluttered up in her mind, like sweet smoke from a long ago cookfire.

"Wen wanted you to have this." He handed her the canvas roll. "He said there was a note inside. He said it was . . . I don't know."

Kila had studied the tools since then, but hadn't discovered any message. But she'd been looking for a note. On paper. And then events had turned into the knotty mess they always did for her, and the idea of a message in the canvas roll had escaped her memory. Until now.

This is boring, Nax sent.

An odd heat now coursed from the base of Kila's spine to the back of her neck and crawled over her scalp. If she still had hair, it would have stood straight up. The fiery chill seemed to burst from the crown of her head, and a gasp escaped her lips.

The familiar feeling converged with a rising certainty. She had never believed in the force of destiny, but she could not deny that she had been meant to discover this message at *this* moment. Father's lockpicking tools and this door were a match. But not in the obvious way. The key to this lock was the message.

She stood and repeated the words she'd just discovered. "Open for Kil's daughter."

Something clicked inside the lock. The door whispered open, showing a lushly appointed apartment within. A fire burned in the hearth, sending red and orange flickers to play across the rugs and tapestries softening the floor and stonework walls.

Kila stepped through, welcoming the dry warmth. Her mercus touch firmed on Cayne's hilt, ready to throw death at the slightest provocation. But again the feeling of familiarity came over her, and she did not feel threatened by the man standing near the window.

"The little raven has come to light upon my sill again. Welcome. Ah, even a Beloved One. An auspicious moment.

I've felt your feats, I've seen visions. Yet I do not know how you are called."

Kila regarded the man, taking in his odd frame. He was very tall, at least seven feet, but thin and long of limb. His clothes were like something she'd seen in mummer's plays, voluminous sleeves, and a lapel slashing diagonally across his chest.

The jacket hung to his knees, exposing silk maroon pantaloons, tightly cuffed at the ankle. His shoes were slim, velvet green, and drawn to points at the toes. His face continued in the same vertical fashion as his body, narrow, drawn down at the chin and out at the nose. Lank gray hair clung to his head and flopped in weak strands upon his shoulders. His eyes drew her focus, for they were emerald green and asparkle with amusement.

"Your name, miss . . . ?"

"Kila."

He chuckled. "Someone named you *Kila?* That's a bit on the nose, if you take my meaning."

"I don't take your meaning. Who are you? Why do I feel like I should know you and this place?"

"Please, sit. And do put that lantern aside. I have rather unpleasant memories of that thing. I warn you, do not attempt to light it, for it will not willingly release your mercusine flow."

That explained what had happened to the lantern-bearer.

He motioned to a pair of chairs, and with an upswelling of mercus, dragged them into the center of the floor, facing the fire. "The cat will prefer your lap, I presume."

Kila sat, putting the lantern on the floor next to her. She

kept a wary eye on the man. She was sure she'd never seen him before. And yet . . . "Have you been to Starside?"

"Not in an age. Not in an age." He clasped his hands on his lap and looked at his shoes for a moment, gathering his thoughts. "But time swirls differently sometimes, and it isn't impossible that you recall this meeting." He rushed on before she could challenge this ridiculous statement. "But never mind that. You want to know who I am. I am Annisforl, Highest of Kil. He raised his eyes to meet Kila's. And you, my dear, are the Champion of Kil, the so-called Despised God, whose blood courses through your veins even now."

She blinked at him, understanding nothing.

"Kila," he said softly. "Kil-ah."

Kila smirked. "You are as clever as any Cheapsgate scoundrel I ever met. Do you think you're the first to notice Kil's name inside mine? But Kil sounds like 'kill' and Kila rhymes with 'smile-ah'." That's how she preferred it, anyway. The way Father and Wen had said it.

"Did your father ever tell you about your mother?"

Pain lanced through Kila's head and she bent double. Annisforl caught her as she tipped forward and was sick on the carpet. She'd done this same thing in Her Enlightened's audience room high up in the Citadel. "Why is everyone so interested in my father?" she said, coughing and wishing she had some water.

Annisforl pushed Kila gently back into her chair. Nax sent a ruffle of annoyance through the bond. She had been sleeping quite comfortably when Kila had spilled her on the floor.

Annisforl hefted himself from his chair and swirled a mercus bolt over her sick-up. It vanished, leaving the scent of lavender in the air. He stepped in front of her, his body blocking the firelight. In silhouette he was a slim shadow, impossibly tall. His eyes gleamed as if lit from within. "I didn't ask about your father. I asked about your mother."

Wincing, Kila pressed her fists to her temples. "He was a locksmith, then a hunter, then a thief. That's all there is to tell."

"You are occluded."

"That's what Sensual Thine and the Voluptuary said. What does it mean?"

"I am going to restrain you for a moment. Do not be alarmed. And please don't stab me with Fate Breaker. . . . And don't roast me with mercus fire."

A band of invisible iron gripped her around shoulders, immobilizing her arms and securing her to the chair. The bolts of mercus were strong, and intricate.

"Kil's teeth!" Kila said. "What is this about?" Her head was swimming and the chamber was too hot. Her brow was damp, but her skin felt cold. "I think I'm going to be sick again."

Nax hissed.

"All will be well, Beloved One," Annisforl said. "Your mistress is occluded, prevented from remembering her mother. You see the pain that causes? I will alleviate it."

What is he doing? Nax sent. *Why do you allow it?*

"Your mother, Kila," Annisforl said, driving a verbal spike through her temples. "Your mother. Your mother. Your mother."

She thrust her heels into the rug and nearly tipped the chair over backward in an involuntary convulsion. Annisforl held onto her arms and set her upright.

Kila's vision blurred with tears, and her tongue curled with bile.

"It will take but a moment," Annisforl said, voice soft and gentle. His haze of mercusine grew and he placed a dry, rough hand on Kila's forehead.

With a plunge just like that of the Hargothe, he speared into her mind. "There it is, a thing of beauty in its own way," he said happily. "And to think I trained for seventeen years to perform this feat for you. The force of destiny ushers us all toward unseeable ends."

Kila did not see the bolts of mercus the man used, for her mind erupted with red light and liquid fire scalded the inside of her head, searing away all thought and sensation.

A BLACK-HAIRED WOMAN swims in the mountain pond, a waterfall plunging into mist behind her. Father stands on the shore, watching. Kila holds his hand.

Kila knows her.

"Mother?"

The memory seems hollow and echoey, remembered from a long distance and through a span of years much longer than Kila's life.

"Mother?"

She sloshes into the water, ignoring the crystal chill biting into her feet and shins. Father does not let go of her hand, but he does not follow her. His grip tightens. "Sweetlight, don't."

Kila strains against his granite hold. Her other hand stretches toward her mother, who treads water just out of reach.

It was like looking into a mirror, seeing her own face on the woman. Those were Mother's eyes, infinite in their depths and speaking of timelessness, as if everything the woman had ever seen had collected there.

"Let her come to me, Wenton Sigh," Mother says. "You are dead and have no further claim to her."

Kila looks back to him, sees pain etched on his face. Love, too.

"Please, Father."

"Beware, Kila. She is selfish."

"Please."

Relenting, he releases her. And vanishes.

Kila spills into the lake. She surfaces, coughing and choking, the chill water stinging her eyes.

"Father Kil's blood runs thickly through you, child," the woman says, wrapping Kila into a comforting embrace. Kila returns it, disappointed to discover her mother such a wisp of nothing, just like herself. Other people's mothers were substantial, warm, dry. Clothed in more than their hair.

"You were once accustomed to this vale," Mother says. "You swam with me, never needing breath. You climbed the cliffs and leapt with the falls, and your days were endless laughter and nights dreamless slumber. Until your father returned to claim you. And then accursed Til rubbed all memory of me from your mind."

They are behind the falls now. Kila didn't remember swimming under, but the cavern pool is as familiar to her as the Warren den she'd shared with her brother. She clambers from the water, shivering, teeth chattering. She wraps her arms around herself and huddles on the smooth stone at the pool's edge. The falls fill the chamber with thunder and mist.

Mother swims close, takes Kila's hand. "Stay with me. Til cannot touch you here."

"I remember you now," Kila says. And she does. She remembers the endless cycle of days, of purposeless youth. The sleepy sun-washed mornings, the ice-lodged winters, the fragrant falls, and raw trout and berries and wild onion. She lived here as feral as a Cheapsgate hound. And mother had taught her nothing. For mother *knew* nothing. The accumulation of time in her eyes is not wisdom at all.

"It is lonely here," the water spirit says.

"I will visit," Kila says. "Someday."

She feels hollow. Like the abandoned tower of Kil's Keep. Strong, old, neglected. Empty.

"Don't go!" Semūin begs. She begins to glow with violet light. Beautiful, wondrous. But cold. Kila senses the allure swirling all around. It is easy to dispel. And in the sour air left behind, Kila feels only pity for her mother.

"Goodbye, Mother. Goodbye, Semūin."

SHE OPENED her eyes to find Annisforl leaning over her, face crinkled with concern. Nax sat upon her lap, also watching. A flicker of relief and amusement crossed Annisforl's face. He straightened and tucked each hands into the opposite sleeve.

"So?" he asked, "Who is she? Who is your mother?"

"Semūin," Kila said.

"Did you say your mother is Semūin?" Quinn asked. The woman stood in the doorway, one hand gripping what looked like a broken-off chair leg. Gian stood next to her, his own blade in hand. His eyes were flat.

Annisforl did not pay them any attention. Surely he had wards set on the approach to his door to alert him of intruders. His gazed was fixed on Kila, the revelation of her mother's name deepening the crow's feet at the corners of his eyes.

Kila merely nodded in response to Quinn's question. The return from that weird dream to this room atop Kil's Keep had been instantaneous. She was left feeling vague and sleepy. But the memory of her mother did not seem odd to her. She'd always known that, hadn't she?

But no. To have a mythical water spirit—and one not noted for mercy toward mortals—for a mother was strange. Wasn't it?

Gian pulled back, face souring. There is resignation there, too, as if he acknowledged a truth he had already guessed but hadn't admitted. He turned away and descended the winding stair.

Annisforl's lips pursed as he considered her revelation. "You do not seem surprised or happy to finally know your mother."

"I don't know her. My memories are like remembering a dream." She stroked Nax, letting the cat's soft ears slide between her fingers. "I don't feel her."

But she did feel something. A pang in her heart. She wished she'd stayed with Father on the shore instead of pulling toward her mother. She wished she'd memorized his face. "He called me 'Sweetlight'. I had forgotten about that." And had his voice always been so gentle when he'd spoken to her? Had he always spoken love directly into her like that? How could she have been deaf to that? Now her eyes ached and she felt again his loss and suddenly missed her brother and their innocent days of thievery.

"Enter, Quinn Peline," Annisforl said. "And you others, too."

Soon, all but Gian and Dunne Yples had crowded into the Highest of Kil's chamber. Pennie's eyes turned toward the ceiling and her head tilted slightly as she reached with her unskilled senses to feel the room. The others eyed Annisforl with open distrust.

"You could have helped us," Henley said. "If you were Kila's ally all along, you could have done something."

"Alas, I am sealed to this chamber by wards and charms not even I can see. The Way of Kil was desperate, and all were sacrificed that I might live and fulfill my duty." He rubbed his palms together. "And now I have done that." With a swift jerk, he removed a garnet ring from his pinky and held it out to Kila. "This is yours now."

Kila did not think before she grasped. Annisforl sighed as he released it, like a man finally setting down an enormous burden.

He said, "The prophecy has not yet been satisfied. But it will be. For good or ill, who can say?"

"About that," Kila started. "We have red-scales and—"

Annisforl shushed her. "I don't know. I don't have any foresight. But look to your companions for answers." He bowed slow. "Lumne calls me to her wakeless realm. Kila Sigh, Highest of Kil, I bid you farewell."

And then he turned to dust.

44

IT WILL BE GLORIOUS

She had planned to leave. To dymense back to Starside and get some answers from Marlow and Her Enlightened Majesty. But dymensing was apparently not a trick easily mastered. So far Kila had managed to give herself a roaring headache and sear her lungs on acrid green smoke.

It was Novitiate Sliy who told her of the visitors coming. When Kila asked how the woman knew, she demurred and said it was only logical thought that informed her opinion, but that, nonetheless, Kila should perhaps clean herself up and make herself presentable to the new Voluptuary, the Coin, and the acting Highest of Til.

Henley had watched the exchange, and when Sliy retreated from Kila's esteemed presence, he told her of coin-talkers. Which meant Novitiate Sliy might be a spy for the Coin, posing as a novitiate. Such intrigue.

But it meant that the Coin, at least, wanted Kila forewarned. She assumed that Sliy had told the Coin about her being named Highest of Kil, which was like being Queen of

Pebbles. Meaningless, since there were no other followers of Kil. She would not go about demanding people bow and scrape, and since she had no idea what doctrine the Way of Kil would promote, she wouldn't be seeking converts any time soon. It was all very ridiculous.

Except Sliy, and Quinn, and even Henley seemed to take it seriously in their own ways. Pennie had even taken to calling Kila "Highest", which irritated her to no end.

"He's called the Despised God for a reason," Kila complained. "I'm not particularly keen to have the association."

It was Quinn who took Kila aside and counseled her on the meeting to come. "Whether or not you want to be Highest of Kil, this is an opportunity for you to stand separate from the other Ways. Mark me, they'll all seek to control you. They fear your power. But anyone can see that Dem-Kisk—whatever it is—is upon us. You must convince them that you do not seek to destroy the world."

Kila wished Gian were there. But he'd gathered his few possessions and stalked into the night. What he saw in Kila, when the truth about her power had been fully revealed, had disgusted him. Or perhaps it had merely terrified him. But he was gone, and with him any advice he might offer.

Annisforl's chamber had held a wardrobe full of enormous frocks. But tucked in the back had been a wooden box. In it, a suit of black. Trousers, shirt, and a slim jacket embroidered in black. Upon each sleeve, a raven.

A pair of soft leather slippers completed the look.

"It's as if he knew your size," Sliy had marveled.

But of course he'd known. Everything but her name, it seemed. Regarding herself in the glass, Kila discovered she rather liked the outfit. She looked a bit like a young lordling, though unmistakably feminine despite her lack of hair. She'd spent perhaps too much time trying to help Sliy grow it back with mercus healing, but the girl couldn't follow Kila's suggestions. Admittedly, Kila didn't know how to explain her instincts on exactly how to accomplish the feat.

"They are here," Sliy said. But Kila had long ago sensed their mercus sparks approaching. She had decided to hold audience here, in Annisforl's chamber. It would force them to climb to her. She liked that.

Her friends formed a greeting party of sorts. All were clean, thanks to mercus feats Sliy had known. Nax slept by the fire, having recently found and eaten a rat.

The Coin came in first, followed by Voluptuary Harrisan Minn, and Dunne Quiv, now acting as Highest. Kila doubted he'd relinquish that title until the day he died.

The three took in the chamber, all looking vaguely uneasy while doing a smart job to conceal it. Kila didn't smile or offer any greeting. She didn't have much in the way of refreshment to offer. Having foreseen this, the Coin opened a basket and proceeded to set up for tea.

"If you could heat this?" she said, tapping the kettle and eyeing Kila.

A subtle move, intended to make Kila do the work of a servant. Quinn had warned of such games. Kila merely blinked.

Henley stepped forward. "Allow me, Coin." He formed the bolts and soon the water was ready. Voluptuary Minn poured.

The tea was good. Kila had not truly felt warm inside since the shriving. She tapped her garnet ring on the cup, sending up a sharp clink. "My advisors counseled me to play coy. But I'm not a very patient girl. Out with it."

Surprisingly, the women deferred to Quiv. He smacked his lips and sat a bit more erect. "Yes, well . . . Raginalt Keel warned us you'd say something like that. Very astute lad. A pity he lacks the spark. He would—"

"Where is he?" Kila and Henley said at the same time.

"He is well. He's helping tend to the wounded at the Tower. He seems to have developed an attachment to one of the Favored. That will not end well for him. She was grievously wounded in the collapse of the tower. And her presence in the Champion's arena—found next to the body of the queller captain—is quite a mystery in itself."

The Coin filled the silence that followed. "Is there a reason we are discussing acolytes and Favored?"

Quiv eyed her, smiling in his stiff-lipped way. "Moving on, then. Highest Fley conspired with Sensual Thine and Voluptuary Sennikt to undermine the Way of Ori with the objective of folding their numbers into the Way of Til. The male Sensuals would eventually be made Donse Masters, and the women enrolled in a new sisterhood." He waved his fingers dismissively as he sipped his tea. "A servant-class of sorts. The merculyns among them to serve as source-taps to Donse Masters where needed."

Voluptuary Minn looked like she'd swallowed a live perch. Quiv made calming motions. "I, of course, helped him further these plans, but merely out of duty. He was Highest of Highests, after all. I assure you, I know every Sensual and novitiate loyal to Thine and Sennikt. Most were killed at Ori's Home. The others have been separated, thanks to Voluptuary Minn."

"What you admit to doing is violating the bylaws of the Synod of the New Pantheon," Minn said. "It's an absolute—"

"Yes, yes. It's a crime against us all," the Coin said. "Let's move along, shall we? This girl expects us to discuss Dem-Kisk, no?"

"What do you have to say on the subject?" Kila asked. Quinn grinned and winked.

"That ring . . ." Voluptuary Minn said, squinting at Kila's hand. "Did you find it in this chamber? Is it a heller?"

"I was given this ring in this chamber."

All three of her eminent visitors leaned forward. Kila obliged by holding out her hand, fingers limp, in imitation of Her Enlightened when she'd bade Marlow kiss her ring. She wanted to laugh.

"That writing there," Quiv said, leaning forward. He gently took hold of Kila's wrist and turned it so he could better read the script. "It's the ancient language of Cigil-Tine. 'Ot Kil, Tuin Pri'—*God Kil, His First.*"

Minn paled and shook her head, leaning away from Kila. Quiv, hands shaking, tried to cover by sipping his tea but only succeeded spilling some in his lap. Only the Coin remained calm, if a bit severe around the eyes. "Highest of Kil. Do you claim that title?"

Kila shrugged. "'Lord of the ash-barrens' has a nicer ring to it." She hadn't planned to reveal the whole Highest of Kil nonsense. Even so, she never would have expected such a reaction. They were taking it seriously.

"It's nothing to joke about," the Coin snapped. "The Synod has held a thousand years, but as surely as time erodes the names from a gravestone, so too have the virtues of the Synod worn away. Nothing remains of that great treaty but the shape. The Way of Til has been lost to corruption, Ori to infiltrations. Only Pol remains as it was: clear-eyed and objective."

"Which is why the Coins of various realms shake loose of your leash at first opportunity?" Henley asked. Kila didn't know what he was talking about, but the Coin obviously did.

"Highest Fley would have agreed with the Coin on much," Quiv said. "He saw the Synod was failing, and boldly moved to consolidate the Ways into one. The One God was Til, of course, but he wished to scrape away the name, which he thought a perversion left behind by the First Race."

"Triumvirate," Kila said. She started to chew her tongue, caught herself and stopped. Holding up her hand, she waggled her finger, making the garnet sparkle. "Perhaps there are four faces of god, and Kil's is supreme. Perhaps god has no face at all. What does any of this have to do with Dem-Kisk?"

None answered.

"Henley?" Kila said.

Her friend removed a single red dragon scale from his satchel and handed it to Kila. "Found in the ash-barrens."

"We have discussed the passages of the prophecy," Kila said. "Most have been fulfilled, some more than once. And yet nobody knows what it means."

Novitiate Sliy stepped forward. "I may be able to add something."

Everyone turned to look at her, Voluptuary Minn suddenly guarded.

"Highest Til held Roya Reth captive in the Til's Tower. He went to her often."

"Roya Reth died at sea," Voluptuary Minn said. "I don't know who's been filling your head with these tales but—"

"She lived, Voluptuary. I assure you. I saw her often when

I was a Favored." She dug in her pocket and pulled forth a copper medallion. "She gave me this and bade me keep it close at all times. And so I have, all these years."

The Coin snapped her fingers and beckoned for the girl to hand it over. Sliy did so, hesitantly. She continued: "Roya Reth never said where she got the medallion. But she was very clear that I should keep it. And so I did." Licking her lips and smoothing her skirts, Novitiate Sliy gathered herself. "And then she taught me how smiles and frowns flashed in sequence could form a code. When I was alone in my chambers, sometimes the medallion would lift from where I had hidden it and spin through a series of smiles and frowns. By and by I became quite quick at deciphering Roya's messages. And I discovered that I could move the coin through a response. Roya and I often had long exchanges. Usually about her childhood and the family she missed. But once, very recently she sent me a different sort of message. 'Soon it will tread upon fields of red.'"

"She sent you a message last night, too," Kila said, now understanding what the woman had been doing late into the night.

"Impossible," Quiv said. "She died in the collapse."

"Roya is not merely flesh. Anyone who met her would know how transparently she existed in this world. She was more like a vergant-kin or a water spirit, loosely tied to the flesh she inhabited. She sent me a final message before she passed into whatever by-world she was bound for. 'Make her run or help her stand?'"

Oly stalked in and meowed loudly. He paused and looked at the people sitting round the room.

The intrusion seemed so absurdly rude—and the timing so bad—Kila was tempted to toss her teacup at him.

Oly has a message from Flaumishtak, Nax sent. *I've already berated him, but he doesn't care. He says that Flaumishtak told him to wait until 'the idiot girl woke up.'*

Flaumishtak said no such thing. What does Oly want? We're having an important discussion here.

Oly swears that Flaumishtak said something like that.

Kila got up and went to stand over Oly. The cat spat at her and turned away. Back to her, he sat and began grooming a paw.

"Something like that, huh? Tell me precisely what he said."

"She's talking to it!" Quiv said.

The Coin merely grunted.

Nax. Make Oly answer me.

Oly says that Flaumishtak said: 'She will learn something in the days to come. Observe and summon me when she's ready.'

Summon?

"Kil be a merry maiden!" Kila said. "Grab every heller you've got, my friends. We have a guest coming."

"Who?" the Coin said, standing and cracking her knuckles. She wore several rings and a crane-shaped bracelet. In fact, all three of the heads of Ways wore hellers. Good.

"My old friend, Flaumishtak, is coming. A demayne."

Novitiate Sliy covered her mouth. Henley pressed his palms to the top of his head and swore. Quinn reached for the dagger that wasn't on her hip. Pennie looked around and asked what was going on.

The mercus green flowed up from the very spot where Annisforl's ashes had been. And then he was there. Hulking over all of them, beastly face with his smoke-wisp hair. The long robe and the hooved feet. Oly mewled in delight and leapt into the beast's arms. "My precious Beloved. You did well." He fed Oly something that smelled of very old fish. Flaumishtak offered Nax a slight bow and flicked her a treat as well. Huff meowed in annoyance, and he, too, received a tidbit.

Don't eat that, Kila sent.

Too late. Nax had already pounced on the treat.

"A Council of the Ways? Quaint," said Flaumishtak in a booming grumble. He nodded to Kila. "And now it has begun. I did not expect this to take quite so long, delicious one."

Kila shivered to hear him speak his nickname for her aloud.

"I'm doing quite well," he said. "I have been doing some killing, here and there. The Hargothe was generous in his negotiations, but I quickly found myself sated. And in truth, the most delectable treat he offered I cannot avail myself of. She is too well guarded in that Citadel of hers." His tone was more annoyed than angry.

He waved his claw in dismissal. "But now I have something much more interesting to occupy me. Training you."

Kila's throat was parched and her nosed burned with his candle-smoke stink. "For what?"

He smiled. So many teeth.

The Coin lashed out with mercus fire. The beast deflected it without moving a finger. Quiv did not attack. He simply backed away until he bumped into the wall. Voluptuary Minn formed wards around herself and the others. Kila noted that Henley did nothing at all. He simply waited.

"Why, my little Highest of Kil, to prepare you for Dem-Kisk. The Despised God is restless in his demaynic hall."

"And he expects me to do what?"

"Free him. Bear him forth, into this world."

Kila laughed. "And why would I do such a stupid thing, even if I could?"

"Because if you don't, the Hargothe will." The beast lifted Novitiate Sliy from the floor with his power and floated her near to him. Voluptuary Minn's wards fell to pieces. "What was it that sweet Roya Reth said?"

"Soon it will tread upon fields of red?" The young woman shook so hard she could barely get the words out.

"True, true. It will be glorious. But I was asking about the *last* thing she told you."

"'The choice is at hand. Make her run or help her stand?'"

"That's the bit!" He sent the girl back and set her on her feet. Her knees buckled and Henley had to keep her upright.

"So to all of you, I ask: what is your choice?"

He didn't wait for an answer before raising a fist to the ceiling and dymensing in mercus green.

45

AN UNSETTLED SEA

The council broke up shortly after. The Voluptuary promised to send some wagons with provisions and supplies. Kila reluctantly accepted the offer. She had planned to leave the island. Perhaps she still would if she could figure out that nifty dymensing trick.

By and by, Nax was again asleep by the fire. The others had found rooms and settled in to rest. Novitiate Sliy was assigned to remain at Kil's Keep, an emissary of the Way of Ori. The Coin swore a solemn oath that Sliy was not, and had never been, a devotee or Spinster of Pol, and that she had never used her medallion to communicate the Way of Ori's secrets to the Coin or to anyone else within the Way. She assigned Spin Moirina as emissary.

Highest Quiv promised to send a man, too, though it might have to wait until things had settled at the Tower. Kila warned him not to move a single man into Kil's Fifth of the Tower. Quiv blinked hard at that, but nodded his commitment.

Late that night only Henley remained with her in the Highest of Kil's chamber, sitting before the fire, sipping watered-down trezz. "It seems you have come up in the world, thief girl."

"Too far up for some."

"Quinn said you and Gian . . . ?"

"I'm just being silly. I'm better off without him. He was too good with his blade. I like to have people around I can beat." She studied her red-headed friend. He was given to long silences, but a new sort of humor had grown in him, too. She liked it. He had a tired way of speaking and walking, but he wasn't weak. He had endured as much as she had. And that made him unique among the people she knew.

They sat that way a long time, not saying much. Their cats slept, the fire burned low.

"We have to kill him," Henley said.

He was speaking about the Hargothe.

Kila closed her eyes. She just wanted to dymense away and escape it all.

I agree with Henley, Nax sent.

Escape. That's why she'd come here to the Garden. To get away from Starside and the troubles that had plagued her there. She wasn't a fool. Wherever she went, trouble would follow. What she didn't know was whether she was the source of the trouble . . . or if she was the answer to it. She didn't want power. She didn't want to lord it over thousands of people.

Perhaps she did have Kil's blood in her veins. Perhaps that made her bad *in her very being.* Maybe that was what Gian had recognized. She had been a thief, after all. But contrasting herself to Thine's viciousness, Fley's blind intolerance, and

Yples's chaotic hate, she could not see how she, of all people, could be the Despised God's chosen one.

Henley was looking at her. "Did you hear me? We *must* kill him."

She did not answer for a long time as she watched the firelight give life to her garnet ring, sending up mesmerizing sparkles of crimson. Kil's blood.

Closing her eyes, she did something she should have done sooner. Much sooner. She released the force-bond upon the soul drifting far to the east upon an unsettled sea. It took no effort at all, and yet it took everything she had. And then he was gone.

Feeling a strange sort of release of her own, she roughly wiped her sleeve across her eyes. "Yes, Henley. I know."

The End of *The Force of Destiny*
Book Five of
Starside Saga